A Willing Executioner

CONNELL NISBET

Published by Connell Nisbet
Copyright © Connell Nisbet, 2019
The moral right of the author has been asserted.
First published 2019

Cover design and photography by Connell Nisbet

ISBN 9780648394709

For Sarah Chang

PROLOGUE

With an almighty kick the ball soared into the sky. Cody Dunbar's left leg remained extended as he watched the ball float high overhead. It disappeared momentarily against the morning sun. He judged the distance, as his uncle had taught him, took two steps forward and leapt into the air. In his mind, he could hear the crowds scream from the stands of the SCG as he rose over the shoulders of the other players to take the mark. It was awesome. For just a moment he knew what it felt like to be Adam Goodes, the world's best AFL player. He felt tall, proud, loved.

Cody moved with a grace that he didn't yet understand. At 14 years old, he was already bigger than most of his mates. The older guys in town gave him a bit of grief, hassled him for the sake of it, but he wasn't afraid of them. He could handle himself, and they knew it. But he was growing so fast he'd need a new Sydney Swans jersey soon. The one he was wearing cut him in the armpits. He'd have to ask his aunty when the time was right. Of course, if she knew he was ditching school to play football in the dry creek bed on the outskirts of town again, all he'd get would be a cuff over the head.

He broke into a steady run as he turned on to Terrence Road, dodging imaginary Hawkes players who came at him from all sides in a well-rehearsed play his uncle had shown him. He had the whole street to work with. Forbes Creek was a dwindling settlement, barely a dot on the map of Central Australia, 120km south east of Alice Springs. No cars came out this way unless they were lost. Every 15 metres or so he'd push the ball against the bitumen. It had to be on just the right angle so the ball would bounce back into his hands without having to alter his stride.

He weaved back and forth across the road. On either side, beyond rusting wire fences, were vacant weatherboard houses, decaying in the sun, broken windows, collapsed verandahs, dusty yards littered with empty beer bottles. Seemed to Cody like the town was getting smaller every year. Some blokes went away for work. Some were locked up. Some just died in their homes. He had grown up with most of the families who once lived in those houses. He didn't like to think about it, because it made him angry. He didn't hate the town. He just wished it could be different. He'd promised his aunt and uncle that he'd get out one day, become an AFL star as big as Adam Goodes. Then he'd come back and make it all better. Everyone would have Swannies jerseys no matter how quick they grew. And the Swannies and the Hawkes would play a match in town every year on a grassy field that would be named in his honour.

He had told his mates Teddy and Yambo he'd meet them down by Harley's Bridge as soon as they could get clear of the principal. He'd ducked out of school earlier than usual so he'd have time to mark out the field and clear away the branches that may have blown down from the gum trees along the bank during the night. The rest of the guys would hopefully get there by mid-morning. They might even have enough players for a full game.

He slowed to a trot as the road petered out to gravel then dust. He moved across the scrub to the shade of the gums along the edge of the creek bed. Beyond the far bank the surrounding desert made its presence felt: bare ochre and low-lying grasses as far as the eye could see, all beneath a vast expanse of blue sky. He jogged along the right bank until it slowly turned east towards Harley's Bridge. He stopped and leaned his back against a tree to catch his breath, waving the flies away from his face. The air was stifling and still. It was going to be a stinker playing in this heat, but he was still excited.

It was then that he picked up a scent lingering in the air. Sharp. Penetrating, but distant. Too difficult to tell exactly where it was coming from. A dead roo, he thought. Must be nearby. Probably hit by a car on the road to Alice, or winged by someone with a .22 during the night. It must have limped onto the creek bed and got finished off by wild dogs. He continued along the bank. Within a few metres he realised the smell was too strong for a dead roo. Cattle maybe. He looked across the sandy creek bed expecting to see the dehydrating carcass of a cow that had collapsed down the opposite bank in a final fruitless attempt to find water. Only sand and the stillness of gum trees.

Somewhere deep in Cody's mind a darkness was beginning to swirl. He knew this smell. A fear crept over his skin. And with it came the images that had plagued his sleep for so long he couldn't remember a time when they hadn't. His feet grew cold, his mouth dry. He was walking into his father's house again.

The stench had greeted him at the flyscreen door. It filled his nostrils and mouth and wouldn't leave. The TV was blaring from the living room, as it always did, but it was jarring with an unfamiliar stillness to the house. He wanted to run, to yell out to his father from the safety of the front yard. Was he drawn by the sound of the TV? The fetid smell? He still didn't know what led him deeper into the house, into that room. To this day he wished someone had been there to hold him back, to prevent him from seeing that – he had never been able to find words to describe what was sitting on his father's couch. Too young to comprehend the feeling of being alone in the company of death, only sensing the horror of it all.

He stepped slowly along the bank of the creek, treading carefully over the exposed roots of gum trees. The flies became more insistent, trying to settle on his lips. He put his hand over his mouth and nose. The stench was now almost unbearable, so hideously familiar. He realised that it was his increasing sense of dread that was actually compelling him forward, when every fibre of his being wanted him to run in the opposite direction. He had to be close. The pale trunk of a large established gum tree blocked his view of the bank further on. Cody pinched his nose, took a deep breath and stepped around the tree.

His ball fell to the ground, bounced once, then rolled awkwardly over the edge of the bank.

An elderly white man was climbing out of the creek. His eyes were screwed shut but his mouth was open, gasping for air. He was clutching at the sand as if something was dragging him back down. He didn't make a sound. Cody stepped back and leaned against the tree because he couldn't trust his legs to hold him up. The man was naked except for a soiled pair of underpants that were once white. A seething swarm of flies covered his thighs. Cody picked up a branch. The fear was receding, replaced by a dull anger that it had happened again. He wouldn't scream this time. He poked at the man's shoulder. It didn't move. He poked it harder, gritting his teeth with contempt. The entire body shifted slightly in the sand and the flies rose up in an angry chaotic mass. Cody stared at the man's thighs, at the torn flesh and bare bones – his legs had been ripped off. A familiar sound erupted from the young boy's throat as he fell to his knees and scrabbled across the dust to get away.

CHAPTER ONE

Deputy Police Commissioner Sven Augerson leaned against the sideboard that lined the wall behind his desk. He sipped on a mug of coffee, oblivious to the rain that lashed the windows of his office on the fifth floor of the *Polititorvet*, the Danish National Police Headquarters. The recent directive of his superiors continued to fall in layers in his mind until any sensible defence or common sense was completely obscured. He glanced at his computer screen. 11am. Detective Birgitte Vestergaard appeared in the doorway. "You wanted to see me?"

"Come in, please. Take a seat." He motioned for her to close the door behind her. "How have you been?"

She held his gaze as she sat in one of two chairs provided for meetings, automatically crossing her legs and placing her hands comfortably in her lap. She had known Augerson for more than six years, and liked him, but she respected his position, so she always felt it best to maintain a professional demeanour with him during work hours.

"I'm fine. Good, in fact, thanks."

"The program going okay?"

"It's a process, apparently." She smiled thinly, but there was warmth in her eyes. Augerson admired her stoicism. God knows if he was in her position, he would have been questioning his own sanity.

"You feel like you're getting on top of things?"

"It has been six months, Sven. I'm absolutely fine. I just want to get on with my job, out there. Get away from a desk." She pretended to tear at her hair, which was immaculately kept, tied back from her face. It was a look that endeared her to her superiors: elegant, sophisticated, discerning. But Augerson knew that behind the refined cheekbones and the piercing eyes was a highly intelligent senior detective with a law degree who was destined to go all the way if she played her cards right. But it was early days and he'd seen other similarly capable officers crumble under less weight.

He watched her carefully before proceeding. As always, she was inscrutable. He knew that what he was about to tell her was not right. In an ideal world, the police community would protect their own, but there were larger forces at work. To his own surprise, it wasn't her feelings he was reluctant to hurt, but her intellect. He knew she wouldn't make this conversation easy for him, and she shouldn't. He had no choice but to plunge in.

"Have you ever been to Australia?"

She cocked her head slightly and answered with a measured uncertainty, "I backpacked there in my early 20s, when I finished my degree. Are you planning a holiday, Sven?" She smiled at him, her porcelain face illuminated from within. Augerson laughed, thinking to himself how much she could achieve on that smile alone. "You have no idea, Birgitte. My wife is ready to walk out on me." He rushed forward when he realised what he had just said. "And I'd love a holiday in Australia but, as you know, with the restructure I'm kind of swamped."

He eventually sighed and pressed on. "A Dane has gone missing down there – former Director of Natural Resources for the EU's energy agency ACER. It's been more than a week since anyone has heard from him, so it doesn't look good."

"Can't the Australians handle it? Surely, they know their own terrain." She kept her voice even, as if they were actually having a conversation that involved her input. It gave her a sense of control.

"He's the brother-in-law of the Commissioner." Augerson leaned back against the sideboard again, allowing the implication to sink in. Verner Holl had run the *Polititorvet* for the past three years and was not shy about giving direct orders to lower staff to achieve his own ends. Officers who had chosen to disobey him found themselves shunted off to distant districts. Augerson didn't need to spell this out to Birgitte. "I need to send someone official to oversee the search, answer any questions they may have. An international liaison officer of sorts."

Birgitte was incredulous for a moment then stared her boss down with a knowing look. She resisted the temptation to ask if this pointless task would have been assigned to her if Max Anders had never existed, or more obviously, if she was a man. "How long will I be gone for?" She couldn't hide the plaintive tone in her voice. It was the first time her veneer had cracked and she instantly hated herself for it.

"Two weeks at the most, I promise. If you're lucky, this guy will turn up drunk in some strip joint within a few days. Consider it an opportunity to show the Ossies how the Danes like to do things. Hands across the water and all that."

She went to say something, but he quickly cut her off. "Birgitte, you should be grateful the Commissioner asked personally for you to handle the situation. It's a huge show of faith on his part. You know how he feels about you. This could be just the gig you need to get back in the good books with the guys upstairs." He regretted it as soon as the words came out of his mouth. He was trying to appeal to the politician in her instead of the police officer.

"The media won't leave me alone just because I'm out of the country, Sven. You know that, don't you?"

"We just think that with Anders' appeal coming up next week it would be best if you were otherwise occupied."

The injustice of it was making her blood boil. She stood up, shaking her head. "Sven, I'm grateful you found a place for me in Fraud, while the psychologists and HR do their thing, but I don't belong here."

She took a deep breath. "I'm sorry, Sven. You have my best interests at heart, I understand that, but you must realise how this looks, to them, out there."

"Orders are orders, Birgitte."

"When do I leave?"

"Tonight. There's a flight at 8pm with a stopover in Hong Kong. Should get you into Sydney sometime Sunday. It's almost summer down there now so you won't be needing your jacket. I'll shoot through all the details within the hour. You'll be meeting with an Australian Federal Police officer... Kingsley... King..." He checked his notes. "Kingsmill.

Detective Anthony Kingsmill. He'll meet you at your hotel on Monday morning and you can go through everything they have at that point."

"And if this guy..."

"Thostrup. Hans Thostrup."

"If Hans Thostrup turns up in the mean time?"

"Consider it a tax payer-funded junket. We've organised some meet and greets with a few of their Federal Departments. And you've got a week or two's leave you can tack on the end of it if you like. Take your time coming back."

She couldn't believe what she was hearing. "Is there anything else?"

"Keep an open mind. I'm pretty sure they do things differently down there. Even the weather, apparently." His attempt at levity fell short. Some days he wished he was back on the street himself.

She walked back to her desk, grabbed her purse and headed in the direction of the vending machine at the end of the floor so Sven and the other Fraud officers at their desks didn't see her walking directly to the bathroom. But when she got there, she closed a cubicle door behind her and sat on the closed lid of the toilet, resting her head in her hands, trying to compose herself. The faces of three children, terrified, pleading, rushed into her consciousness. She gritted her teeth as her hands began to shake. She could hear their tiny fingernails scratching against wood. And always Anders' deep laughter, confident, knowing. She wrung her hands, twisting at the wedding band that she now only wore to keep up appearances. Eventually her breathing slowed to a steady rhythm. Within a few minutes she was washing her face at the basin. She stood tall and stared herself down in the mirror. There was the strong, intelligent senior detective that other, more experienced, officers admired and new recruits looked up to. This was a setback, no doubt, but she knew she could make it work for her, or at the very least, prove to herself that she was bigger than the petty politics of the Danish police force. As her father had always told her, lead by example. And, of course, she could hear her mother chiming in – "never let them see you crying".

Salina Heysmith came to, emerging from a hideous montage of dreamscapes and memories, her senses heightened by a searing pain she couldn't immediately locate, as if her skin was alive with fire. Her hands brushed at her thighs, but she felt numb and clouded and clumsy. She opened her eyes. Dead leaves, dampness, the smell of fecund earth. Her hands moved more violently, in counterpoint to her own intention. As she tried to scratch away the burning pain, her hands were trying to move separately but were unable. She looked down with horror: her wrists were taped together, her bare legs and feet were covered in angry red ants that were crawling all over her skin, hundreds of them, biting her incessantly. She could feel them under her blouse. It was all she was wearing. She tried to scream but couldn't. Only a guttural moan that echoed in her own head. Her tongue was obstructed and she could taste dirty fibres. Her mouth was taped open with a gag of some sort wedged between her teeth. Panic shot through her limbs. She began to struggle wildly, rolling herself across the ground. She got up on one knee but the earth kept racing up to meet her. Every time she fell, the urge to fight escalated. Before she could even register a need to escape, her body was already reacting.

It took 10 minutes to brush most of the ants from her body. Once she had regained her balance, and screamed at herself to stop panicking, she had the wherewithal to snap a branch from a sapling and lash her legs with it. Then she had scraped herself against a tree until she had crushed most of her attackers. As she did so her mind raced, trying to work out where she was and what had happened to her. She was still alive, she kept saying to herself, so there was still hope.

It was suffocatingly humid. There were trees all around her but nothing like the bushland around her home in the northern suburbs of Sydney. Here, the foliage was luminescent green, the leaves broad and glowing with brilliant light. The air was shrill with the incessant screeching of cicadas. Beyond the tree canopy she could just make out cliffs of ochre blazing in the sun. Her mind raced with associations that made little sense. She remembered brochures in the hotel where she was staying for the conference. Images of magnificent palm trees set against orange-brown cliffs. No. The trees were growing out of the cliffs. The hotel offered tours to a remote national park a few hours outside of Darwin. The realisation of where she might be suddenly terrified her more than the fact that her wrists and mouth were taped. She was bound and gagged in a jungle somewhere in the Northern Territory, literally in the middle of nowhere.

She steadied her breathing again and tried to think rationally. The conference. Did it have something to do with the conference she'd been attending in Darwin? Potential off-shore mining rights in the Timor Sea. The legal firm she worked for, Blake, Patterson & Walker, represented Katercorp. Her mind was now racing. They were meeting with representatives of all the major mining corporations to lobby the Northern Territory Government. Barclay Industries, a potential rival to any deal in the region if the government gave the green light, was at the conference. How could anyone know of her relationship with its lead counsel? It didn't make sense. Everything was a mess. She had wanted desperately to use the trip to Darwin to tell Jason everything. She hadn't got the chance.

Oh Christ, she thought suddenly. Was he tied up somewhere nearby? Could he help her? Her heart beat violently at the thought of him possibly being in greater danger than herself. She stood still and tried to listen through the wild cacophony of insects and curious cawing of unfamiliar birds. Water was rushing somewhere way off in the distance. But no human sounds. She desperately hoped that he was okay. Whoever had abducted her was nowhere to be seen. But how far away were they? How much time did she have? What the hell did they want?

She looked again at her hands. In her panic she hadn't noticed the thin metal wire, that ran from her wrists off into the jungle. She pulled on it but there was no tension. She was tethered to something, like an animal. Oh god. She felt violently ill.

She began to follow the wire through the trees. The foliage was so thick she had to bend over to walk and hold her hands out in front of her to clear a path. The earth was moist and hot under her feet, and mostly even, but she sensed she was heading slightly downhill.

Within a few minutes she emerged on the muddy banks of a swollen creek. The wire disappeared into the brackish water. On the other side was a raised bank of mud held together by the roots of trees that formed an impenetrable green wall. She lifted the wire and began to pull on it. It slowly rose up out of the creek, dripping with water. It formed a hard line into the foliage opposite. She had found the source.

If she crossed the creek, she could find what it was attached to, but something inside told her not to get into the water. The sun was disappearing behind the cliffs. She staggered back to where she woke up to see if she could find a fire trail. She only managed to get a few feet further beyond the clearing when the wire prevented her from going any deeper. She felt hopeless, confused and sick with self-loathing. She fell to her knees weeping, knowing that her past had finally caught up with her.

It was raining even harder as the cab pulled up in front of a modern apartment block in Vesterbro. Birgitte paid the driver and made the dash from the back seat to the security door but still managed to get drenched. As she let herself in she realised she only had two hours to pack her bags and get to Copenhagen Airport to check-in for her flight. She ran up the four flights of stairs, unlocked her door and threw her wet jacket and scarf on the console in the hallway.

The spacious two-bedroom apartment belonged to a colleague of Birgitte's who had suggested she rent it when she and Tomas separated. It came furnished, which saved Birgitte the pain of being surrounded by the furniture they had bought together over the years. But it meant the apartment wasn't a home, it was just somewhere to stay until she got herself sorted. She kicked off her shoes, dried her hair with a hand towel from the bathroom and got busy.

Within 15 minutes she had cleaned out the fridge, taken out the garbage, and booked another cab for 4.30pm to allow for the Friday afternoon traffic. She grabbed her luggage from the wardrobe in the bedroom and began to pack. She couldn't remember the last time she ate but she didn't have time to worry about that. Suddenly she realised she didn't know where she last saw her passport. She rifled through the drawers of her desk in the living room. But then remembered it was with all her important papers in the bottom drawer of the wardrobe in the bedroom.

She checked her watch and figured she had just enough time to shoot off a couple of emails.

While her laptop was warming up, she changed into a dark pair of trousers and a cream blouse. She felt frazzled but presentable enough to travel. She sent off a short email to her mother, telling her that she would be out of the country for at least the next week.

For a moment she considered sending Tomas an email, just in case he tried to get hold of her and couldn't. A horn blasted in the street outside. Her cab had arrived earlier than expected. There was no point writing to Tomas, she decided. It would only open another round of tense correspondence that she would rather not deal with from the other side of the world. She packed away her laptop, ran around the apartment turning off the lights and the heating, then gathered her luggage and wheeled it out the door.

By the time she climbed into the back of the waiting cab she could feel her frustration getting the better of her. Her situation was beyond unreasonable. She was being treated as an inconvenience to her superiors, a very public inconvenience, and she resented it.

The driver looked over his shoulder, "Copenhagen Airport?"

"Yes, please," she said, managing a polite smile. "Departures."

He nodded. The cab pulled away from the curb. The storm had passed over the city but it was still raining steadily. Birgitte double checked her handbag to make sure she definitely had her passport and ticket.

She sat back and took a moment to try to get some perspective. She was being churlish and she knew it. It was natural to be upset at their decision. Yet in all honesty, had she been the Commissioner, would she have treated a senior detective like herself any differently in similar circumstances? She liked to think that she wouldn't have, but the more time she spent in that managerial headspace the more she began to compromise her own principles. It surprised her to think how quickly they could be shuffled down the order of competing priorities. There were, as Sven had suggested, greater forces at play at that level. And this was how she needed to think if she was going to get ahead.

As the cab pulled onto Sjaellandbroen, an unwanted thought occurred to her: perhaps she wasn't ready for upper management. Perhaps this entire episode only served to confirm the suspicions of a few superior officers disgruntled by her rapid rise through the ranks over the past 12 years – she was nothing more than a pretty face, a diplomat's daughter, who liked to play police officer. Her father was right, she would have been better off pursuing a legal career.

Tomas would have preferred it if she had become a lawyer also, particularly given they had met at law school. But he had been considerate enough to keep those thoughts to himself most of the time. His greatest virtue during their relationship was his respect for her to make her own decisions.

Poor Tomas. It couldn't have been easy being married to her. They both worked long hours, but her job put her among society's refuse and in harm's way on a weekly basis. He had been incredibly patient and understanding, even in her desire to hold off on having a family.

The thought of children reminded her again of Anders, his smug face, calculating eyes. And with that her empathy faded. An all-too familiar anger stirred inside of her, tinged with resentment and bitterness. Not at Anders for causing so much pain and grief for so many people. Nor the tabloids, that had portrayed her as an ambitious woman who put her career above the safety of children. But at Tomas, who in the heat of their last and most spiteful argument had suggested there was an element of truth in the media's accusations.

He had had no right to judge her. Nobody did. They had no idea what she was going through back then. A pathological killer had singled her out for attention in one of the most publicised criminal cases in modern Danish history. It saddened her to think that for all his stoicism up to that point, Tomas had balked when she had needed him most.

She stared down at the boats moored on the marina as the taxi made its way on to Amager toward Copenhagen Airport. The truth was, she missed him horribly. What she missed was his faith in her. It had given her so much strength. And, if she was to be entirely honest, she only had herself to blame for the loss of that.

Birgitte was in the seat she had requested, on the aisle near one of the front exits of the plane. She was trying to read the file on Commissioner Holl's missing brother-in-law, but was struggling to concentrate. The middle-aged man beside her, a dour businessman from Odense who had commented on her blouse as she put her jacket and laptop in the overhead compartment, had fallen asleep after the second meal was served, and was snoring unevenly.

She had been grateful at first. His attempts at conversation after take-off were limited to his line of work – photocopiers – and how impressed he was with her figure, for a woman of her age. Fortunately, his overt interest in her breasts evaporated the moment she told him she was a senior detective with the Danish Police. He was suddenly intrigued by his in-flight magazine.

But now, as his bulbous head lolled onto her shoulder for the umpteenth time, his breath stinking of pickled fish and spirits, she wondered if it was too late to request a different seat. She carefully pushed him back into an upright position. He snorted and coughed then resumed his unsettled snoring.

Birgitte returned to the file. It was sparse; basic facts written on a legal pad gleaned from short phone interviews with the missing man's sister and the HR department of the EU's Agency for the Cooperation of Energy Regulators (ACER). There were also a handful of images and articles printed from the internet, with a few scribbled notes in the margins from the Commissioner.

Hans Thostrup. 67 years old. A Danish national. Caucasian with silver hair. Six foot one. Approximately 95kg. No defining features or marks.

The photographs confirmed as much – an office shot for his security pass, a family snap, probably taken at Christmas within the past five years, a business magazine profile from the conservative newspaper *Berlingkse*, and a few press-conference images taken from a distance. He would have been attractive in his youth, Birgitte thought. Now he was on the distinguished side of handsome. Intelligent eyes, long nose, strong jaw line. He exuded an authoritative air of calm judgement – someone that less capable people would listen to in a crisis. In the Christmas snap there was a kindness to his face that Birgitte hoped wasn't just a trick of the camera.

As Sven had mentioned, Thostrup was a former Director of Natural Resources for ACER. A short bio printed from its website highlighted an impressive professional background, predominantly in the energy sector. He had joined the EU in 2001 and rose steadily, promoted to more complex portfolios every 18 months or so. It was a distinguished career no doubt assisted by a Master in Economics from the Cambridge University, and a Bachelor of Economics with First Class Honours from Copenhagen University. He was highly respected by his colleagues and counterparts from other nations. The journalists who regularly covered energy-related stories had summed up his tenure as Director of Natural Resources as a period of global and regional turbulence that he had handled with distinction.

According to his sister, Katerine Holl, he was still an avid tennis player, and kept himself healthy with long walks around the affluent suburb of Oesterbro in Copenhagen, where he had lived for the past six years.

19

Birgitte yawned and rubbed her eyes. The cabin air was getting the better of her. It must have been about 1am back home. She ordered another water from a passing stewardess.

Thostrup was married for 33 years. No children. Sadly, his wife, Margarethe Thostrup, an accomplished economist in her own right, had passed away from breast cancer 18 months earlier. Apparently he had immersed himself in work for several months following the funeral then suddenly announced his retirement. No one could judge him for this, but his decision to take a holiday in Australia had struck his sister as odd. She hadn't questioned it because she knew he needed time alone, and figured Australia was as good as any place to finally grieve properly. So, why Australia, thought Birgitte.

There was an email from Emirates confirming a Hans Thostrup had flown to Australia from Copenhagen via Dubai on Wednesday October 22, arriving in Sydney Friday October 24, and another from the East Wind Hotel in Sydney providing the dates for the two nights that a Hans Thostrup had booked and stayed the previous week. And then nothing.

What had alarmed Thostrup's sister was the fact that he had agreed to phone her on the following Thursday, October 30, to discuss her son Jorg's plans to study Economics at the University of Copenhagen. He doted on the boy and would not have missed the call intentionally. There had been no email contact since he had arrived in Sydney. His sister had phoned the hotel from her home in Copenhagen, but they explained that he had checked out on the 26th as planned on the previous Sunday. It was out of character, and her husband, Commissioner Holl, agreed. When the Commissioner went in to work on the Monday he wrote to the Federal Police in Australia to see what could be done. Over the coming days he was told that two officers in Sydney had been assigned to investigating Thostrup's whereabouts but by Friday nothing had been turned up except to confirm his time at the East Wind. There was a printout of an email from the Commissioner, suggesting Birgitte be sent down to Australia to keep the investigation moving at an appropriate pace – there was no mention of Anders' appeal.

As Birgitte closed the file and slipped it back into her bag at her feet, she felt she had gained insight into Thostrup the financial whiz, one of a rare breed who brought a level of sophistication to the bureaucratic machine of the EU. But she didn't have much sense of the man himself. She wondered for a moment whether her father, Jan, may have had any dealings with him, then made a mental note to email him when she landed. Even though Jan had retired, he had an incredible memory for people, particularly people of importance in government. He might just be able to provide a light sketch in terms of Thostrup's personal attributes. She had gleaned the profile piece from *Berlingske*, but it had obviously been vetted by the powers that be in the EU to ensure very little personal information was provided. It was mostly about his thinking behind crucial policy decisions that defined his tenure. Perhaps that was intentional on his part as well. Maybe the most she could tell from all of this was that Hans Thostrup was a once-powerful man who knew how to keep his private life private.

Salina Heysmith was on her knees scraping the metal wire against a rock, checking it occasionally to see if she was making any progress. But the wire comprised fine threads that were wound around one another to form a durable rope of metal. The sun had gone down and she was struggling to see in the half light of the approaching evening. The screeching had stopped but the birds had become more raucous and now she was being attacked by mosquitoes. She felt like she was trapped in some exotic aviary. Occasionally she heard thumping noises through the trees. She would stop scraping and listen but it never amounted to anything. She continued scraping violently against the rock.

It was only $250,000, she said to herself. She could raise the money if she had to. It would take a few days but she could raise it. She felt a sudden flicker of irrational hope. Jason's family had money. Surely. She almost burst out laughing with hysteria. Jason's family. His wife. Her parents. The life that Salina had so deeply envied. Christ. It was ridiculous. The ramifications of all the poor choices she had made over the years were rising up to overwhelm her. It had nothing to do with the mining conference. She had borrowed money from the wrong people to cover her gambling debts and now they had come to collect.

She had liked to think that if Jason knew about her predicament he would do anything to help her. But deep down she knew he was too self-absorbed to really care. Did she seriously think he'd leave his wife and kids for someone like her? She had dug this hole for herself and it was up to her to get out of it.

She hadn't noticed the wire moving through the leaves behind her. It confused her when it slipped out of her hands and she couldn't find it among the debris around the rock. Then she felt her wrists lifting against her own volition. She was being pulled through the jungle. No. Not now. She needed more time. She tried to wrap a leg around a tree but the tension on the wire was increasing steadily. She fell to the ground and it continued to drag her over the cooling earth. She managed to get up and jog along so that it didn't pull her so hard. The fear was rising in her throat. She ran ahead and quickly ducked around a tree twice to tie off the rope but it was pointless. The wire grew taught but continued to retract. There was nothing she could do but let herself be dragged back down the slope. It pulled her to the creek's edge.

It was much darker now but she could just make out the opposite shore. She was on her knees in the mud, weeping into her gag, breathing heavily through her nose. The wire pulled less intently now. She dug her heels into the mud for the sake of not giving in entirely but it was pointless. She was dragged into the shallows. The wire stopped moving. The water was warm, dark and soothing on her insect-ravaged skin. She pulled at the wire in the foolish hope that it might come loose but she only disturbed the water across the width of the creek with her splashing. Then she froze. On the far shore, down by the waterline, something was moving. In the twilight it was too difficult to make out what it was but she heard a hideous heavy slithering sound and the slightest splash.

Salina Heysmith's mind was a riot of images and thoughts but her body was perfectly still. Before the water exploded around her she wondered what had become of the Jimmy Choo shoes she'd been wearing before she was abducted.

CHAPTER TWO

The suburbs had slipped by his window unnoticed, manicured stretches of healthy green lawn, low brick fences, wide driveways, well-kept gardens. Street after street of three-bedroom, single-storey homes. Far enough out of the Sydney CBD to raise a family, but too expensive to renovate upwards. Then it suddenly turned grey. One side of the street gave way to a monolithic reminder of how it could all go so wrong.

He had parked the car, killed the engine. Then settled back into his seat as he had done so many times before, just under different circumstances. Across the street one drab cyclone fence after another, each topped with loose spirals of razor wire. Several fences in, the sheer walls of the Frazer Correctional Facility for Women rose up like some sort of homage to communist architecture. Property prices weren't heading north in this area any time soon.

Detective Tony Kingsmill had been sitting there for two hours. He turned the engine over again to stop the battery from dying. If this had been a stakeout, he wouldn't have had the radio on. But he probably would have been eating the same pastries. A plastic takeaway container filled with baklava that he'd picked up from a Lebanese sweet shop continued to tempt him. He bit into his fourth and made a hollow vow to never buy them again. Then it occurred to him what she might be eating inside, beyond all those grey fences. His mind began to race with scenarios that made his muscles twitch.

Of course, he could have parked the car in the lot, walked into the facility, and sat down with her to find out exactly how she was coping. But he knew he wouldn't. At the very least he could have written her a letter. He had balked at this as well. He had no idea where to start or what to say. Letters had never been his thing. He didn't even like responding to emails from friends. And what was the point? She was doing her time. The best he could do was hope that she gets by okay. In 18 months she would be eligible for parole. Good behaviour. Out in two years. But he knew that the chances of her moving with the wrong crowd, whether out of a need for protection or through her own family connections, were sadly quite high. He turned the radio up.

"Northern Territory Greens Senator Bill Fennimore has accused the Minister for Trade Frank Howard of getting into bed with multinational mining corporations. The accusation comes as the Northern Territory Government prepares to meet to consider new gas exploration licences in the Timor Sea three kilometres off the coast of Arnhem Land. Several multinational companies have been lobbying the State Government since June, arguing it will bring billions of dollars to the region in investment and employment opportunities. However, environmental groups and the Greens argue the project will have dire consequences for the marine life and social welfare of the Indigenous communities. Business commentators are undecided as to which of the two biggest companies, Barclay Industries or Katercorp, will secure the deal if it goes ahead. Frank Howard was not available to respond to Senator Fennimore's accusations. The Northern Territory Government will meet on Monday to discuss the proposal which..."

He flicked through the stations until he found some music he could tolerate. Classical. His legs were stiff with sitting for so long and his lower back was beginning to ache.

This was ridiculous, he thought. He was achieving nothing. Just being maudlin. His curiosity was sated, he'd seen where she was staying. He didn't need to sit out the front with his head in his own lap. Of course, the first few weeks were going to be frightening for her. There was nothing he could do about it out here. He put the car in gear, dropped the park brake and pulled out into the street. As he drove away he mentally kissed her forehead and told her not to worry.

Forty minutes later, as he pulled into his own drive, his phone rang. He turned the engine off and answered it.

"Kingsmill."

"Tony, it's Superintendent Carolyn Miller."

"Everything okay?"

"Sorry to bother you on your Sunday."

"No problem. I was just out in the garden."

"I wasn't sure whether you check your emails over the weekend, but I sent you some details on that missing Dane,

Hans Thostrup. Local NSW officers are handling it. Constables Harris and Donleavy. Do you know them?"

"I've worked with Harris and I know Donleavy socially. They're stationed at the Cross from memory."

"That's right. Listen, it's not much to go on in terms of background, but I thought it might help if you were completely up to date before the week starts. Are you still good to meet with Detective Vestergaard at the East Wind Hotel in the morning?"

"I am. Any changes to the schedule?"

"No, she flies in this afternoon. You meet with her at 9am tomorrow. We'll touch base here after lunch."

"Fine."

"And, Tony?"

"Yes?"

"I promise this is a blip on the radar. Once we find the Dane, and this Detective Vestergaard heads back to Europe, we can sit down and have a chat about your role."

He held his tongue. "That's fine, Superintendent. I'm happy playing liaison officer for as long as it takes."

"You're a dreadful liar, but I appreciate your patience."

He hung up. He'd been a Federal Officer with the AFP for three weeks now and still had no idea what his actual role was. Part of him was in no hurry – after 13 years with the New South Wales Police, six of them as a Detective in the Middle Eastern Organised Crime Unit, he'd experienced enough high drama for one lifetime. Still, he couldn't afford to be complacent for long. He was all too aware of the arbitrary forces that governed the decision-making above him. Despite Miller's reassurances, he was sure she was only keeping his interests in mind out of expediency. Just as he was sure she hadn't phoned him on a Sunday afternoon to give him a friendly heads-up, but to let him know she could phone him whenever she felt like it. He got out of the car and walked inside. Suddenly he felt incredibly tired.

From her room on the 16th floor of the East Wind Hotel, Birgitte had a clear view of Circular Quay and Sydney Harbour.

She had been sitting in an upholstered armchair by the floor-to-ceiling window since 4am, unable to sleep. As the sun rose over the Pacific Ocean the city below slowly came to life, ferries began to pull out from the finger wharves, the traffic on the Harbour Bridge steadily thickened and by the time her alarm clock began bleating at 8am it actually felt like Monday morning.

She mentally thanked Commissioner Holl for doing the right thing in terms of accommodation. Her room was a welcome respite after 36 hours of travel. Following a seven-hour stopover in Hong Kong and a nine-hour flight into Sydney, she had trudged through Customs and Immigration the previous afternoon feeling as if she had been disassembled and put back together slightly incorrectly. She had gone to bed by 6.30pm. It was obviously going to take a few days to adjust.

She turned on the TV and found a local 24-hour news channel. There was no mention of a missing European in the main headlines. And there had been no further emails from Sven. So, as far she could tell, Thostrup still hadn't been found. She wondered if he was waking up in a similar hotel somewhere else in Australia, oblivious to the fuss he was causing.

Another voice inside her was beginning to articulate darker thoughts – was he in danger and were they moving fast enough? Was she already partly responsible for another person's demise? She took a long shower and reassured herself that until she knew more, speculation was counterproductive.

Tony Kingsmill negotiated his way through a bustling crowd of middle-aged Chinese tourists who had gathered at the entrance to the East Wind Hotel. He was a good head above most of them. He had his father to thank for that – Ernie Kingsmill was a strapping lad back in the day, or so Tony's mother liked to remind him. Tony's solid frame filled his suit jacket comfortably, accentuating the broad line of his shoulders. Fortunately the length of his legs saved him from looking like an ape. The guys on his touch football team used to joke about the heaviness of his walk – he preferred to call it being 'sure-footed', 'earthy' even, which they thought was hilarious. Despite the jokes they knew that when speed was called for he could outsprint guys half his age. He looked after himself at the gym, boxing mostly – it gave him the bulk up top for the heavy hitting but ensured he could still move nimbly when he needed to. If he could just rein in his love of Lebanese sweets, he'd be quicker still, but that wasn't going to happen any time soon – he wrote it off as an occupational hazard. As he stepped through the sliding glass doors he wondered if his days of sprinting blindly down alley ways after bikie drug dealers were all behind him. It only made him want to train harder. He simply wasn't ready to let himself go like some of his colleagues.

The foyer of the hotel was a contemporary cathedral to tourism: a vast interior of travertine, flooded with natural light courtesy of three-storey windows. It could have been any luxury hotel in the world except for the over-sized artworks of outback Australia hanging on the wall behind reception.

Swanky place, he thought. It reminded him of his cousin's house in Maroubra, except the East Wind probably cost less to decorate and was a damn-sight more tasteful.

There was no sign of Harris or Donleavy.

He took a seat in a leather armchair by the window and opened his folder that contained the material Miller had sent through the day before. He gave it another read through. There really wasn't much information they could constructively act upon.

He checked his watch. 8.58am.

An attractive woman in grey trousers and a white blouse emerged from the elevator bay. She carried a black bag over one shoulder. Tony figured she was in her early 30s, well-bred, self-assured and very fit. It didn't occur to him that she might be the woman he was supposed to meet. He found himself staring at her as she walked into the lobby. It wasn't just the length of her legs or the curve of her breasts against her blouse that he found captivating, but the way she carried herself. She was comfortably self-assured without being too self aware. He continued to watch her as she stopped and looked about at the other people sitting in the armchairs around him. Suddenly she caught his eye and smiled. As she approached him she said, "Detective Kingsmill?"

He stood up without thinking and said, "I am."

She reached out her hand. "Detective Birgitte Vestergaard, Danish National Police."

He shook her hand, quietly hoping she hadn't noticed how hard he'd been staring at her. "Welcome to Australia. Was your flight okay?"

"It was very long but, thankfully, I've slept well."

Early 40s, she guessed, looks after himself, knows how to dress, confident but relaxed. And nice eyes. "Shall we get started?"

"Of course. There are two local officers handling the case who are due here any minute. I said we'd meet them in the lobby cafe over there."

He led her to a raised carpeted area where leather armchairs and low tables were set in a casual fashion around a grand piano. As they stepped up into the cafe Tony said, "It must be refreshing to see the sun."

Birgitte smiled. "It was minus 15 in Copenhagen when I left."

"In Sydney we don't get out of bed for anything less than 20."

She laughed. "You certainly have it good down here."

As they were about to sit down at a table, two uniformed officers arrived from a back entrance to the hotel. Birgitte figured the woman was in her 20s, slight, officious looking. The guy was a bit older, but judging by his vacuous eyes and loping gait, less intelligent. He ignored Birgitte and shook Tony's hand. "I still don't get it."

"What's not to get?" Tony replied.

"You could be running the Middle Eastern Unit," Donleavy said. "You bloody well should be. Why would you bail a sure thing like that and join the Feds? I couldn't believe it when the guys told me."

"It wasn't a sure thing."

"And to work for Carolyn Miller. She's back, isn't she? And they promoted her?" He shook his head in disbelief.

Tony let the conversation fall flat. "Nathan, this is Detective Birgitte Vestergaard from the Danish National Police. This is Constable Nathan Donleavy and Constable Kate Harris. They're looking after all the enquiries in regards to Mr Thostrup here in Sydney."

Birgitte smiled and shook both their hands.

Tony noticed that Harris was being particularly professional, obviously nervous at meeting a senior female officer from Europe. There weren't too many role models for young women in the NSW Police force.

Donleavy still focused his attention on Tony. "What's Miller got you doing? Cleaning her car?"

"Not sure yet. But for the time being I'll be making sure that Detective Vestergaard gets all the assistance she needs so we can find Mr Thostrup as quickly as possible."

Donleavy took the hint and backed off.

They sat around the table.

A young waitress approached, but Tony raised his hand to suggest she wouldn't be required.

Birgitte leaned forward in her chair and said, "It's probably best to make it clear from the start that I am only here as liaison. I don't want to tread on anyone's toes or get in the way. And although my English is quite good, I may not catch everything you say, so please, be patient with me."

Constable Harris nodded then turned to Tony, who gave her the floor. She brought out her notepad, but tried to look like she didn't need it.

"We were notified of Mr Thostrup's disappearance on Wednesday, November 5. Apparently, his sister reported him missing on the previous Friday – October 31. Called here from Denmark because she hadn't heard from him in a week or so. It was out of character. She phoned this hotel in fact but he had already checked out. We're not entirely sure where he's got to next."

"Have you spoken to the staff here?" Birgitte asked.

"We did, but we didn't come up with anything except to confirm his check-out date as October 26. You're welcome to talk to the Head Concierge yourself." She flicked through her pad. "His name is Michael Kapolos."

"Thanks. If that's okay with you?"

Tony asked Birgitte, "What can you tell us about Mr Thostrup?"

"Until recently he worked for an energy agency within the European Union called ACER, where he was Director of Natural Resources, but is now retired. He's been married for 33 years, but his wife passed away from cancer 18 months ago. According to his sister, he was down here trying to clear his head on a long-overdue holiday. He's had a difficult couple of years by the sound of it."

"Is there a chance he may have taken his own life?" Tony asked.

"When I spoke to the Head Concierge," said Harris, "he remembered Mr Thostrup as being polite and warm. He certainly didn't give off the impression of being depressed. But we have been keeping an eye out for any bodies found in Sydney in the past few days."

Harris paused for a moment to collect her thoughts, cleared her throat then took a short breath. She turned her attention to Birgitte, she said. "If you don't mind me asking, is there something we don't know about this guy? It seems kind of serious to have a detective come all the way from Denmark at such an early stage. He may not even be missing."

Birgitte smiled and felt a bit embarrassed. "Actually, his sister, the woman who raised the alarm, is married to my boss's boss, the Commissioner of the Danish National Police."

Harris nodded knowingly.

"So what did you do to get the shit stick?" Donleavy asked.

"Sorry?" She wasn't sure she had heard him correctly.

Harris shook her head and looked away. Tony didn't have a chance to warn their new colleague about Donleavy. If he did, he would have told her he was one of those guys who would never amount to much, and knew it, so he was constantly trying to level the playing field by undermining the authority of everyone around him, particularly women.

"You must have done something to get such a crap detail," he said.

Birgitte looked him in the eyes and held his gaze.

"Constable Donleavy, is it?" She spoke carefully as if trying to find the right words in a foreign tongue. "In Denmark, when a high-profile national goes missing overseas we take it very seriously. I can only hope, for Mr Thostrup's sake, that the Australian police are as concerned as we are."

He smirked awkwardly then shifted in his seat, like a teenager.

Tony chimed in. "We certainly are, Detective Vestergaard. I can assure you that Constable Donleavy will be doing everything he can to find Mr Thostrup as quickly as possible."

He had almost been tempted to let him squirm a little longer, but he figured they would all have to get along together for the next few days at least.

Tony was impressed with how Detective Vestergaard handled Donleavy. There was something about her he immediately admired, but couldn't quite put his finger on. Many of the women he'd come across in the force hardened over the years, but that didn't always suggest strength – there was a brittleness to them, a suggestion the cracks they tried so hard to conceal could one day cleave open without any warning. Detective Vestergaard possessed an inner steeliness that was innate rather than defensive.

He noticed the ring on her left hand. It contained a small but pronounced diamond, nothing ostentatious, but at least a carat. Must have cost some guy a few months' salary, he thought.

Birgitte realised Tony was looking at her wedding ring.

"Thank you, Detective Kingsmill," she said to catch his eye while deftly placing her hand behind her bag. "I'm looking forward to working with all of you."

Donleavy stood up and turned to Tony. "Is that it? We need to be getting back to it."

"Just let me know if any John Does turn up that meet his description. And keep us posted if there are any developments from your end. I'll contact you if I hear anything new."

Donleavy nodded curtly to Birgitte then walked out of the cafe.

Harris waited for Birgitte to stand up before doing the same. "Have you been to Australia before, Detective?"

"About 20 years ago."

"Well, welcome back. And I'm sorry that our men haven't changed a bit."

Birgitte smiled. "I'm sure Constable Donleavy and I will get along just fine – with your help, of course. And I meant what I said: I am looking forward to working with both of you."

As the two officers left the hotel through the back entrance Tony apologised for Donleavy. "Some of our guys are a bit old school."

"It's fine. We don't have much to go on yet. I can almost understand his attitude. It must seem odd to have someone like me landing on his doorstep at such an early stage."

"He knows better."

She took a smart phone out of her pocket. "I've already bought a local sim card. This is my number. I'll let you decide whether you think either of the two constables need to call me direct."

Tony typed the number into his own phone. "Thanks for this. I'll text you with my number when we're done here. Probably best, for the time being, if the juniors work through me. Shall we talk to the Head Concierge?"

"He seemed like a decent guy, polite. Not overly friendly at first, but I put that down to the fact that he'd just flown here from Europe. He always smiled when I nodded to him in reception."

The Head Concierge of the East Wind was immaculate. From his waxed hair, slicked back from his brow, to his tailored uniform. He was in his early 30s and obviously took as much pride in his outward appearance as his position in the hotel. The East Wind was an international chain. He clearly felt his prospects were brighter than most. He stood with his feet hip-width apart, hands clasped comfortably behind his back. Balanced and in control. This was his domain and the Federal Officer's questions were beginning to bore him. He turned his attention to Birgitte who had barely said a word since Tony had introduced her.

"Do you mind if I ask where you are from in Denmark?" he asked with a wry grin. "I couldn't help recognise your accent."

Birgitte's eyes glazed over but her smile distracted his attention. "Copenhagen. Arhuse originally, but mostly Copenhagen."

"Ah, The Little Mermaid." He laughed as he said this as if it was some private joke between them.

Birgitte offered a little laugh in return. She gave Tony a quick look, requesting the opportunity to question her new friend. He nodded as if to say, "Be my guest".

"I know you have explained this to the other officers, Mr Kapalos, but if you wouldn't mind walking us through Mr Thostrup's movements again, as far you can remember them. Anything could be helpful to us at this stage."

"Of course, and please, call me Michael. Would you like to see the room he was staying in? I believe it's not occupied at the moment."

"That would be good."

He motioned to the elevator bay to the left of the reception desk. As he strode across the travertine tiles he produced a print-out from his jacket pocket. "Mr Thostrup checked in on October 24. In the morning, 10.30. We'd organised a transfer from the airport. I was on duty."

The elevator chimed. The doors opened. He stood back as they stepped in then followed. He pulled at a security card on a retractable wire attached to his belt and swiped a dark section of glass on the console. Then he pressed the button for the 23rd floor.

"He'd booked a Superior Room with a Harbour view. When he was checking in he told me that he loved the

Harbour and was looking forward to waking up to it each morning."

The elevator felt like it was barely moving. But they all watched the numbers slowly rising over the door.

"So he'd been here before?" Tony asked.

He continued to direct his answers to Birgitte. "He said he lived here back in the 70s for a short while."

"Did he say what he did for a living back then?" she asked.

"I'm sorry. I didn't think to ask. I just said it was great to have him back in Australia."

The elevator slowed and the doors opened.

"It's along here."

They stepped out into the elevator bay and then turned left down a long corridor that looked identical to the one on Birgitte's floor.

"The Superior Rooms are second only to the Premier Suite, which is upstairs. Twenty-four hour butler service, if that appeals to you."

"Sounds wonderful," said Birgitte.

He gave her a knowing look as he used his swipe card to unlock the door. He held it open for the two officers. Birgitte exhaled loudly as she took in the view. "It's so much more impressive than my room."

"I might be able to do something about that."

"Not bad," Tony muttered. He wasn't too sure what they would be looking for, as the Dane had officially checked out. The room had probably been used several times since, but at least the guy was talking.

Birgitte stood by the window. "Did Mr Thostrup ask for any services while he was here? Did he get you to book any tours, anything like that?"

The Head Concierge checked his printout again. "He dined in the main restaurant on the first night. Spared no expense by the looks of it. The twice-cooked pork belly is extraordinary. You must try it while you're here."

Birgitte stared at him carefully as he spoke. He was suddenly more interested in his printout than looking at her. "He used the buffet all three mornings he was here, but he didn't book any tours through us. He did use the gym twice and the pool once though."

"So nothing else that you can remember?" She nodded to his printout. "That isn't on his record."

"Nope. It's all here." He looked at his watch then to the door.

"Did you get a chance to chat with him much?"

"There are several hundred guests here on any given day."

Birgitte smiled at him. "I understand, but you strike me as a man with a memory for the guests you like and it sounds like he made at least a bit of an impression."

"I'm not sure why I remembered him in the first place, to be honest. Like I said, he was a polite guy. Kind of warm in a bit of a stiff, upper-class kind of way, I guess." His face lit up. "He did mention he wanted to go to Adelaide to visit a friend."

"Did he say when?" Tony couldn't help interjecting.

"No. He just said he had an old friend he might catch up with."

"Did you organise a hotel for him from this end?" Birgitte asked.

"I might have suggested one. I really can't remember."

"Safe to say it would have been part of the East Wind chain?"

"Probably."

They both laughed at this to ease the tension.

Birgitte asked. "Can we get a copy of that print-out?"

"Of course. I'll get you a fresh one as soon as we're downstairs." He seemed grateful that the questioning had stopped. He led them out into the corridor. "So how long will you be staying with us?"

"Hard to say, I'm afraid," Birgitte said. "But I'll be sure to ask for you if I need help with anything."

"I'm here Tuesday to Sunday. And you can reach me outside of hours if it's really important. For the case or anything at all."

They rode down to the lobby in silence.

As they stepped out into the reception area Birgitte touched the Head Concierge's elbow to get his attention. "Could you please also check that he isn't staying at one of your hotels in Adelaide, or anywhere else in the country. It could save us a lot of running around."

"I'd be more than happy to. Won't take a minute."

He moved off in the direction of the offices in the far corner of the lobby.

Tony laughed. "He'd probably be willing to run you around Sydney in a rickshaw if you like. I can suggest some good hills."

"I hope you don't mind me asking about the hotel in Adelaide."

"Not at all. I'd be surprised if it had even occurred to Donleavy to ask. Harris is quicker, but she's not that experienced. Would you be able to call Mr Thostrup's sister in Denmark to find out who he might know in Australia?"

She looked at her watch. "It's still too early, but I can call her later this afternoon."

The Head Concierge came back with a fresh printout but told them that the Dane definitely wasn't booked into any of their hotels in Australia and that a flag would go up on the system if he did. He would call her personally if that happened. She thanked him for this. He made a point of giving his card only to her, then excused himself to assist with the check-out of a large group of elderly Americans who were milling around the reception desk like lost sheep.

Tony and Birgitte stepped through the main doors into the driving bay. Tony suddenly clicked his fingers. "I'm sorry. I should have got him to get me a copy of that printout as well. Stupid of me. I'll be two seconds."

He spotted the Head Concierge heading back towards the office. Tony caught him up.

"Mr Kapalos?"

The Head Concierge turned but didn't bother to smile. There was no reason to.

"I'll need a copy of that printout as well, if you don't mind."

When the Head Concierge came back out with another printout Tony stared at him hard and kept his voice down.

"You seemed pretty cagey when my colleague asked about services up in the Dane's hotel room."

"It's all on the printout."

"Cut the crap. I know how hotels work. Did he ask for any special services?"

The Head Concierge paused and looked discreetly for any management staff that might be within earshot. Tony was tired of this guy's shtick. "Listen, I don't give a shit if this is how you pay your rent, but this guy has been missing for a few days so if you organised a hooker, I need to speak to her today."

Birgitte sat at the desk in her hotel room, her laptop whirring slowly to life. She watched the ferries bobbing about down in Circular Quay as she waited to get online. It was 4pm. She had considered having a short nap to take the edge off her jet lag but decided to force herself to stay awake until at least nine that night.

She was still perturbed. She had watched Detective Kingsmill's altercation with the Head Concierge earlier that day from outside. It was subtle but he'd definitely pressed the man for more information. Yet when he came back out he simply waved the printout and said, "Got it". She had waited for him to say more, but he just folded the paper up and put it in his pocket.

"What's next?" she asked.

"I've got a few unrelated matters to attend to, another case. And I also have to check in with my boss back at the office. You're okay to call Thostrup's sister?"

"Sure. I'll do some digging on his first time in Australia as well."

"I'll get one of the staff to start contacting all the hotels in Adelaide, too, there can't be that many of them. It's a much smaller city than Sydney."

"Do you have any thoughts as to what might have happened to him?"

"It's really too early to tell. It doesn't seem right that he should just disappear, but at the same time, he could have booked a tour from anywhere, so he's out of reach. Or he's gone bush with a friend."

"Gone bush?" Birgitte asked.

"Out of the city. Into the country."

"And not contacted his family?"

"We're following all the right leads. Nice work up there, by the way. I couldn't get 'boo' out of the guy."

Birgitte gave him a querulous look, only picking up two thirds of what he was saying.

Tony realised he'd have to drop the colloquialisms and speak more carefully. He said, "You got him talking. It helped."

"Thankfully," she said, smiling, "it would appear Constable Harris' observations on Australian men are accurate."

He laughed. "I'll bear that in mind. Are you okay to have the afternoon to yourself?"

"I'm sure I'll manage."

"I'll call you if I hear anything."

She had watched him get in his car. A feeling of disappointment descended on her. He seemed like a capable officer, and even a good man, but she was concerned he may have issues with trust, either because she was a woman or he just preferred to work alone, which could cause problems if there were any serious developments. She decided to give him the benefit of the doubt and see how he behaved the next time they interviewed someone.

Her browser popped up on screen. She opened her email. Nothing from Sven. There was little point updating him already. He preferred it when there was actual news to report, something to go on. She resisted the temptation to check the Danish sites for news on Anders' appeal.

It suddenly occurred to her to see if Thostrup had a LinkedIn account. He might be recently retired but he seemed savvy enough to want to maintain a profile, even if it was maintained by an assistant. She kicked herself for not thinking of it earlier. There were several Hans Thostrups but she recognised the third in the list. She clicked on his name and scrolled back through his career carefully, making notes as she went.

Five years as Director of Natural Resources at ACER, 14 with the EU all up, six years at Energistyrelsen – the Danish Energy Agency, several more mid-level roles for large mining corporations across Europe. Then she spotted what she was looking for. He had had been a Financial Officer at Central Gas Co from 1976-1978, based in Sydney. It looked like he moved around the country a lot.

She brought up the company's website. They had plants outside of Adelaide as well as in the Northern Territory and the top part of Western Australia. There was a history tab. It had black and white photos of drilling equipment dating back to the 50s. But there was no mention of Thostrup or who he might have worked with.

She checked the bedside clock then calculated the time in Copenhagen – 6am. She picked up her phone and dialled Katrine Holl's number that was in her files.

"Hello." The voice sounded slightly alarmed.

"Ms Holl. It's Detective Birgitte Vestergaard, Danish National Police. We spoke on the phone earlier in the week."

"Yes. Yes. Have you found him?"

"No. But I am in Australia now, working with their Federal Police. I take it you haven't heard from him then?"

"No. I'm getting very worried."

"I can appreciate that, Ms Holl. We're doing everything we can. We've noticed that he lived in Australia in the mid 70s. Can you tell us anything about that?"

"It's a long time ago. It was with some multinational firm, Gasco or Gas Light."

"Central Gas Co."

"Yes. That's it. I'm not entirely sure what he did for them, but it would have had something to do with finance. That was his thing. But there was nothing out of the ordinary. His wife moved with him for the duration of the role. They lived in Sydney. She used to say that the heat got to her."

"Do you know if he is still in touch with any one from those days?"

"I'm not sure. He's travelled so much. He has former colleagues he stays in touch with all over the world." The line when quiet for a few moments. Birgitte waited.

Ms Holl said, "There was a gentleman he mentioned more than others, a German man who had started with him at Gas Central Co at the same time – he loved the wine country outside of Adelaide so much that when his contract was up he stayed. Hans might have planned to meet up with him."

"Can you recall his name?"

"Gunther? Gun... Gunner Mendelson."

"You wouldn't have any contact details, would you?"

"I'm sorry, I don't."

"That's okay. I'm sure there can't be too many Gunner Mendelsons in that part of Australia. One more thing. Would your brother have been likely to travel with an old friend on a whim?"

"Are you suggesting that he's not missing, Ms Vestergaard?"

"Not at all, but I'm hoping there is a simple explanation to all of this."

"Since his wife died I have kept a close eye on him. The depression, the grief really weighs on him – not that he would ever admit it. He doesn't like me to fuss so he always calls, every week. I didn't expect to hear from him all the time but as I explained to my husband, he had agreed to call me on the 30th of October. I marked it in my calendar. He simply wouldn't be that inconsiderate. I hope for his sake we are wasting your time, Ms Vestergaard."

"So do I, Ms Holl." And so do the taxpayers of Denmark, she thought. "Thanks for your time. I will be in touch the moment I hear anything."

She felt deflated by Ms Holl's tone. She brought up the home page for Berlingske. There was nothing on Max Ander's appeal. Then she foolishly clicked on to one of the tabloid sites and felt her heart sink.

Tony turned into a back street in Kings Cross, the red-light district east of the city. At this time of the afternoon Maison

Road was quiet, almost serene, lined either side with ageing jacaranda trees and restored terrace houses. The cafes on one side were deserted. In the evening the street would be bustling with all manner of nightlife. As Tony walked up the hill he read off the house numbers on the right. The narrow street turned left at the crest into a laneway that served as the back entrance to the strip clubs along the main road of the Cross. He was familiar with most of them. In his youth he'd spent enough time with his mates carousing the Pink Pussycat and Porky's for him to realise that women could move beautifully when they were dying inside and men could earn respect for behaving like animals. The street stank of rotting garbage, stale beer and urine.

Three houses before the turn was a recently restored terrace with an elegant brass plate by the door, which read 'The Silken Touch'. Tony stepped through the wrought-iron gate and up a short flight of steps to the front door.

He felt that Detective Vestergaard had been right to press the Head Concierge on Thostrup's extra-curricular activities, but he wasn't entirely sure of the protocol for overseas police officers when dealing with organised crime. He figured it was best if he pursued this line of enquiry on his own and he wasn't comfortable having to explain that to her on her first day in Australia. If it did prove useful, he'd fill her in later.

He rang the buzzer and waited. The door opened. A tiny Asian woman wearing a see-through red slip and matching panties appeared behind the security grill.

"Federal Police. This isn't a raid. I just need to talk with one of the girls."

The woman didn't unlock the grill. She turned on her four-inch heels and disappeared down a dark hallway. She called out something in Cantonese. He could hear doors opening and closing and scurrying feet and urgent muffled conversations. Eventually a large Chinese man in his mid 30s stood in the doorway, stone-faced.

Tony tried again. "I'm Detective Anthony Kingsmill with the Federal Police. I was hoping to have a short informal chat with a girl here by the name of 'Heaven'."

The bouncer stared at him as if he didn't understand English.

"I could get a warrant but it really isn't necessary. We're just trying to locate a Danish gentleman who may not want to be found. I was hoping Heaven could fill in some details as to his whereabouts a week or two ago. I promise, I'm not interested in your business. I just need to speak to the girl and I'd like to do it as discreetly as possible."

The bouncer turned around and yelled out in Cantonese. A tiny face appeared from one of the doorways in the corridor.

Tony called out to her. "Heaven? I just want to talk about one of your clients. A Danish man. I need to find him. You are not in any trouble at all. Just a quick chat."

The bouncer unlocked the security door. Tony stepped into the hallway as a stocky Chinese woman wearing oversized reading glasses appeared at the top of the stairs.

"What you want? We good for this month."

"I don't care about that. I need to talk to Miss... Heaven here for a few minutes."

"We good this month."

"Yeah, I get it. And I'm not here for that." He turned to the bouncer. "Can you explain?"

The bouncer barked up the stairs in Cantonese. The woman eyed Tony warily. "Five minute. She on my time. You cost me money."

"It will be quick, I promise."

He turned to the girl down the hallway. "Do you want to do this here or in the cafe down the street?"

She reminded him of one of the girls from his school days – a pretty face but with a slightly nasty edge to it that some guys found incredibly hot. She disappeared inside the room. The door closed. When she came out she was wrapping herself in a gaudy purple robe. She led him down the hall to the back of the house. The kitchen was cluttered with unwashed soup bowls and takeaway containers. It smelled of cold dishwater. There was a rice cooker steaming away in one corner. She opened the back flyscreen and stepped out into a small cement backyard that was lined on both sides by a decrepit paling fence. There were several clothes horses draped with burgundy towels drying in the sun.

She pulled a pack of cigarettes and a lighter from her gown. In the daylight Tony figured she was 22 at most.

"How's your English?" he asked, trying to adopt a non-threatening tone.

"Okay." She eyed him, warily placing a cigarette between her lips and lighting it.

"Been here long?"

"What you want?"

"One of your outcalls last month. The East Wind Hotel on about the 24th or 25th of October. Remember it?"

"Maybe," she said, breathing smoke through her nose.

"Please, Heaven. I'd prefer it if you played nice. I'm looking for a gentleman. A Danish man. Apparently, he booked your services."

"I see lot of men," she said flatly. "Every day."

"Do you remember a Danish guy at the East Wind Hotel or do we have to do this down at the station?"

Suddenly she smiled at him, a practiced smile that was supposed to melt his resolve.

"You say you play nice." She stroked his upper arm and looked up at him with an inviting smile.

"I need details, Miss."

"It'll cost you." She let her robe fall open so that he could see that she was only wearing a lace thong.

He grabbed the cord of her robe and did it up so tight she squealed. Her cigarette fell from her lips.

"It'll cost you if you don't start cooperating," he said. "I don't think the boss lady would appreciate a raid later this week and every other week after that because you want to be coy. So quit wasting my time."

She stepped back from him. Her dark eyes flashed with hatred but then her bottom lip started to wobble. This girl played so many roles she didn't know how to behave.

"He was old man. He pay cash. One hour."

"What did he want?"

"He didn't say."

"He drew you a picture? What did he want?"

"Didn't matter. I gave him massage but then he couldn't get it up. He start crying. He talk to himself whole time. About some woman."

"Name?"

"Maggie something. He said, 'Sorry', and he gave me $50 tip. I left."

"How long were you in his room for?"

"Half an hour. No more. He pay for one hour plus tip."

"He didn't ask for anything weird? Didn't say anything else?"

"He say a lot, but I don't understand. He upset about this woman."

"It was definitely Maggie. Not anything else?"

"It sound like Maggie. But he was blubbering like little baby," she said with contempt.

"Was there anything else?"

She considered his question, and was obviously tiring of her own routine. "He seemed like nice man, but very sad."

"Was he drunk? Did he smell of booze?"

She nodded. "There was scotch beside bed. Half empty."

"Did he ask for you again in the days afterwards?"

"No."

"Ask boss lady if he contact here again." Tony frowned as he realised he was beginning to talk in broken English. "Ask your boss if any other girls here went to the hotel."

He followed her back inside the terrace house. The madam was in the hallway barking into a mobile. The girl interrupted her to ask Tony's question in Cantonese.

The woman glared at them both. "Nothing. No. He no ring back. She give him bad time. I lose customer. Now leave."

Tony thanked the girl and the bouncer whose expression hadn't changed since he'd arrived. The screen door slammed behind him and he could hear the boss lady yelling out to each of the rooms what he could only guess was "The pig has gone, get back to work".

He stood out on the street. He couldn't help but feel for Thostrup. To lose someone you love for whatever reason was soul-destroying. The grief, the loneliness, the torment of physical desire that doesn't let up regardless of your personal circumstances. The guilt that follows. Some things were best left behind closed doors.

His phone rang. It was one of his colleagues from the office. They had been calling all the hotels in Adelaide. Apparently a Hans Thostrup had stayed at The Grace Hotel on North Terrace for two nights a fortnight ago. But according to the manager there, he'd checked out on October 28 and hadn't mentioned where he was heading next.

Tony rang Birgitte as he walked back to his car.

"Yes." She sounded agitated as if he'd interrupted her in the middle of something more important.

"It's Detective Kingsmill," he said. "Am I disturbing you?"

"Not at all," she replied, closing her web browser on her laptop. She couldn't unread the article in Extra Bladet she had just seen but she needed to put it and all the other Danish tabloids out of mind as quickly as possible. She cleared her throat. "I'm sorry. It's the jetlag."

"Of course, I understand. I've just been informed that Mr Thostrup stayed at The Grace Hotel in Adelaide from the 26th to the 28th of October. Are you up for another flight?"

She laughed wearily. "I'll manage. I have spoken to his sister in Copenhagen. She mentioned a gentleman by the name of Gunner Mendelson, a former colleague."

Tony wrote the name down in his pad as Birgitte talked. "They both worked for a company called Central Gas Co back in the mid 1970s. Apparently he still lives somewhere around Adelaide. She thought they might have planned to meet while he was in Australia. Could be worth speaking to him while we are down there. Hopefully he can tell us where Mr Thostrup is or at least what he's been up to before he disappeared."

Tony thought about the young woman he'd just interviewed. He knew he probably should share what he had learned with Detective Vestergaard but somehow it didn't seem right. Thostrup had lost his wife and was obviously just trying to move forward in his own way, privately. If it had no bearing on the case, there was no point in bringing it up. He decided to sit on the information for a while longer. Quietly he hoped that it wouldn't need to come out. He pictured Hana Shakib alone in her cell at the Frazer Correctional Facility for Women and thought about all her lies, so tangled in good intentions and darker motivations that it would make little sense to an outsider. Some things were best kept private.

"I'll book some flights for first thing in the morning and text you the details," he said. "Thanks for doing the research and calling Thostrup's sister. Here's hoping he's just out fishing with an old friend."

The trap door slammed shut with a brittle clang. Inside the long metal cage, a three-metre crocodile thrashed about with the bloodied carcass of a chicken still protruding from its mouth.

A man in a khaki shirt and chinos, with a rifle slung over one shoulder, stood beside the cage on the bank of the creek, admiring the animal's brute strength and ferocity.

"Take it easy, my little friend. Enjoy your snack. I won't be gone long, then you can go about your business."

The beast sat motionless for a moment then lunged at him, bashing its snout against the cage.

The man didn't flinch. "Don't be like that," he said, laughing drily. "Or I'll put a tiny bullet in your thick fucking skull and let the ants have their way with you. And where's the dignity in that?"

He turned and strode through the trees along the bank, pushing the palms out of his way with his hand. Despite his long limbs and bony frame, there was a languid agility to his movements as he stepped between the trees.

He came to a clearing where he had moored an aluminium dingy. The sound of the outboard engine shattered the stillness of the jungle. He drove the boat slowly up the creek, past the caged crocodile, and round a gentle bend. The air was thick and humid, where the sun broke through the canopy it blazed violently against the water. He searched the luminescent wall of foliage on the left bank until, a few hundred metres on, he spotted the tree where he had set up the winch a few nights earlier. He could see the steel wire lying slack on the mud, leading down to the water's edge. He used a long wooden pole to hook the wire up from the bottom of the creek. Then, tickling the throttle gently as the wire ran through his hand, he began tracing its full length.

A hundred metres further along the creek the wire turned toward the bank and disappeared deep under the water. He cut the engine. "So this is where you live, my little friend. I believe you have something that belongs to me."

He cast the anchor, made sure it would hold then tied off the line. Then he waited. When the water was finally still and the only movement he could sense was the myriad tiny insects flitting erratically in the broken sunlight he took hold of the wire. He scanned both banks of the creek and the surface carefully for other crocs before plunging his hands into the water. After a minute of pulling on the wire at different angles, straining against the anchor line, it started to give. He sat up and pulled lengths of the wire steadily into the boat. Eventually, through the tannin-stained water about a metre down he caught sight of a pair of slim pale hands taped at the wrists. He let go of the wire and watched as the hands turned gracefully, continuing to rise slowly to the surface until he could see long thick strands of black hair swirling between pale arms. The body rolled. The bloated face of Salina Heysmith neared the surface. She appeared to be staring up through the water at the sky, her final expression was one of dull horror.

He carefully lifted her out of the creek by her wrists. One of her legs had been ripped off at the hip, the other, crushed and torn, was curled up to her stomach at an odd angle. Her wet blouse, littered with weed, did little to conceal her nakedness. He admired her breasts and lifeless eyes then drew her close, taking her in his arms. The boat rocked gently under his feet as he pressed her body to his. For a minute or two they swayed, drunken lovers dancing in an empty bar, his face buried in her matted hair. He inhaled the smell of wet mud and death. Eventually, he let out a dull indecipherable moan, mired in pleasure and anguish. Letting go of the moment, he rested her broken body in the bottom of the boat.

The engine erupted once again as he turned the boat around and drove back along the creek to recover the winch. Once it was in the boat and he'd cleared away all evidence of his ever being there, he drove back to the metal cage, but when he opened the trap door the crocodile refused to budge. He poked it roughly with the end of his rifle. "Don't sulk, my little friend, one bird for another is a fair trade, eh?"

The crocodile backed out of the cage with the chicken still in its mouth. The man raised the rifle to his shoulder and lined the sight up between the beast's eyes, following it carefully as it slithered heavily into the creek and swam around the bend. The man walked back to the boat. He drove along the creek to the original clearing. There he climbed out, threw his catch over one shoulder like a butcher with a calf and walked up through the jungle to a dark SUV parked on a disused fire trail. Within several minutes the body was packed and sealed in a custom-built refrigeration unit in the back of the vehicle, to be preserved in a state of partial decay for the long journey south. When he had hidden the boat among the foliage and gathered his rifle and winch, he felt a sense of satisfaction with his work. It had been a very productive weekend. He settled in behind the wheel. It would take two days to cross the country from Kakadu in the Northern Territory down to the bottom of South Australia, then just out of Adelaide he'd head east across the border into Victoria. Easy money, he thought, quietly laughing to himself at the months of preparation that had led to this point.

CHAPTER THREE

The road up into the Adelaide Hills hugged the contours of the undulating landscape, through neat orchards, vineyards and olive groves. Wispy clouds drifted overhead, providing little shade from the blazing sunshine and relentless heat.

As Tony drove, Birgitte sat beside him, trying to make sense of his behaviour in Sydney the day before. She remembered being underwhelmed by Australian men when she had backpacked around the country in her early 20s. Many of them were lovely to look at, with their sun-bronzed skin and toned physiques, but they clung to a 1970s attitude towards women, as if the fairer sex should be wrapped in cotton wool or shielded from information their tiny brains couldn't comprehend. She hoped Detective Kingsmill was better than that.

Occasionally she glanced at him. Beneath the dry humour and the laidback charm was a sadness; nothing overt, a subtle resignation in the eyes as if something or someone had dampened his spirit. Perhaps for this reason she had decided not to raise her concerns about his altercation with the concierge at the East Wind Hotel. She rubbed her face with a restless hand, wiping her bleary eyes. Thanks to the jetlag she had been awake since 2am, her mind racing with potential scenarios that might be worth pursuing. She had been eager to discuss the case with him on the flight from Sydney to Adelaide but despite her best efforts to stay awake, she had fallen into a deep sleep as soon as the plane took off. She awoke with him gently pressing her shoulder and calling her name. They had already landed.

As they had stepped off the plane he suggested she adjust her watch again by half an hour. She looked at him, bewildered. "Forward or backward?"

"Backward."

It wasn't much of a time shift but it still managed to tilt her further from her own axis. She had to remind herself it was actually Tuesday.

They had rented a car at the airport and drove into the centre of the city, which was as she remembered it: quiet, peaceful and very pretty. Tony had booked two rooms in the Parkview Motel on North Terrace, then they walked up the street to interview the owners of The Grace Hotel, where Thostrup had stayed.

Gillian Beaumont and Charles Hanning were a married couple who had formerly worked in PR before taking the plunge to start their own boutique hotel. They had converted an old print shop and warehouse into modernist industrial accommodation designed to appeal to travelling executives. Unfortunately, the interview didn't provide much in terms of fresh leads, only confirming that Thostrup was last seen on October 28 when he checked out of The Grace. However, Ms Beaumont had said that Thostrup looked sad when he left, which Birgitte found interesting.

"Sad at leaving?" she had asked.

"No," she replied. "He said his wife had died of cancer not so long ago. I think he was struggling to come to terms with it all. He was just lonely, I guess, and missing her."

"Did he say where he might be going next?" Tony asked.

"I had a chat to him about Kakadu and possibly Uluru," Mr Hanning replied. "He said he'd been before, but he'd like to see them again. Outside of that, he didn't seem to have any concrete plans."

Birgitte became a little alarmed when her colleague began to press them about possible visitors Thostrup may have had in his room. He wasn't being aggressive, just persistent, but it bothered her, and them. They responded awkwardly as if they were being accused of running an escort service out of the hotel. When he was confident they were telling the truth he wrapped up the interview, thanking them for their time.

As he pulled the car onto a dirt road that led through several acres of eucalypts Birgitte finally said, "Can I ask you a question?"

"Sure."

"This morning, when we were at The Grace Hotel, why were you pressing the owners so hard about visitors?" Lack of proper sleep was making her irritable and suddenly she was in no mood for games. "Is there something you're not telling me?"

Tony concentrated on the road, which was heavily corrugated, slowing the car down to almost walking pace as he negotiated the rivulets in the dirt. He looked across to see that she was staring at him, obviously without any intention of dropping the subject. He considered brushing over it with a joke but he was beginning to realise she wasn't the sort of officer you kept information from.

"Thostrup had a visitor at the East Wind during his first night in Sydney," he said.

"I'm listening."

"A prostitute, goes by the name of Heaven," he said. "I thought he may have done the same while he was in Adelaide."

The front of the car dropped into a small pot hole with a bang that jolted them both in their seats. Tony wrestled with the wheel and accelerated. The wheels spun momentarily but then the car lurched upwards and was able to pull it on to smoother ground.

"A prostitute? At the East Wind?" she asked, making no attempt to hide her consternation. She braced her hands against the dashboard. "When did you learn of this?"

"When I spoke to the Head Concierge," he said, finally realising how bad this must look to her. "After we'd both spoken to him."

She shook her head. "At what point did you intend sharing this with me?"

"I'm sharing it now."

"I can't be going into interview like that with only half the information, Detective Kingsmill. Not only does it look bad in front of people, I won't be able to pick up on what is really being said. It's hard enough that English is my second language."

"I honestly didn't think it would amount to anything."

Birgitte was really surprised by his lack of judgement. It jarred with her initial opinion of him, and her first impressions were usually razor-sharp. She cursed the jetlag, but still wanted to know how she had got it so wrong. "Why couldn't you have pressed Kapalos for that information while I was there?"

"I could have, but I don't think it would have got the same result."

She found his arrogance astounding. "Why didn't you at least tell me afterwards, when we were outside the hotel?"

He cursed under his breath as the underside of the car grated against a rock he should have seen. He accelerated awkwardly up the steep incline. Eventually the road rounded the crest of a hill and he was gradually able to pick up a bit of speed and regain control.

"Listen," he said, "Kapalos suggested that Thostrup contact a brothel in Kings Cross called The Silken Touch, so I dropped in yesterday afternoon on my way back to the office. Fortunately, the girl he hired was there so I spoke to her. She remembered going to the East Wind but said Thostrup couldn't perform – he was too drunk and upset with grief for his late wife."

She turned away from him. "*Jesus Kristus*, I'm here following the investigation and you leave me out of a key interview."

"At the time it was hardly a key interview."

"But suddenly it is now?" She took a deep breath to contain her anger. The dreadful road was now rattling her nerves as much as the lack of sleep. "At this stage, talking to anyone who has seen Hans Thostrup in the days leading up to his disappearance is crucial."

"I was hoping it would amount to nothing. I just didn't want to get you involved in this side of things on your first day."

"What side of things? Do you think that we don't have prostitution in Denmark, Detective Kingsmill? I can assure you we have far more liberal attitudes to the industry than Australia. Or did you think you were doing me a favour? Is this some sort of misguided Australian chivalry."

"It was a basic line of inquiry I wanted to get out of the way so we could focus on the bigger picture."

Birgitte stared at him in disbelief. "And what if it is crucial? What if we've lost a day because you either don't trust me or don't think I can handle the information? I seriously hope for your sake that Mr Thostrup is okay."

Up ahead Tony saw a wooden gate across the road. He pulled up, grateful for an excuse to get out of the car. He pulled the gate back and considered ripping it off its hinges. At what point was he supposed to explain that blokes like Kapalos aren't likely to 'fess up to anything to do with hookers in front of a beautiful woman? She was being unreasonable. He got back in the car, drove a few metres passed the line of the fence and got out again. As he slammed the gate shut behind them he remembered Miller's tone when she had first told him to act as liaison officer for a Danish fly-in. He found himself surrounded by over-zealous women hell-bent on telling him how to do his job.

Without another word between them, they drove up through the eucalypts, which soon gave way to neat rows of vines. They eventually arrived at a white bungalow with a wrap-around verandah and corrugated tin roof. It sat near the crest of a hill on a clearing of manicured lawn. There was a dusty dark blue SUV in front of a garage to the left of the house. It was an idyllic setting with views over the trees back towards Adelaide.

Before they got out of the car Birgitte said, "I want this to work, Detective Kingsmill. But you have to be open with me and treat me as you would any other colleague, regardless of my nationality or my gender."

"It's got nothing to do with that."

"Doesn't it?"

They got out of the car. The heat was stifling. Birgitte realised she couldn't afford to alienate her only connection in the country on their second day. Her face softened slightly as she walked around the front of the car and approached him. "What I'm trying to say is that I'm sure there are ways of doing things in Australia that are different from how we do them in Denmark, and I can respect that, but I need to be kept informed so I can do my job efficiently. Like you, I have to answer to my superiors as well."

She set off across the towards the house. When he caught up to her he asked, "Are you this tough on all your colleagues back in Copenhagen?"

"You thought that was tough, Detective Kingsmill?" she replied, smiling. "That's very sweet."

He chuckled despite himself. "You can call me Tony, if you like," he said, feeling slightly sheepish at getting so angry earlier. "I'll obviously still call you Detective Vestergaard."

"Birgitte is fine, Tony. I'm sure we can get over this little hurdle. You're not the first man I've worked with."

As they approached the steps to the front verandah an elderly man in blue jeans, a check shirt and gardening gloves appeared from around the side of the house holding a pair of secateurs and a single-stem rose.

"Detective Kingsmill?"

"Mr Mendelson," replied Tony, reaching out his hand. "Thanks for agreeing to talk with us on such short notice. This is Detective Birgitte Vestergaard from the Danish National Police. She's helping us with our enquiries." Mendelson shook hands with both officers then offered Birgitte the rose. "From my garden out the back. I was going to put it in the hall, but I'd be happier if you took it. I've stripped off the thorns. You're quite safe."

His accent, even after several decades in Australia, was still distinctly German. There was a warmth and sincerity to his manner that Birgitte liked. She smiled and accepted the gift.

"Come up onto the verandah. We can talk out of the sun. I won't be able to stay out there much longer myself. Was the road in okay?"

Tony laughed. "Bit of a challenge."

"We had some heavy rains earlier in the year. I need to do something about it. It's easier going downhill if that's any consolation."

There was a white wicker table setting by the front door. They sat down and Tony began to elaborate on their phone conversation about Hans Thostrup.

Mendelson listened carefully, his brow furrowing as he took in the details. Birgitte figured he was in his early 70s. The skin on his face was slightly translucent but his eyes were still clear and sharp. His aquiline features would have been quite appealing in his younger days. Eventually he sighed, genuinely perplexed.

"He contacted me a few weeks back by email, to say he wanted to catch up. I had no idea he was even in the country. We haven't seen one another for something like seven years. Last time I was in Belgium in fact."

He looked at Birgitte, whose face was beading with perspiration and said, "I'm so sorry. You must be sweltering. Would you like some ice tea?"

"Thank you." She would have preferred for him to keep talking, but she was struggling. He disappeared inside.

"You're not going to pass out, are you?" Tony asked.

"We do have summers in Copenhagen, Detective Kingsmill. Sorry... Tony. It's just a bit of a shock to the system."

Mendelson returned with a tray holding a jug and three glasses. Birgitte drank steadily until she could feel the cool liquid working through her system. She exhaled heavily, slightly embarrassed at her inability to cope with the heat and her lack of sleep. She looked out over the vines. "What grapes are you growing?"

"A small batch of chardonnay. A friend crushes it for me and another makes it. I get about 200 bottles a year. Nothing extraordinary, but it keeps me busy. My family back in Frankfurt tell me they like it. I think they are being polite. You can try some if you like."

"A little early for me, thanks," Birgitte said.

"So you didn't meet up with him then?" asked Tony.

"He said he'd call me when he'd settled in. I figured he planned to be here for a few days. But he never rang. And I never bothered to even ask for his number. I just assumed he was busy doing other things. It's been a long time since he's been here."

"Yes," said Birgitte. "We understand he worked here with you in the 70s for Central Gas Co?"

"That's right. I was an engineer, and he was in the finance department. I think we were both escaping everything we knew back in Europe."

"Do you know of any other acquaintances he might still have from those days?"

The old man stared out into his garden, thinking. "Gaerets went back to Holland. Newman to Boston. I stayed here, obviously. Wait here a moment, I have some old photos that might jog my memory."

The flyscreen door flapped behind him.

"Are you concerned about Mr Thostrup?" Birgitte asked.

"I don't know, to be honest," said Tony. "It's been two weeks but nothing is screaming out at me that something has gone wrong, aside from him not calling his sister. He doesn't have a mobile. He's getting over a deceased wife. He's on holiday. I'm quietly hoping he calls his sister out of the blue from the other side of the Nullarbor and apologises. But..."

"But, what?"

"Just a gut feeling."

"Tell me."

"He'll turn up when he's ready."

"So there's no point looking?"

"When I was a kid, a great uncle of mine with Alzhiemers went missing one day – literally left the house to buy a carton of milk and never came back. The whole family hit the streets looking for him for days. I didn't see the point. He could have been anywhere. Seventeen days later a cleaner for a supermarket chain found his body in a fire-stairwell off the car park. The building next door was being gutted for a new development and a builder had stacked refuse in front of the fire door, blocking the exit. The poor old bugger was a war veteran and he perished in a supermarket car park."

"That's awful," she said. "But I'm sorry, what's your point?"

"Thostrup will turn up eventually, but it won't be through anything we're doing here."

The old man came out with a handful of photographs. He rested them on the table as he put his glasses on. He considered each photo until he found one that might be of interest.

"This is us on site at a mine in Coober Pedy. That's Hans, me, Gaerets and there's Newman on the left."

They passed the photo around.

"Here's another. Christmas party, later that year."

"Who are the women either side of Mr Thostrup?" asked Birgitte.

"The pretty one on the left was his wife, bless her. Maggie. She passed away a year or so ago, I believe. Cancer. The other one is Hans' sister, Katrine."

Tony went to say that she was the one who had contacted them but Mendelson kept talking. "Silly woman. Couldn't keep her nose out of Hans' business. She was only here on holiday for a few weeks but we were all ready to send her to the airport after a few days. Never liked her. High strung. Constantly worrying about her little brother despite the fact that he was far more accomplished than anyone in that family. But she did well for herself back in Denmark, apparently. Married some policeman who made quite a name for himself. Hans said it only made her more troublesome. He loves her, but even he prefers her in small doses."

He looked at them both. "You don't mean you're out here because she rang the alarm bells? Silly cow. Sorry, but she always got my blood up."

"So you think Mr Thostrup is not in any danger?" asked Birgitte.

"Listen, I don't know. As I said, he never got a hold of me after that first email, but he's a very capable man and I believe he was just enjoying his retirement away from the EU and memories of Maggie. I certainly hope he's okay."

Tony had helped himself to the other photos. "Who is this gentleman? He looks familiar."

"He should. That's Nils Brekman. Owns Katercorp."

"Jesus. He's worth a quid now."

"You're not wrong. We always knew he'd do well, but not that well. He's competing with Barclay Industries for the Timor Sea deal up off Arnhem Land at the moment. Or at least he will be if the Northern Territory Government gives the go ahead. But if you want my opinion, for what it's worth, it will go to the Chinese, if not directly then through some local subsidiary. They've got their claws into Africa. I'd say within 15 years they'll have most of Australia working for them as well. Sorry," he said, sipping his ice tea. "I shouldn't talk shop; force of habit. And I don't have anything against the Chinese as a people – hard workers, but their methods are a tad ruthless even for an old German like me."

Birgitte asked, "Do you know if Mr Thostrup is still in touch with Mr Brekman? Would he be planning to meet up with him as part of his holiday?"

"I'm really not sure. It's not beyond the realms of possibility. Hans kept in touch with a lot of his former colleagues. Much more than I have."

"Do you know where Katercorp is based?" asked Tony. "The head office?"

"Probably Sydney. They have sites all over Australia. There isn't really much more I can tell you. I'm very sorry if this hasn't been helpful."

Tony stood up and pulled a card from his wallet. "If you think of anything that might help or if Mr Thostrup contacts you, please tell him to call us immediately."

"Thank you for the ice tea," said Birgitte. "And the rose."

"Before you go." He went inside for a third time and came out with a bottle of wine. "It's a 2012 Mendelson Vineyard Chardonnay I've been hanging onto for a while. Bit of a lottery as to how it's holding up. Perhaps you can let me know how you liked it."

Once they were back in the car Tony started laughing. "Seriously, do all men trip over themselves to impress you."

"Not all of them, no."

As they drove back down through the vines, he said, "I'm sorry, about earlier. I shouldn't have gone off on my own like that. I wasn't trying to shut you out, I actually thought I was doing the right thing."

"It's okay. I'm glad we talked about it." She yawned into her hand and struggled to stay focused. "So where to next?"

"We should try to get a hold of Nils Brekman at Katercorp if we can, see if Thostrup has made any plans to meet up with him. I'll touch base with the guys back in Sydney. I asked them to run a check on his credit cards and ATMs. Hopefully he's used one of them in the last two weeks."

Birgitte crossed her arms and nestled back into her seat, rapidly losing the will to battle her fatigue.

Tony negotiated the corrugations in the road more carefully on the way down. Several minutes after closing the gate to Mendelson's property, he noticed Birgitte was fast asleep.

She was definitely a force to be reckoned with, Tony realised, looking over at her. It was actually reassuring to be working with someone so switched on and committed. He pulled the car back onto the main road and headed back towards Adelaide. Every so often during the drive he found himself watching her sleep.

The temperature in Adelaide continued to creep up into the early afternoon. Tony was standing in the shade of a sandstone church a few blocks up from the Parkview Motel, reading up on Katercorp on his smart phone.

He and Birgitte had arrived back at the motel just after midday. She was embarrassed that she had slept so deeply in the car, but obviously she needed more rest. Tony suggested she take a proper nap in her room for another hour or two as there wasn't much more they could do at that point. She didn't have the energy to argue.

As she had closed the door to her motel room, Tony set off across the car park and along North Terrace. Despite the heat, he had felt like stretching his legs after the drive. He'd also got to thinking about Hana Shakib. Something about watching Birgitte asleep in the passenger seat had reminded him of their time together. He hoped the walk and the research would get his mind back on the job.

From what he could glean from the website Katercorp was one of the largest locally owned mining firms in Australia. It focused solely on natural gas and operated sites across the country as well as off-shore. It was set up in the 80s and had grown steadily through the 90s. When Nils Brekman took the helm in 1998, he made headlines for dramatically restructuring what was already believed to be a hugely profitable business. His gamble paid off. The company now employed several thousand workers and posted annual net profits in the billions.

There was a head shot of Brekman beside a brief summary of his career. At a glance, Tony figured early 60s, possibly European descent. His face was thin, his bones pronounced; he appeared almost brittle, but there was a steeliness to his eyes – a serious man, in a dry way. The bio mentioned he was Dutch by birth, raised and educated in Australia, an engineer by trade.

Tony dialled the contact number of their Head Office in Sydney and asked to be put through to Brekman. After several transfers he got hold of Brekman's EA, a woman by the name of Judy Hastings, who explained that Mr Brekman was on his way to Kingsford Smith Airport where he would be boarding a flight for the US. Tony asked if he could be put through to his mobile. She hesitated. Tony couldn't believe the arrogance of these corporate bigwigs. He reminded her that he was with the Australian Federal Police and it was an important matter.

Eventually, a man's voice came on the line. The connection wasn't very clear. Tony thought he could hear passing traffic noise in the background.

"Nils Brekman?"

"Speaking."

"Mr Brekman, it's Detective Tony Kingsmill here. I'm with the AFP. Do you have a moment to talk?"

"Barely. I'm about to board a flight and I'm already running late." He was short of breath and Tony could picture him pulling luggage from the back of a hire car.

"This won't take long."

"Okay, Detective, what can I do for you?"

The line became clearer as Brekman entered the departures lounge of the airport.

Tony said, "We are investigating the disappearance of a Danish national by the name of Hans Thostrup."

"Hans? I've haven't spoken to Hans for a few years."

"You used to work together back in the 70s, is that right?"

"That's correct, we worked for Central Gas Co for a couple of years, down in Adelaide."

Tony could hear a muffled conversation between Brekman and the check-in staff. He waited.

"Are you still there?" Brekman asked. "Sorry about that. They're holding the flight for me."

"When was the last time you heard from Mr Thostrup?"

"Would have been at least two years ago, maybe a bit more. I had dinner with him in Lubjliana in Slovenia, where he's based. Works for the EU on their gas division."

"So he hasn't tried to contact you in the last few weeks, to meet up here in Australia?"

"No. I had no idea he was even here. Is he all right?"

"We're hoping so, Mr Brekman. Just trying to trace his movements as best we can."

"I wish I knew more."

"We've spoken to Gunner Mendelson who suggested we talk with you. Do you know of any other mutual acquaintances Mr Thostrup might be likely to contact if he is in Australia?"

Tony waited while Brekman considered the question.

"Not really. Hans was better at that kind of thing."

"Well, if you hear from him, could you please tell him to contact the AFP immediately. His family back in Denmark are obviously concerned."

"Of course. Can I call you on this number if anything comes to mind?"

"I'd appreciate that."

"I don't think they're going to hold my flight much longer, Detective. I seriously have to get a move on. Sorry I couldn't be more helpful."

"Thanks again for your time, Mr Brekman."

Tony leaned back against the church wall. He was about to call the office in Sydney to see how his colleagues were getting on with tracking Thostrup's electronic transfers, when he thought of Hana again.

For several minutes he seriously considered calling the prison – if only just to hear her voice – but he knew it was all too complicated. As his former boss on the Middle Eastern Organised Crime Unit, Richard Hartford had told him – he'd definitely dodged a bullet when their 18-month investigation into the Retif twins came to a head. Ironically, he had those two thugs to thank for saving his career. If one of their drug deals hadn't gone sour and ended in a shoot out in a Westfield car park, Tony still would have been involved with Hana. Up until that day he had no idea she was related to the family he'd had under surveillance for more than a year. The arrest of the two brothers brought down the extended family, which to his disbelief, included their first cousin, Hana Shakib. She was arrested and charged with falsifying tax returns on the brothers' scrap metal business. He still refused to accept that she did this willingly, but as she had refused to speak to him since that day, he had no way of confirming this.

Hartford was the only person in the NSW Police who knew of his friendship with Hana. And, as he rightly pointed out, if Tony had gotten any closer to her, regardless of how innocent their friendship may have been at the time, he could have been implicated in family's illegal operations. It could have ended his career and even landed him a bunk in Silverwater Jail. It was a sobering thought to say the least. He'd only ever wanted to help Hana and it tore him up that he couldn't have done more before her trial.

Funnily enough, Birgitte's comment in the car about misguided chivalry had cut deeper than she could have known, which was why, he realised now, he'd got so angry with her on the way to Gunner Mendelson's house. He couldn't help wondering what she would make of his involvement with someone like Hana.

Suddenly his phone rang in his hand.

A woman's voice asked, "Detective Kingsmill?"

"Yeah, who's this?"

"Kate. Constable Kate Harris. You said to call if we found anything."

"What have you got?"

"Well, I've been doing that general search of recently reported deaths of unidentified elderly males across Australia as you asked."

"And?"

"Apparently, there's a body of an unidentified white male possibly in his early 70s that's been sitting in the Alice Springs mortuary for more than a week unclaimed."

For a moment he pictured his great uncle, the war veteran who had survived the horrors of the Kokoda Trail, lying dead in a concrete stairwell for 17 days – unclaimed. "Shit. Cause of death?"

"Still being examined. He was found on the outskirts of an old mining town about two hours out of the city."

"Can you get in touch with the local guys there and send through a photo of Mr Thostrup, see if it marries up? Give them my number and tell them to call me direct if it's a match."

Birgitte was in a deep sleep. She was on trial for the murder of the three Svedbo children in an early modern European court. Max Anders was the prosecutor and he had a jury of peasant mothers hanging on his every word. He was showing them enlarged images of tabloid articles that accused her of putting her own career above the safety of society's most innocent. They shook their heads with disgust. As he showed them photos of the tiny corpses, the women turned pale and began to weep. Suddenly, the children in each image awoke from death to plead for justice. The women screamed and fainted. People in the gallery booed at Birgitte and threw rotting vegetables at her. The executioner stood to one side, a leather mask covering his face, but she recognised his eyes and the shape of his frame. It was her father. She felt so ashamed.

Her husband, Tomas, was dancing around the gallery in a harlequin's costume dry humping all the women he could get his hands on. "How do you like it?" he kept screaming at her. "You'll get yours, you filthy bitch."

Anders had finished his deliberations to raucous screams from the gallery for Birgitte's blood. The sentence is announced but she can't hear it because the courtroom has already erupted as people leap over the wooden barriers to attack her. She falls to her knees in the dock, peering out through the railings. She is the only person who notices that Anders is slipping out of the courtroom with a child in each hand. He looks over his shoulder with that grin that she knew all too well, then he laughs. It resonates around the courtroom but only she can hear it. Her father the executioner is practicing his swing, bringing the axe down hard on a block of wood, again and again.

She awoke to a loud banging. She stared about the motel room. It was still daylight. Still Tuesday. She checked her watch – 3.16pm. Someone was hitting the door very hard. She crawled off the bed, still dressed, and opened it. Tony was out of breath as if he'd been running.

"They've found Thostrup."

"Where?" she asked, wiping sleep from her eyes and trying to brush the hair from her face. The images from her dream continued to berate her.

"In a desert town outside of Alice Springs, in Central Australia. He's dead."

A few minutes later, when she had washed her face with cold water, she asked him to explain exactly what he'd been told.

He was sitting on a chair across from her as she sat on the edge of the bed. He'd got his breath back. "A Constable Anne Smith from Alice Springs rang and said she'd been given my number by Harris back in Sydney – I'd asked her to send through the image of Thostrup."

Birgitte had no idea what he was talking about. "Why Alice Springs? I don't understand."

"Sorry," he said. "I'll go back a bit. Constable Kate Harris, who you met yesterday, had phoned me earlier. Said she'd learned of a body that had been sitting in the mortuary in Alice Springs for a week or so, an unidentified male in his early 70s. She thought it might be Thostrup so I told her to send them a photo and get back to me."

"And it was a match?"

"Yeah. The forensic pathologist says we'll need better identification than that, but for the time being, they're confident it's him."

"How did he die?"

"Bled to death apparently, from wounds to his legs. But the forensic pathologist's report isn't finished. I told them we can be on a flight in the morning and that we'll need to meet with the pathologist and whoever is in charge of the investigation."

"They told you all this when you were next door? You could have woken me when Constable Harris phoned you."

"I was out researching Katercorp."

"Did you get in touch with Nils Brekman?"

"Yeah. We had a quick chat – he was about to board a flight for the US. But Thostrup hadn't got in touch so there was nothing new Brekman could tell us."

"Did he sound..."

"Suspicious? Not at all. At that point, I didn't know Thostrup was dead. That being said, Brekman was surprised at hearing his mate had gone missing and was concerned for his safety. He promised to call if he hears anything that might help."

He stood up and walked to the door. "I'll need to get us on the first available flight to Alice Springs."

Birgitte stayed in her room and began taking notes from their conversation. She decided not to email Sven until she was absolutely certain that the body in Alice Springs belonged to Hans Thostrup. She went into the bathroom and looked at herself in the mirror. She winced at the sight of herself. She tried to calculate how many hours she'd slept in the past 48 and couldn't.

So they'd found Hans Thostrup. It saddened her that he was dead. His overwrought sister would be devastated. Now she hoped it was a simple case of explaining his death as accidental, so she could get back on another long-haul flight and go home.

CHAPTER FOUR

The four-seater, twin-engine plane taxied along the runway of Alice Springs Airport. Under different circumstances Birgitte might have enjoyed the flight north over Central Australia – the vast expanses of parched earth, occasionally buckled by ragged ridges, glittering in parts with salt pans. The rare sightings of dark pools of water that could hardly be called lakes and the thin rivers that barely flowed into them. It was desolate and beautiful.

The plane eventually rolled to a halt in front of a small terminal several hundred metres from the main airport. Birgitte stood up and stretched, checking her watch. It was just past midday – and it was now Wednesday. Ever so slowly her body was adjusting to the shifts in time she had experienced in the past few days. Although she had slept better the night before, she still found herself getting groggy and irritable at odd hours. Again she had hoped to talk to Tony about the case but this time he'd fallen asleep during the flight.

There was a police car waiting for them on the tarmac. A bull of an officer in a short-sleeved khaki uniform was leaning against the bonnet with an Akubra hat shielding his eyes. His arms were folded across his chest and his legs were crossed at the ankles.

Birgitte followed Tony down the stairs from the plane door. She figured it had to be at least 42 degrees on the runway. Flies buzzed around her face. She tried to brush them away but it was pointless; a sizeable colony were already riding on Tony's broad shoulders and down his back. The heat of the tarmac burned through her shoes as they approached the local officer who hadn't budged.

"Steve Quintock," he said not offering his hand.

Tony and Birgitte introduced themselves. He gave them a perfunctory nod as if was passing them on a highway then he opened the driver's door and got in without another word. Birgitte frowned at Tony as if to ask, "What the hell is wrong with you people?"

They eventually collected their luggage from a trolley and put it in the boot. Birgitte opened the back door of the patrol car, leaving Tony to sit in the front. Quintock started the engine. They drove off the tarmac onto a service road, through a cyclone fence and on to the main road out of the airport.

"What can you tell us?" asked Tony when he realised the officer needed some prompting.

"One of the local kids found him Monday a week back – the third of November, from memory. He was in a creek about three hours out of town." His voice was flat, his demeanour disinterested.

"Had he been in the water long?" asked Birgitte.

Quintock snorted. "Love, there ain't been water in any creek round there since God wore short pants."

"What time was he found?" asked Tony.

"Some time round 10am. Little snot-nose fucker was wagging school. Meeting up with the rest of his deadshit mates to kick a football round. Only thing the little turds are good for."

"And the body? Is it still at Alice Springs Hospital?"

"I'm not taking you to a fucking drive-in." He looked into his rear view mirror. "Unless that's what you'd like."

Birgitte stared out the window, ignoring him. Her mind was too clouded to deal with a Neanderthal like Quintock – four flights in five days was almost more than she could bear.

"Have you been out to the crime scene?" asked Tony.

"Listen," he said with irritation in his voice. "I've only been told to pick you up and take you to the mortuary. I can't help you beyond that. You'll have to speak to Smith."

"Is he in charge?"

Quintock chuckled with derision. "He's a she, and she couldn't manage a fuck in a brothel."

They drove through the centre of Alice Springs in silence. Eventually Quintock pulled into the car park of a mid-sized hospital. He cut the engine, got out and strode into the reception area as if he was on his own. Birgitte and Tony followed at a distance, still bemused by his attitude. Tony decided there was no point apologising for every obnoxious bloke in the country.

An elderly nurse on the front desk gave them directions to the mortuary at the back of the east wing.

They walked along the bare corridors following the signs over each of the doorways, until they were admitted into section marked 'Mortuary'.

Tony asked a passing nurse if the forensic pathologist was available. She disappeared through a pair of doors. A few minutes later a pallid-looking man in his mid 50s emerged from the same doorway. He looked slightly lost in his lab coat and his thinning hair was stained with nicotine.

"Were you looking for me? Neal Brannigan, forensic pathologist." He shook their hands, then rubbed his nose which was covered in a chaotic web of splintered veins that suggested to Birgitte that the climate out here gave him an insatiable thirst. He stared at them with flat eyes. "Can we make it quick; I've got a lot on."

Quintock was nowhere to be seen so Tony introduced himself and Birgitte, and explained their connection to Hans Thostrup. The doctor looked over Tony's shoulder as he spoke as if he was waiting for someone more important to call him away. With a phlegm-riddled cough he cleared his throat and ran through the basics of the body's arrival at the hospital in a droll voice, until Tony held up his hand.

"So Mr Thostrup's body was found last Monday," he asked, checking his notes. "Thirteen days ago. And the autopsy wasn't performed til last Friday, and it's... what? Now Wednesday, and we still don't know what happened?"

Brannigan didn't like his tone. "Firstly Detective, I've been a little busy here thanks to a meth-lab fire last Wednesday that saw four people horribly burned, and a head-on between a sedan and a mini-bus on Friday which killed six. We don't have the resources to devote to Mr Thostrup, whose identity was only discovered yesterday. Secondly, due to the nature of his injuries, I am not about to rush to any conclusions. You'll know what I'm talking about when I show you."

He led them through several doors into a small windowless room. It was much cooler, almost cold. Birgitte's skin crawled with a curious familiarity – the beginnings of autumn in Copenhagen. The connection was jarring. There were several trolleys of varying size pushed into the corners and the far wall was lined with steel doors. Brannigan excused himself for a moment and returned with a manila folder, which he opened out on one of the trolleys. It contained paperwork and photos of the crime scene. He stepped across the room, opened one of the steel doors and pulled on the handle of a tray, sliding it out to its full length.

Birgitte approached the body of Hans Thostrup. He lay on his back, his arms by his side. As she took in his profile and followed the line of his torso, her mind automatically stepped up a gear and began to process every detail – the tone of his skin, the state of decay. She moved closer and felt her stomach lurch. Thostrup's legs had been ripped off midway up the thigh. It wasn't a clean cut. There were ragged pieces of flesh hanging around the severed bones in his legs. She held her breath so she wouldn't throw up.

"Thresher," grunted Quintock from the doorway. He was eating a chocolate bar he'd fetched from a vending machine.

Brannigan looked up, smiling. His crooked yellow teeth shone in the fluorescent light of the mortuary. "Hey, Quino. Yeah, I thought it might be, too, at first. Until I found this."

Quintock moved into the room as if suddenly it was his investigation.

The doctor pointed to a small trolley pushed over by a far wall. On a green cloth was a white triangle the size of a large coin. "It was lodged in the left femur."

"What is it?" asked Tony.

"Take a look."

Birgitte stared closely at it. "It's a tooth. Wild dogs? You call them dingoes?"

Brannigan laughed then began coughing again. "Yep. It's a tooth alright. But if we get dingoes with teeth like that, I'm moving to Afghanistan."

Quintock looked at her and chuckled drily.

The doctor returned to the corpse and continued to prod at the splintered thigh bones with a thin metal implement. "I'd hazard a guess, at this stage, to say it belongs to a shark. A bloody big shark. But I'm still waiting on confirmation."

They looked at the body again, struggling to comprehend the situation. Birgitte thought about the Hans Thostrup she had come to know if only through bare facts and vague impressions from his sister and the hotel staff who had dealt with him over the previous weeks: a warm, distinguished man who had achieved so much in his life time, an inspiration to his colleagues, a man who had experienced love and loss and had handled both with dignity. She stared at the shredded scraps of skin and torn flesh that had curled in the sun. The horrific nature of his demise demanded she be objective. She didn't really know this man at all.

"Was there any blood at the scene?" she asked, almost to herself. She looked up from the body.

The doctor directed her to the crime scene photographs in the file. There were several shots. The first, taken back a few metres from the gums that lined the bank, showed Thostrup seemingly climbing out of the creek. The next was a close up of his face, his expression one of frozen agony. The third was of his severed thighs. There was no blood in the sand or anywhere around the body. The others were of different parts of his body, and the whole scene taken from down in the creek bed. In the background Tony noticed three police cars up on the bank and kids cycling beyond the cordon.

"I'm thinking he bled out, possibly where he was bitten, that is on a boat somewhere, probably off the South Australian coast," said Brannigan.

"Why the South Australian coast? It wouldn't have happened at an aquarium?" Birgitte asked.

"There aren't any great whites in captivity. The coast of Adelaide is closest – I might be wrong about where it happened but that's for you guys to work out."

"So we're assuming it's a great white?"

"Like I said, I'm just waiting confirmation."

Birgitte asked, "How long has he been dead?"

71

"That's the other mystery."

"How so?" asked Tony.

"As you pointed out, he was found last Monday. He was in a makeshift mortuary down near Forbes Creek until we could get a car out there to pick him up on the Thursday. It's not much more than a shed in a paddock, and unfortunately the fridge down there is still on the blink. I've called the council but they reckon it's the responsibility of the Territory to fix it. I don't think anyone's in a real hurry. Usually only houses the locals. We don't get many international dignitaries here." He grinned at Quintock who sniffed his approval.

"So when I started the autopsy on the Friday I couldn't be confident as to the time of death. The signs of decomposition are a bit all over the place. However, there's no sign of other animals so I'd say he would have been dumped not that long before he was found – within a day at the most."

Tony said, almost thinking to himself out loud, "He checked out of The Grace Hotel on the 28th. Then his body turns up on the 3rd. It would take what? About 20 hours to drive up from the coast?"

"Sixteen to 17," said the doctor. Quintock concurred with a lazy nod from the doorway.

"So he probably died between the 29th and the 1st. It also rules out him being killed off any other coast line. There wouldn't be time to get him across from WA."

The doctor considered his theory and muttered, "We'll see."

Tony put his card on the trolley next to the shark's tooth. "Would you mind giving me a call as soon as you have any more information?"

"You'll get my report when everybody else does," he replied, guiding them out of his mortuary and patting his chest pocket for cigarettes. He turned at the door.

"See you at training, Quino?"

"Not unless those cigarettes get the better of you."

"6pm sharp – bring your A-game."

"Fuck you."

Brannigan set off down the corridor.

Birgitte and Tony walked behind Quintock back through the hospital to the entrance.

Tony asked Quintock, "Will someone be able to take us out to the crime scene?"

"Already sorted," he said, barely looking over his shoulder.

A stocky, stunted officer with a cool, boorish manner was waiting in the reception area with her hands on her hips. Quintock nodded to her and continued outside. Birgitte figured she was in her late 20s, naturally overweight, but probably very strong for her size. Her face was full but her features were pinched and her eyes were wary. She was clearly overcompensating for the thugs like Quintock whom she had to work with every day. Then Birgitte noticed the bruising under her left eye. The swelling must have come down in the last day or two.

The officer reached her hand out to Tony and Birgitte. "Constable Anne Smith. I spoke to you yesterday on the phone, Detective Kingsmill."

They all shook hands.

"You've seen the deceased?"

Tony exhaled. "Not good."

She looked at Birgitte, measuring her up as a female officer. Birgitte sensed she'd already formed a negative opinion of her, but she was still too affected by what she'd just seen in the mortuary to care.

"I can take you out to Forbes Creek in the morning," said Smith. "And you can talk to the boy who found Mr Thostrup if you like."

"We can't go today?" asked Birgitte.

The constable directed her answer to Tony. "It's a four-hour round trip and it's already just after 2pm. Best do it in the cool of the morning."

"Okay," said Tony. "Can you suggest a place to stay?"

"Settler's Arms in the centre of town isn't too bad. I can drop you off if you like."

"Thanks, we'd appreciate it," said Tony.

As the main doors of the hospital slid open he asked, "Have you already been out to the crime scene?"

"I was the one who called it in," she said with a hint of pride. "I happened to be in the area that day on an unrelated matter."

She motioned to a patrol car parked between two ambulances. Quintock had already dumped their luggage by the boot and driven away.

They walked across the driveway in the shade of a cement awning. It shielded them from the sun but not from the heat. Birgitte pulled a bottle of water from her handbag and paused to take a long mouthful. They waited for her. She put the bottle back in her handbag. "What were your initial impressions?"

Again Smith made a point of avoiding eye contact. "He looked desperate. As if he was trying to climb out of the creek, but he'd obviously been dead for days." Her voice was cold, matter of fact, but Birgitte could sense the young officer was no less affected than they were; she was just too wary of how it might look if she showed it. She unlocked the boot of the patrol car and helped them load their luggage.

Birgitte nodded to Tony, suggesting he sit in the front with Smith. He agreed and opened the passenger door.

As Smith settled in behind the wheel, Tony asked, "How did you get the shiner?"

"One of our regulars in the drunk tank took a swing at me."

"Charming."

"Prick didn't have the guts to swing at Quino or Mackay, or Davo."

Sounds like a fair fight, he thought, four sober cops against one inebriated local.

Birgitte asked from the back seat, "Was there anyone there when the body was found?"

"It's pretty remote," said Smith. "If the kid didn't feel like playing football, we may not of discovered the body for days. Lucky for us he had nothing better on."

The patrol car pulled out of the driveway, onto the main road.

"Who's heading up the investigation?" asked Tony.

74

"Senior Sergeant Frankston, but he's on the Gold Coast until Friday."

"Holiday?"

"Why would you need a holiday from this place?" she said with a droll voice. "He's at a conference. We've had a two new bikie gangs setting up shop in Alice over the past 18 months. He's trying to get the most up-to-date information on which gangs are active in drugs, which gangs are connected to international organised crime. That sort of thing."

"I didn't know you guys had bikies out this way," said Tony.

"They go wherever they can find a market apparently."

"Enterprising bastards, aren't they."

"One of their meth labs caught fire at the start of the week, out passed Braitling."

"The pathologist mentioned that."

"Still don't know whether it was rival gangs or just some dopey tweaker mixing the wrong chemicals. Frankly I don't care if they all set themselves on fire – less work for us."

Birgitte was fascinated by the slow response to Thostrup's murder and was beginning to get frustrated at the lack of concern.

"Tony, have you seen anything like this before?" she asked, wanting to get the conversation back on track.

"The Dane? Well, I've seen my fair share of car accidents when I first started out on the force – people who've lost their limbs, been crushed beyond recognition, but I've never seen someone who's been fed to a shark while they were still alive. It's almost incomprehensible."

He was right, she thought. It almost too difficult to accept. How could someone feed an elderly man to a great white shark? And why only his legs? If the killer, or killers, was looking to dispose of a body, he would have left it in the ocean for the shark to destroy the evidence. If it was a revenge killing then why stop at just the legs? This was no crime of passion. It was well thought out, meticulously researched in fact.

They sat in silence as they drove through the city. The more he thought about Thostrup's corpse the more Tony could sense a dull formless anger stirring within him. An old man – not unlike his own father – had been tortured and dumped. For what? What could possibly justify such a brutal death? He'd long ago accepted there were vicious people out there who lacked a conscience, empathy, a sense of compassion. And there were others even further along the spectrum away from decency who actually got a thrill from hurting others. One of the reasons he'd joined the force as a young man was to stop people like that.

He realised he hadn't spoken to Miller since Monday night when he'd told her he and Birgitte were heading to Adelaide the next morning. She would want to know that Thostrup had been found so she could break the news to her boss, Commander Barton. Tony wondered if it was worth suggesting he be allowed to pursue the case through to the end. The victim was a Danish national, and the crime had probably been committed across two states, so in effect, it was Federal in nature. If he knew Miller at all, she wouldn't give him the opportunity. The longer he was kept floating in his new role the more secure her own position would become.

They pulled into the car park of the Settler's Arms Motel, a two-storey red-brick block that wrapped around a pale blue swimming pool. Tony got the luggage out of the back and thanked Smith for the lift. She told she'd be back for them about 9.30am the next day. They watched her drive out of the car park and back onto the main road.

Tony turned and looked up at the rooms. "Welcome to Shangri-La. I hope you like Four X."

"Four eggs?" asked Birgitte.

"It's a beer... forget it. Desert humour."

Birgitte wrinkled her nose at him but didn't pursue it.

After they had checked-in, they wheeled their luggage up a flight of concrete stairs to two adjoining rooms on the top floor. Birgitte unlocked her door and said. "So what do we do now?"

"Nothing much we can do til the morning," Tony said, pulling at his shirt which had stuck to his chest with sweat. "I suggest you check in, cool off as best you can. As for me, I'm going to get changed and take a nap under the air-conditioner in my room. Knock loudly if you need anything."

Birgitte watched him close the door. She wondered if she could ever get used to the pace of life in Australia.

In the evening Birgitte took her laptop down to the pool area to do some research. She would have stayed in her room to work but there was an underlying odour of urine and stale cigarette smoke. When she had stepped outside she was surprised by the coolness of night air. She grabbed a dark cardigan to throw over her shoulders.

Down by the pool there were several white plastic tables and chairs scattered around for guests. An elderly man in black swimmers and a matching cap was doing languorous laps, oblivious to the cold. Each time he turned his head to breath between strokes she was reminded of Thostrup's face in the mortuary. She set herself up on a table down one end and typed 'great white sharks' into the search engine. After reading news accounts of recent attacks off the West Australian coast she found a clip on YouTube that had been filmed by an onlooker.

It started with the image of a young woman who had had no idea how much danger she was in moments before but was now swimming for her life. She was only a few metres from the safety of the boat where her friends were screaming at her to swim faster. Their hands reached out to her in desperation but they could see what was about to happen and no amount of screaming could help.

The shark had been cruising the waters 11 kilometres off the shore of Chile when two large boats filled with backpackers cut their engines. It was a sweltering hot day. A few of the cockier guys stripped off their shirts and leaped into the iridescent blue water. Soon enough, anyone who was able was bobbing about in the ocean, grateful for the cool change. They had been in the water for about 20 minutes when the call went out.

One of the deckhands had squinted through the sunlight as he thought he saw something breaking the water 30 metres away. He ripped off his sunglasses and grabbed his binoculars. A large dorsal fin was cutting a slow but purposeful swathe through the water towards the boats.

It wasn't so much the word "shark" that sent a jolt through group, but the way it was screamed by a grown man as if it was already too late. There was chaos as more than 20 kids swam frantically for the boats, splashing the water wildly. Tour staff hauled the swimmers up one after the other. Some fell on the deck screaming hysterically. Those who had the energy stood up and leaned over the gunwales to help the few who were still in the water. It was only then they realised the danger they had been in – the great white was now only 10 metres away and there was one girl left in the water.

She had always prided herself as a strong swimmer. She had the ribbons in her bedroom to prove it. Perhaps that's why she had swum further from the boat than the others; she had been confident she could get back without too much hassle. Only now the water felt like wet sand and her limbs like jelly. No matter how hard she kicked her legs the boat didn't seem to get any closer.

She could see the fear in their eyes now. The guys were calling out for her to keep swimming and to not look back. She was almost there. But the girls on the boat were looking behind her, not out on the horizon, directly behind her. They were no longer screaming but stared ashen faced at the water.

A hand grabbed her wrist and for a moment she felt genuine relief. Safety.

"That stuff will give you nightmares," said Tony as he moved around the back of Birgitte's chair to the edge of the pool.

Birgitte was startled. She wondered how long he had been watching her. The YouTube clip went dark. All she could hear through the tiny speakers on her laptop were the screams of the people on board the two boats. Then it was over. Two minutes of utter horror that had been viewed by tens of thousands of people across the world.

"She survived," Tony said as he squatted down and ran his fingers through the water. He'd showered and was now wearing a pair of chinos and a thin black jumper over a t-shirt, which accentuated the thickness of his upper torso. "In case you were wondering."

Birgitte stared at him, slightly appalled. "You've seen this?"

"Yeah. Sharks have been 'trending' in Australia for years." He gave a lopsided grin and stood up, wiping his hand on his trousers. "I read an article about it too. She didn't quite make it to the boat in time, unfortunately, but where the camera goes dark what you don't see is her leg being ripped off, which actually allowed the guys to lift her to safety."

"I can't believe the person with the camera kept filming," said Birgitte, slowly getting her breath back.

"Crazy times."

She leaned back into her seat and laughed nervously. "I was going to go for a swim to warm up, but I'll think I'll take a shower instead."

She closed the laptop. "That bottle of Mendleson Vineyard Chardonnay is in my room. Would you like to have a glass with me down here?"

"Sure."

She stood up. "I'll be back in a minute."

He watched her as she walked up the stairs. She was wearing a thin skirt that sat neatly over her hips. He couldn't help wondering how good she'd look in a black one piece doing laps in the motel pool. A voice inside his head reminded him to keep it professional.

When she came back down carrying the bottle and two glass tumblers from her room, he noticed she'd quickly applied a bit of lippy and taken her hair out of her ponytail for the first time since they'd met. She had beautiful dark hair that made her skin appear paler than usual.

She poured the wine into both tumblers. He pulled up a chair beside her so that they were both facing on to the water. They raised their glasses and watched the old man swimming back and forth across the length of the pool. Thin veils of steam rose up over the illuminated water.

"A little sharp," Birgitte said, pursing her lips.

"I've never been enough of a connoisseur," he said. "Whatever takes the edge off."

They sat in silence for while. Eventually she said, "It was such a horrible way for him to die."

"Thostrup?"

She nodded. "The guy we're looking for – he must be some sort of sociopath."

"I've seen a lot worse acts committed by ice-fuelled bikie gangs," Tony said. "I'd be wary about profiling at this stage. We still can't be certain that it's the act of one man."

Birgitte conceded the point. She didn't really want to talk shop with Tony but she wasn't sure how to broach anything personal. "Back in Sydney Constable Donleavy implied that you were in between jobs. Is that right?"

"It's an odd situation," Tony said, stretching out his legs and crossing them at the ankles. "I'd been with the NSW police for a long time, about 13 years – the last six of which in a task force focused on Middle Eastern organised crime. I was getting tired, jaded, I guess. There was a lot of politics and I really just wanted a change. Needed one, because of a few factors." His voice trailed off as he thought of Hana. "A job came up with the Federal Police – Liaison Officer. I thought it might give me the shake-up I needed. It was a maternity-leave position, nothing set in stone. But I put my hand up and got it. Only thing was, the woman who was going on leave – Carolyn Miller, she lost the baby at the last minute. I had already left the NSW Police and was officially employed as a Federal Officer but she insisted on returning to work immediately and there was no precedent for how to handle the situation. The guys upstairs got nervous so they promoted her. Now she's my boss and I don't actually have a role within the department. I don't think there is even a budget for an increased head count."

"How is she coping?"

"Hard to say. She's a tough one, that's for sure, but I can't help feeling she's come back too early."

"To early for her or you?"

Tony looked across at her, unsure of whether his thoughts would be best kept to himself. "I'm not a woman or a doctor but I would have thought a couple of months might have helped."

Birgitte was fascinated by his situation and wondered how Sven and his superiors would have dealt with it if something similar had happened in Copenhagen. How would she have handled it? She recalled the horrible fights she'd had with Tomas just before they broke up over her reluctance to start a family. She tried to block it from her mind.

"It can't be easy for you. A male officer being unsure of his future, because a woman in a senior position lost a child."

"She wasn't senior to me when she was pregnant."

"You don't think she deserved the promotion?"

"No. I don't," Tony said calmly. "Not because she's a woman, or because she lost a child, but because it was done out of expediency – fear of political reprisals or a law suit. Now she's trying to rise to the occasion and prove she's management material."

They both stared at the water. The elderly man climbed out at one end, his skin and swimsuit sagging from his bones. He wrapped himself in a towel and left the pool area. Birgitte was suddenly aware that they were alone together – it felt good. She reached over and filled up his glass.

She raised hers and said, "To Gunner Mendelson's vineyard."

He laughed and raised his glass. They settled back into their seats.

"So what does your husband do for a living?" he asked, trying to keep the brightness in his voice.

"He's a lawyer. Environmental law."

"Smart guy."

"We met at law school."

"You're a lawyer?"

"I never practiced, much to my father's annoyance, but I am qualified." She looked at Tony. "You sound surprised, Detective."

"Not surprised, but genuinely impressed, and to be honest a little intimidated." He said this with a self-deprecating smile that made her feel warm and confident. His eyes were suddenly very clear to her. He continued to look at her. He could see her as a younger woman. She would have been stunning, but time had made her more beautiful in a way he couldn't describe – there was a depth to her demeanour that stirred something in him.

He cleared his throat. "So what does your husband think of your chosen profession?"

"He's been supportive," she said, turning away.

Tony wasn't convinced. He watched her as she began scratching at the label on the wine bottle. For a moment she was back in Copenhagen mired in a world of emotional anguish. "The truth is we separated nine months ago."

"I'm sorry. I didn't realise."

"It's okay. It's the first time I've admitted it to a stranger..." She looked away, tucking a length of hair behind her ear. Then she realised what she had said. "I mean someone who doesn't know me well. It feels – different to what I'd expected. Bit of a relief, really."

When she looked back at him he couldn't tell if her eyes were wet with emotion or if the lights of the pool were playing tricks.

"Were you together long, if you don't mind my asking?"

"Married for nine years – if you count the separation, together for just under 12."

"Any kids?"

"No."

"It must have been difficult."

"It was. All too complicated for words. How about you, Detective Kingsmill? Is there a significant other in your life?"

He felt the ground shift slightly under his chair. But he figured if she was big enough to share her personal problems, it was only fair he meet her in the middle.

"I met someone a little while back, but let's just say it didn't go according to plan."

"Where did you meet?"

"I took up an evening class to learn Arabic for work when I was still on the Middle Eastern Organised Crime Unit. It was a mistake in itself. I should have applied for classes through the department but I wanted to get on with it privately.

"I told the teacher and the other students I was in construction, and that I wanted to learn Arabic to get on better with my crew. Didn't say much more than that. Turns out the teacher, an Egyptian lady by the name of Naima took a bit of a shine to me."

Birgitte smiled at this and gave him a knowing look.

"Not for herself. For her niece. Apparently she was always trying to set up her younger sister's daughter with students from her class. I played along not thinking anything of it until we were introduced – and this girl was stunning, outgoing, smart as whip."

He stared into the water and savoured the memory of that night for a moment before proceeding. "She was in the final year of her CPA."

Birgitte didn't know what that was but didn't want to interrupt him. Tony realised and explained, "She was studying to be an accountant. Anyway, her Aunt Naima suggested she earn a bit of extra cash by tutoring me in Arabic an hour a week. And, without thinking, I agreed."

"She didn't know you were a police officer."

"I didn't know how to tell her. And to be honest, I was really just enjoying her company too much to risk spoiling it. It was the first time since I'd joined the Middle Eastern Unit that I was learning about Egyptian culture in Australia outside of bikie gangs and drug syndicates. It was stupid of me. I shouldn't have lied to them in the first place and I sure as hell shouldn't have kept lying to Hana."

"Hana was the girls name?"

"Yeah. Hana Shakib."

"It's a pretty name."

"She's a very pretty girl."

"Are you in love with her?"

Tony wondered why it was so easy for women to ask such personal questions. He crossed his legs and stared into the pool. He couldn't give her a straight answer because he didn't know how he felt, so he just shrugged. "We didn't really have chance to take it too far."

"But you still care for her?"

"Perhaps in a more brotherly way than I once did." Saying it out loud made him realise how much he had cared for Hana in those first few months. It was the closest thing he'd come to a serious relationship in more than a year.

Birgitte was sincerely intrigued. "How does she feel about you?"

"I'm not sure. We haven't spoken for a while."

He wanted to talk it out but at the same time he had no interest in picking at a wound he'd rather see scar over. So the conversation crumbled away into silence.

Birgitte felt for him – he was obviously still hurting and was incapable of putting that hurt into words. She knew the feeling, or at least something similar. She reached across and touched his hand to bring him back into the moment. "What are our plans for tomorrow?"

Tony coughed and sat up in his chair, slightly invigorated by her touch and embarrassed by the course of their conversation. "Well, let's see. Smith will take us out to Forbes Creek. It's a two-hour drive, I'm guessing we'll be there for at least two hours so we should be back in the city by mid afternoon. Frankston isn't back till Friday so we may have to wait until then before anything else happens. Have you contacted your boss back in Copenhagen?"

She tucked another strand of hair behind her ear, not yet willing to allow the moment they'd shared to pass so easily. "I have. He's probably already spoken to the Commissioner. It's best that he breaks the news to his wife. She'll probably want to come out here to escort her brother's body home and try to find out more about his murder. I hope we'll have some answers by then. Do you have any theories?"

"Not at this stage. There isn't much to go on. I'm keen to follow it through and I've written to my boss to suggest as much, but I'm also wary of getting involved. It's now a local matter. My job was to keep you informed of developments as we looked for Mr Thostrup. We've found him so I'm not sure what happens next?"

"You're not even curious?"

"I'm curious, but I'm also a realist," he said, recalling Quintock's attitude. "I don't know how things work in Denmark, but here you have to respect who is in charge of the investigation and stay out of the way if you're not a part of it. As much as I'd like to pursue it, part of me really just wants to get back to Sydney and settle into my new job, whatever the hell that may be."

"But what if we know something that might be of help?"

"I reckon that's what Frankston wants to find out on Friday."

They both noticed the bottle was empty. Birgitte considered suggesting they have another drink in a nearby bar.

Tony stood up and said, "You must be tired. It's been a hell of a day."

She looked a little disappointed but resigned herself to the fact that tonight she would be sleeping alone. "It has. I'm going to do a bit more research." She opened her laptop again.

"Don't watch too many of those clips," he said, unlocking the gate to the pool area.

She smiled, perhaps a change of nightmares was what she needed.

CHAPTER FIVE

A solitary roadhouse shimmered in the distance. He'd been on the road since dawn, covered 250km or so. He was making good time, but his tank was running low. He pulled off the highway and cruised up to one of the petrol bowsers. The station was empty but there were a few cars parked out the front of the cafe. He recognised a couple of the SUVs from the highway.

Out of the cabin the heat was stifling. Blowflies settled on his shoulders and hair as he pulled the pump from the bowser and began to fill his tank. He stretched his legs and cricked his neck.

He'd left Kakadu in the Northern Territory on the Tuesday morning and it had taken two days to drive south across the country to reach Coober Pedy in South Australia. Now it was Thursday. It was a formidable schedule, but the pay-off would be worth every aching muscle.

On the way into to pay he noticed a girl sitting on a backpack in the shade of the awning. She must have come out while he was filling up. She looked about 19 years old, wore a thin sun dress scattered with flowers, and was drinking a bottle of Diet Coke through a straw. She had long legs, soft, tanned skin and her hair was long and slightly burnished by the sun. As he passed her he caught a hint of sweet perfume. She pretended not to notice him.

He grabbed some chocolate bars for the drive. He figured he'd stop for lunch in Port Augusta, another 300km further south. The attendant was a scrawny bloke who didn't bother looking up from his magazine.

"$183," he mumbled.

He pulled out his wallet.

There was a security camera in the corner of the ceiling behind the attendant, but he could tell it was a dummy set up to deter shoplifters. He paid cash for the petrol and snacks.

When he turned the girl had come inside and was flicking through the magazines by the door. She looked up at him expectantly as he got closer. Her eyes were a pale hazel. "You heading to Port Augusta?"

"I am."

He stepped past her, out into the heat. She stuffed the magazine back in the rack and followed him. "I could do with a ride. The last guy kinda left me stranded here. I can chip in for petrol. A little."

He kept walking to the SUV, calculating his journey. It was another eight and half hours to Mildura. He'd sleep on this side of the state border and be on the Murray River by mid morning the following day. He'd make contact with the client again once he was well clear of the region.

She watched him walk away from her, disappointed. She really liked the way he walked. He was thin and wiry but she could tell there was plenty of muscle under the khaki shirt and dusty chinos. He moved like a leopard. But it was his eyes she was drawn to. He had knowing eyes, like he'd seen things. He was perfect for her next ride.

"I won't be a nuisance, mister," she called out to him. "You'll barely know I'm there."

He turned and leaned against the front of his car.

She moved towards him. "Don't you want some company?"

"Thought you said, I'd barely know you were there."

"You won't but you will, and that's a good thing for long drives." She smiled sweetly and bit on her lower lip.

"Just to Port Augusta. No further."

She squealed and clapped her hands then ran back and grabbed her backpack, slinging it over one shoulder.

He walked to the back of the car and lifted open the back door.

As she got closer to the car she hesitated. "I usually like to sit with my pack, if you don't mind. Kind of has my whole life in it. I can put it at my feet."

He shrugged and went to close the door. She slipped the pack from her shoulder.

"Sorry. I'm being silly."

She peered inside the back of the SUV. There was a long refrigeration unit with a padlock on it, a camera bag, a duffle bag and a swag – still plenty of space for her pack. He took it from her shoulder and placed it inside then shut the door.

She walked along the side of the car, running her fingers along the duco, feeling slightly elated. It was going to be an interesting day after all.

They got in. He started the engine and pulled back onto the highway.

He wasn't outwardly good looking, she decided, but all the more intriguing for it. He had a nice line to his nose. His lips were a bit thin for her liking but his hands were enormous and that drove her a little wild. Ever since she'd let Darren Bilford shag her in the back of the Minimart where she used to work she had a thing for guys with big hands.

The ride was nice, too, she thought. Not completely new, but it didn't look cheap. The console was all digital.

"Sweet wheels," she said.

"What?"

"Your car," she said, meekly. "I like it." She went red and felt awful. What was she thinking? She was coming across as a silly little girl. If he found out she was only 18 he'd probably kick her out on the side of the road.

She sat in silence for a while, but it made her nervous.

"What's in the fridge?"

He continued watching the road ahead. "Work."

"What sort of work?"

He grinned to himself. "An environmental sample from up north."

"Why do you lock it up?"

"So it doesn't get stolen."

"Is it worth much?" She looked across at him expectantly but he didn't answer. "Sorry. I'm just making conversation."

She stared out the window at the scrubby bushland, biting her nails. When she was about to give up on talking to him all together, he said, "It's worth plenty to the people who pay me."

He finally looked at her and she felt a little swimmy in his gaze.

"I'm Susie," she said. "In case you were wondering."

"I wasn't." He returned his gaze to the road ahead.

"Where's your accent from?" she asked.

"Where do you think?"

"Europe, maybe."

"Yeah? Whereabouts?"

"Germany?"

"No."

"Belgium?"

"Wrong again."

"Are you Dutch?"

"Not exactly."

"You're not from Holland?"

"My family was, some way back," he said. "If you must know, I'm Afrikaner."

She didn't understand.

He smiled at this. "I'm from South Africa. You do know Africa, don't you?"

She nodded.

"Well, I'm from the southern part. Have you ever met someone from South Africa before?"

"No, but I know you usually beat us at cricket and rugby."

He nodded. "We are good for some things."

"I was born in Adelaide," she said, responding to the question she had wanted him to ask. "But my family moved to Alice Springs when I was a kid. I'm visiting friends in Port Augusta."

It was all lies but he didn't care. She was right. It was good to have some company for a change. When he was younger, girls like her never looked at him the way she was looking at him now.

They drove in silence for a while.

"Do you mind if I put the radio on?" she asked. "Makes the journey go faster."

"If you like."

She leaned forward and turned on the stereo. She flicked through the stations until she found one that played pop music. "This okay?"

He shrugged.

"Can I put the window down?"

He turned off the air conditioning.

The hot wind blew her hair around her face and teased the straps on her shoulders. She put her hand into the wind, pointing her fingers into the current so the force of the air made her hand move up and down like a dolphin in a wave. He smiled at her, which made her giggle nervously.

Her laugh reminded him of a glass wind chime from his childhood.

"What happened to your last ride?" he asked.

"Nothing much. He bored me."

"Was he going in to Port Augusta?"

"Said he was."

"Not concerned about bumping into him at the next petrol station?"

"It's a big enough town. He'd be half a day ahead of us by now anyway. He was a bit of a creep."

She motioned over her shoulder. "Where did you collect your sample from?"

"Wetlands up in near Kakadu."

"What for?"

"There's a mining project up that way. I'm assessing potential damage to the region."

"You travel much?"

"All over."

"Must get kinda lonely on the road all the time."

"I don't mind it. Better than sitting at a desk."

"Doesn't your wife miss you?"

He grinned.

She reached for the radio. "I love this song." She turned it up and began singing along.

They drove along for another hour or so just listening to music. Eventually she succumbed to the heat. He watched as her head tipped slowly forward, then lolled to one side, her tiny hands twitching in her lap. He turned the music down.

The wind had blown her thin dress up around her thighs, and the sun caught the fine gold hairs above her knee. She twisted and murmured in her sleep. Her left thigh emerged from the hem of her dress as she turned, so slowly he thought it would never end. Her panties a pale shade of pink. He could feel his blood pumping harder through his veins.

The road was dead straight, barely requiring attention.

He looked back at her.

A thin sheen of perspiration was forming on her cheeks, which had reddened in the heat. A length of damp hair clung to the contours of her face. A trickle from behind her ear, ran down her neck to her shoulder, it gathered speed over her collar bone and slipped down between her breasts. She wasn't wearing a bra. A strap slipped from her shoulder and he could just make out the edge of one of her nipples.

The wind chime was tinkling in his mind. The flyscreen door to the general store in Masosobane swung open. Nyeleti came out with a broom in her hand, her father had told her to sweep the entrance. At 15 she wasn't quite in possession of her own body. At times it seemed to belong to the gaze of every man who entered the store. But occasionally she would move in a knowing way, enjoying the line of her own legs, the fullness of her breasts. Young Zachary was sure she was at her most knowing around him. His father nodded to her as he stepped up onto the verandah.

"Your father in?"

She stepped back from the door. "Out back."

"Stay here," he muttered to Zachary.

He would have only been 12 back then. He was always waiting for his father as he did his business in the backrooms of local shops and bars. The old man's uniform gave him unlimited access to every shop and every house in every village for 350 square kilometres – his "jurisdiction" he called it.

The door slapped shut. Nyeleti continued to sweep the dust from the boards, suddenly bored by her duties. Zachary watched the muscles in her calves tense and relax with every sweeping motion, fascinated. She leant the broom against the mud adobe wall and took a seat on the top step of the verandah, tucking her dress between her long dark thighs. He couldn't look away but didn't know what to say.

"What are you staring at?" she asked glumly.

"Nothing."

"I'm nothing am I? Figures."

She licked her thumb then proceeded to wipe the dust from each of her toe nails so they looked freshly painted against her dirty bare feet.

When his father emerged from the store again he was holding a can of Coke. He tossed it to Zachary who caught it and cracked it open. He offered a sip to Nyeleti but she was staring up at his father.

"Later," he said, stepping down in to the street.

She smiled so openly as if this was the one moment she was truly herself.

"I'll be waiting."

Zachary waved at Nyeleti and followed his father up the street. It was the last time he saw her smile. The next time he saw her there was a rubber tyre shoved tight over her father's bony shoulders and he was being pushed through the yard at the back of his store. The tyre was quickly filled with petrol from a can. The old man slumped to the ground, too beaten by life to put up a fight. Nyeleti was screaming for it stop. But it didn't. It never stopped until his father was done. The stench of burning flesh had repulsed him the first few times but young Zachary got used to it eventually. He didn't know what became of Nyeleti after that, but he had always remembered her beautiful smile.

"Wake up. We're here."

Susie rubbed her face and stared blearily around her. A service station on the outskirts of a rural town. Wide streets, dust and gum trees. They all looked the same after a while. Another friggin' dump.

"This Port Augusta?"

"Yep."

He got out of the SUV and pulled the pump from the bowser.

She climbed out and moved round to the back. She opened the hatch and dragged out her back pack. She looked at the fridge. It seemed awfully big to just hold soil and water samples. The padlock was brand new.

She peered around the back of the car.

"Thanks for the ride. Sorry I slept for most of it."

He didn't say anything.

"Are you heading on to Adelaide?" she asked, making no attempt to hide the disappointment in her voice.

He shook his head.

She stood waiting, staring at him, not sure how to proceed.

"You're not visiting friends, are you?" he asked as he watched the meter on the bowser tick over steadily.

"Not here. Further on."

He sighed. "I'm heading on to Mildura tomorrow, but I'm not stopping in a town tonight. I'll be camping in the bush. Sorry about that."

"I could sleep in the car. I don't mind, seriously. There's plenty of room next to the fridge."

The thought made him smile. He shrugged.

"It's your funeral."

She ignored his comment and threw her backpack back into the car, cheered in the knowledge she might make it all the way to Melbourne in almost one stretch, and quietly excited that her journey with her new companion wasn't over yet.

"I can buy you lunch, if you like?"

"Sure."

"I've just got to take a pee – I mean, use the ladies. Meet you in the cafe."

She ran across to the amenities. Inside she quickly checked her face in the mirror over the basin. She was hot and a little red but she hoped she looked okay to him. She splashed cold water on her face to freshen up. She stepped into one of the stalls, locking the door behind her. She lifted her dress, slipped her panties down and sat down.

As she peed, she noticed a thin smear of dirt across the inside of her right thigh. She looked at her hands, there were similar smears across her knuckles. Like wet dust. The window had been down for most of the trip, she reasoned, and there was a lot of dust in the car. She had probably just wiped her face in her sleep then brushed her knuckles on her thighs. She couldn't remember if there had been similar marks on her face before she had splashed water on her cheeks. An awkward feeling shifted in her belly, but she dismissed it. She was being silly. She had a ride all the way into the city with a gorgeous older man. That was all that mattered. She spat on her hands and wiped the smear away from her thighs and knuckles. Tonight they would be sleeping out under the stars together and anything could happen.

For two hours Constable Smith had been driving across a relentless, arid landscape scattered with ragged shrubs, tufts of spinifex and hillocks of fine red sand. Occasionally the road would rise over a low ridge, revealing thousands of square kilometres of desert then it would meander down the other side and straighten out again. It was a monotonous drive punctuated only with the stench of rotting carcasses that managed to seep through the air conditioning – cattle that had strayed too far from the herd, roos stunned by the headlights of road trains in the night.

Birgitte sat in the back, her mind racing along several divergent paths as it always did when she first encountered a victim of a brutal murder. Some of her responses were empathetic. She could only imagine the fear Thostrup must have felt prior to the actual attack. How long was he in the water for? Had he been conscious? For his sake, she hoped he was out cold. Did he even know why he was being killed? The police officer in her was assessing the evidence – the wounds on the corpse that indicated intent, while also gauging what sort of person they may be looking for. And of course there was the natural fear that rose up without warning as the realisation that the killer was still out there and someone else may be suffering as badly as Thostrup while she was sitting in a patrol car with Tony heading across the desert.

She didn't like to admit it but she was deriving a certain satisfaction from the adrenalin that was pumping through her body. For the first time in more than six months she was part of an active murder investigation. Despite the circumstances, or perhaps because of them, she felt alive, focused and eager to redeem herself in the eyes of her superiors back in Copenhagen. Of course, as a liaison officer there was little real field work she could do, but as long as they let her visit the crime scene and interview the boy who found the body, she was confident she could bring valuable resources to the table.

She genuinely hoped it was a stand-alone crime – an execution or payback for a personal debt, something from Thostrup's past that may have finally caught up with him – mostly because she couldn't bear the thought of another person suffering as he had done. But a tiny voice inside of her was already beginning to taunt her. It was suggesting the real reason she wanted this to be a stand-alone murder was that she couldn't handle the mind games that came with chasing another killer whose work wasn't complete. That taunting voice belonged to Max Anders.

They slowed at a road sign marked 'Forbes Creek' and turned off the highway onto a narrow road heading south east. Birgitte stared out across the flat landscape searching for a roadhouse or a homestead. But there was nothing. It was hard to believe anyone could live out here, she thought. Perhaps it was the emptiness that made her think of Tomas, his long silences that would descend on their home for days at a time. She would be too busy to notice at first, coming in late at night, seeing him sleeping in the bed, then leaving first thing before he awoke. It never occurred to her that anything was wrong – because she hadn't taken the time to look. On weekends he would busy himself with his own chores that conveniently gave him further time to himself. And when they were together there was only silence, at the time misconstrued as the comfort of a secure relationship. How did she not see the signs? Had she chosen to ignore them? Was Tomas aware the whole time? He had complained just before the end that he was most alone in her company. It was an awful thing to say and it stung to hear it, but now she was beginning to understand.

As her racing mind encountered the mire of those cold, expressionless days it slowed to a crawl and she felt the desire to sleep. She rested her head against the window and was about to close her eyes when she noticed a large angular structure rising up violently from the earth about 300 metres from the road. It was surrounded by several corrugated tin sheds at its base. The tower was several stories high and leaned against the sky like the neck of a construction crane. It was dark with rust, a long-discarded relic of heavy industry that looked like it might collapse at any moment but was sadly more permanent than the low-lying dunes around it, which shifted with the prevailing winds.

"It's the old Masser mine," Smith said, realising both Tony and Birgitte were watching it with dull fascination. "Forbes Creek grew up around it in the 50s and 60s. It did okay for a while, apparently."

"What were they looking for?" asked Tony.

"Asbestos, would you believe."

"Seriously? I didn't even realise it was a mineral."

"Before the general public got wind that it was carcinogenic there were several mines across Australia supplying the construction industry. This one was set up by a Hungarian immigrant looking to strike it big. But the demand dropped off for obvious reasons so by the 70s the place was a ghost town. Then the Northern Territory Government began relocating Indigenous communities here in the 80s, mostly families that had been kicked off the land for the mine in the first place."

"Was it safe?" asked Birgitte.

"I guess they figured as long as the asbestos was still in the ground, it should be okay. Not too sure how much went into the prefab walls used in the homes though."

The road swung away from the mine towards a line of single-storey houses that stretched either side of the road. A shotgun-peppered sign that had almost entirely faded marked the entrance to the town. Birgitte squinted to read the words: "Welcome to Forbes Creek. Building a new future for the Territory".

"As you can see, this place isn't exactly flourishing," said Smith. "Apparently the Government is looking to close it down all together."

"Closing a town?" asked Birgitte.

"It's considered a remote community. Remote communities need Government services which cost taxpayers' money."

"Where will the residents go?"

"They'll be encouraged to move to other settlements closer to the Alice, or at least closer to existing services that the Government can afford to run."

"And what about their connection to the land?" asked Birgitte.

Smith didn't have an answer.

They drove down a main road lined with red dust and dying grass. Beyond short wire fences bloated women sat on the front steps of weatherboard houses staring at kids riding bicycles in the street. The houses had paled to bone white in the sun while the tin rooves blazed with rust. Other kids, shirtless, played in the dirt, their bellies protruding over their shorts. Scrawny teenagers gathered in circles, hovering over mobiles. Forbes Creek was a part of Australia Birgitte hadn't seen on her first trip. She was staring at a world that was surreal to her. Poverty in the desert had a distinct ochre stain that lingered on the mind. Smith raised a finger from the steering wheel occasionally but no one waved back.

Within the space of two minutes the car reached the other side of the town to where the road met the edge of the dry creek bed at a bridge. All that was left of the cordon was tattered lengths of police tape tied around the trunks of two gum trees. Tony remembered the photos at the forensic pathologist's lab. The crime scene in those shots had looked both dramatic and comic at once: a two-ring circus that inspired only partial curiosity. Three kids riding their bikes in lazy circles on the peripheries for something to do. An officer standing on the inside of the tape making sure they didn't get too close. The kids out here would know how it worked: one or two cop cars meant a beating, probably a domestic, but three meant death.

But the scene out here was deserted.

Smith pulled the patrol car over and switched off the engine. They stepped out into the heat. Birgitte noticed the stillness. The air didn't seem to move. She tried to imagine the creek in full flood but couldn't. It was the sun-parched skeleton of a long-dead waterway. And it seemed the town itself wasn't far behind.

Smith walked over to the bank, the flies descending on her shoulders unnoticed. "He was just down there."

She took a camera out of a pouch on her belt. "These are the shots I took before anyone else arrived."

As horrific as it was for Birgitte to see the Dane's body in the morgue, it looked worse to picture it in the dry creek bed. The scene had clearly been staged as some sort of macabre joke, his hands clutching at the sand, his mouth open as if gasping for his last breath of air.

"How long did you say it would it take to drive here from the ocean?" Birgitte asked.

"About 16 hours," said Tony.

"Then he was posed like that before rigor took hold."

The implications of what they were dealing with were beginning to sink in.

Smith pointed further out into the creek. "The kid who found the body is over there. I called him earlier and asked him to meet us out here."

Three kids moved dolefully along the creek bed, passing a football back and forth.

Tony and Birgitte stepped down the embankment and headed out across the coarse sand. Eventually they met out in the middle. The tallest of the three, a boy of no more than 14, stepped forward with the ball in his hand. He wore a Sydney Swans jersey that was grey with sweat and grime. He looked serious, Birgitte thought. No, humourless. What was there to find funny out here, particularly with what he'd seen recently?

Tony asked, "You Cody Dunbar?"

The boy nodded.

"I'm Detective Tony Kingsmill, Federal Police. This is Detective Vestergaard. We need to ask you a few questions about what you saw last Monday when you were out here."

"I told them other coppers what I saw."

"I get that, but now you need to tell us."

The boy stared at them hard, mistrustful. He began to toss the ball up into the air and catching it as if the action calmed his nerves or gave him the confidence to talk to adults in authority.

"Came down here to meet up with these fellas." He nodded his head in the direction of the other two teenagers who were staring at them in silence.

"From school?" asked Birgitte.

"Yeah."

"Why here?"

"Ground's level. No oval with grass for 200 kilometres."

"How often do you meet here?"

"Dunno. Most days, I guess."

"Did you see anyone around that morning?" asked Tony.

"Nuh."

"When was the last time you'd played here before that?"

He thought for a moment and turned to his mates. "Day before."

"Sure about that?"

The three boys nodded.

"Did you see anyone hanging about then?"

"Nuh," said Dunbar. "Wasn't looking but."

"What about over the last few weeks? Anyone who wasn't a local pass through?"

"No one comes here, except you lot. And you leave on the road you come in on."

Tony brushed the flies from his face, "Okay, the Monday then. What time did you find the body?"

"Reckon it was round 9.30am. Dropped my bag off at school. Saw the principal then came down here."

"What were you seeing the principal about?" asked Birgitte, trying to keep the conversation friendly.

"Wagging."

Tony shook his head and turned to Birgitte to explain. "Not attending classes."

"Truancy?"

"Yeah."

She gave the boy a knowing smile. "I wasn't a fan of school myself at your age."

"Rather be practicing," he said.

"You play the AFL?"

He started to laugh. "Just AFL."

"Sorry. I'm from Europe. We don't have AFL over there. Are you good?"

He looked at the ball as the two boys behind him nodded. One of them piped up. "He got Best and Fairest for the region three years' running. They reckon he'll represent the Territory soon."

"That's terrific," said Birgitte. "Listen, Cody, what can you tell us about that morning that might help us find who did it."

A shadow slipped across his face. Tony stepped toward him and gestured for the ball. "May I?"

He handed the ball over.

Tony said, "Gentlemen, we need a moment with Cody alone."

He gripped the ball between both hands took two long strides forward and booted the ball in the air. At first the three kids stared as the ratty looking ball shot higher than they'd ever seen it go, then Teddy and Yambo bolted across the sand after it.

Tony called out to them. "First one to the bridge back."

They laughed as they ran, trying to jostle one another out of the way.

"You got a good boot," Cody said warily.

"I used to play State, in a former life. So, what can you tell us?"

"I was heading out here from school like I said."

"How long does it take?"

The kid shrugged. "Fifteen, 20 minutes."

"And there was no one out here?"

"Nuh. But the smell. I could smell him from back there." He pointed back along the line of gum trees on the edge of the bank. "I didn't see him but, until I was on top of him." He looked at Birgitte. "What happened to his legs?"

"We're not sure yet," she said. "But we're hoping, with your help, we can find out."

"He looked so strange."

"I'm sure it was a shock."

"It's not my first," he said with finality.

Tony asked, "Did you touch the body?"

He looked down and toed the sand with his sneaker.

"Did you touch the body?" Tony asked more firmly. "Move it in any way?"

"I poked it with a stick, you know, to make sure it was dead."

"Did you notice anything else at all?" Birgitte's tone was conciliatory.

He shook his head. Birgitte thought he suddenly looked like a little boy.

"Cody?"

He looked at her with a sullen, confused expression.

She said, "I'm sorry you had to see what you saw. It wasn't right."

His two mates scarpered back across the sand passing the ball back and forth to one another.

Tony called out to them. "So who was first?"

They looked at one another and cracked up laughing. They were so used to playing together the idea of competing had been forgotten as soon as they'd reached the ball.

Tony turned back to Cody. "Call if you think of anything."

The kid put the card in his pocket and turned back to his mates. They passed him the ball and he kicked it as hard as he could into the air. As his two mates set off after it like kelpies rounding sheep he turned to see if Tony had been watching.

"You've got a pretty good boot yourself," he said. "Keep at it. And try not to miss too much school, yeah? You can't play footy forever."

He chuckled at this then turned and ran off after his mates.

Birgitte looked over that the line of decrepit houses that marked the edge of town.

"He must have driven through the night. Possibly placed the corpse there before sun up and been back in Alice Springs, maybe, within a few hours."

"He might not have stayed in Alice though," said Tony, thinking out loud. "He could have camped in the bush and driven back without stopping in any town, except to get petrol perhaps. Even then he could have carried tanks with enough fuel for a round trip."

"Round trip from where?"

"Adelaide maybe."

They spotted Constable Smith stepping crab-like down the embankment. As she walked across the creek bed towards them she called out, "Did you find out anything new?"

Tony shook his head. "Have you checked with the principal to verify the kid's story?"

"I phoned him the day after. He says he talked to the boy at about 9am and he was gone by 9.10am. It takes 15-20 minutes to get here on foot."

Birgitte asked, "Would there be any one round here who might have seen something during the night? A car must have driven up here at some point."

"We canvassed the locals," said Smith. "But no one had anything to tell us."

"That doesn't mean they didn't see anything," said Tony. He turned to Birgitte. "Any ideas now that you're here?"

"It's not making any sense. If Thostrup was being tortured for information, surely the body would have been hidden somewhere even less visible than this. If it was a revenge killing or a crime of passion, why stop with just his legs? He's been punished, up to a point, then staged. The killer obviously wants the body to be found – but several hundred kilometres away from the murder scene? What purpose does that serve? What does it say about Thostrup or his killer?"

Tony followed her line of reasoning. "Do you think the killer knew Thostrup? Knew he was in Australia? Or was it random; wrong place, wrong time."

"A thrill kill?"

"Maybe."

She shook her head. "It all seems too staged for any part of it to be random. It looks like a message. I just have no idea who it is meant for. And what it is saying."

She looked at the houses again, struggling to think why anyone there would be threatened by the body of a dead Dane.

Smith said, "I spoke to Senior Sergeant Frankston before I picked you up. He wants to meet with you both tomorrow morning."

"Fair enough," said Tony. "Shall we head back?"

"Do you mind if I have a moment at the scene alone?" she asked.

Tony nodded. "Of course."

Constable Smith and Tony walked back to the car as Birgitte made her way to the edge of the creek where Thostrup's body was found. She squatted down, looking up the embankment. She couldn't see the houses which meant even if the residents were alerted to a set of headlights at a strange hour, or the noise of an engine, they couldn't have seen him once he had the body out of his car.

From what the forensic pathologist had said about the difficulty he was having determining a precise time of death, she wondered if the killer had a refrigeration unit in his car. It would have to be one of several options worth bearing in mind. She pictured a car large enough to contain a fridge that could hold a body – or at least three quarters of one. It would have to be a van or an SUV. To travel so many kilometres it would need to be reliable; less risk of being pulled over by the police. He was a brazen killer but someone who didn't take unnecessary risks. He liked to be in control, a step ahead. Somehow he knew the body would be found within a day or two. He needed it to be, which is why it was staged. Had he been here before and seen the kids playing football? In the police report there was no evidence of footprints or tyre marks. It was way too thorough to be a first-time murder or a reactive crime of revenge. Despite her eagerness for this to be a one-off, the awkward feeling in her gut told her that there

103

would be more bodies. She stood up and took in the scene one last time, committing as many details to memory as she could.

In the distance, further down the creek bed Cody Dunbar leapt in the air again over his two mates to catch the ball mid-flight. Birgitte watched him for a moment and wondered if his opportunities would improve if the Government relocated his community elsewhere. She sighed and walked back over the coarse sand to the patrol car. As she climbed in she asked Smith, "The unrelated call you mentioned?"

"Yeah?"

"What was it about?"

The brilliant streaks of amber and ochre on the western horizon were fading as rapidly as they'd come as Susie emerged from the bush in a fresh sun dress of pale apricot. She was carrying a bathroom bag and drying her hair with a small hand towel. The dress she'd been wearing during the day was draped over one shoulder. It was still warm but soon enough she'd need to put a jumper on. Her backpack was propped against the back tyre of the SUV. About 40 minutes ago they'd pulled off the highway and driven several hundred metres into the bush, far enough so that the headlights or campfire wouldn't be seen by anyone driving along the highway.

She put away her dirty things and began rubbing moisturiser into her shoulders. Her new companion was on his hands and knees blowing into the base of a low but growing camp fire, paying her no mind.

"What's for dinner?" she asked. She felt refreshed having washed the dust from her skin and was quietly elated about the evening ahead.

"I picked up some steaks at the roadhouse," he said, noticing her for the first time since she'd emerged from the bushes. "Where's the water? We'll need it for cooking."

She tossed the moisturiser on top of her backpack and disappeared back into the scrub. When she came back a few moments later, lugging the 25-litre water tank she had used to freshen up, the fire had doubled in size. He was dragging a large dead branch across the dirt as if it was a stick. He placed one end carefully over the coals.

"Oughta do us for the evening," he muttered to himself.

Susie noticed that there two steaks wrapped in plastic sitting on a couple of plates by the fire, along with a fry pan, a dented billy and two cups. The steaks must have been in the fridge all afternoon. She peered into the back of the SUV. The fridge was still locked. He'd taken out his swag and bag and set up a space for her to sleep in the back.

She watched him as he moved to the edge of the fire. "Can I ask you something?"

He threw a splash of oil in the pan and rested it in the coals on the edge of the fire. He didn't say "no" so she continued. "Why won't you tell me your name?"

"You hadn't asked."

"What's your name then?"

"None of your business." He chuckled at his own joke, knowing his evasion would only draw her closer.

She leaned against the back of the SUV, with the tube of moisturiser in her hands. She began rubbing the cream slowly into her upper arms. "Whereabouts are you from, in South Africa?"

He looked up as he unwrapped the meat from its packaging, and considered how much he should tell her. "A few hours out of Jo'burg."

"Like a small town?"

"More of a village. But we moved around a lot. So several villages, I guess. None that you'd know the name of."

"What did your dad do for a living?" She had pulled up the hem of her dress and was working the cream into her thighs gently with the heel of her hand.

"He was a policeman...," he said, his voice drifting off with the memory. "A captain in the South African Police. The Captain – that's what everyone called him."

"So he was a good man," she said absently as she turned to rub the cream into the back of her legs, pointing her toes like a ballet dancer.

He laughed heartily at this as he threw the two steaks into the pan. They sizzled over the crackling of the fire. He watched the smoke swirl up into the darkening sky then spoke into the flames. "My father was the meanest son of a bitch that ever lived."

She winced at his tone. "I'm sorry. I didn't mean anything by it."

She returned the moisturiser to her backpack and walked to the opposite side of the fire. He went to the back of the SUV and pulled out two foldaway chairs. He set one up for Susie to use and placed the other near the fire so he could sit and watch the steaks.

He eventually drew the pan from the coals and served up two plates.

They ate in silence.

He got up and poured water from the tank into the billy can and rested it in the coals then returned to his meal. Eventually he said, "I can't work out if you're very brave, travelling out here all alone with a complete stranger. Or whether you're incredibly stupid."

She placed her plate at her feet. Then looked at him with a slight air of defiance because she didn't like the tone he was taking with her. "I reckon I'm a pretty good judge of character. Should I be nervous around you?"

He chewed on a piece of gristle he held between his fingers. Sucking the meat from his teeth, he said, "Just can't figure you out. I hope you're smarter than you look."

"What's that supposed to mean?"

"In my experience, silly little girls can become a big nuisance very quickly."

"I'm older than I look," she said petulantly. "Like I said, I'm just trying to get to Melbourne and you seemed like a nice guy."

"Thought you said you were only going as far as Port Augusta."

"Well, it's none of your business where I'm going in the end."

"Is that so?"

He tossed his plate into the dirt and stood up, scratching his crotch. She watched his fingers work their way around the shape of his genitals. She felt herself getting heated again.

"I'll wash up if you like."

She busied herself with the plates and cutlery and the water tank while he poured two cups of tea and stoked the fire.

She was flustered. She wanted him to like her, to want her, and now he was being so rude as if he never wanted her around in the first place. This had all been a big mistake.

He handed her a cup of steaming hot tea. She took it but didn't bother to thank him.

"Where have your manners gone, Missy?"

"I said thank you. You didn't hear me."

"When I was a child, if I didn't say my pleases and thank yous my father would lay into me with a belt so hard I couldn't walk for days. I was quite the polite little man. And a pretty fast runner for my age." He grinned into the fire. The flames made it look like a leer that made Susie's skin begin to crawl.

"Your father sounds horrible. What about your mother? Did she just let him do that?"

"I never knew my mother."

"How could you not know your mother?"

"She wasn't around when I was old enough to remember, and my father said she wasn't worth knowing."

"I'm sorry."

"For what?"

"You grew up without a mother, and your father used to beat you with a belt. That's awful."

"It's all I knew," he replied in a matter-of-fact tone. He used a branch to turn the logs in the fire. "Made me who I am today."

One of the smaller logs rolled out of the fire towards Susie, sending tiny embers spiralling up into the night. Before she even had a chance to react he had closed the gap between them and pushed the log back among the coals with the toe of his boot.

"I owe my father a hell of a lot," he said, sitting back down.

She was slightly alarmed by how swiftly he moved and spoke without thinking. "I think your father wounded you deeply."

The words possessed more maturity than she thought she had. She stared at him for fear of looking away.

He watched her carefully. "Don't be making presumptions about my life, Missy."

Her eyes flickered brilliantly in the fire light. "Have you ever been in love?"

He laughed openly at this. "Now you're just being a silly brat."

"I am not." She felt wretched. In one sentence she had gone from appearing womanly to being a silly little girl again. She wanted to run away from him, but suddenly realised she had nowhere to go. "I want to go to sleep now."

"Suit yourself."

"Thank you for dinner," she said with mock politeness. She climbed into the back of the SUV and dragged her backpack up after her. It was too hot for a sleeping bag and she was too upset to make any sort of bed for herself. She lay back looking at the ceiling, listening to the hum of the fridge beside her. This was not how she thought the night would play out. She began to cry quietly to herself.

She thought of her mother for the first time in days, and wondered if she missed her at all. They had had a dreadful fight before Susie had told her to go to hell and had run out of the house for what she believed would be the last time. She was so upset she had left her phone behind. It was liberating at first, but now she missed her mother horribly and wanted nothing more than to be able to call her to beg her to come and take her away from this horrible man.

Something was digging into her side. She cleared away a drop sheet and saw a long thin canvas bag with straps at either end. She undid the straps and her heart began to beat wildly. She crawled out of the SUV backwards and almost fell off the tray. He was still sitting by the fire, mesmerised by the flames.

"Why have you got a gun in your car?" she asked timidly.

He looked up at her. "Like I said, I was up north, in the wetlands. Crocs everywhere. Some really nasty bastards. Had to be sure I could get my work done."

She didn't know whether to believe him.

"It's not loaded," he said. "I can show you, if it will help you sleep any easier."

"It's all right," she said sullenly. "It just gave me a fright."

She moved across the clearing, went to sit down in the chair but didn't like the fact it was so far from the car and that she couldn't quite see him through the smoke and the flames. She picked up the chair, came around the other side of the camp fire, a few feet from him and settled down into it, watching him warily. "I can't sleep."

"It's still early."

They sat listening to the fire crackle.

"Do you find me attractive?" she asked suddenly. She was leaning forward on the chair, staring at the dirt between her feet. "Is that why you're being difficult?"

His mouth twitched in what could have been a smile. He held out his palms as if to say, "You've caught me, now what are you going to do with me".

She tucked her hair behind her ear and looked over at him without turning her head. Her breathing was laboured and she could feel the warmth of the fire on her skin. She was drowsy but aroused. It was as if she could hear every sound around their camp, sense every vibration.

"It's okay if you like me. I want you to." She smiled when she realised how this must have sounded. "I meant I want you to like me... but I do want you, too."

His chair creaked as he leaned back into it, crossing his feet at his ankles, staring at her as she stood up and moved towards him.

She slipped the straps slowly from each shoulder. The dress lowered down a few inches but didn't fall at first, the fabric held by the fullness of her curves. She gave a demure wiggle and the dress fell to her feet. She giggled at her own nakedness and brushed her hair away from her face with one arm. He watched her breasts rise and fall with the gesture.

She stepped closer, straddled him and rested herself down on his lap. She barely weighed anything. He could smell her cheap perfume, and the overcooked steak on her breath, as she began to kiss him clumsily. She ran her fingers through his hair and drank in his scent – oily, animal, earthy. She licked his neck and grated her teeth against his cheek, pretending to bite him. He took a handful of her hair and pulled her head back beyond the point of comfort. She began rubbing herself against his crotch, partly out of desire but partly in the hope that he would let go of her hair. When his hands slid down her back she pulled away playfully and started to fumble with his belt and zipper. The size of him alarmed her at first. She took it in her mouth but her inexperience irritated him. He pulled her up by the elbows and allowed her to lower herself onto him very slowly. A low groan escaped her throat as she tried to gauge how much of him she could bear. She pressed her thighs against him to raise herself up until he was almost free then she relaxed and lower herself down again. He sat back and let her move over him as she wished. When it became too much he lifted her up. She was surprised by his strength. With a deft movement of his body and wrists she was suddenly on all fours, with her face pressed into the dirt and dangerously close to the burning coals. A guttural scream burst from her throat as he thrust himself deep into her. The pressure against her cervix was excruciating. He had a firm grip on her hips, pulling her into him as he shoved his way forward, pushing her away only far enough to pull her in again. She tried to grab at his arms, but he was too strong. Her screams for him to stop did nothing. It was as if he was oblivious to her presence. She felt like a rag doll with no will of her own. She could smell her hair singeing on the edge of the camp fire and her mouth was filling with dirt as he shoved her head down with one hand.

She continued to scream as his violation of her continued in ways she would never wish on anyone. And suddenly he was done. He was on the other side of the fire, pissing against a tree. She could hear him move around, whistling to himself. She had curled into a ball, her insides aching and so much of her skin smarting she couldn't begin to assess her own injuries.

"I watched my father beat a man so badly once that his entire family promised to do whatever he wanted if only he would stop." He was standing over her, his voice even, almost calm.

She slowly used her knees and elbows to try to move herself across the dirt away from him but she didn't have the energy.

"This guy had ratted my father out to his superior. Silly kaffir – chose the wrong officer. It got back to the Captain soon enough so when he next visited the village he decided to teach the man, and every other stinking animal within earshot, a very basic lesson about power. It wasn't pretty, but it was certainly effective. When he had finished beating him he strung him up from a tree in the main street. The guy kicked for ages."

He was standing over her with his hands on his hips as if instructing a class of young men on combat.

"I know what you're thinking – no, he didn't kill him. He cut him down while he was still twitching. Left him a little simple, of course, but he was no trouble at all after that."

He spat into the fire.

"I learned all I need to know about power by the time I was 14."

He moved back to his seat and settled in. "Academics call it the monopoly of violence. Very effective. And if you really know what you're doing you don't even need to be that violent – it is the suggestion of violence that will allow you to have your way. Not that I've ever cringed from doing what was necessary, but it's a question of efficiency. Why expend the energy if a suggestion is just as effective?"

He looked down at her as if noticing her for the first time. "Would you like another cup of tea?"

CHAPTER SIX

Senior Sergeant Ron Frankston did his best to keep his mood elevated, but it wasn't easy. Three days on the Gold Coast, even if it was mostly spent in the function rooms of the Novotel, had given him a taste of the good life. His hotel room had been so close to the beach he could smell the ocean. He woke up each morning before the dawn and jogged barefoot along the shoreline, the sea breeze filling his nostrils, then he sat on the sand and watched the most glorious sunrises he'd seen in decades. It was soul-restoring. Meeting with so many other police from around Australia had invigorated his sense of duty as well. He wanted to be doing more, and just as importantly, to be seen to be doing more.

He peered out of the window of his cluttered office in the heart of Alice Springs. He had an unimpeded view of the main road at street level. Hardly inspiring. Six years of drunk and disorderlies, domestic violence, petty crime. Six years of bone-wilting heat. Six years of goddamned blowflies. His mind was made up. Crushing the organised crime syndicates operated by bikie gangs was his ticket out of the Northern Territory and back into the real world. If the conference was anything to go by it was set to be one of the hottest topics in crime, outside of terrorism, for the next 10 years. That meant bigger budgets and more chances to increase his profile. He'd turned 53 at the conference – celebrated with a couple of beers by himself in some dingy singles bar along the promenade. He was running out of time and he knew it. Thankfully, a pack of animals just outside of Braitling had decided to blow themselves up in a meth-lab the previous Wednesday, which was all the impetus he needed to start his own task force. But his first order of business was the Thostrup briefing that was set for 11am.

He checked his watch. 10.48am.

He got up from his desk, grabbed his manila folder of notes and reports from the conference and stepped out into the 'briefing room'. It made him want his shake his head in disgust. The briefing room was little more than a few desks pushed out of the way to make space for a cheap whiteboard. The thought of budget constraints made him want to run out the door for the east coast immediately. On the board were photos of the elderly corpse found out at Forbes Creek, in the mortuary, and one shot of him when he'd been alive. Frankston studied the photos carefully, musing to himself that if any of the locals had been found out at Forbes Creek in a similar state, it wouldn't have generated much interest at all, probably wouldn't even landed on his radar. But a Danish national was different. It suggested darker forces at play. His mind ran through several of the lectures he'd attended on the Gold Coast, looking for signs that this might fit into a broader context of organised crime.

Half an hour later he was leaning against a desk, listening to Constable Smith as she relayed her findings from several days ago to a small group of officers and their two guests. He'd been introduced to Detective Kingsmill and Detective Birgitte Vestergaard as they arrived, but was reserving his judgement as to the potential merits, or otherwise, of their involvement for the time being. Quino had made his feelings known from the outset. The "guy was a wet rag" and the "dyke from Denmark had a great rack, and spoke kinda funny, but he still wouldn't mind giving her one". Quino was a necessary evil in Alice; a mindless oxen who could be relied upon to do some of the heavy lifting and muddy work that came with the Territory, but this wasn't the sort of case he should be involved in. Frankston made a mental note to keep the big lug busy with other duties until this was sorted. The other decision he had made from the outset was to keep the details about the cause of death out of the media for as long as possible. He didn't need a TV and internet shit-storm on his hands.

Constable Smith wrapped up by saying that Dr Brannigan from the Alice Springs Hospital had confirmed that the tooth found in the Dane's leg did in fact belong to a great white shark. Given the time of death they felt that the Thostrup must have been bitten somewhere off the coast of Adelaide on about October 28, then transported straight up the highway.

"So," sighed Frankston, "Detective Vestergaard, what can you tell us about our victim?"

Birgitte stood up and introduced herself to the rest of the group, some of whom she hadn't met. As she was about to take the floor, she noticed several other whiteboards, pushed to one side of the room, all of them littered with photos of recently deceased victims in other cases. She wondered how long Thostrup would remain on top of that list.

"I was brought in because the victim's brother-in-law is the head of the Danish police. It hasn't hit the headlines back home as yet, but it will only be a matter of days before it does. So I feel we need to move as quickly as possible."

The officers in the room stared at her blankly. It obviously wasn't her place to suggest how fast they should be working. She was an outsider, a foreigner. She put this to one side and continued. "Mr Thostrup was a retired CFO who, until recently, worked for ACER, an energy agency within the European Union. His background was in the energy sector, particularly mining. He lived and worked in Australia in 1976-78 for the Central Gas Co, but hadn't been back since. His wife passed away from cancer about 18 months ago. He was here on holiday. He flew into Sydney on October 24, where he stayed at the East Wind Hotel for two nights. We couldn't ascertain much about his movements during this time, except he did organise for a prostitute to visit him on his first night in Sydney. The woman, who goes by the name of Heaven, works at a Kings Cross brothel called The Silken Touch. She said she was paid for an hour but only stayed for 30 minutes as Mr Thostrup was too grief stricken to perform."

A couple of the male officers had smirked at the mention of a prostitute called Heaven, but then stopped smiling when Birgitte mentioned impotence.

When she had their full attention again she pressed on. "He flew to Adelaide on the 26th and stayed two nights in The Grace Hotel on North Terrace. Again, we don't know his exact movements over this period but we do know he contacted an old colleague from his Central Gas Co days – a Mr Mendelson, who lives in the Adelaide Hills. But Thostrup never followed through on his original email to meet up. He either hadn't got round to it or he had already been taken. And unfortunately that's all we know."

Frankston said, "Thanks for that. Detective Kingsmill, anything you'd like to add?"

Tony stood up. "Judging by the wounds Thostrup suffered, he was possibly strapped to some device and fed to the shark off the back of a boat, maybe a trawler. Apparently the Adelaide police are questioning charter operators to see if anyone remembers a customer who requested a boat that could handle big game, and they're checking CCTV footage around the hotel on the dates in question, but as yet there is no investigative team working the case in full. If they could get one together it might be worth canvassing the brothels around The Grace Hotel to see if any of the girls can provide information as to his last-known whereabouts closer to the time that his body was found."

"So," Frankston said to the room, "any ideas at this stage?"

Suggestions were thrown around, tentatively at first, but then with more confidence: gangland execution, bikers calling in a debt, a drug-fuelled thrill killing.

Frankston listened, nodded where he thought appropriate.

Tony said, "Is there any significance to where the body was found? Seems a bloody long way to drive to dump a body. The killer was taking a hell of a risk."

"At this stage," Frankston said, "We can't rule out multiple killers. It could be gang related, as Smith suggested. Do we know anything about Mr Thostrup's financial situation? Was he a gambler?"

"The sister didn't mention anything," said Birgitte slightly baffled by where the conversation was heading.

Tony could see she was perturbed but was eager to keep Frankston on side. "We could get the local guys in Sydney and Adelaide to show his photo around the casinos, check security footage of the relevant dates. It does seem a bit improbable that a guy from Denmark could get himself into that much trouble within a week of arriving here."

"Still," Frankston said, not willing to let a Federal cop dismiss his idea, "I think it's worth looking into. I'll contact my equals in Sydney and Adelaide to get the ball rolling. We'll want someone to talk to that Mendelson gentlemen as well. Make it official."

Tony considered himself slapped down. He looked at Birgitte who was watching Frankston carefully.

Frankston lifted the manila folder. "As some of you already know, I've just got back from the Gold Coast for a conference on bikie gangs and organised crime. It's well documented that international crime syndicates have got their claws into the east coast drug market. For the benefit of our guests, we've had a few gangs roll into to town over the past 18 months, making their presence felt in the hotels and the tattoo parlours and the like. The meth-lab that went up in flames was attached to a gang that goes by the name of the Rising Phoenix who hail from Queensland and have connections to Lebanon. There's also talk that the Bloodline gang, who come from Melbourne originally, maybe looking to force them out.

"That being said, I'm concerned that our Danish friend may be involved in some way with this increase in activity. It looks like an execution. For what – I don't know. But he's been fed to a shark then dumped in broad daylight."

Birgitte moved towards the whiteboard. "I agree it looks as though he has been executed, but his background doesn't marry up with the crimes you're talking about. He's a former Director of Natural Resources for the EU. Why would he be involved with bikie gangs in Australia?"

"That's what we need to find out."

Birgitte was flustered with Frankston's refusal to look beyond the context of his own neighbourhood. "So you are treating this as a stand-alone murder?"

"At this stage, I don't see how else we can treat it."

"The killer is still out there."

"Obviously. And we need to find them."

"But you're confident that they are not going to kill anyone else? That they haven't already abducted someone who may still be alive?"

"Ms Vestergaard, I'm confident I know my city and I know how to manage a murder investigation. There are groups here,

116

unwanted elements, that you are not aware of. You flew in, what, a week ago? Please don't presume to know how things operate in Australia, and particularly not Alice Springs. I assure you, we are as concerned as you are about the murder. Now, I believe Mr Thostrup's sister in Denmark has been notified."

"She has," replied Birgitte, resisting the temptation to walk out of the briefing. "She's flying out to escort his body back to Copenhagen."

"Can we line up an interview with her when she arrives?"

"I believe she will be here tomorrow afternoon. I'm sure she'll be more than eager to clarify her brother's reputation as a respected member of the EU's energy community."

Frankston stared at her hard. "Your assistance to date is appreciated."

He turned to Tony. "Where can we reach you both if we need you?"

"We're staying at the Settlers Arms Motel. I'll leave my details up on the board."

He shook their hands, grateful they'd both be out of his hair. "I'm sure I don't need to remind either of you," he said, then turned to the rest of the group, "any of you in fact. If the media contact you, send them directly to me."

As Birgitte left the police station she was ropable. It wasn't that the Australian police were incompetent, she was reasoning with herself, but when an overworked investigative team has another case dumped on them it's easy for details and important connections to be missed, which isn't helped if the senior detective has a preconceived idea of what may have happened.

Tony caught up to her on the steps outside the station. She turned to him and said, "Thostrup isn't the type to be involved with gangs. He has no history of gambling or credit problems. None of his behaviour suggested he was in a desperate state or linked to organised crime. He was simply abducted while on holiday. Someone knew he was here and that his death would cause a problem for someone else. I don't know who, but it was definitely a message to someone. And if the point isn't made clear enough, there will be more bodies before we know it."

"Frankston seems capable, Birgitte. I'm sure he'll work that out as soon as he gets his head around the case. He's only just come on board and he's obviously a bit excited about the conference he attended. Perhaps you can outline your concerns in an email."

"I don't like it, Tony," she said with frustration.

"There isn't anything more we can do."

"So what now? Should we head back to Adelaide to see if we can find out which boat was used?"

"Frankston has that covered, Birgitte. It's out of our hands."

She looked deflated.

Tony said, "Listen, it's Friday, almost the weekend. Why don't you book a tour out to Uluru, check out the Rock and the Olgas or maybe Kings Canyon."

"What? Suddenly become a tourist?" she said. "I can't do that. I need to be around for Katrine Holl." She didn't admit how much she was dreading that meeting, particularly now she could see where Frankston was heading with the investigation.

Tony said, "Well, I've got to touch base with my boss back in Sydney to find out what the hell I'm doing." He gently squeezed Birgitte's upper arm. "Try to switch off from it all, if you can. You were sent to find Hans Thostrup and you've found him. Well done, by the way."

As he turned to walk back into the station she said, "You were right."

"How so?"

"He just turned up."

"Sorry?"

"You said Thostrup would just turn up, but it won't be because of anything we're doing."

"Try not to think about it too much. Sometimes it's how these things play out."

If Friday had been difficult for Birgitte, Saturday was worse. Although Commissioner Holl had arranged for her to collect his wife from the airport in the afternoon and take her to the mortuary to formally identify her brother's body, Mrs Holl obviously had had other ideas. The distraught woman had arrived in Alice Springs first thing that morning, having changed flights in Singapore without notifying anyone. Extremely jet lagged and with her nerves on edge, Mrs Holl had caught a taxi straight to Alice Springs Hospital where she demanded in broken English to see the body of her brother. After several phone calls by staff and a string of heated threats, she was permitted to identify his body, which only upset her even more.

Birgitte had been reading a newspaper in a cafe near her motel, trying to enjoy the first bit of down time to herself since arriving in Australia. She hadn't expected Mrs Holl to arrive until after 3pm, and was finally coming to terms with her minimal role in the investigation when Tony phoned her to say she better get to the hospital quickly because Mrs Holl had arrived and was causing a scene. By the time Birgitte had reached reception, she was told by the staff on the front desk that Mrs Holl had already left, demanding to see the officer in charge of the investigation. Birgitte ran outside and caught another taxi to the police station. The desk sergeant explained that Mrs Holl had turned up about an hour before and abused him in broken English because Senior Sergeant Frankston didn't work weekends. Then she'd stormed off threatening legal action. Birgitte hailed a third cab and directed the driver to the Marionet Hotel a few blocks up from the police station, hoping that Mrs Holl may be there. She wasn't surprised when the concierge explained that Mrs Holl had taken one look at the lobby and refused to check in. The last anyone saw her she was wheeling her luggage down the main road in 43C heat.

Birgitte had been at a loss for what to do next so she returned to the hospital on the slim chance that Mrs Holl would eventually calm down and agree to meet with her as originally planned. By mid-afternoon Birgitte had given up. If Mrs Holl chose to ring her then she would do everything she could to help, but until then there was nothing else she could do.

Beside the hospital was a memorial garden that celebrated the native wildlife of Central Australia. It was an entire desert compressed into a few hectares, complete with sand dunes, small forests of red gums and a thoughtful selection of flowering plants and shrubs scattered either side of broken-gravel walkways. Despite the heat, it was a peaceful respite from an otherwise difficult day. Birgitte was walking through a copse of Mallee gums when she heard a familiar sharp voice speaking in Danish. It came from the other side of a red dune that rose up from a nearby path. Birgitte stepped carefully up the loose incline. As she reached the crest she could see Mrs Holl standing with her back to her down in the hollow of several dunes. She was wearing bone suit pants and a white blouse. The matching jacket was draped over her luggage nearby. The suit looked like wool. She must have been sweltering. The woman was uncomfortably thin, with dirty blonde hair that had shifted to dishwater grey. She held herself as if she was in a boutique dress shop on Strøget berating a surly shop assistant.

"It's outrageous, Verner" she spat into her phone in Danish. "Utterly absurd. Hans' body was left in a cinder-block shed for three days before these Neanderthals brought him here, and this place isn't much better... it's not right... they'll be hearing from our lawyers, I assure you."

Birgitte waited, not wanting to alarm her.

"No, I'm not staying at that hotel," she snapped. "I know you organised it, but I won't do it. It was just hideous. You can't expect me to stay there after what I've seen. I can't believe you've let me come out her on my own ... I know you're busy but ..." She began to weep hysterically. When she had composed herself she said, "His face was so peaceful, but they said he was fed to a... he was fed..." She couldn't say the words, then she howled, "Why would someone do that to Hans?"

Birgitte felt awkward for intruding on a deeply intimate moment of grief. She turned to walk back over the dune out of sight when Mrs Holl suddenly realised she was not alone. Her fragile face quickly hardened. "Yes, I've found her. She's here. Watching me. Couldn't you have sent somebody else?"

She knew that Birgitte would have heard but offered no apology as she struggled to walk up the dune in her heels. Birgitte tried to meet her midway and they both slipped awkwardly down into the hollow. "He wants to speak to you. It's my husband, the Commissioner."

Birgitte took the phone.

"What's going on?" His voice was distant and weary with sleep.

"There were a few crossed wires, Sir, but I have found your wife." Speaking in Danish had a soothing effect on her own mind. She realised how taxing it had been these past few days having to translate all her thoughts into English. "I believe she's identified her brother's body and has also been to the police station."

"She said there is no one there to assist with the investigation."

"It is Saturday, Sir, and I've literally only just caught up with her. If you like, I can get her settled into a hotel, we can have a chat and start making some inroads with the local police, together."

"That would be good. And Detective Vestergaard?"

"Yes, Sir?"

"Please be patient with her. She's taking this very hard."

"Of course, Sir. I'll notify you immediately of any developments."

Mrs Holl had lost the will to stand. The heat had worn away what little resolve she had left after the flight and the scenes in the hospital and the police station. She slumped into the hot red sand and wept into her knees. Birgitte sat down beside her and drew out of her bag a cold bottle of water she had brought with her from the hospital cafe. Mrs Holl took the bottle and drank greedily.

"Have you eaten?"

She shook her head. Birgitte could see the child in Mrs Holl and wanted to put her arm around her but knew it wouldn't last very long so she just suggested they get out of the sun. Mrs

Holl followed her, wheeling her bag through the sand, muttering the word "brutal" over and over. Birgitte wasn't sure if she was referring to the heat, the landscape or the demise of her brother.

Twenty minutes later they were sitting in the cool of the hospital cafe. Birgitte had ordered two cold drinks and a salad for Mrs Holl. She was slowly regaining her composure. Birgitte walked her through the search for her brother, choosing to leave out any reference to prostitutes for the time being. For a moment she understood where Tony had been coming from and wondered if she hadn't been too hard on him that day in the Adelaide Hills. As she tried to explain the current state of the investigation, she was careful to remind Mrs Holl that it was very early days, so they needed to explore every avenue.

"I don't understand why they are pursuing motorcycle gangs," she said, picking disdainfully at her salad. "Hans had no reason to interact with criminal elements."

"I understand but, like I said, it's an avenue that has to be exhausted before it can be ruled out."

Birgitte couldn't believe she was defending Frankston's approach.

Mrs Holl looked up at Birgitte. "I can't help feeling more should have been done to find him. If more resources were allocated when I first raised the alarm, Hans wouldn't be in that morgue."

"I can appreciate your feelings, Mrs Holl, and I haven't had a chance to express how sorry I am for your loss, but I didn't get here until November 9 and they believe he may have been killed around October 28. There was nothing anyone could do."

"You're quite skilled at that aren't you, Detective Vestergaard?" she said curtly, looking out the window.

"Skilled at what? I don't understand your question."

"It's nothing," she said. She pushed the half-eaten salad away from her as if it was full of lice. "It just seems that every time you come under fire, you manage to wiggle your way out of it."

"I'm sorry you feel that way, Mrs Holl. If you're alluding to the Max Anders case, I was cleared of any wrongdoing in court."

Without warning, Mrs Holl changed tack. "Did you speak to Gunner Mendelson as I asked?"

Birgitte realised she would have to watch her step. Grief aside, Mrs Holl was a nasty piece of work who took pleasure in using her elevated position as the wife of the Commissioner to turn people inside out without suffering the consequences.

"We did," she said. "He talked at length about his and Mr Thostrup's time together at Central Gas Co, but there was nothing he said that seemed relevant to your brother's disappearance."

"I never liked him."

"Who?"

"Mendelson," she said abruptly. "Smarmy little man, thought he knew everything."

Birgitte recalled Mr Mendelson's opinion of Ms Holl and it only endeared the old man to her even more. "I'm sorry to hear that."

"Don't patronise me, Ms Vestergaard."

Birgitte decided it was time to get on the front foot. "Someone knew your brother was here, I'm sure of it. Do you remember him mentioning a Nils Brekman?"

She shook her head then sipped at her coffee, which also appeared to leave a bitter taste in her mouth.

"They worked together at Central Gas Co but he's now very powerful – he's the CEO of a large mining company called Katercorp."

"Well, have you spoken to him?"

"Not yet. Mr Mendelson mentioned him in passing and I thought your brother may have been in touch. It's a long shot, but I will pursue it."

"When?"

"First thing Monday."

"Why not today?"

"Because we are in Australia, and I have to be seen to be going through the correct channels. It will be a fraction slower than either of us would like, but it will mean there won't be any repercussions if and when it gets to court."

"If or when, Ms Vestergaard?"

"Mrs Holl, I'm not in the habit of making promises I may not be able to fulfil."

"You've done it in the past."

Birgitte wanted to say that she was doing everything she could to learn from her mistakes but it would only give Mrs Holl more ammunition.

"We're not in Denmark," Birgitte said with more firmness to her tone than she would normally allow. She took a breath before continuing. "Please trust me, I will do everything in my power..."

"I'm sure you think you will but if it's not enough and my brother's death goes unpunished because of your inability to rise to the occasion, I assure you, my husband will be the first to hear about it. And I don't need to spell out how that may affect your career." She stood up. "I need to find another hotel in this godforsaken hell hole."

She grabbed her luggage and stormed out of the cafe. Obviously Birgitte was paying for lunch.

The main campus of Melbourne University was mostly deserted. The lecture halls were empty, the cafes, coffee carts and food courts closed. Occasionally the odd student could be seen carrying a satchel of books to the library or heading back to the car park, but Saturdays in November were generally a quiet time. The second semester had almost drawn to a close and the examination period didn't officially start for another week.

As he drove across the campus he smiled to himself. For someone who preferred his own company, his last 48 hours had been somewhat crowded. He had realised the girl's fate was sealed the moment he had told her he was heading to Mildura. It was a matter of expediency. That's not to say there was no pleasure in the final act.

Afterwards, he had slept well, but made sure he got up before the dawn on Friday. In the chill night air he'd taken his shovel from the back of the SUV, and proceeded to break the earth beside the smouldering remains of the campfire. After an hour of digging he tipped her body into the shallow hole. He stepped down into it and used a bowie knife to slash at her abdomen three or four times, ensuring the gases wouldn't build up, bloating her stomach and breaking the top soil within a few days. He couldn't afford to risk a wild dog smelling her corpse, digging it up and dragging it to the edge of the highway. At that point, the only body he wanted discovered was still in the fridge of his car. He stepped out and rolled the bloody stone into the hole before filling it back in. Then he scattered loose earth over the coals and cleared away any sign of a camp. By the time the sun had come up over the desert he was back on the road and still on schedule.

The drive into Mildura had been uneventful. He spent the afternoon in a park reading a newspaper. He was pleased to see there was still no mention of a body found in Alice Springs. The story would probably break in the next 24 hours. The later the better. In the early evening he drove into the bush just outside of town and crashed out, but was sure to get up at 3am on the Saturday. Once the second package had been placed where he knew it would be found, he had set off for Melbourne.

In the city he had put the SUV into storage and picked up a large second-hand van. The next collection had been made with relative ease. And now he was on his way back to the SUV to transfer the goods. Then he would make his way up towards Bourke in northern New South Wales. As he pulled out of the university grounds he looked over his shoulder into the back of the van. Beneath a greasy tarpaulin lay the third instalment of the project. He would contact the client that afternoon to ensure the next payment was on its way.

CHAPTER SEVEN

The private dining room of Atlas restaurant boasted uninterrupted views of Circular Quay, The Rocks and the Sydney Harbour Bridge, but the Northern Territory Minister for Trade's eyes were set squarely on a thin stack of Polaroids. He pushed his chair back to give his bloated stomach room to digest and sucked audibly on his teeth. In the past two hours he had devoured enough seafood for three people and washed it down with two bottles of expensive German riesling. He continued to scrutinise each image, one after the other, grinning occasionally.

Across the table Sam Westlake watched the Minister with satisfaction and a growing sense of pride in his own achievements. For all the industry's wrangling it only took a bit of homework on his part to determine exactly which currency the Minister preferred. Few people knew of the Minister's private collection, and fewer still would ever have guessed – given his reputation as a rough and tumble 'man of the people' – but apparently it made quite the retirement fund.

A pretty young waitress appeared at the door. Westlake called her over and touched her elbow, slightly stroking her skin through her blouse.

"Bring out a bottle your aged chardonnay. It's not on the list. Marty will know the one I mean."

She gently extricated herself from his fingers and slipped out of the room.

"So, Frank. It's quite a collection, yes?"

Frank Howard looked up almost in a daze. "Fucking brilliant. How'd you do it?"

"You don't want to know," Westlake laughed. "But the provenance of each work is in order. Some of the bigger pieces you probably recognise."

"You know, I met him once. Some fucking meet and greet or the launch of another fucking regional initiative. Extraordinary man. He was sitting in the dirt doing his thing, you know. Didn't even bother to look up at the cameras or the visiting dignitaries. I mean, fuck, the Northern Territory

Minister for Trade drops by and, Jesus, I think the Federal Minister was there that day as well – that cunt Postecopelou, whatever her name was – not that it matters now. Anyway, this prick doesn't even acknowledge us. But, fuck me, if he wasn't painting the most extraordinary picture I've ever seen."

Westlake was chortling with feigned admiration when Marty Reynolds, the chef and owner of the restaurant, appeared with a bottle of aged chardonnay and two fresh glasses.

"Gentlemen, how was lunch?"

"Fucking fantastic," said Howard, trying to hold his train of thought.

"It was exceptional as always, Marty."

"I'd love to stay and help you with the chardy but the kitchen needs me. Even on a Sunday we get hammered. Not that I'm complaining." He poured two glasses, slapped Westlake on the back. "We good for Tuesday night?"

"My assistant will call to confirm."

"See you then."

Howard picked at the bones of the snapper with his fingers as he continued to stare at the Polaroids. "It was this one." He tipped the image towards Westlake. It was Untitled 6, an enormous canvas depicting a coastal section of the northern most tip of Arnhem Land. "I'm no art critic, but this just fucking blows me away. The colours... the..." He waved his hand about searching for the right words, then muttered, "...the vibrancy. I mean, it looks like a fucking kid could do it, but there's something about this guy. And at Sotheby's last month one of his early works fetched a ridiculous amount."

"Well, if I've done my sums correctly, that little collection there will mean you own about 42 per cent of his works, all purchased anonymously over the past six months. We didn't want to be too greedy, might catch the attention of the market. But I'll send you a list of all the owners of his remaining works so you're free to bid for them when the mood takes you."

"On my salary?" he chuckled. His face softened. "Did you know he's on a dialysis now, apparently. An hour and half a day strapped to fucking machine just so he can piss straight. Poor bastard."

"They say he doesn't have long. And that his best works are behind him."

Westlake used a fork to pry a morsel of lobster from a half shell near his elbow, slightly surprised at himself for not spotting it sooner. "Actually," he added with a grin, "his best works are in front of you."

Howard didn't care for Westlake's humour. Never had. "What's it all worth?"

"That's not important, Frank. It's what they'll be worth when he's gone."

"Just curious," he said, draining his glass. Westlake reached across the table and filled it again.

"So," Westlake said with a contented sigh. "We can rely on your support come Tuesday?"

Howard snorted and waved the Polaroids at him. "These are on their way up north?"

"Flying overnight. You'll have them by midday tomorrow."

Howard stood up, tossed the photos on the table and steadied himself on the back of the chair. "Good grub. You'll get this, yeah?"

"It's on us."

"Tell Nils I'm not happy he didn't show."

"Discretion is the better part of valour."

"Don't be such a fucking ponce. We both know that this deal means a damn sight more to him than it does to me. The least he could have done is show me the goddamned respect and turned up for lunch. Thinks I'm just a fucking miner who came into politics on a whim? He owes me more than a bunch of coon paintings. And I'll be sure to collect – at my convenience, not his. You can tell him that from me."

Westlake listened carefully to the vitriol in the man's voice, gauged his hunger, his frustration and determined that it was time. "Truth be told, Minister," he said, standing up. "Nils is unaware of our little lunch meeting."

Howard's bleary eyes suddenly sharpened. The two men stared at one another for several moments. Both men knew exactly where they stood. Howard suddenly burst out laughing. "Fuck me. You've got a pair, haven't you?"

Ten minutes later Westlake was still at the table sipping his chardonnay. Through the window he could see the Minister waddling slowly along the promenade back to his hotel, where a Thai girl would be waiting for him – another of the Minister's predilections when he travelled to big cities. Westlake always liked to wrap up his business lunches with dessert. And the images she'd capture of them together would provide Westlake with the insurance he needed to secure the deal.

Dr Julie Barnett was intrigued. The woman's corpse lying on the steel table in front of her was a paradox. Conflicting evidence was calling to her from all directions, but was also distorted by the course of time that had passed between death and the arrival of the body at the forensic pathology unit of the King George Hospital in Melbourne.

The corpse had been discovered just outside Mildura, about an hour east of the border between Victoria and South Australia. It was bloated from being in the Murray River for what looked like a matter of days but the flesh wasn't as decomposed as Barnett would expect. The ball of the left femur had been ripped from the pelvis, leaving rags of torn skin and flesh around the exposed bone. Elsewhere the skin was split and extremely bruised in several places from what looked like bite marks, some of the other limbs were broken, and the bones in the face had been crushed. The damage to the skull could have been inflicted solely by a large animal or that damage could have masked a blunt-force trauma. She had mulled this over while proceeding with the examination but the fact that there were nothing larger than domestic dogs in the area where the body was found continued to niggle at her. What bothered her even more was the weed she had discovered in the mouth. She was pretty sure it wasn't growing in the Murray. Perhaps the body had been moved at some point. But from where?

Her phone rang. She considered not answering it but she recognised the number.

"Hey, Sweetie."

"My toe hurts."

"Which toe, Darling." She tucked the phone under her ear and returned to the corpse on the trolley.

"My big toe." Her four-year-old daughter was always stubbing her toe – she was going through a phase where she refused to wear shoes.

"Were you running in the house?"

"No," she said, mortified that her mother may think poorly of her. "Well, maybe, but it was Caesar's fault."

"Caesar made you stub your toe?"

"Uh-huh."

"Well, mummy has just given your big toe a special kiss from here at work so I'm sure it will be all better soon. And you tell Caesar to stop chasing you in the house or I won't take him for a walk when I get home."

"When will that be?" her tone was one of exasperation.

"It will be a few more hours, Sweetheart. Mummy's very busy."

"But it's Sunday. You said wouldn't work Sundays anymore."

"I'm sorry, Pet. But I couldn't get out of this one. Can you put your father on."

There was a loud clattering as her daughter dropped the phone and ran looking for her ex-husband. She noticed a slight discolouration on the wrist of the corpse's arm. She moved around the table and noted a similar effect on the other wrist. It was barely perceptible to the human eye. She examined the skin more closely, there were fine strands of a grey material. She took a pair of tweezers from a nearby trolley and carefully peeled off one of the strands from the left wrist.

Eventually a gruff voice came over the line. "Yeah."

"Hey, David. Thanks again for helping out."

"It's not part of the agreement."

"I know that, David. But you know what it's like here."

The line went silent. Neither of them had the energy to argue any more. She placed the strand in an evidence bag to be analysed more carefully. "Anyway, I just want you to know I appreciate it."

"I'm doing it for her."

"I get that, but still, thank you."

She put the phone down and exhaled until the stress in her shoulder where she had held the phone lessened to a dull ache.

She referred to the witness's statement, a Gavin Whitaker, captain of a paddle steamer, The Eureka, which ran cruises up and down that part of the Murray River for tourists. He said he'd spotted a foot protruding from the bank a few kilometres along the river from his base in Mildura. It was down by the waterline. He reckoned he wouldn't have seen it if the tide had been any higher. She studied the photos of the crime scene. By the time the police and forensic crew had arrived the tide was much lower so it looked like the body had been speared into the bank. Judging by the darkness of the mud above the water line, there was a one metre variation in tide. She imagined the scene six hours earlier when the river was full.

It brought to mind a case she'd read about during her student days of a man in the Northern Territory whose car had broken down on one side of a flooded creek crossing. He had tried to swim across on dusk to get help but slipped on the causeway. His two little kids had watched him float away. What was left of the torso and head was found two weeks later shoved up a hole in the creek bank 100 metres from where he had fallen. A local croc had seen its opportunity and grabbed the man as he fell into the water. From what she had read up on the creatures, they preferred fresh meat to rotting flesh but when they attacked larger animals, they had been known to rip off limbs to devour immediately before storing the rest. The forensic pathologist's report had detailed the damage inflicted by the crocodile in crushing its victim and the difficulty in ascertaining the cause of death. Had the man hit his head on the causeway? Had he drowned while unconscious in the water? Or was the crocodile a killer that had to be destroyed? The similarities in that corpse and the one lying in front of her were disturbing. But there were no crocs in Victoria and even if one had escaped from a private zoo, as far-fetched as that sounded in her mind, how long would it survive in the Murray? Only a saltwater croc could do this sort of damage. The idea was absurd. But the alternative theory was just as crazy. Had the woman been taken by a croc up north and the body moved so far afterwards? Barnett knew the answers lay in the weed she'd removed from the mouth and throat. She sealed the sample in a clear container, which she then addressed to the lab for analysis.

It was the heat of the sun that brought him round. The dryness in his mouth. The sensation of his skin slowly burning. The sunlight was so bright when he opened his eyes that he closed them again, unable to deal with a new reality that was utterly foreign to him. His mind tried to process what his eyes had seen for only a moment. Parched brown earth, so much sky. It didn't make any sense. He slowly opened his eyes again. Parched brown earth as far as he could see, stretching uninterrupted to a warbling horizon, the searing heat buckling any semblance of form in the distance.

James Freedmont carefully raised himself up on one elbow and shielded his face from the sun with his forearm. His limbs felt unnaturally heavy, cumbersome. He realised he was naked except for his underpants – nothing to protect him from the sun's rays. Again, he looked around in the hope there might be a tree to provide some shade, a shrub even. Nothing.

As he struggled to sit up he noticed a thick bracelet attached to his right ankle. He tried to take it off but it was strapped too tight. He gave up. It was some sort of electronic device encased in heavy-duty black plastic. A tiny red light pulsed steadily over the locking mechanism. He rested his head on his knees, closed his eyes again and tried desperately to remember what he was doing before... all of this. Slowly images came to mind, distant recollections as if from childhood.

He was on campus at Melbourne University. It was a Saturday – he had been doing a group assignment in the library for his International Relations major. Astrid Marillo had touched his hand under the table while that impossible bore

Suravin Kampor continued to dominate the discussion, banging on about everything he'd recently read on Chinese trade in Africa. Astrid's dark Italian eyes were so full of promise as she caught James's attention. When she was sure Kampor wasn't looking, she faked a yawn of operatic proportions. James tried not to laugh and had to pretend that he'd dropped his pen. Chuckling into his lap, he noticed Astrid's denim skirt had ridden up high on her thighs. He stopped laughing, fascinated. He closed his eyes. He couldn't be doing this. She'd only broken up with Tom Barclay the previous week. They were mates, good mates. It would be the death of their friendship if he tried anything on with Barclay's ex.

A flash of jealousy and resentment raged through James's mind. Barclay had everything: he came from money – a lot of money. His old man was some sort of mining magnate, owned large chunks of Queensland apparently. Like his father, Tom had been educated at one of the top private schools in the country, where he'd excelled at most of his subjects, as well as sport. He had his mother's good looks and his father's sense of entitlement, which at their age was construed as confidence. Most frustrating of all, he was for the most part a decent guy. Everyone on campus thought he was a rock star. By comparison James was a gangly kid from Broadmeadows who had had to work his arse off at the local state school to get into Melbourne Uni. He'd done all right, he was in the top five for most of his classes, but there was always a sense that Barclay did better without even trying. Ever since the two of them had met up at a football match and bonded over a shared love of the Celtic Rangers, James had deferred to Barclay on everything. It was the natural dynamic of their friendship, something he'd never questioned, until now. Frankly, he couldn't see what Barclay saw in him; maybe he liked slumming it to stick it to his parents. Just once, James wanted to taste some of the success that seemed to come so naturally to his mate.

They'd finished their group work by midday and after 20 minutes of internal anguish, he'd finally asked Astrid if she'd wanted to meet up for a drink in the city that evening. She said couldn't and he could feel his self esteem crumpling like a metal drum at 20,000 fathoms. He wanted to disappear into the pavement, but she suddenly said he could come over and help her with one of her essays at her house. The crumpling suddenly reversed and he thought he might explode. He had watched her walk across the main lawn, her gorgeous arse swishing about in that tiny denim skirt. The gorgeous arse that Barclay used to crow about in the pub on weekends.

James had been mesmerised by Astrid Marillo since their first semester together. He couldn't believe Barclay had never noticed how he looked at her. She was way out of his league, the sort of girl who dated the captain of the rowing team or the head of the student council or guys like Tom Barclay. The poor guy had been gutted when she'd dumped him. It was the first time he'd experienced anything close to public failure. James had consoled his mate but would have been lying if he wasn't pleased that Barclay had been brought down a peg or two, closer to his level. For the first time he felt they were competing on a more even playing field.

He was on his way back across the university, feeling 10-foot tall when he noticed a blue van parked on the side of a utility road. The driver, some blonde guy in his late 30s, dressed like a tradie, was standing beside it, staring at his mobile, shaking his head, obviously lost. It was a big campus and the internal roads could be confusing. James normally would have kept going, but he was feeling so good about Astrid that he crossed the lawn and asked the guy if he needed any help. Apparently, he was looking for the Clancy Building. There was some power outage he had to sort out. The guy had sounded foreign. Perhaps, Dutch or South African. James remembered apologising, telling him he wasn't familiar with the Clancy Building. The guy said he had the address written down in his log book. He opened the back of the van and started rummaging around. Then he had stood up and tried to get better reception on his phone. James wasn't really paying attention. He was trying to guess what Astrid's nipples might look like – she was an Italian blonde so they might be really tight and pink, like he'd seen on his laptop or they could be that broad dusky brown he loved from those European movies from the 70s. The maintenance guy said he had the place marked on his map but his phone kept cutting out. He pointed to the book in the back of the van and said the address was on the page flagged with a pen.

The last thing James remembered was leaning into the van and opening the book to a blank page, then he was hit so hard from behind he blacked out.

He took a deep breath and tried to think rationally about his situation. He couldn't be too far from help. It was just a question of in which direction. The sun was directly over head so he couldn't tell which way was north. He knew that if he stayed there, not only would he continue to burn, he'd probably dehydrate in a matter of hours. He recalled the news story from a few years back about the two teenagers in outback Western Australia who had run out of petrol while out hunting roos. They had perished within two days. Their corpses were found in the ute with a note saying that they loved their families and were sorry. They never realised they were only two kilometres from a homestead with running water. He tried to shut this out of his mind. There at least had to be some shade somewhere within walking distance.

He went to stand up but as soon as he put weight on his left foot a searing pain shot up his leg and he fell to the ground screaming in agony. The bracelet on his right ankle had distracted him from the swelling of his left ankle. Parts of the skin were broken in round welts. The guy who had abducted him must have smashed it with a hammer or a mallet. He felt nauseous at the thought but the sense of dread that had lingered beneath the confusion earlier was now draining the blood from his face. If he didn't get moving immediately, he was going to die out here, alone.

After several agonising attempts he managed to stand up, putting all of his weight on his right leg. He slowly hopped forward. Occasionally he would lose balance and his left foot would automatically take the weight. He screamed and fell each time. Within minutes he was sweating profusely. He knew he was using too much energy, but he had to keep moving.

He berated himself as he hobbled across the arid plain. How could he be so stupid? He could hear his father laughing at him drily for once again being so naive and his mother butting in, telling him not to pick on the boy. His parents. Did they even know he was missing? They didn't expect to hear from him until the following week. Astrid wouldn't raise the alarm. She'd assumed he'd got cold feet, because deep down she knew he was just a hopeless virgin who didn't know the first thing about pleasuring a woman like her. He felt awful for betraying his mate Tom. When he got back to Melbourne he'd fess up about what he'd done and do his best to convince Tom that Astrid wasn't worthy of a guy like him. They could both do better.

He felt like he'd been hobbling for a couple of hours when he stopped to get his bearings. His shadow was starting to shift under his blistering feet. He must have been heading south-east for a few kilometres. It didn't seem right. He felt that he should have been moving north. He didn't know why. It just felt safer to be heading north. He looked about him but nothing had changed. It was as if he hadn't moved at all. His skin was burning but there was nothing he could do to make it stop. He began to panic. He could have been anywhere and no one would know that he was missing. He didn't even know how long he'd been unconscious. Was it Sunday or had several days passed since he was knocked out? He started to shuffle in a slightly different direction just to feel that he was in control of his own situation but he was beginning to realise it was hopeless. He fell to his knees and began to scream with fear and helplessness.

CHAPTER EIGHT

Birgitte stood on the bank of the Murray River watching The Eureka shunt past. The colonial-era steamer was one of several operating along the river. It collected tourists from Mildura and transported them back to a time when gold was sluiced from the earth by hand. The steamer had been beautifully restored, painted the colour of sand with a rich burgundy trim. The polished brass railings shone in the early morning sun. A throaty rumble issued from the engine, which was working steadily to keep the boat at half speed, pushing out a plume of smoke that swirled against a clear blue sky. The captain, a grey-haired man wearing a dirty white boiler suit, leaned out of the cabin assessing the distance from the far bank. Further back along the top deck a small group of Serbian tourists who had been enjoying breakfast were now staring across the water at Birgitte, who was standing within the perimeter of a crime scene marked by blue and white police tape. They grabbed their phones and cameras and moved to the railing, snapping as many shots as they could. One woman in a fluoro sun visor pointed to the waterline convinced she could see a body, but her husband, an oafish man wearing a matching visor, told her to stop being so stupid – it was only a submerged log. She was visibly disappointed. A stick-thin man in a red tracksuit yelled out to Birgitte in broken English, wanting to know what had happened. They all waved their arms, trying to get her attention but she did her best to ignore them.

It was an uncomfortable start to the week, first thing Monday morning, staring down at the dumping ground of another victim. The similarity between the scene here and at Forbes Creek was not lost on her. Large, established eucalypts leaned out over the murky brown water, which was flowing steadily. It was a remote part of the river 20 minutes' drive from town. The nearest houses were several hundred metres back from the bank. The body had been found on the Saturday, possibly by the same captain who was now guiding the steamer around the next bend.

As the stern disappeared beyond the tree line, taking with it the rumble of the engine and the excited conversations of the tourists, a familiar stillness returned to the river, dry heat, silence, as if the air and the all the sounds it carried had been stripped away. It was the same eerie feeling she had experienced four days ago outside of Alice Springs.

She took hold of a low branch and carefully leaned out over the muddy water, peering back at the edge of the bank. The tide was on the way out but still covered the hole where the body had been first spotted. She looked up to the houses to assess what the residents may have been able to see if they had been alerted by some noise in the night. It was too difficult to draw any inferences from the scene. She pulled herself back in and wiped her hands on her trousers as she ducked under the tape. She didn't feel vindicated, nor triumphant that her theory was playing out as she had imagined it. A woman had lost her life in the most horrible of circumstances and there was no dignity in her makeshift burial.

Further along the bank Tony was talking with the forensic pathologist who had flown up from Melbourne, an angular looking woman in her late 30s, a Dr Barnett. She was showing him several photographs, pointing at the bank then comparing the different shots. Birgitte walked along the line of trees towards them.

The past few days had been hectic. After finding a hotel to Mrs Holl's liking on Saturday afternoon, Birgitte had returned to her own motel room to compile a fresh report for both Sven and Commissioner Holl. She knew she would have to keep them abreast of every detail as quickly as possible for fear that Mrs Holl would skew their judgement with her own interpretations of the evidence. She had made a point of telling Mrs Holl that engaging with the media at this point would only hinder the investigation into her brother's death. The grieving woman had replied with a snide remark about Birgitte's media profile back in Denmark, which Birgitte had no choice but to ignore.

Tony had knocked on her door at one point early that evening to suggest they grab a bite to eat, but she had already started to research Nils Brekman, his company Katercorp and mining in Australia in general; it was their only lead so she wanted to keep going. She spent several hours at it that night but didn't turn up anything that linked Thostrup's death to the local mining magnate, beyond their time together at Central Gas Co. As she prepared to go to sleep, she wondered if the Northern Territory Police were actually reading the situation better than she wanted to admit. Could Thostrup have been singled out for extortion? He certainly wasn't short of funds. But it still seemed too far-fetched that a bikie gang setting up a new chapter in Central Australia would target a wealthy tourist holidaying in another state.

Sunday had started off smoothly enough with a much-needed sleep-in until 9am, but then she had Senior Sergeant Frankston on the phone wanting to know how Mrs Holl knew so much about the case and if there was any way of getting her to back off. Her incessant calls to the station were distracting his staff, which was now disturbing his weekend. Birgitte had phoned Mrs Holl and only succeeded in making her angrier by suggesting she let the local police handle the investigation. She empathised as much as possible but she couldn't openly admit that she didn't like what the locals were doing either. She reiterated Tony's line that there was a process that had to be respected.

She had just fallen back into bed when her phone rang again. She considered putting it on silent but saw that it was Tony. He didn't bother with formalities.

"Another body has turned up."

"Where?"

"Interstate again. This time in Victoria, just outside of a small town called Mildura. Are you still at the Settler's Arms?"

"Yes. Where are you?"

"At the station. Constable Harris came through once again with the goods."

"What can you tell me?"

"An unidentified woman in her mid 30s. She was found stuffed in a hole in the river bank. A passing boat driver spotted her foot sticking out of the water."

"Do they know how she died?"

"Not yet, but the forensic pathologist, a Dr Barnett, has said the woman's injuries are consistent with an attack by a saltwater crocodile. The thing is, there aren't any crocodiles in the Murray River, nor anywhere else in Victoria. She thinks the woman may have been killed up north somewhere – Far North Queensland or in the Northern Territory – Cape York, Kakadu or Arnhem Land maybe – it's too early to tell. It might have even been in a private zoo. We're waiting on lab tests on weed found in her mouth and throat."

"Jesus, Tony."

He paused before asking, "Any chance of you catching another flight with me?"

"I'm not really a part of the case, Tony. Neither are you. And I thought you wanted to get back to Sydney."

"I did, but hear me out. The way I see it if one body turns up – it's a local case. Frankston's in charge. But if two bodies turn up in different states and the murders are connected – that's definitely Federal. It would make sense for us to be across the developments in both cases. At least that's what I'm planning to tell my boss," he said with a note of humour in his voice. "And if you are right, then they're going to need all the help they can get."

She needed time to think it through. Was she acting beyond her remit? Would she get on the wrong side of Sven and the Commissioner if she stayed? Or did she owe it to Thostrup and his sister to find more answers? Furthermore, was someone else already at risk of being brutally slain by a killer acting with impunity?

"Birgitte? Are you still there?"

"How do we get there?"

"I've already a chartered a flight from Alice Springs airport. We can leave at 6pm tonight."

She had decided to follow her intuition, but then wrestled with how to handle Mrs Holl. She didn't want to get her hopes up or have her feeding partial information back to the Commissioner in Copenhagen, or worse, talking to the media. Mr Thostrup's body was due to be flown back to Denmark on the Tuesday. Birgitte figured she might just have enough time to get to Mildura and back before Mrs Holl even knew she was gone.

Now, as she walked along the bank of the Murray River, her mind was processing all the latest information. As confident as she was that this was the work of the same man, she was determined to keep her own theories at a distance from the evidence until she was certain. In the shade of a large eucalypt Dr Barnett was explaining the discrepancies in calculating the time of death. Birgitte waited for a pause in the conversation and asked, "If the killer kept the body on ice – refrigerated – for a few days, long enough to get from one end of the country to the other, would that throw out the calculations?"

"Definitely," she said. "Judging by the state of decay, she was in the water for about three or four days after death but I can't tell whether that was here or in the crocodile's lair, which could be thousands of kilometres away. And I don't know at this stage how long she was out of the water – on ice, as you say – in between."

"So it's hard to say when the body was dumped, beyond it being found on Saturday morning," said Tony. "No eyewitnesses have come forward either, apparently. Which means it's even harder to work out how far he's driven since."

He looked back at the line of houses then at the river. He was coming up blank and it was beginning to bother him. "Are we looking for some crazed killer with a thing for wildlife?"

Birgitte shook her head. "It's too orchestrated. The bodies are being staged. There is no rage in the execution."

He looked at her with incredulity. "No rage? Thostrup's legs were torn off while he was alive, and a woman was possibly fed to a saltwater crocodile. Do you know how big those things are?"

"Yes, there is violence in the act of being eaten alive, Tony, but there is no rage in the execution of the crime. It's incredibly calculated. We mustn't confuse the act with the intent behind it. That's what he wants."

"What do you mean?"

"He wants us to be horrified by the act, to think that he is capable of anything, so that we are blinded to his methodology."

"Which is?"

"I'm not entirely sure yet but, if this is the work of the same killer, there is definitely a pattern forming. He's doing this intentionally. The cause of death, the dumping of the bodies interstate. He's sending a message to someone or perhaps to different people, but he's also doing as much as he can to slow down the investigative process at the same time. At the very least he's hoping we don't connect the two murders. As long as it is interstate and so incredibly bizarre there's less chance that different police forces will think to cooperate quickly enough to stop him from completing his task."

Dr Barnett was listening closely, impressed with Birgitte's quick, rational reasoning.

"You mentioned the Hans Thostrup case," she said. "I found sticky threads on the wrists of this woman. I'm thinking it might be residue from electrical tape. I'll get in touch with the pathologist in Alice Springs and see if they can detect anything similar on Mr Thostrup. If it is tape and the killer has used the same roll on both, or even something similar, then we may have a connection. It might take a few days to coordinate."

Birgitte appreciated the fact that Dr Barnett was thinking along similar lines but made a conscious effort not to get her hopes up at such an early stage of the investigation.

She took the photo of the corpse from Tony. The lifeless eyes stared back at her, void of any desperation or fear. They had been too late to help her.

"Do we have any idea who she is?" she asked.

"We're running a search on missing women that fit her description," he said.

"She looked healthy, outside of her injuries," said Dr Barnett. "Well bred, almost. So you can rule out drug addicts or the homeless, if that helps."

Birgitte wondered if a forensic pathologist's ability to develop an image of a person's life from their decomposing corpse was a talent or a curse. Would it blur her clinical judgement to humanise the victim, or help her ascertain a clearer understanding of the circumstances surrounding the cause of death?

The grating sound of car tyres braking over gravel caused them to turn. A dark-blue unmarked police car pulled up in front of their own two vehicles and a tired-looking detective in his mid 50s stepped out. He was wearing ash-grey trousers and a cheap short-sleeve business shirt, which didn't conceal his undershirt. The look was topped off with fake aviator sunglasses. Birgitte noticed the forensic pathologist's face tighten at the sight of him.

"Julie."

"Jack."

He took off his glasses and stared hard at Tony.

"Who the hell are you?"

Tony introduced himself and Birgitte. As Tony explained their reasons for being there, Birgitte watched the local detective carefully. Senior Sergeant Jack Braithwaite's face was flabby and pale, probably from late nights drinking scotch in front of the television. His eyes were tiny, sharp and cold. He obviously didn't care much for Dr Barnett, and he was even less impressed that a Federal officer had dropped in on his command. He stepped over to the edge of the bank and peered into the water as if all the answers were submerged there for him to access when it suited him. He walked back to them, expressionless.

"A young woman was found here two days ago, shoved up a hole on my river bank," he announced. "Now, at this stage, we don't know how she got here, or how she died. We don't even know who she is. What we do know is she has been tortured, brutally beaten and dumped."

"And one of her legs has been removed," Dr Barnett interjected. "Possibly by a..."

"Your croc theory," Braithwaite said with wry bemusement.

"Her injuries are consistent with a saltwater crocodile attack," she said firmly. "And not just because she is missing a leg. The other contusions and fractures all suggest significant trauma, probably by a large animal. An animal with the crushing capacity in its jaw to break several bones and rip limbs from their joints."

"There aren't any saltwater crocs in my river, Julie."

"I'm aware of that, Jack. That's why I'm waiting to hear back from the lab on the weed found in her mouth and throat. I don't believe it came from this river."

"And until that evidence is confirmed as such, it's just a theory, yeah?"

"Yes."

"I don't build a case on theories, Julie. You know me better than that. And I sure as hell don't want some journo from the Mildura Times leading with 'CROC ATTACK' or 'MURRAY MONSTER' in tomorrow's paper." He turned to Tony. "Which brings me to you two. Until Dr Barnett's 'theories' are proved plausible, there is no connection between this murder and the one outside of Alice Springs, as you suggest, so as far as I'm concerned this is a local matter."

He put his sunglasses back on. "Now I can't stop you guys from doing what you think is necessary, but if you get in the way of my investigation in any way whatsoever, all hell is going to rain down on you from a very great height. Won't it, Julie?"

She didn't respond.

He turned to Tony. "Where are you staying while you're here?"

"The Riverside Motel." He handed his card to the senior detective. "You can reach either of us on that number."

Braithwaite took the card but didn't bother looking at it before shoving it in his pocket. He walked back to his car without another word. The three of them watched as his car pulled away with a flurry of dust.

"What did he mean by all hell raining down on us?" Birgitte asked.

"Senior Sergeant Braithwaite is very protective of his turf and he's well connected," replied Dr Barnett, "So much so that he's given the Victorian coroner a few headaches in the past. He's shut me down on more than one occasion when he's felt the evidence might require the involvement of outsiders. It's his way of maintaining control for as long as it takes for him to get all the kudos for solving homicides in and around Mildura."

Tony asked, "How long will it take to verify the weed in the woman's mouth and prove her injuries were the result of a saltwater crocodile?"

"A few days at least, which means I better get back to it. I've also got a four-year old at home in Melbourne who hates me being away for any length of time. Sorry I couldn't shed any further light on the situation."

She gave them both her card, got into her rental car and did a swift u-turn back on to the road into Mildura.

Between the trees along the bank the bow of The Eureka appeared again on its return journey, pushing a low rise of muddy water from its hull, which then splayed out in a wide wake from the stern. The Serbian tourists had seen enough of rural Victoria for one day, they lazed about on bench seats or played with their phones. In the cabin the captain made a point of keeping his eye on the river ahead. What he'd seen a few days ago would stay with him for years to come. He didn't need to be reminded of it so soon. It wasn't until the steamer had disappeared beyond the next bend that small waves slowly lapped against the bank where Birgitte stood.

"It's playing out the way he wants it," she said, almost with admiration. She turned to Tony. "The Northern Territory police are treating Thostrup as a gang-related murder, and the Victorian police want to keep their investigation to themselves. No one is doing anything to stop the killer because they don't want him to exist."

Tony's brow furrowed as he realised how this must look to an officer like Braithwaite. "As modus operandi go, it's hard to comprehend – sharks, crocodiles, driving all over the country to dump bodies in random locations. I don't blame them for being wary. Without evidence or a some sort of motive it looks pretty untenable."

"I hate to say it, Tony but we don't have time to wait for the evidence. As strange as that sounds. Someone else could be in danger."

"We don't know that."

She gave him a stern look.

He held up his hands. "It looks likely, I'll admit, but I wouldn't be taking that line with any of the locals."

She stepped past him and headed back to the car. "We need to find out who this woman is; there has to be a connection between her and Thostrup."

"If this guy has been killing people interstate, where the hell do we start? It's a big country, Birgitte. If you hadn't noticed."

They opened their doors and climbed into the car.

"We start with the regions with saltwater crocodiles. You said they were all up north?"

"Do we rule out private and public zoos?"

"I think so, at this stage. If he's brazen enough to feed Thostrup to a shark in open waters, I'm confident he'd be working in the wild on this as well."

As he started the engine Birgitte said, "I'm sorry if you think I'm being obsessive about this, but I've been right before when everyone else refused to read the evidence correctly."

"Yeah? And what happened?"

"Three children suffocated to death while police, like Senior Sergeant Braithwaite, debated the most suitable course of action."

They drove back to Mildura to the Riverside Motel. Tony called Constable Harris and told her to start researching missing persons who resembled the description of the woman found in the Murray River. He then forwarded the images of the woman that Dr Barnett had sent to him. Birgitte wanted to learn more about crocodiles, where they lived, their feeding behaviour and basically how a crocodile might react to being fed a human being. She took her laptop to the motel cafe and spent the next few hours reading zoological and museum websites. They met up for lunch and went over the MO again to see if any further connections could be made.

On the way back to their rooms in the afternoon, Tony decided it was time to bite the bullet and contact Hana in prison. He wanted answers so he could put that chapter behind him. It was causing too much of a distraction in his life.

As he got to his door he said, "I'm going to call Miller, try to pitch your theory, see if she gives me some room to move on this."

"Do you think she'll go for it?"

"I'll let you know how I get on."

"Good luck."

Tony let himself in to his motel room. He sat on the edge of the bed and rested his elbows on his knees, bringing up the number on his phone. Without analysing it any further, he dialled. He listened to the dial tone for an interminably long time. When he finally spoke to the receptionist and explained that he wanted to speak to Hana Shakib, she put him on hold. He waited several minutes. The receptionist eventually came back on and told him Hana Shakib wasn't available. He thanked her and ended the call. So that was that, he thought.

He was about to call Superintendent Miller when it occurred to him there was no reason why Hana couldn't have taken the call. He could feel himself getting angry at being fobbed off by the prison staff. He stood up and began pacing around the room. Why the hell wouldn't they put him through? He considered phoning again to demand to speak to a supervisor, when it finally dawned on him – Hana still didn't want to talk to him.

He shook his head and laughed to himself. He knew he'd lied to her about his vocation, but he wanted a chance to tell her the truth. It infuriated him that she was shutting him out. If anyone had explaining to do it was her. At the very least he deserved to know why she would risk her own future by getting involved with her cousins. Had they physically forced her to cook their books? Had they threatened to hurt her?

Tony went into the ensuite to wash his face. He took a deep breath. There was no point getting worked up over something he had no control over. He'd made the call and for today that would have to be enough.

Above the sound of the running faucet he thought he heard yelling. He turned the tap off. Through the walls he could hear a woman's voice raised in anger. For a moment, he just put it down to motel life then he realised it was Birgitte.

He ran out the door and along the car park. Birgitte's door was open. She was standing in the centre of the room with her hands on her hips talking angrily in Danish at her laptop, which was set up on the bedside table.

On the screen a middle-aged man in a suit was sitting at a desk staring flatly at the camera on his computer. The man shook his head and responded calmly. Tony had no idea what they were saying but Birgitte looked flabbergasted, ready to kick the computer across the room.

Tony's phone rang. It was Miller.

"Kingsmill."

"Tony, it's Superintendent Miller. Where are you?"

He stepped outside into the car park but could still hear Birgitte talking heatedly from her room.

"Mildura. I was just about to call you."

"Mildura, Victoria? What the hell are you doing there? I thought you were in Alice."

"Another body's been found."

"Another shark victim?"

"No, the pathologist reckons this woman, an unidentified female in her 30s, was taken by a crocodile."

"In Mildura?"

"That's the thing. She's waiting to hear if the woman was killed in some other location and dumped interstate, like Thostrup."

The line went quiet. Eventually Miller said, "Listen, Tony, I know we haven't clarified your position as such, but that doesn't mean you get to pursue your own investigation on a whim. You were told to escort Detective Vestergaard and assist in the search for Mr Thostrup. He's been found and the Territory Police are across it. I now have Vestergaard's boss, a Sven Augerson, wanting to know why she isn't returning his calls. And I'm not some international messenger service. I need you to get her on a plane back to Alice Springs so she can ensure Thostrup's body leaves Australia as planned. And I want you back in the office as soon as possible."

"And what if the murders are connected?"

"I take it the Victorian Police are investigating the body in Mildura?"

"They are, but no one is making the connection. Birgitte... Detective Vestergaard feels there could be a killer working interstate. I think she might be right."

"If it helps, give me a summary of your concerns and I'll email it to the lead investigators in both cases and they can draw their own conclusions. But your work there is done. Do you understand?"

He considered arguing the case further but he didn't want to get on the wrong side of his new boss in the first two weeks. "Yeah. I got it."

He hung up. Thick clouds had rolled in during the afternoon. He could feel the electricity in the air as the large drops of rain spattered against the bitumen. With a flash of lightening and delayed rumble of thunder a steady downpour was unleashed on the country town. Tony considered stepping into the deluge to wash away the frustration and disappointment; instead he walked back into Birgitte's room. She was sitting on her bed staring at the carpet between her feet in disbelief. The video call was over.

"Was that your boss in Copenhagen?" he asked.

She nodded.

"Did he say it's time for you to go home?"

She nodded again. He wanted to put his arm around her.

She looked up at him, replaying the conversation in her mind, trying to make sense of it all.

It was early evening in Copenhagen. Sven had spent the afternoon trying to contact Birgitte but had only succeeded when he was on his way out the door for the day. Birgitte didn't like what he had to say.

"Sven, you told me to find Thostrup and I did. Now we need to find his killer. Surely, the Commissioner wants to know who killed his brother-in-law."

"I told you to liaise with the local officers to assist with the search," Sven said. "No more. No less."

"So now that Ander's appeal is over and I'm out of the headlines, you want me back in Copenhagen?"

"We're confident the Territory Police in Australia are going to find out what happened to Mr Thostrup..."

Birgitte cut him off, "He was fed to fucking great white shark, Sven. His legs were ripped off at the thigh. Then he was dumped in a dry creek bed in the middle of nowhere, several hundred kilometres away. This is not a normal murder."

"I saw the photos, Birgitte," he replied calmly. "It must have been horrific. We have no idea what or who Mr Thostrup may have been involved with, but we do have a direct line of communication with the Australian police who will keep us up to date with any developments. You don't need to be there."

"And what of this other body?"

Sven had looked almost reluctant to even ask. He sighed, "What other body?"

"A woman in Victoria, further south east of Alice Springs. The forensic pathologist is confident she was killed by a crocodile several hundred kilometres away and dumped interstate, like Thostrup."

Sven rubbed his eyes and shook his head. "Be that as it may, Birgitte. You are not there to lead a murder investigation."

"But no one can see the connection, which means not only will they not find the guy who killed Hans Thostrup. They won't stop him from killing more people in the meant time. The guy could be preparing to kill someone else as we speak."

"Birgitte," Sven barked, getting angry with her for the first time in their six-year working relationship. "Enough. There are murders taking place all over Australia and Denmark which are not your responsibility nor mine. Now I've just had Commissioner Holl on the phone. Apparently his wife has no interest in you escorting her back to Copenhagen, so you're done in Australia. Get yourself on a plane back to Denmark, today, now. Got it?"

She was about to beg but he saved her the indignity by hanging up on her. She was so tired of all the politics, the myriad unrelated reasons for not doing strong police work. She stared into Tony's eyes wanting him to make it all go away, but knowing that he couldn't. They were out in the ether together.

Tony said quietly, "Do you still need to go back to Alice Springs to escort the body back to Denmark?"

She shook her head.

"Well, there's a charter flight to Sydney tonight. We can sort out international flights in the morning."

He didn't know what else to say so left her alone in her room.

Birgitte finally exhaled and settled back into her seat as the pilot brought the small plane to its desired altitude, heading east across the country to Sydney. It was 10pm. Tony was beside her, resting his head against the window, trying to get some sleep. It had been a bumpy ascent out of Mildura because of the storm which had only increased in ferocity during the late afternoon. Birgitte had resisted the temptation to grab Tony's hand as the plane lurched and dropped then lifted again for five very long minutes. Short flights on small planes usually didn't bother her but this had been particularly rough. Now that they were up over the clouds she did her best to take her mind off the ascent.

Sven's tone at the end of their video call had reminded Birgitte of her father when she had finally worked up the courage to tell him she was going to join the police force fresh out of law school instead of joining the diplomatic service as they had discussed. Jan was calm at first, then, when he realised she was serious, he shut down and wouldn't listen to "anymore of her nonsense". He simply couldn't envisage any other path for her. As he saw it, she had an extraordinary mind, anything less would be a waste of her talent. There was no point discussing it; if she couldn't see the opportunity she was throwing away then she just needed to trust his judgement until it dawned on her. He had the audacity to suggest that she would thank him for his insight in the long run.

Birgitte recalled being ropable that her father could be so bloody minded and arrogant. It was ironic, she felt at the time, considering his career was built on his ability to assess multiple possible alternatives, determine the most suitable course of action then convince everyone around him to get on board.

But when it came to Birgitte he had blinkers on – he assumed there was only one possible outcome, and it was her shortcomings that prevented her from seeing it. Her mother, Loll, did her best to mediate but eventually threw her hands in the air in frustration at both of them and went and stayed in their holiday house in Aarhus for the weekend. They could sort it out for themselves. Her poor mother – stuck in a house with two wilful creatures who couldn't see eye to eye at the best of times. Tomas had remained on the periphery, slightly bewildered by the combative nature of Birgitte's relationship with her father. He had only been seeing her a short while at that point and thought it best to offer his support by listening to her. She appreciated his measured approach but would later realise that it amounted to a reluctance to get involved.

Sadly, her father had never come to terms with her decision. Now that he was retired he'd learned to let it go albeit begrudgingly. His daughter was a police officer, probably the smartest police officer in Denmark as far as he was concerned – and that was a damn pity. The criminals didn't care, neither did the victims most of the time; their lives were too shattered to notice. It was an utter waste. The memory no longer rankled her but it still made her sad her father couldn't appreciate what she was trying to achieve in her own right.

She didn't want Sven to be disappointed with her either. Before Tony had come into the motel room she had just accused Sven of being a puppet for the Commissioner. She now regretted saying it, but at the time she couldn't understand how such an astute detective could switch off his capacity for reason so easily, not to mention his compassion. Lives were at risk. They were trained to protect people from harm. Politics shouldn't come into it.

Despite Sven's own criticism of her, she wasn't so arrogant to assume that the Australian police on the ground couldn't solve their own investigations. It was the fact that they refused to consider the possibility that there was one killer working beyond the limits of their individual jurisdictions. They may come to that realisation themselves eventually if they scrutinised the evidence correctly. The image of the woman's dead eyes reminded her that they could already be too late. Birgitte was certain someone else had already been abducted.

Her mouth went dry as her hands began to tremble slightly on the arm rests. It was happening again. She was thinking like a killer. She couldn't pinpoint how it happened, god knows she'd tried, but somewhere during her most intense investigations she realised she was a step ahead of her colleagues because she'd made the leap from reading the evidence for proof of past action to determining patterns of potential future behaviour in real time. It was what enabled her to catch up with, and at one point almost overtake, Max Anders in his quest to kill 13 children over that horrible summer. The investigative team of which she was a part was dealing with the same evidence – tiny, decomposing bundles of flesh scattered across the city, each child wrapped in the same sheets of canvas, tied with mariner's rope, and deposited under the floorboards of different houses. But at some point, she couldn't recall when, she was already convinced that the next victims would be siblings and that if they could only determine from which family, then they could stop the murderer in time.

No one had listened then either.

She looked at Tony and wondered what he must think of her. Was he humouring her until he could get her on a flight back to Copenhagen? She didn't think so. He appeared to trust her judgement and be equally contemptuous of the politics that slowed down effective police work. She considered him a solid officer – did the necessary legwork to help close as many cases as possible. His tenacity was tempered by a pragmatic acceptance of human behaviour, which included the day-to-day running of a police station even if it grated against his nerves at times. From what he'd told her these past few days he'd spent so much time on the streets that there was little that could surprise him, but it was mostly cases of domestic violence, drug-related homicides, armed robberies and organised crime. The only serial killers he'd experienced were in the pages of police journals and airport novels. She could tell he would rather be back at his desk in Sydney getting his head around the latest stage of his career but she knew he was also deeply disturbed by the fact there was probably a killer out there whose work was by no means complete. She watched him sleep. He was a good man. It made her feel better to know that there were still good men in the world and it gave her a sense of security to know he was sitting so close to her.

And now she was going back to Copenhagen, back to the media fallout from Anders' appeal. Sven had told her that his appeal was unsuccessful, which she already knew. Against her own better judgment she had followed the case in the Danish tabloids online. The commentary about her performance from certain journalists was no less biting than it had been in the past. What hurt her most was the amount of crucial information that was not released to the media, details that could have affected the public's perception of her. And of course the details that only she and Anders knew. It was a hideous bond that had formed between them, one that Anders had hoped would secure his release or perhaps he only hoped it would torture her a little longer – their shared secret. He thrived on cruelty and given his current incarceration, it was the best he could do. Birgitte refused to let him get the better of her. One thing the trip to Australia had afforded her was distance from her recovery, long enough to appreciate the police psychologist had done an admirable job of helping her compartmentalise the issues so she could address her guilt, anger and frustration in more digestible portions. She wondered what the doctor would say if he ever learned the full truth.

The evening traffic on the southern end of Pitt St was barely moving. The rain that had swept in over Sydney an hour before was now settling into steady drizzle. Jason Pender emerged from an unmarked doorway set into a narrow lane. He paused under an awning to adjust the belt on his suit trousers and check his business shirt was tucked in properly. Satisfied, he walked out of the lane and onto the street, discreetly looking to see if anyone might recognise him.

Normally a quick fuck of a pretty little Japanese girl at Tiger Lily would have set him right before going home to the kids, but his day had been particularly unbearable so it barely took the edge off. His boss, Reginald Barclay, the CEO of Barclay Industries, was refusing to budge on his request for more shares leading up to the Timor deal, which was frustrating enough, but now he had to go home and explain as much to Trudy. The thought quickly cancelled the momentary pleasure he'd enjoyed 20 minutes earlier. As his wife had so constantly reminded him, this was their one chance to set themselves up for good. All the work he'd put in to date was useless if he failed to renegotiate his contract to include a higher proportion of shares prior to the Northern Territory Government giving the green light.

He stepped between the bumpers and was about to head up to Goulburn Street when he spotted Sam Westlake sitting in the window of a Spanish tapas bar. Or had Westlake spotted him? He couldn't be sure. He suddenly panicked that Westlake may have seen him coming out of the back entrance to Tiger Lily, unsure of where the guy stood on such things. He smiled awkwardly and waved. There was no avoiding a conversation. Westlake nodded, watching him through open bi-fold windows with reserved expectation. As Pender stepped onto the pavement he quickly rationalised with himself that all Westlake could have seen from that distance was him walking out of a laneway. He could have been coming from anywhere west of Pitt St.

"Just been in a meeting down in Haymarket," he said, laughing as if it was some shared joke. Westlake grinned and motioned to the seat opposite. Pender entered the bar and sat down. There were several other patrons at the surrounding tables but it was noisy enough not to be overheard. The two men shook hands. Pender shifted in his seat and stared out at the traffic. He didn't know what it was about Westlake that made him uncomfortable but he could never really settle in his company. Perhaps it was the fact that he admired the guy too much – he exuded such a sense of control that he could intimidate anyone. Pender ran a hand through his thick damp hair, sweeping it back from his face. He was a good looking guy and he knew it but in Westlake's company he felt like he was back at school trying to impress the cool kids.

Westlake waited for him to relax. "Have you eaten?"

"Trudy has dinner waiting for me at home."

"Do you have time for a glass of wine?"

"Of course."

They exchanged pleasantries while the staff brought a bottle of Rioja to the table with a tray of olives. When they were alone Westlake leaned across the table.

"How's Reginald?"

"He's Reginald," Pender said curtly.

Westlake offered a good-natured smile. "He strikes me as someone who doesn't budge on a position unless it's to his benefit."

"That's about the crux of it."

Westlake leaned back, swirled the glass and held it to his nose before setting it back down on the table. "I have it on good authority that things are about to heat up."

"How do you mean?"

Westlake ignored the question. Pender could be so tedious at times. "I need to know where you stand."

Pender took a mouthful of his wine because his mouth had been dry since he'd sat down, then he remembered to smell the aroma and felt ridiculous for even trying.

Westlake said, "You do realise that by midday tomorrow, if our Reggie hasn't changed his position – and we both know that our Reggie isn't in the habit of changing positions – you'll be plum out of luck, while the rest of us will be deciding what's the best season for baccarat in Monaco."

"I spoke to him today."

"And?"

"And nothing," he said bitterly. He knew how this must look.

"Well," Westlake said, sipping his wine, "the offer isn't open-ended. But at least it's an offer, which is more than you're getting from Barclay."

"I don't know."

"Yes, you do. You can man the fuck up and take control of your future or you can let Reginald Barclay keep you in his pocket for the rest of your career."

"It's a hell of a risk."

"With a hell of a return – that's how risk works." Westlake resisted the urge to roll his eyes. It was like dealing with a 13-year-old, and he'd had no patience for teenagers even when he had been one himself. He chewed slowly on an olive, thinking back to his first conversation with Salina Heysmith three months previously. Dreadful night, all that hysterical weeping, her oscillating between feeble justifications for her actions and raw self-loathing, the sheer terror that comes when an addict finally realises the darkness that surrounds them is merely the hole they've dug for themselves.

And then – a light and a ladder.

It had actually saddened him to see what little resistance her conscience held to the idea he had presented that night. At the time she spoke of Pender with the derision she usually reserved for hotel porters, but the thought of her most immediate debts being cleared was too tempting. She agreed to getting close enough to Pender to find out what drove him. Westlake never explained to her that he intended to use this information against him, to gain access to the inner workings of Barclay Industries. Or better still, to bring Pender over to his own side.

Westlake wondered if Salina ever gave a thought to that night herself. Did she see Westlake as a saviour? Or did she ever pause long enough to notice whether the ladder he'd offered her was helping her out of her situation or leading her deeper down?

"I need an answer, Jason."

"What if I the answer is 'no'?" He looked at Westlake, almost expecting to be told that everything would be okay – at least their friendship wasn't at risk.

Westlake peered at him curiously then motioned to his own face with his fingers. "You have a little something on the corner of your mouth."

Pender brushed his lips and checked his hand. Nothing. He looked expectantly at Westlake.

"Still there."

Pender turned and checked in the reflection of the bi-folds but still couldn't see anything. He could see himself laughing in the glass as Westlake asked if he'd been eating Japanese. By the time he turned around his smile was gone and Westlake was on his way out the door. He'd left more than enough money to cover the bill. Pender slumped in his chair. What had been sold to him as a positive deal was now looking like a mill stone he would be tying to his own neck, but given his wife's demands and the closing window of opportunity it seemed to be the best alternative.

As Westlake climbed into the back of the waiting Limousine he was confident that Pender would come on board by morning.

CHAPTER NINE

The first ferries of the day pulled out from Circular Quay and made their way past the Sydney Opera House. Birgitte was standing in the window of her suite at the East Wind watching the morning sun gradually lift the colours of the harbour. It was hard to believe that little more than a week ago she hadn't even heard the name Hans Thostrup. Now she had travelled from Copenhagen to Sydney, then back and forth across Australia on what felt like a fool's errand to find him. She was partly grateful that she was heading home alone. The thought of having to spend another minute in Mrs Holl's company put her nerves on edge.

She sat back down at the desk and read over the report she had been writing for Sven. She'd been up since 5am working on it. It rankled her to think that this hastily crafted statement, which contained more questions than answers, would signal the end of her involvement in the case. It was not the way she liked to work. She pressed 'Send' and leaned back in her chair. It was Tuesday morning in Sydney so Sven probably wouldn't be in the office to read it until she was on her flight to Hong Kong, which was due out at 8pm that night.

She checked the clock on the bedside table: 9.32am. She looked at the state of her nails. Perhaps it was time to avail herself of the hotel's spa facilities; maybe even a one-hour massage was in order. She opened the directory from the bedside table and was about to dial for reception when there was a knock on the door. "Now what," she thought.

As she opened the door Tony stepped past her into the room followed by Constable Harris.

"Salina Heysmith, 32, from Sydney. Last seen in Darwin in late October," he said with conviction. "I've sent an image to Dr Barnett in Melbourne. We should have confirmation within the hour."

Harris was carrying a folder. She shook Birgitte's hand and produced a photo of an attractive but cold-looking brunette in her mid 30s. Birgitte quickly went to her luggage and dug out copies of the photos from the pathology unit for comparison.

It was hard to tell given the woman's horrific injuries but the bone structure certainly looked similar.

Harris opened the folder and began gleaning pertinent facts from the missing persons report. "Ms Heysmith is a senior lawyer with Blake, Patterson & Walker, a law firm on Bridge St."

Tony peered down on the traffic below the window. "You can almost see the office from here."

"She was up in Darwin for a three-day conference. It finished on a Thursday and she was due to go on holiday to Bali direct, so no one reported her missing until late the following week."

"Who reported it?" asked Birgitte.

"A Ms Handley-Smythe, the missing woman's sister. The whole thing was slowed down because they thought she was on a beach somewhere sipping cocktails, but the airline confirmed she never boarded her flight."

Birgitte turned to Tony. "Could you get a body from Darwin to Mildura in the time-frame we're dealing with?"

"It would take some long-haul shifts, but it's doable, just," he said. "It's also a question of whether he could physically commit both murders. Thostrup went missing from Adelaide on about October 28 and Heymsith was found on November 15. So the killer would have had to feed Thostrup to a shark, possibly off Adelaide, driven up to Forbes Creek via Alice, dumped the body then driven up to Darwin, abduct Heymsith, feed her to a croc somewhere nearby then get halfway back across the country to dump her body in Mildura. All within a space of three weeks."

"He might have an accomplice," suggested Harris. "If only to help him with the driving."

Birgitte shook her head slowly, deep in thought. "He could be anywhere in the country now with another victim. You need to talk to Heysmith's family, friends, her colleagues as soon as possible. The killer chose her for a reason."

"We can't interview anyone until we can confirm it's her."

"You can ask about the fact that she's missing. They don't need to know she's been found."

Tony and Harris both looked at her expectantly.

"No, Tony. I'm flying out tonight. I can't be involved any further. Sven will crucify me."

"We can interview at least two or three people who may know something. You can help me write a summary based on the most up-to-date information for the investigating teams in Alice and Mildura – a parting shot. I'll drive you to the airport by 6pm. What do you reckon?"

She paced about the room, torn between her need to the right thing by her superiors and her need to do the right thing by her own moral code.

She grabbed her jacket and handbag. "Let's talk to her employer first."

Within the hour Birgitte and Tony were in the reception area of Blake, Patterson & Walker, a corporate law firm that overlooked the harbour from the 33rd floor of one of the newest skyscrapers in the city. They had been waiting anxiously for 20 minutes when a well-dressed woman with an officious air approached them.

"Mr Patterson will see you now."

They followed her down a narrow, glassed corridor to a spacious office that had a clear view across Sydney Harbour to the North Shore. Gregory Patterson stood up from behind his desk and came around to greet them. He was in his late 50s, fit and full of energy. Birgitte figured he would have been quite the athlete back in his day. He wore an expensive, tailored suit, but the jacket was off and his sleeves were rolled up. He gave the immediate impression of a man who is comfortable taking charge and getting things done.

"Detectives Vestergaard and Kingsmill, is it? Sorry about the wait." His eyes were clear and engaging – a look he probably reserved for his top clients.

He shook their hands then directed them to a setting of black leather Barcelona chairs by the window.

As they sat down he called out the door to his Executive Assistant. "Catherine? Can we have some ice water in here, please? Would either of you like tea or coffee?"

"Water is fine, thanks," said Birgitte. She peered around his office. "What sort of clients does Blake, Patterson & Walker represent?"

"Blue-chip mostly," he said. "Multinationals and Australian corporations, across a range of industries."

He was comfortable being direct and professional with them both, but Birgitte noticed that he seemed to take her in more intently than Tony. Not in a seductive way, but in attempt to get her measure, as a woman. He was obviously used to young female lawyers being smitten in his company. She held his gaze but gave nothing in return.

"To be entirely honest," he said, "I wasn't aware that Salina was missing until the other day. We're all very concerned for her safety."

Tony nodded then leaned forward, resting his elbows on his knees. "According to the Missing Person's Report, Ms Heysmith was last seen on November 6 in Darwin at a conference. Were you there that day?"

"I was in Darwin, but not for the conference. We have an office up there and I was dropping into to oversee some operational matters. I did catch up with the staff, who were attending the conference. On the Thursday night from memory. We had dinner at a restaurant in town. Pablo's, a seafood place, I can get Catherine to check the details if that helps."

"How did Ms Heysmith seem?" Tony asked

"Her usual focused self. She has a brilliant legal mind – one of our best. Thorough, tenacious. Likes to win." He grinned warmly at Birgitte as if he wanted her to understand that he admires intelligent, ambitious women.

"Do you have any ideas where she might be?" Birgitte asked.

"I really don't know. She'd booked a week's holiday to Bali, was supposed to fly out that night, after dinner. But they say she never made the flight."

"Do you know why she had planned a holiday at this particular point in the year?"

"It was long overdue apparently. She's the type that needs to be told when to take leave. I have to admit I didn't think the timing was brilliant, but my partners reassured me that we knew where to reach her if we needed her."

"And you didn't need to?"

"No."

His EA returned with a tray of glasses and jug of water which she set out on the glass table between them. Patterson proceeded to pour the water. "I feel a little foolish now not knowing she didn't even get to Bali, but we were busy here so I just assumed she was lying on a beach enjoying herself."

Birgitte waited for the EA to leave and close the office door behind her, before asking, "What was the conference about?"

"Off-shore mining rights. We've been helping a client who's in the process of lobbying the government for approval of a new gas site in the Timor Sea."

"And what was Ms Heysmith's involvement?"

"She's our lead solicitor for the client. In fact we're expecting to hear later today if the Northern Territory Government will give the green light or not. I'm really hoping Salina is okay so she can hear the news as well. She's put a lot of work into it."

Birgitte looked across at Tony who was writing notes in his pad. Mr Mendelson had mentioned something about a mining deal in the Timor Sea. She asked, "What is the name of the client she is representing?"

"Katercorp."

Tony stopped writing. They were both processing the information, trying to remember exactly what they had been told in the Adelaide Hills. Tony looked at Patterson and said, "The CEO is Nils Brekman, yes?"

"That's correct," he said, looking a little concerned that they already had information on his client. "But I believe Salina does most of her work with their legal team."

"How long has Katercorp been a client?"

"I'd have to check my records, but it's been at least five years."

"And Salina? How long has she been representing them on your behalf?"

"She started about 18 months ago, and we hired her specifically to look after Katercorp."

"Why was that?" asked Birgitte.

"She has an exceptional record in the energy sector. It was quite a boon when we got her on board."

"And Katercorp have been satisfied with her performance to date?"

"As far as I'm aware. Very satisfied." He no longer looked as intently at Birgitte – he was beginning to realise there was more to their interview than he first thought.

"What was she like to work with?" asked Tony.

"Very professional."

"And as a person?" asked Birgitte.

Patterson considered the question carefully then responded in a very measured way. "I think Salina is great. She has a beautiful, sharp mind and loves what she does. But she can be a little difficult to be around. In her defence," he added quickly, "a lot of the more focused lawyers can be difficult. Basically, Salina doesn't suffer fools, as they say, and she has a tendency to assume everyone she encounters is a fool until they prove otherwise. Makes her a little difficult to be around, socially."

Birgitte looked at him carefully, knowing he had more to say.

He stared down into his glass of water. "I hope I'm not talking out of turn here."

"It will be treated as confidential, Mr Patterson," Tony said. "We're just trying to get a sense of who she is, to help us rule out certain possibilities and focus on others."

He looked up at him. "Well, I've found her to be very dark at times. Moody. More so than most. I never asked if she is medicated, but I wouldn't be surprised if she has been diagnosed bipolar."

"What makes you say that?"

"I've met a few, and the ones whose meds aren't quite right can be a challenge to be around. I don't have an issue with mental illness but, in my experience, the mood swings can exacerbate the uglier aspects of a person's personality. So when she is busy, she gets a little manic and more than a little insufferable."

"How so?"

"High minded. Thinks she has all the answers. There is only one way of seeing things and it's hers. She's clashed with the partners several times. Fortunately for her, however, and much to my colleagues' annoyance, she's usually right, and people do come round to her way of seeing things, but when she's manic she lacks the social finesse to bring people on board in a more reasonable way."

Birgitte wondered if Patterson would have spoken differently if his top lawyer was a man. Would a similar 'high mindedness' be taken as sign of confidence, to be laughed at over drinks at the end of the working week? She recalled one of her old uni friends back in Copenhagen, Ana. She'd been diagnosed as bipolar the month she accepted a job with a top corporate firm. She had chosen to keep the news a secret from her employer for fear the stigma of mental illness would put her at a further disadvantage in an already challenging industry. Birgitte didn't like Patterson's casual sexism or his attitude to mental health, but she didn't get the impression he was lying or trying to obfuscate with his answers.

"Did she seem unduly stressed when you last saw her, on the Thursday night?" she asked. "Manic, as you suggest?"

"We work 80 hours a week for clients with annual returns bigger than most African states. We're all dealing with a certain level of stress. But no, she was no more high-minded than usual. If anything, she seemed a little on the uncertain side. Less confident in herself – not in her job, if you know what I mean, as if something outside of work might have been bothering her. I never got a chance to ask."

"What about relationships," Tony asked. "Do you know if she was seeing anyone?"

He shook his head then looked out the window, avoiding their eyes.

"According to her sister," Birgitte said. "She had been seeing someone – a man who was married. Any ideas who that might be?"

"I tend not to pry into my staff's personal affairs."

Tony leaned forward. "Could it have been someone from this office?"

His face had darkened slightly, his eyes flicked across the harbour as his mind rapidly tried to calculate how much he should be saying.

Birgitte and Tony watched him intently. Tony looked at his watch quickly and said, "Mr Patterson, I don't mean to be rude, but we are on a very tight schedule here and this is only the first of several interviews we need to conduct today."

He looked at him and nodded. There was no avoiding the subject. "There was some drunken talk at the dinner that night, that she had been getting very close to a lawyer for one of the other firms. I didn't think too much of it because I believe she's professional enough to know better. To be honest, I laughed it off at the time."

"Do you have a name?" asked Tony.

"Jason Pender, Lead Counsel for Barclay Industries, another mining company. If it turns out there is substance to the rumour, I'll definitely have to have a word to her."

They could see his mind processing the ramifications as he spoke. "The thing is, if this deal in the Timor Sea goes ahead it will be Katercorp and Barclay Industries competing for the rights – there are others, smaller fish, but they can't really cut it at this level. It'll be worth billions over the next decade or two."

"So the lawyer representing one firm, who has gone missing, may be having an affair with the Lead Counsel of the other firm," said Tony. "You're right to be concerned, Mr Patterson. That could have some serious consequences."

The confident veneer had begun to crumble. Patterson was clearly trying to comprehend the gravity of a situation he should have been across much earlier.

Birgitte changed tack. "Did you know a Hans Thostrup, a Danish gentlemen who used to work for Central Gas Co in the mid 70s?"

"Was he the guy they found outside of Alice Springs?"

"Yes."

"I read about that in the paper yesterday. I didn't know him."

"Nils Brekman did," said Tony, keen to keep him on the back foot. "They were old friends."

"Jesus, do you think something has happened to Salina?"

"We're following all leads at this stage," he said.

"I assure you, despite the sums involved, these companies wouldn't behave like union thugs on a construction site – they're some of the biggest mining companies in the Southern Hemisphere."

"Have you spoken to Mr Brekman recently?" asked Tony.

"We talk occasionally. I believe he's in the United States for the rest of the week. If you need to speak to him I can get Catherine to give you his office number on the way out. If you can't reach him, there is always his 2IC, a guy called Sam Westlake. I'll get you his details as well. There really isn't much more I can tell you."

They stood up and thanked him for his time. Birgitte noticed the virility of the man had faded over the second half of the interview. Obviously the tolerance and empathy he showed his star lawyers was perquisite on their ability to secure lucrative clients. She wondered if he really cared for Heysmith's welfare now that she was a potential liability to the Timor Sea deal.

By midday they were driving east of the city to the affluent suburb of Point Piper. Birgitte was keen to meet with Jason Pender, the man with whom Salina Heysmith was supposedly having an affair. When they had called his office at Barclay Industries, his EA told them Mr Pender was working from home that day and would organise an interview for 12.15pm. Along the way they discussed the interview with Patterson, both excited they had discovered a link between their two victims. The sums involved, if the Northern Territory

Government were to approve the deal, would certainly amount to a motive, but for who?

They pulled into a gated driveway. Tony announced their arrival into an intercom system. The wide slatted gate opened slowly. They drove down a steep path of imported stone to a three-car garage. The house was boxy, modernist, finished in several shades of grey, with spiky yukkas and cycads jutting out against the flat exterior. Tony thought it looked cold and soulless.

A surprisingly young man in jeans and a polo shirt with an upturned collar greeted them at the front door. If it wasn't for the slight grey at his temples, Jason Pender looked like he'd barely finished university. Tony thought Pender had the entitled air of private school kid who came from money. He greeted the two detectives with feigned warmth at the front door, stepping out onto the stoop, pulling the door closed carefully behind him. He led them around the front of the house to a small succulent garden that rose up from a bed of white pebbles. He obviously wanted the conversation to be out of earshot of his family. "Yes, we were involved. But it wasn't for very long," he explained.

"'Were?" asked Birgitte.

"Well, I was in the process of winding it up." He nodded towards the house. "It was getting complicated."

"How long is 'not very long'?" asked Tony.

"Three, fourth months." He realised how all of this must have sounded. "Listen, I'm as worried as everyone else about her welfare, but I can't have my family know about our... little fling."

Birgitte gave him a knowing look. "We understand, Mr Pender."

Her manner put him at ease. Since they'd arrived he was sure it had something to do with his meetings with Westlake. Now it seemed it was only about Salina, which restored his confidence. He looked at Birgitte steadily, trying to assess if they were of a similar kind. She smiled at him. "When was the last time you saw her?"

"It was on the Thursday night at the conference."

"How would you describe her? Generally?"

"Salina is... complex. She has a really sharp mind. She's very attractive," he chuckled boyishly at Birgitte, "obviously. But she can be a little difficult to deal with – what comes across as arrogance is more insecurity in her own talents, but she is a very good lawyer."

"What does she get up to in her down time?"

"What down time?" he laughed, genuinely relieved that the interview had nothing to do with the Timor Sea deal.

"How does she like to unwind?"

Pender peered back through the window that fronted onto a living area. "She likes anything that gets her adrenaline going."

"Skydiving? Race cars?" Birgitte prompted. "S & M?"

His pupils dilated momentarily. He liked the detective's interview technique. He figured she'd be super-fit under her blouse and trousers. He wondered what the best approach would be to getting her confidence. "Listen, I don't even know if I should be saying this..." he said, coughing into his hand as his eyes flitted about.

"Try us," said Tony, bluntly.

"She has a thing for blackjack," he said.

Tony looked at Birgitte and they both considered Frankston's gambling angle on Thostrup.

"Poker machines or casinos?"

"Either. Both. I've been to Star City with her on occasion."

Tony interrupted to explain Star City was Sydney's big casino down on the harbour.

Pender continued, "But I got the sense she preferred to play alone. And I've seen her on the pokies a few times. She really seemed to know what she was doing."

"What sort of money are we talking?" Tony asked.

"She never said, but I'd hazard a guess and say it could be in the tens of thousands."

"Annually?"

He nodded gravely. "Could be more. It not about the cost with her." He looked at Birgitte. "It's the rush – even when she's losing. If anything, it's exacerbated when she's losing because the stakes are even higher. I don't get it, to be honest."

"Did you ever lend her money?"

"Hell, no."

"Did she ever ask?"

"In a round-about way. She pressed me to leave my wife so we could buy a property together. I was pretty shocked given we'd only been fooling around together for a little while. I thought she knew that it was just a fling. But when she suggested we start looking at houses I realised it wasn't working out. In hindsight it makes me think she wanted some security she could secretly borrow against."

"Where does she get her money?"

"She earns a six-figure salary. What bank wouldn't give her a line of credit?"

"Do you know if she dealt with loan sharks? Organised crime?"

"I wouldn't think so. She wouldn't be that stupid."

"By stupid you might mean desperate?"

"Do you think that's why she's gone missing?"

It was the first time he'd looked concerned for her safety.

"That's what we're trying to find out."

"I figured she was just trying to get away from it all for a few days and people were overreacting."

The front door opened. An attractive woman in her 40s appeared. "Darling, everything okay out here. Do your guests want something to drink?" Her tone implied she was used to him having secretive meetings under her nose.

Pender turned and managed a sincere smile. "No thanks, Sweetheart."

She disappeared back inside the house.

"Why are you working from home today, Mr Pender?" Tony asked.

"Sometimes I can get more done."

"You're expecting to hear from the Northern Territory Government, about the Timor Sea mining deal, is that right?"

Pender could feel the blood pumping through his heart and hoped it didn't show on his face. "We are in fact. A lot of work has gone into it."

"I can imagine. If it goes ahead there is a lot of money to be made."

"We're not there yet by any means," he said. "Government approval is just the first hurdle."

Tony cleared his throat. "I have to say, Mr Pender. The fact that the lawyer for one mining firm is sleeping with the Lead Counsel for the competition, over a deal worth billions, is going to raise a few eyebrows with your superiors, if not your spouse."

Pender gave a nervous laugh. "It happens plenty in our industry. The long hours. The trips away. There isn't really anything I can tell you. Like I said, it was pretty much over."

"Did she know that?" he asked.

"I'd suggested as much. That was why she was flying to Bali – to think things over."

"Not that she had any say in the matter."

"Listen, she was at the conference then she went missing. I didn't see anyone with her or see anything that raised my suspicions at all. If she didn't go to Bali, I just figured she had changed her mind at the last minute. Did you check to see if she flew anywhere else? Macau perhaps? Or Vegas?"

Birgitte hoped that they weren't giving anything away by not being surprised. "We're already looking into it."

Tony asked, "Can we reach you if we have any further questions?"

The two men exchanged cards. He walked them back to their car. As Birgitte opened the door she turned and asked, "Do you know a Hans Thostrup?"

"Should I?"

"He went missing in Adelaide a few weeks ago."

He shook his head.

"He was an old friend of Nils Brekman apparently."

The lawyer didn't say anything.

"They found his body in the desert outside of Alice Springs. He'd had his legs ripped off at the thigh – he'd been fed to a great white shark apparently, while he was still alive. If you think of anything that may be related to Ms Heysmith's disappearance be sure to contact Detective Kingsmill immediately."

He looked genuinely horrified by what Birgitte had just said. He nodded dumbly and walked back into his house.

As they got in to the car, Tony muttered, "Classy guy. Do you think he knows anything he's not telling us?"

"Hard to say. To be honest, I don't think he cared too much if she was missing or not so long as she wasn't in his way anymore."

"Nice bombshell, by the way."

"Not sure if it hit the target."

"So where to next?"

Birgitte checked her watch. They had little more than five hours left. "Let's see if we can get a hold of Mr Brekman. Here's hoping he has more to tell us than when you spoke to him when we were in Adelaide."

The offices of Katercorp filled the top six floors of a glass skyscraper on the west side of the city. The waiting area to Nils Brekman's office provided views over the Parramatta River and the suburbs that sprawled out towards the Blue Mountains.

Tony was checking his watch with irritation. It was almost 2pm. They'd been waiting for 15 minutes. If they didn't get some clear answers on Heysmith's connection to Thostrup by 5pm it would all be over. Birgitte was staring down at the Cockatoo Island, deep in thought, when the attractive EA who had told them earlier to "wait just a moment" finally returned.

"Mr Westlake will see you now."

She opened the double doors behind them to a vast office. At the far end, behind a broad desk sat a slick looking man with soft features and sharp eyes. He was wearing a white business shirt with brilliant red braces, which would have looked pretentious on most men, but he had the confidence to pull it off. His complexion was tanned in a healthy way, possibly from running marathons or ocean swimming. Tony thought he looked the type.

Westlake ushered them in while still talking on his mobile. "Yes, yes. They've just walked in. No, like I said, there is nothing to worry about. I'll call you later."

He hung up the phone and stood up to walk around the desk and greet the two detectives.

"Welcome to Katercorp."

They shook hands and Westlake directed them to the two armchairs perched at angles across from his desk. He returned to his seat and said, "I'm afraid Nils is in Texas this week. I'm looking after things in his absence."

Birgitte was disappointed the CEO wasn't there to take questions. Something about Westlake bothered her, but she didn't know what. There was something reptilian about him. The eyes set too far apart, perhaps, or the thinness of his lips. She decided it was his overall demeanour.

"So you've heard about Salina Heysmith?" asked Tony, "The lawyer for Blake Patterson & Walker who has been missing since last week?"

He offered a look of concern. "Have there been any developments?"

"We were hoping Mr Brekman, or yourself, could help us with our enquiries."

"Of course. What would you like to know?"

"Do you know Ms Heysmith well?"

"Only professionally speaking. She's been helping out for a few months. Very capable solicitor."

"You didn't deal with her socially?"

"We've had a few drinks after work on occasion. Nothing too intimate, colleagues at the pub kind of thing."

"How would you describe her?"

"Sharp. Quick-witted. Congenial, in a professional way, as if she doesn't ever really switch off from being the high-flying solicitor type. But I like her."

"Any reason to think she might be in trouble?"

He leaned back in his chair and gave it some thought. "I really don't know her well enough to say. Despite her outward charm, I've always felt there's a darkness behind the eyes, you know. Probably prone to a little too much thinking at times." He gave a dismissive laugh. "But like I said, I barely know her."

"What about Mr Brekman?"

"He deals with her even less than I do; mostly she works with our legal team."

"Is there any chance we could speak with him today?" Birgitte asked.

Westlake checked his watch, considered the time difference then picked up the handset to his landline phone. He dialled a few numbers then settled back.

A thin voice came over the speaker. "Sam? How's things? Any news?"

"Not yet, Nils. Soon," he said smiling politely at Birgitte. "Listen, I'm just in the Sydney office with two police officers, we're on speaker phone. You're with Detective Kingsmill, who is with the Federal Police, and Detective Vestergaard who is here all the way from Denmark."

"Detective Kingsmill," he said. "I spoke to you the other day."

"That's correct."

"Any news on Hans?"

"He has been found," said Tony, looking at Birgitte, trying to remember how much was common knowledge and what needed to be kept secret. "I'm sorry to say, he was murdered. I can't say too much as it's an active investigation, but his body was found outside of Alice Springs."

"Jesus. Do you have any ideas what happened?"

"We're working on it around the clock."

They waited as Brekman processed the news. "There isn't any more I can really tell you. Like I said I hadn't seen him for a couple of years."

Birgitte was annoyed that they weren't able to interview Mr Brekman privately, but she didn't want to make a fuss given that they shouldn't have been there in the first place and they were running out of time. "Good afternoon, Mr Brekman. It's

Detective Vestergaard speaking. We'd like to ask you a couple of questions about Salina Heysmith."

"The lawyer for Blake, Patterson & Walker?"

Westlake chimed in, "The one in the same."

"Of course," said Brekman. "She's been helping us on a potential mining deal in the Timor Sea. What would you like to know, Detective?"

"Were you aware that she's been missing since last Thursday?"

"I had no idea."

"She was last seen at a conference in Darwin where she was representing your firm in regards to the Timor deal of which you just spoke."

"That's really worrying. Do you have any ideas where she might be?"

"She was supposed to be in Bali on a holiday but she never made the flight."

"I've been in the States since last Tuesday so I'm not entirely across the day-to-day operations. Has Sam been able to clarify her movements up til Thursday? Have you spoken to her boss?"

"He has and we have, thank you," she said.

Tony asked, "Were you aware she had a thing for blackjack?"

"No, I wasn't. Can't say I see the appeal myself," he said drily. "Was it a problem?"

"We're not sure at this stage."

Westlake looked up over their heads. His EA had appeared in the doorway.

"Excuse me, Mr Westlake." Birgitte and Tony turned in their seats. She looked smug and a little excited. "You might want to turn on the ABC News."

Before Birgitte or Tony could say anything, he grabbed a remote and turned on a TV that was set against the wall by the door. The national 24-hour news channel came on.

"Can you hear that okay, Nils?"

"Sure can, Sam."

An elderly reporter in a suit and tie was standing outside a government building. He looked like he was struggling with the humidity as he spoke to camera.

"In a surprise turn around, the Northern Territory Government have announced they will be accepting applications for exploration licences in the coastal waters off Arnhem Land. The decision to allow mining operations in this part of the Timor Sea is certain to be a contentious issue in the months ahead. Business analysts are forecasting figures in the billions over the next 10 years for whichever mining firm secures the right to drill for gas."

The shot cut to a press conference where Northern Territory Minister for Trade Frank Howard, standing in front of a blue curtain flanked by an NT flag and an Australian flag, said, "It's a windfall for the people of Arnhem Land, a windfall for the Northern Territory, and a windfall for the country." The report crossed to scenes of mangroves as the reporter outlined the impact the decision may have on opposition groups. Westlake turned down the sound. His face was glowing. He started to clap slowly as if his rugby team had just walked in a try against an incompetent opposition.

Nils screamed down the phone, "Finally, some good news!"

The EA was jiggling in her heels, resisting the urge to run around the desk to hug her boss. Westlake grinned at her. "Sweetheart, break out the Moet, we're celebrating. And call and confirm the private dining room at Atlas. Tell Marty to get the key to his cellar ready."

"Yes, Mr Westlake. And congratulations. I know how much work you've put into this."

"You don't know the half of it. But you've been a huge help."

As she disappeared from the office Brekman's voice erupted through the speaker. "I can't believe it. That difficult bastard Howard came through. Don't know what you said to him, Sam, but thank you."

"It wasn't me, Nils," he said, smiling at Birgitte and Tony. "It just makes good sense for the region. I think he finally worked that out for himself."

"Christ, that's good news. I'll need to wrap things up here and get back home asap."

"Before you go, Mr Brekman," Tony cut in. "We haven't quite finished here yet."

Hearty laughter came down the line from Texas. "I'm sorry. You have to understand how much work we've put into lobbying the Government. It's incredible news. Where were we?"

"The disappearance of Salina Heysmith."

"Awful business." The line went silent for a while as Brekman composed himself. "There really isn't anything more I can tell you."

"So she has never spoken to you about concerns she may have had with the deal," Birgitte asked, "or if anyone was pressuring her in anyway?"

"Not at all. Sam? Has she said anything to you?"

"No, Nils. Can't say she has." He looked at Birgitte. "I don't want to be rude but, given the announcement, we are suddenly under the pump to get a lot of work done in a very short space of time. As Nils has said, there isn't anything more we can tell you at this stage. Of course, if we hear from Salina, we'll contact you immediately."

Before they could protest, he said, "Nils, the schedule is in place so things will be well underway by the time you get back."

"Thanks, Sam," he said. "Detectives, do you mind if we cut it short? I'm sorry if this appears callous. I am as concerned about Salina as you are."

Tony said, "That's okay. Thanks for your time."

The line went dead.

"I hope we were able to help in some way," Westlake said standing up and motioning to the door.

Birgitte wanted to ask the 2IC more questions but Tony gave her a look that said, "now isn't the time". They both stood up and shook Westlake's hand.

"Thanks for your time," said Tony. "We'll be in touch if we hear anything. And don't hesitate to call if something comes to mind."

Birgitte turned at the door. "So what happens now, with your Timor deal?"

"We'll it's not in the bag by any stretch of the imagination. Now we have to write up a tender so we can go in the running with our competitors, try to convince the Government why we'd be the best company to run the show."

"Who is your biggest competitor?"

"That would be Barclay Industries." He guided them out into the reception area, not in the least interested in the conversation.

"Barclay Industries?" said Birgitte. "Jason Pender is the Lead Counsel for Barclay Industries, isn't he?"

"I believe he is."

"Were you aware he has been having an affair with Salina Heysmith?"

Westlake paused for a moment, smiled then pressed his hands together, doing his best to appear unflappable. "What they do in their own time is their own business."

Tony asked, "It doesn't bother you that they're both privy to information that could dramatically affect the outcome of this deal in terms of competition in the tendering process?"

He resisted the temptation to roll his eyes. Frankly, he was surprised and a little disappointed that Salina had developed real feelings for Pender. It had added a layer of complexity to an already intricate plan. When he heard that Pender had broken it off he felt genuinely relieved. Their relationship was of no further use to him. He offered the officers his most reassuring expression. "I'll be sure to raise the issue with our lawyers when next we meet. Now, I'm sorry, but I seriously have to get on."

He pressed the button to the elevator. "If I hear anything from Ms Heysmith, I will contact you immediately."

Birgitte and Tony stepped into the elevator slightly bewildered. When the doors closed Birgitte asked, "What just happened?"

"We just got railroaded out of our own interview." He pressed the button for the lobby. "Do you believe Westlake?"

"About which part?"

"The affair."

"Hard to say. He didn't seem too concerned."

"He didn't even seem too worried that she had gone missing either."

The doors opened. They walked through the lobby and out into the street.

"I'm struggling to comprehend," said Birgitte, "how they could be more concerned with the Government approval than the death of an old friend or the fact that a colleague is missing."

"We are talking billions of dollars over the next few decades. That's a lot of money in each of their pockets."

"Only if they get the tender."

Tony considered this then looked at his watch.

"How are we going for time?" she asked, even though she already knew the answer.

Tony was pacing around Birgitte's hotel suite as she sat at the desk cross-referencing notes she'd made on her laptop with scattered piles of paperwork. For the past two hours they had sifted through all the evidence they had gathered since the morning.

"Well, it has to be something do with that Timor Sea deal," said Birgitte emphatically.

Tony stopped pacing. "I agree with you, but I think Patterson was right – two of the biggest mining companies in the country are hardly likely to risk potential revenue in the billions behaving like union thugs on a construction site. So far both victims have links to Katercorp, not Barclay Industries."

"But if the killer knew about Heysmith and Pender then it could serve to scare off both." She knew she was clutching at straws as soon as she said it. "It might be worth contacting the CEO of Barclay Industries. See if he's missing any staff."

Tony thought it was a long shot but waited as Birgitte brought up Barclay Industries' web page on her laptop. "Reginald Barclay is the CEO."

"What time is it?"

"It's just after five." She gave him a concerned look as if to say, "We've run out of time."

He shrugged. "Let's give it a shot; we might be lucky."

As Tony dialled the number from the Contact page she stood up and went to the bed to put the last of her clothes in her bag, then she collected her toiletries from the bathroom.

Tony was patched through to the CEO's EA who tried to tell him that Barclay was unavailable. Tony decided to drop the missing-person angle and told her it was in regards to a murder investigation. She put him through immediately. When Barclay picked up it sounded like he was in a pub at closing hour. Tony put the phone on speaker.

"Barclay speaking."

"It's Detective Tony Kingsmill of the Australian Federal Police, Mr Barclay. I was hoping to have a quick chat about the murder of Hans Thostrup."

"I can't say I've heard of him."

"He's an old friend of Nils Brekman, CEO of Katercorp."

"I know Nils. Probably best if you speak to him."

"Did you know Salina Heysmith?"

"Name rings a bell."

"She's the solicitor for Katercorp on the Timor Sea deal the Northern Territory Government have just approved."

"It's great news, isn't it? What about her?"

"She's been missing for over a week, since the conference in Darwin in fact. Do you know the one I mean?"

"I do. Are you suggesting I might have had something to do with either of them?"

"Not at all, Mr Barclay, but I'm sure you can appreciate we are trying to find out what happened."

"I really don't know anything, but I'd be more than happy to meet with you for a face to face in the next day or two if that helps."

"It might, but in the mean time, are all your staff accounted for? Anyone associated with your end of the lobby group not turned up to work in the past few days?"

"In fact, I'm with them all now. We're kind of celebrating if you can't tell."

"So no one is missing?"

"We're all here."

"I hate to ask this, Mr Barclay, because I don't want to cause alarm, but what about your family or friends."

"I assure you Detective Kingsmill, I'd be the first to call the police if anything happened to my family."

"Would you mind giving each of your immediate family a call just to be on the safe side, then give me a call back on this number?"

There was a pause as he weighed up the inconvenience to his schedule. "If you insist."

"I insist. And thank you."

He hung up. "It's a long shot but we'll see if he comes back with anything. You all packed?"

She was looking through her handbag, checking she had her phone, passport, ticket. "Pretty much." She looked anxiously at him, almost guilty. "Is there anything more I can do to help?"

"Not really. I'll write up a report tonight, shoot it through to Miller and she can forward it on to Frankston and Braithwaite if she thinks it stacks up."

"I'm sorry it couldn't have worked out differently. I really don't feel good leaving the case as it stands."

Tony laughed, shaking his head. "What case? We did our best with the resources we had."

"Did we? What if someone has already been abducted? I can't help feeling that we were on the cusp of sorting this out."

"What are you going to do, Birgitte? Your job is waiting for you back in Copenhagen and I'm due back at Goulburn Street." He made a point of picking up her luggage to wrap up the conversation. There was no point discussing it any further.

They drove out to the airport in silence. Occasionally, Birgitte looked across at Tony as he negotiated the afternoon traffic. She didn't know what now bothered her more – leaving the case unfinished or leaving Tony before she could really get to know him. None of it seemed fair, but there was nothing she could do about it.

After an uncomfortably slow drive where the traffic had slowed to a crawl, he eventually pulled into the short-term parking lot and killed the engine. They got out of the car and he helped her with her luggage. When he walked her to the glass doors of the entrance, she put her bags down and turned to him.

"I want to thank you for everything you've done. It would have been a horrible trip without your assistance."

He stopped abruptly, suddenly feeling quite awkward. "My first gig as a Federal Officer has been intriguing to say the least."

"You have my email, so please, keep me informed of any developments."

"You really are a glutton for punishment."

"I just want to see that this killer is stopped before any more people are hurt."

He stopped smiling and thought that under other circumstances he would handle their farewell differently.

They shook hands and for a moment they looked into one another's eyes. Birgitte withdrew her hand before the urge to kiss him on the cheek got the better of her. She picked up her luggage. "Take care, Detective Kingsmill."

"You too."

Tony's phone rang. He held up his hand for her to wait.

She watched him as he listened intently to what he was being told. His face became more grave than she'd ever seen it, then he wrapped up the conversation.

"That was Barclay," he said. "His family are all accounted for but a mate of his son's hasn't been seen since the weekend. A guy called James Freedmont. He was at Melbourne University on Saturday then no one heard from him."

"If he was abducted on Saturday, how far could the killer get since then?"

"In three and half days? Anywhere across the country," he said, then he remembered where they were. "You have to catch your flight."

She picked up her luggage but continued to work on possible solutions. "He'd be heading out of state and looking

182

to kill him somewhere remote then dump the body somewhere else within a matter of days."

"So that's New South Wales or South Australia."

"I'd take a guess that he's more likely to move away from where he's been or crossed through."

"WA or Queensland?"

"It would help if we had a make of car or even some description. It has to be a large SUV or a van. Something that can hold a fridge."

"Do you think he could still be alive?"

"Three and half days. We could be lucky."

They both knew that Thostrup and Heysmith were probably killed within 48 hours of being abducted.

"I'm sorry, Tony. I wish I could be more helpful." They heard her flight being called. "If I think of anything I'll email you from Hong Kong. You should have it by the morning."

"Thanks," he said. "And I'm sorry."

"What for?"

He didn't know how to say it. He just shrugged. Birgitte reached forward and kissed his cheek, then held him in her arms for a moment. "Go," she said.

He turned and ran back out of the terminal.

Birgitte picked up her luggage and headed for the check in.

On the way back to the city Tony spoke to a senior detective from Missing Persons, explaining the background of the case. The detective promised to text him Freedmont's parent's details. Tony then called Miller and explained the developments. She tried to berate him for going against her orders but he kept reiterating that a young man was missing and in immediate danger.

As he pulled in to the car park of the Goulburn Street office he got a call from Dr Barnett.

"The tape residue I found on Salina Heysmith's wrists?"

"Yeah?"

"It matches residue found on Thostrup. You have your connection."

"Can you email me the details so I can forward it on to the two investigative teams?"

"Within the hour."

Birgitte was right. He couldn't believe it. She'd been a step ahead of everyone. And now she was on a flight back to Copenhagen when they needed her most.

The flames curled and flickered lazily. A log which had been burning slowly, eventually collapsed, sending a spiral of sparks upwards through the smoke. He watched them rise until his eyes were drawn by the depth of the night sky. It was nights like these that he missed the Madikwe, the National Park north-west of Rustenburg. For all its wildlife, Australia had nothing on southern Africa. So many nights of his youth camping out, like this, under the stars, but there the darkness beyond the campfire would be bristling with the sound of wild dogs, lions, elephants, and depending exactly where he was, any number of animals trying to survive the night. These were the basic laws his father had shown him to be true: strength outweighed weakness, cunning outweighed complacence, patience outweighed desperation. There was a hierarchy in the animal kingdom of which he was very much a part. His father illustrated the point whenever he got the chance. It was only a matter of time before Zachary would be expected to prove that he had been paying attention.

One afternoon they had driven into a remote village. His father never mentioned why they were there but Zachary, by the age of 15, had come to recognise the look in his father's eye that would precede another violent reckoning. Like flamingos by a waterhole, the peaceful scene outside a cafe erupted as Zachary's father stepped out of his vehicle. Women grabbed their children and stumbled over plastic stools to get away. Tables and cups clattered to the ground as men herded together for safety then took their chance and ran in all directions. Among this sudden chaos, a boy not much older than Zachary sat frozen against the wall, his eyes so wide and white with terror that no one noticed he had pissed himself in his seat. He couldn't have run if he wanted to – his walking stick had been knocked away in the melee, without it the raw stump at the bottom of his left shin would shudder uselessly over the ground as he hopped desperately, hoping that someone older or more crippled than himself might fall down behind him and be sacrificed instead. Not today.

Zachary's father stood over the cripple, glaring at him, his hand hovering over his holster.

"It's time, boy," was all he said.

Zachary stepped forward, lifted the boy by his armpits and dragged his scrawny body into the car. As they drove away, Zachary knew the townsfolk would eventually settle back into their routine of sitting about, preparing meals, waiting for whatever came next in their squalid lives.

They drove into the hills about five kilometres out of the village. The Captain never gave Zachary an express order as such. He simply stopped the car and handed him his pistol. Zachary climbed out of the passenger seat, dragged the boy, who was now wriggling like a dog, out of the back of the car. When he let the boy go he fell onto his hands and knees and began crawling in the dust. Zachary watched him, momentarily fascinated by the stump – the obscene suggestion of a limb that never was. Zachary had expected his own pulse to quicken at this point but the opposite happened. It was the calmest he had ever felt in his life. He cocked the pistol, sensed the weight of it in his hand, raised it and squeezed the trigger. He didn't appraise the moment for significance as it was playing out. His father was right, it was time. Two more bullets in the head to be sure as he had seen his father do on several occasions. He climbed back into the car. When he went to hand the pistol back, his father raised his hand. The gun was now his. They drove on in silence. He didn't need to know why the boy had to die, it was enough that he had done something to incur the wrath of the Captain – the order of things had been threatened momentarily, but now they had been put right again. So this was what it meant to be in control.

Over the following months Zachary developed a greater understanding of his father's world view by living it directly. He soon likened himself to a leopard in his willingness to wait, to stalk his prey carefully then strike when the moment was right. Of course, as he matured he dismissed these ideas as the arrogance of youth. Over the years he realised he was a somewhat different beast. Not unlike the leopard, but more willing to move into new territory and meld with different surroundings, there was a fluidity to his nature that enabled him to adapt quickly. His father had noticed it early on and resented him deeply for it. The leather strop came down harder and more often. The lessons were no longer designed to teach but to remind him who was boss. Zachary was under no illusions that he was immune to the fate of so many others if he stepped one foot too far out of place. However, accepting the shortcomings of his father – the fact that he was driven by rage and drunk on power – and realising his own potential was the most important lesson in the young man's life; one that came to him in a moment of clarity. He spat into the fire at the memory.

He was somewhere east of the midway point between two outback towns – Bourke and Cobar, at least 70 kilometres from the nearest homestead. He had turned off the highway at about 3pm that afternoon and driven overland for about 10 kilometres across a vast expanse of desert, tracking the flashing red dot on the GPS until a woman's smooth voice announced that he had reached his destination. He had cut the engine but left the air-con running. According to the read-out on his dashboard, it was 46C outside. He closed his eyes and napped in the car until the sun went down, then he got out and set up camp. He'd brought enough firewood, water and food to get him through the wait ahead.

Now, as he threw another log into the burning coals, he turned to look at the figure curled up on the ground a few feet behind him. The skin was blistered with third-degree burns, the lips cracked and bleeding, the tongue swollen and slightly protruding from the mouth. It looked like a flayed cat in a rural Chinese market. It was still breathing, barely.

He took out his bowie knife and stood up.

James looked up at his abductor with terrified, desperate eyes, unable to react.

When the SUV had arrived out of nowhere, he had already given up hope of being saved. He was drifting in and out of consciousness, hallucinating with the heat and in excruciating pain. He didn't believe what he was seeing. His heart swelled at the thought of holding his parents in his arms again and he had closed his eyes, resigning himself to the care of an unknown Samaritan. But nothing had happened. He tried to call out to the driver who hadn't moved but he was too far gone to make any sense. When it finally occurred to him that the driver in the car was his abductor, he made a pathetic attempt to crawl away. Now as the man stood over him with his knife, James wished for him to cut his throat and spare him the agony of another day in the desert.

With a firm grip on the knife he leaned down and sliced the GPS bracelet from the boy's ankle. He could hear a low, guttural whine issue from his throat. It could have been a question or another plea for help but the boy's tongue was too swollen to tell. Might just have been the last bit of life escaping from his lungs with a wheeze. He went back to the fire and took a seat. He'd be back on the road by early morning at the latest. He'd already mapped out the spot for the boy's corpse – a stretch of the Darling River where it flows into Bourke. The body would be found within 12-24 hours. Soon it would be time to contact the client. As agreed, the first two instalments had been paid in to a private cryptocurrency account on the dark web. With the discovery of the third body the final instalment would be made, by which time he would already be on a flight out of the country. Regardless of how his client's plan played out he would be long gone and $2M richer. But experience had told him, it was too soon to be gloating over the end game yet. He had to stay focused. Still, as he stared into flames, he couldn't help wondering what his father would think of him now.

CHAPTER TEN

Tony arrived at work slightly hung-over and in no mood. He sat at his desk and reluctantly scrolled through all the emails that had built up over the previous week – administrative messages, Federal Police newsletters, regional updates. He thought about Birgitte, what she had achieved in the short time she had been in Australia. It made him angry that she hadn't been listened to from the outset. As far as he was concerned they needed more detectives like her on the force – intuitive, perceptive and willing to think outside of her own self-interest. They would have a better chance of finding James Freedmont. He felt out of sorts knowing she wasn't there to challenge his ideas or to offer an alternative point of view. He recalled their conversation by the pool at the Settlers Arms Motel in Alice Springs; he was genuinely impressed with her ability to get him talking about things he was more comfortable keeping to himself. In his mind's eye he watched her walk up the stairs to get the bottle of chardonnay from her room. It was an image that had played in his mind more often than he'd care to admit, that and the look in her eyes just before he suggested they call it a night. It hadn't occurred to him at the time that she may have been interested in him, but now he kicked himself for not making some sort of gesture.

"Misguided chivalry," he muttered to himself as he continued to scroll through his inbox. He came across a meeting invitation from Miller sent earlier in the week. It was entitled MOVING FORWARD. It was scheduled for 3pm Wednesday. He had to check his calendar to realise it was for that afternoon. She wanted to formally address the issues of his role with the AFP. It sounded ominous, but he didn't really care anymore. The conversation with Sam Westlake the previous day had been playing over in his mind. The man's arrogance. His dismissive nature. It rankled Tony's sense of better judgement. It wasn't that he just didn't like the guy. There was something in his behaviour, particularly in his handling of Nils Brekman. Westlake obviously liked to be in control. He had wanted to be there when Brekman was interviewed. He wanted to shut it down as soon as it moved in an awkward direction. Westlake knew something. He had to.

Tony decided that an impromptu visit to Westlake might be enough to rattle his composure, make him say something he wouldn't otherwise. It was 11am. Across the heads of his colleagues he could see into Miller's office. She was meeting with her manager, Commander Andrew Barton, an ageing officer of the old school, who had a soft spot for his direct reports. Tony realised this might be the last chance he had to move forward with the case. He slipped out the door without her seeing him.

Forty five minutes later he entered the lobby of Katercorp. He caught the elevator to the 26th floor. Westlake's EA recognised him from the day before and asked him to take a seat while she contacted the 2IC. He chose to stand by her desk to make it very clear he was in a hurry. After a few anxious moments she put the phone down and said, "Unfortunately, Mr Westlake is in the middle of an important meeting. He could be another two hours. He asked if he could call you later."

"Perhaps you need to make it clearer that I'm with the Federal Police investigating a murder."

She picked up the phone again.

Tony could feel his blood begin to heat up.

The receptionist took a deep breath, realising that she was stuck in a difficult position. "Mr Westlake apologises but he insists that he can't meet with you right now."

"Really."

Tony marched across the foyer and into the office area, ignoring the receptionist who was calling after him. He stepped into Westlake's office.

"We need to talk."

Westlake peered up from his desk, looking pale and bewildered.

"I said no meetings," he muttered.

"We need to talk further about the murder of Hans Thostrup and the disappearance of Salina Heysmith."

Westlake's hands were shaking as he shuffled papers aimlessly on his desk. "I told you everything I know."

Tony stared at him, suddenly thrown by what he was seeing. Westlake looked as if he'd just witnessed a car accident. His confidence had evaporated.

"Mr Westlake, is everything okay?"

"Yes," he said. "I've just had some very bad news. I really need to be alone right now."

"Anything I can help you with?"

"No. It's a personal matter."

The EA came in behind Tony. "Mr Westlake, I explained to the detective that you were busy but he wouldn't listen."

"It's okay, Judy."

"But I didn't want you to think that..."

"It's okay," he snapped. He stood up, desperately trying to regain some of his authority. "That will be all, Judy. I've got it."

She turned and walked out into the foyer, visibly rankled at being yelled out for trying to do the right thing.

Westlake came round from behind his desk. "Detective Kingsmill, as I explained yesterday there isn't anything more I can tell you. Really."

"Salina Heysmith is dead."

Westlake didn't even flinch. "That's awful news. I'll notify Mr Brekman immediately."

He talked like an automaton, as if some part of him had slipped into the driver's seat to maintain the illusion of control while the rest of him scattered and crumbled.

Tony stood his ground. "Do you know anything about these murders that you're not telling us?"

Westlake shook his head slowly. "I have no idea what's going on," he said quietly.

For once Tony believed him. "Mr Westlake we are concerned for the safety of a young man by the name of James Freedmont."

Westlake stared out the window onto the city below barely listening.

Tony continued. "Do you know him? He's a friend of the son of the CEO of Barclay Industries."

Westlake ran his fingers through his hair. "Sorry?"

"Freedmont. James Freedmont. Do you know him?"

"No, I don't."

"We think he may be in considerable danger. Is there anything more you can tell us?"

Westlake slowly shook his head, walked back to his desk and sat down. He stared at his computer with distaste, as if it was soiled.

Tony wanted to press him for more information but didn't know what else to ask him. "Well, you have my details if anything occurs to you."

He excused himself and walked out of the foyer. If Birgitte had been there she may have known how to press Westlake for more information. The man was clearly in shock. None of it made any sense.

Tony walked across the street and got into his car. As he turned the engine over he saw Westlake step purposefully out of the building, talking urgently into his mobile. He hailed a cab. As one approached he almost stepped in front of the bonnet to get the driver's attention.

Tony swung the car round and followed the cab at a safe distance. It moved around Darling Harbour and north into the city. Tony thought he might be driving to the office of Blake, Patterson & Walker but the cab swung up the hill towards the Royal Botanic Gardens.

Tony pulled the car over as the cab stopped at a set of lights. Westlake paid the driver cash and got out. He ran across Macquarie Street, through the large steel gates that opened onto the sprawling gardens that stretched down to the harbour's edge. Tony followed him on foot.

He thought he'd lost him through the trees but then he spotted Westlake's white business shirt as he entered the rose garden. This part of the Botanic Gardens didn't get as many visitors, even during lunch hours. Most people walked or jogged along the promenade down by the water, or gathered at the restaurant and cafe in the palm grove. You had to know the rose garden was there.

Tony leaned into a sandstone pylon that formed a pergola over the rows of flowers. Suddenly he spotted Jason Pender approaching from the other side. He must have come in from an entrance further down Macquarie Street. The two men didn't waste time being cordial. Tony wasn't close enough to hear what they were saying but Westlake was clearly agitated and Pender was listening carefully. Tony was intrigued that the 2IC for Katercorp was secretly meeting with the Lead Counsel for Barclay Industries. It immediately suggested corporate collusion, on a grander scale than Pender having an affair with Salina Heysmith. He tried to replay the previous day's interviews in his mind to see if there was anything to suggest the two men knew one another.

Without warning Westlake grabbed Pender by the shirt front and threw him up against a pylon. The lawyer yelled back at him, "I don't know anything. I have no idea what you're talking about."

Westlake held him a moment longer then shoved him down to the ground and stood over him talking in a low voice. Pender looked up, frightened. Tony wanted to get closer. He had to hear what they were saying, but there was no way of doing it without giving himself away. Westlake pointed a threatening finger at Pender then turned on his heel and strode out of the rose garden.

Tony didn't know whether to follow him or wait to see what Pender did next. On an impulse he decided to stay with Pender; he figured he was the weaker of the two and therefore more likely to do something more overt.

The lawyer slowly got up and dusted himself off. He looked confused and angry. He paced about, took his phone out of his pocket then put it away again. He walked out of the gates and hailed a cab heading up Macquarie Street. Tony didn't have time to get back to his car so he hailed a cab himself. He told the driver that he was with the cab in front and didn't have the address so he needed to stick close – anything else would have sounded absurd.

The two cabs moved along Hyde Park, turning left onto William Street after St Mary's Cathedral. Something important was playing out and Tony was desperate to know what it was but for once he would just have to go with it and hope that it would lead to a breakthrough.

The cab in front continued east out of the city towards Point Piper. Soon enough Tony recognised the street they were on. He told his driver to pull up on the next corner as Pender got out of the cab and ran into his house.

Tony walked back along the street. The cement-rendered wall around the perimeter of the property was too high to scale. He stood out on the drive and waited, thinking what to do next. He decided to wing it. He pressed the buzzer on the driveway intercom.

After a few moments Pender answered.

"Who is it?"

"Detective Kingsmill."

"What can I do for you, Detective?"

"We need to have another conversation."

"Now isn't a very good time. Could I call you later, perhaps?"

"I'm afraid I have to insist, Mr Pender. There have been some developments and we could really do with your help."

Tony waited for what seemed like several minutes. Eventually the gate slowly opened. Tony walked down the drive. Pender was at the front door, looking distracted, trying to maintain an air of professionalism.

"Is your family home?" Tony asked.

"No. They're out. Trudy is visiting her mother with the kids."

"We can talk inside then."

"Of course."

He led Tony into a vast living area lined with travertine. It reminded him of the foyer of the East Wind Hotel. Oversized sofas were almost dwarfed by the expansive canvases on two walls – abstract artworks that were probably original. There was a TV on the far wall that could have passed for a small cinema screen. The living area opened out on to a deck that overlooked a lap pool but he barely noticed it because the back of the property faced directly on to the water looking across Sydney Harbour to Taronga Zoo.

Pender offered him a seat on the sofa. He stared at Tony hard, wanting to know what could be so important as to be interrupting what was proving to be a difficult day.

"Do you know a young man by the name of James Freedmont?"

"Should I?" he asked curtly.

"He's a friend of your boss's son."

"The name doesn't ring a bell."

"He went missing from Melbourne University on Saturday. We're concerned he may be in some danger."

"What's this in relation to, Detective Kingsmill?"

"Mr Pender, Hans Thostrup, an old friend of Nils Brekman was found murdered outside of Alice Springs a week ago. Salina Heysmith went missing shortly after and now James Freedmont has disappeared. Clearly something is going on and we believe it might have something to do with both Katercorp and Barclay Industries."

"What do you want to hear?"

Tony couldn't hide the anger in his voice. "I need you to tell me if you know what's going on."

"I told you yesterday. I have no idea where Salina is."

"And you've never heard of James Freedmont."

"No, I haven't."

"Are you even concerned for the welfare of Ms Heysmith?"

"Are you here to judge me, Detective Kingsmill?"

"She's dead, Mr Pender. She was murdered a week ago. Her body was found in the Murray River in Mildura."

Pender lost his composure for a moment. "Why didn't you tell me yesterday?"

"We were waiting confirmation of her identity. I shouldn't even be telling you now, but another person is missing and we really need to get to the bottom of this as quickly as possible."

Pender stared at his hands. His mind was elsewhere.

"Mr Pender, I need to know your connection with Sam Westlake."

Pender didn't move. His breathing was even. "I know him through our dealings with the lobby group."

"Is that all?"

"We've played squash once or twice." He thought back to their first meeting at the Marion Hill Courts. Jason had been playing there for years and had never seen Westlake within a mile of the place, which was why he was surprised to bump into him off court one morning. Westlake had suggested a friendly game and they'd played together every two months ever since. They had initially joked about how it might look, as they both worked for two of the biggest mining firms in the country, but Westlake reassured him that it was all in the spirit of competition and had never talked business on court. It was all about the game.

"So you know him outside of work as well."

"We're not that close. I've known him for a few years."

"Where did you meet?"

"At university."

"So you've known him for how many years?"

"About 15, on and off, but I haven't seen much of him until this Timor Sea deal came up. He's really just a professional acquaintance." He looked up at Tony, confused by his own recollection of events. Did he bump into Westlake that day or was he waiting for him at the courts? He thought about the other night on Pitt Street and could feel his stomach lurching. He turned to Tony. "How did she die? Salina?"

"We can't say at the moment. Is there something I should know about you and Sam Westlake and this Timor Sea deal? Something you're not telling us?"

He laughed nervously. "Like what?"

"Like anything that will help us find James Freedmont."

A phone rang in another room. For a moment they stared at one another. Finally, Pender said, "I think I need to get that."

Tony watched him leave, bewildered by his behaviour. He stood up and looked around the living room. He could see Pender through a doorway talking on the phone in his home office. He had moved behind his desk and was looking at his

195

laptop. He hung up the phone and stared at the screen. Tony moved out onto the deck to wait outside, frustrated by the stilted pace of the conversation. Sailing boats glided past, tacking at an orange buoy that was within hundred metres of Pender's house. He saw the Manly ferry cutting its way past Middle Head. It looked serene.

When he turned back Pender was standing behind him, ashen faced. "You'll have to leave."

"Sorry?"

"Something's come up. I can't talk now. If anything comes to mind, I'll call you. I can't be of any further help to your investigation."

"Mr Pender, are you aware of the gravity of the situation?"

"I assure you, I'm very aware."

He hurriedly walked across the living room and opened the front door. "Now. This interview is over."

First Westlake; now Pender. Tony was baffled. "Is there something wrong, Mr Pender?"

"Not at all," he said, exhaling heavily, trying to get his breathe back. "I'm sorry. The news about Salina, the stress of the Timor deal. I really just need to lie down. I want to be alone right now. You must understand."

"If there's something that you're not telling us, now is the time to change course."

Pender stared at Tony. There was a slight flicker in his eye. Tony tried to determine what it was as he stepped out the front door. It was fear. Pender was terrified but was doing his best to hide it.

Tony turned to press him further but the door was already closed. Without a warrant or a clearer idea of what he was looking for there was little else he could do but leave. He walked out onto the street, completely bewildered by the day's developments. He looked at his watch. Shit. It was 2.30pm. He had to get back to the office for his meeting with Miller.

The wall behind Superintendent Miller's desk was lined with framed certificates and commendations, reminders for all who entered her office they were in the company of a high-achieving, accomplished officer. The few certificates Tony had received over the years were 'filed' in the bottom of a drawer somewhere in his apartment.

If he had to describe Miller in one word it would be "corporate". Try as he might, Tony wanted to admire her – it would have made his situation easier to handle – but for all the awards and baubles she had received, he could only see a cold, ambitious statistician, someone who could make the numbers stack up in her favour.

"British" was the other word that came to mind. She had migrated from Yorkshire to Australia as a teenager. For all her years in Sydney she still maintained an austere air, an aloofness that was difficult to warm to. He often wondered if she would have cut it back in England as an officer. Were her type rewarded over there or ostracised.

She stared at Tony, processing what he had just said, her tiny dark eyes gave nothing away. He looked at the line of her long nose and at her weak chin. She reminded him of someone from a Dickens novel he'd read as a kid but he couldn't place it. Her face was incongruous with her body, which was sinewy to the point of concern. The muscles and thick veins in her in her neck were testament to the hours she spent in the gym every night, probably burning away a lifetime of petty resentments. He had to remind himself that she had only recently lost her pregnancy. But beyond his natural responses of empathy, he struggled to feel anything for her.

"So?" she asked, almost petulantly. "Where is it at now?"

Tony wasn't sure how she'd take the news so he just dove in.

"Well the Forensic Pathologist in Melbourne, Dr Barnett, has confirmed that Salina Heysmith was killed by a saltwater crocodile, most likely up in Kakadu. The residue on Heysmith's wrists matches the residue on Thostrup. So we have a direct link between the two murders. Missing persons are interviewing family and friends of James Freedmont, trying to find eyewitnesses at the university but he went missing on a Saturday so there weren't many people around. I've suggested they talk to the CEO of Barclay Industries and the senior staff at Katercorp as well."

"What for?" Miller looked slightly affronted that the investigation was proceeding at a pace without her approval.

"Thostrup was an old friend of Nils Brekman at Katercorp. Heysmith was a lawyer representing Katercorp. She was also having an affair with the Lead Counsel of Barclay Industries. James Freedmont is a friend of Tom Barclay, the son of Reginald Barclay, the CEO of Barclay Industries."

"So you think it's extortion?"

"Hard to say at this stage," he said. He didn't want to tell her about the two interviews he'd had earlier that day. He wanted to email Birgitte and hopefully catch her when she got to Hong Kong or back to Copenhagen at the latest. "Both firms were part of a lobby group pressuring the Government to get approval for off-shore mining rights in the Timor Sea. It could have something to do with that. But as one of the lawyers explained to us, it's not likely that either firm would behave like union thugs on a construction site."

"I've spoken to the lead investigators in Alice and Mildura and they appreciate the information you've sent through."

Tony resisted the temptation to snort with derision. "Is there any way of ramping up the search for James Freedmont?"

"It's with the right department. You've done well, Tony, but I think it's time you backed away from the investigation."

She leaned back in her chair. The social niceties were dispensed with. It was her meeting now.

"I've been talking with Commander Barton about your role and there is a genuine concern we don't have a budget for an increased head count. He's spoken to a few of his colleagues and they think there could be a space in Identity Theft coming up in a few weeks."

"Identity Theft? I have no interest in working in that field. I have no experience or expertise."

"They'll provide all the training."

"This is ridiculous. I came across to take your role."

"Which no longer exists."

"Because the people upstairs promoted you."

"Careful, Detective."

"This is absurd," he said out loud to himself. "I'd be better off going back to the NSW force."

She looked at him coolly as if to say, "That's always an option," but resisted the urge. Instead she offered a wan smile and said, "Listen, I'll admit, it's not normal but be that as it may, we have to find a solution."

"So you get promoted and I get shuffled off to some bureaucratic backwater. Looks a bit convenient don't you think?"

"I'll let your implication slide, this time, Detective. But I'd strongly advise that from this point forward you think very carefully before you speak." She leaned forward in her chair. "I've been with the Federal Police for eight years now. It can be a rewarding place to work if you play your cards right. I'd suggest you take the position with Identity Theft, as the Commander has suggested. I'll be sure to put in a good word for you."

Tony stood up. "Thanks for your time. I think it over and get back to you."

He walked out of her office, a bundle of tightened muscles and grated nerves.

After work he was still too wired to go home. He strode across the city, his mind racing. He was ready to walk away from it all. If his transfer to the Federal Police had been a mistake then perhaps it was time to take his uncle up on his offer to work as a labourer for his construction firm for a while, get out of the game altogether. He was 44, still young enough to make a go of something else. He simply didn't have the energy or the wherewithal to compete with political animals like Carolyn Miller or Sam Westlake. The people who seemingly made the world turn did so because they lacked any consideration for the people around them – the people they deemed inferior. Apparently compassion and empathy slowed down the play of the ball. They might miss their opportunity to shine. He sensed their desperation and it made him sick to the stomach.

With no particular destination in mind he crossed George Street and headed up the hill into the narrow streets and laneways of The Rocks. He could feel the anger steadily welling within him again. He thought of Hana and for the first time he was genuinely furious with her. It was like a spark to a powder keg. She had to have known what she was getting herself into. She'd probably been doing the books for the Retif twins since she first started at university. It was no wonder she had no intentions of talking to him. She couldn't possibly explain away her behaviour. He looked back over all the times he met with her and now saw deception in every smile and burst of laughter. How could he have been so blind? Birgitte was right, he did suffer from a misguided chivalry. He felt like a complete chump.

As he reached the top of the hill he stopped to get his breath and realised his anger was getting the better of him. If he wasn't careful it could turn to bitterness and resentment and that was the last thing he needed. He'd seen it happen to other officers on the force and he knew it wasn't worth it. He wasn't the first guy to fall for a deceitful woman and he wouldn't be the last. And as to work, tonight wasn't the night to be making decisions about his career.

He looked around and realised he was on Cumberland Street. The East Wind Hotel was just a few hundred metres further on. He thought of Birgitte and he could feel his mood lifting a little. He decided to have a drink in the lobby bar. He wasn't the sentimental type but he did like the idea of salving his wounded pride in the place where he had met her.

As he entered the lobby he noticed there was a brighter energy to the hotel in the evenings. Guests were stepping out to explore the city while others came in from a day of sight-seeing. Tony walked across the travertine and up into the cafe which operated as a bar at night. He pulled up a tall chair, rested his elbows on the mahogany and ordered a beer from a thin Indian waiter who then brought him a shallow bowl of peanuts. Tony settled back into his seat and sipped his beer slowly. He looked at the cafe and thought back to his first meeting with Birgitte, Harris and Donleavy. So much had happened in the past two weeks. When the beer was gone he ordered another.

If he had the money, he mused, he should have taken a holiday between leaving the NSW police and joining the Feds. He couldn't think for the life of him where he'd go but he could feel his shoulders relaxing just being in the company of tourists. He drained his second beer and decided to leave before he was tempted to book a room. He paid his bill and headed back through the lobby. As he reached the glass sliding doors Birgitte appeared, with tote bags full of paperwork hanging from each shoulder and more paper in her arms. "Tony!" Her face shone with appreciation.

Tony had to stop himself from hugging her. "What are you still doing here?"

"I was about to call you. I cancelled my flight last night. What are you doing here?"

He felt embarrassed. "I was in the neighbourhood, thought I'd have a beer."

"I'm so glad I've caught you. We need to talk about Darwin."

"Birgitte, it's over. I'm off the case," he said, then added. "I don't think we were ever on it. I'm getting transferred."

"Transferred?" she asked, perplexed. "Where?"

"Identity Theft."

"Do you know anything about Identity Theft?"

He shrugged. "I'll learn, apparently."

"But what about the boy, James Freedmont."

"It's with Missing Persons. They're in touch with the family."

"But if they're anything like the Danish police, they're not going to move fast enough."

"Birgitte, it's now Wednesday; he's been missing for six days. It's only a matter of time before his body turns up in a creek or a river somewhere – it's Thostrup and Heysmith all over again. I'm sorry. You should have stayed on your flight."

"I'm still here, so we may as well talk about it. But I just need to speak to reception first." She smiled at him. "I can't believe we've bumped into one another."

She crossed the lobby to the reception desk. Tony was surprised at how down he had become without her positive energy to buoy him up. He was incredibly grateful to see her. Part of him wanted to convince her to walk away from the case so they could just spend one night talking about other things. He wanted to get to know her away from bloated corpses and self-serving corporate types.

When she came back she said. "Can you give me 10 minutes to settle into my room then come up? I don't want to discuss the case in the lobby. It's room 2002"

As she turned towards the elevator she asked, "Shall I order some dinner?"

"Why not."

She stopped. "Tony?"

"Yeah?"

"Please don't give up on this yet."

He smiled. "Do I have a choice?"

She laughed and headed for the elevator bay. He walked back to the lobby bar with a slight spring in his step and ordered another beer. He felt like a detective again.

CHAPTER ELEVEN

Tony knocked and waited. Eventually, Birgitte opened the door. She stepped back for him to pass.

"Sorry about the mess."

The bed and the surrounding furniture were scattered with stacks of paper. She moved past him, still unpacking her tote bags, trying to sort through the material she had brought with her. At a glance Tony could see printouts of annual reports for mining companies, geological survey maps, newspaper articles and acts of legislation. He rested his satchel by one of the armchairs and took a seat.

A few minutes later there was a knock at the door. Birgitte asked him to answer it. A young girl in a dark uniform rolled a dining trolley into the room.

"I'm famished," said Birgitte, crouching down to compare two documents. "I haven't eaten all day." Tony gave the girl a tip and began to set up their dinner on the desk near the front door.

When they were alone again Birgitte said, "I ordered steaks. Medium rare. And a pot of coffee for afterwards. Is that okay?"

He smiled. "Read my mind."

As they sat down to eat she said, "So, tell me about your day?"

"You're not going to tell me why you're still here?" he asked.

"Not yet," she said, smiling. "I need to be brought up to date first."

Birgitte listened and took notes as Tony ran through the course of his day. She couldn't believe what she was hearing. Westlake and Pender had known one another for years. She knew Westlake had lied about the affair, she just didn't know to what extent. So, he and Pender had both lied about crucial aspects of their business dealings. It created a direct, albeit secret, link between the two biggest firms in the Timor Sea deal and therefore altered how they should be reading all the evidence to date. She was particularly interested in the two men's shifts in mood during their interviews with Tony. She asked him several times for more details, but even then, she couldn't work out what any of it meant.

By the time Tony said, "...and that's when I ran into you", they had finished dinner and were halfway through their coffees.

Birgitte curled her feet up under her thighs and stared intently into her cup, deep in thought. "That's extraordinary."

Then she looked up at him. "You're brilliant. And I'm sorry about Carolyn."

"Thanks," he said. "But I'm not sure where that leaves us."

He grabbed the glass percolator and topped up their cups, then gave her a look which said, "Well?"

"I couldn't do it, Tony," she said finally. "I couldn't fly back to Copenhagen knowing that the Freedmont boy hadn't been found. I don't care what happens when I get back to Denmark. And I promise I won't get in your way, but I need to see this through."

"Have you spoken to Sven?"

"I emailed him last night to tell him I would be back a little later than planned, that I needed time to think about my future. He thinks I'm in Hong Kong."

"So, what have you been doing?"

"I started to go through all the material we gathered yesterday and I'm convinced, it definitely has something to do with the Timor Sea deal. I'm sure of it. And from what you've just told me about Westlake and Pender, we're on the right track. I'm just not sure how that aspect fits in with what I've found."

She got up from the table. "The problem has been that we haven't been able to determine who all the potential players might be, which makes it near impossible to find a motive for the killings. So I spent the day at the State Library, researching the mining industry in Australia, and further afield. Who are the main companies? What are their specialities? I looked at the boards of directors, and executive staff of all the main firms, then did a quick background check on each of them –

just the stuff I could find online: newspaper files and press releases."

She moved around the bed, gathering up select print outs, discarding others. "I researched the government approval process – which ministers of which department have to sign off on these deals, like the one in the Timor Sea. What would they have to gain or lose?"

"Hence, the mountains of paper," said Tony.

She came back to the table. Tony cleared away the plates so she could lay out several pages at once.

"According to the legislation I've looked at, if a proposed mining site is more than five kilometres off shore, it is a Federal matter." She patted a piece of legislation. "It would require considerable scrutiny and a lot of stakeholder management."

She then moved this document to one side and drew out a map of Australia. "However, the site Katercorp and Barclay Industries are interested in is 3.8km off the coast of Arnhem Land, which means it falls under the jurisdiction of the Northern Territory Government."

She quickly grabbed another document, similar to the first.

"The Northern Territory legislations states that the Minister for Trade is responsible for the approval of an exploration licence. That is this gentleman." She found a printout of a photo of a corpulent man in a suit and placed it in front of Tony. He vaguely recognised the guy from the TV.

"Frank Howard," he said.

"Now from what I can gather, for the past few years there has been talk in the industry that there could be sizeable reserves of natural gas in the Timor Sea if they could only dig deep enough to find it. Up until recently the technology wasn't available. But even if it was, without an exploration licence nothing could happen. Now given the political sensitivities of the area – contentious issues about the environment and the local Indigenous communities – the Northern Territory Government weren't about to just give these licences away. So apparently a few of the bigger mining firms decided a collective approach would be best. They formed a lobby group, which has been meeting regularly to develop a convincing business case for the government. They were actually in Darwin when Hans Thostrup turned up in Forbes Creek."

"Then Salina Heysmith went missing," said Tony, "which would explain the possibility of her being killed in Kakadu."

"Exactly. But no one was aware of either crime at the time. And then the Northern Territory Government approved the deal."

"Basically, it's now a bun fight between the firms within the lobby group," said Tony.

She stood up and began to walk around the room with her coffee. "That's what I was thinking as well. So far, we know the two biggest firms involved are Katercorp and Barclay Industries. But neither are likely to extort the other and both are being targeted. I asked myself, who else was at the conference?"

She drew out a copy of the agenda. As they both leaned over it he could sense her perfume on her skin.

"But we've questioned all of these firms," said Tony.

"I know," she said. "Stay with me. We're almost there. I then did some research to find out who owns these companies."

She showed Tony the list she had compiled. He read through it quickly, recognising several of the names. He said, "Still, most of these smaller firms are either owned or directly affiliated with major multinationals who wouldn't stoop to killing the opposition."

Birgitte shook her head. "I'm worried you're basing your ideas on an idealistic assumption of corporate behaviour."

"Multinationals won't risk their profit margins in the long run with something as risky as murder. That's not idealism; its realism of the most capitalist kind."

"But an individual within one of those corporations might. We're assuming the company behind this is following corporate protocols, when the act itself belies it."

"Which brings us back to this list, and short of interviewing every executive within each firm in the hope that they suddenly confess, we're kind of stymied."

"Which is why I started to compile another list showing where each of these multinationals is based."

Tony scratched his head and began to read the list out loud: "Australia, the US, Britain, France, Saudi Arabia." Then he shrugged. "You've lost me."

"It was something Gunner Mendelson said. It's been bothering me since we were in Adelaide."

"About Nils Brekman? Hans Thostrup?"

"No," she said, looking at him with a sense of triumph. "China."

He stared at her blankly.

Birgitte grabbed the agenda. "Where are the Chinese firms on this list?" Then she grabbed the list of parent companies. "Or this?"

Tony was beginning to feel a little stupid because he still couldn't make the connection.

"Tony, China has the most rapidly growing economy in the world. It is desperate for resources to fuel this growth – in quantities they can't source themselves. They're relying on vast amounts of imported raw materials. As Mr Mendelson said, they've been operating in Africa for years. One of the reason's Australia's economy is proving so resilient in the GFC is its reliance on Chinese money. State-owned subsidiaries of major Chinese companies are setting up here to extract iron ore and uranium. They're also funding very large off-shore gas projects off the north west of the country on the understanding that if they help develop the infrastructure, they will receive an agreed amount of gas for the next 25 years. It simply doesn't make sense that Chinese mining companies already set up here wouldn't be at least interested in this deal."

He was beginning to see the picture Birgitte was drawing for him.

"Is it too small?" he asked. "Sure, it will be worth billions over the next few decades, but perhaps the return on investment doesn't warrant their involvement."

"I considered that," she replied, crossing the room to find a pad she'd been writing on. "Here's a full list of all the mining companies operating in Australia, and here's the list of attendees at the conference and the parent companies. There are four companies that would more than likely be interested in a project of this size that didn't attend the conference in Darwin. Of those four, there is one that stands out."

She pointed at a name midway down the first list.

"Xancorp?" Tony asked, staring at the page. "Never heard of them."

"Why would you? They've only been operating in Australia for three years."

She pulled out an article from a business magazine. "It says here they were a surprise last-minute bidder for a failing gas company 18 months ago. No one knows anything about them, except the CEO is this guy – third from the left." She turned the page so Tony could see an image of a group of middle-aged Asian men in suits standing in front of a modern glass building. Third from the left was a man in his 50s – stern faced, slightly uncomfortable in front of a camera, his hands hanging heavily from his cuffs: a photographer's nightmare. Tony gleaned the caption; it was the opening of a research facility into natural gas at a university in Perth, funded by Xancorp.

He read the name out loud to himself: "Xian Lao."

"He's a Permanent Resident but obviously Chinese by descent."

Tony shook his head. "I don't get the racial profiling on this."

"You still don't you think it was odd that no Chinese firms were at the conference, attempting to lobby the Northern Territory Government?"

"I guess, but you're only considering this because Mendelson has a gripe with the Chinese. Maybe you've both got issues with racism. What it says to me is that there is even less of a connection between Xancorp and the mining deal and therefore less of a connection with the murders. What would they have to gain?"

"Seriously, Tony? What would a Chinese mining firm have to gain from the two biggest local mining companies backing out of the deal at the last minute?"

"But what about the other companies at the conference? Surely they're still bigger than a company that is barely on the radar."

"Not if Xancorp is backed by the Chinese Government."

Tony sat down again. "Birgitte, you're making my head hurt. Do you really want to start a diplomatic shit-storm by accusing the Chinese Government of plotting to kill the competition in a local mining deal?"

"It might not be the Chinese Government, directly. But if Xancorp is being bankrolled by someone in China, the Government would have to be involved in some way. The State owns everything or at the very least someone in Government would have to be paid off to look the other way."

"But hang about," said Tony, "Thostrup and Heysmith were both found before the Northern Territory Government approved the site. What would have happened if it had been knocked back? I'm not sure about the going rate for contract killing, but it can't be cheap. It would have been an immediate loss on investment."

"That's been bothering me as well," said Birgitte, turning to the computer and beginning to type. "But I did notice something else when I was reading up on this earlier today. That research facility in Perth isn't the only project Xancorp have funded recently. They've also paid for a new wing at a university in Darwin."

"So?"

"It would give the university more international appeal, attract more students to the city and therefore bring in more money to the region – who would benefit from that sort of news?"

Tony looked at the screen. It was an article from the Courier Mail. Xian Lao was standing beside the Northern Territory Minister for Trade, Frank Howard.

Tony grinned, shaking his head. "Jesus, the Northern Territory Government."

"It doesn't equate to a direct bribe," said Birgitte, "but it certainly suggests that Xian Lao may have had his eye on this deal for some time and didn't want anything to get in his way."

"What about Westlake and Pender?"

"I'm as surprised as you are that they obviously know one another, but I'm not sure what the connection might be between them and Xancorp."

"So how do you want to proceed?"

"Let's talk to Mr Lao. See what he has to say."

Tony shook his head and laughed to himself. He was enlivened by the coffee, but more by the pace of Birgitte's mind. She was something else. She looked at him triumphantly, her eyes shining with a brilliance that made it difficult for Tony to look away.

She smiled confidently and said, "If we can't catch the killer, let's find the guy who's paying him."

When Birgitte and Tony arrived at the Floating Lotus restaurant the staff were clearing tables for the end of service. The maitre d', an attractive young woman in a silk top and long black skirt, guided them between the large tables to the back of the restaurant where the door to a private dining room was flanked by two glass tanks holding enormous crabs. She held up her hand politely for the detectives to wait. She opened the door and slipped inside.

Tony could see a large setting for 10 being cleared of dirty dishes and empty wine bottles. It was noisy inside as a group of middle-aged Chinese businessmen in suits were preparing to leave. They were jovial and warm with one another, laughing loudly at something one of them had obviously said about the maitre d', who was making her way between them to the far corner of the room. She approached a heavy-set man in a dark suit. He lowered his head to listen to her then looked across the room to the door. Tony recognised the guy from the article Birgitte had shown him earlier. It was Xian Lao, CEO of Xancorp.

The businessmen slowly proceeded to say good night to their host who shook each of their hands. He didn't laugh or even smile but was respectfully silent. The men filed out of the room paying no mind to Birgitte or Tony.

The maitre d' came back and held the door open for them. Birgitte and Tony stepped into the room, which now only contained a handful of wait staff.

Xian Lao was a large man, bigger than his photo suggested. He may have once been athletic but he was now carrying excess weight, which he concealed beneath an expensive tailored suit. Birgitte figured he was no more than 55, but it was difficult to tell, because his complexion was smooth while the skin around his eyes looked weathered. His face was expressionless, his eyes almost dull.

Birgitte decided to hold back as Tony approached the CEO.

"Mr Lao? I'm Detective Tony Kingsmill with the Australian Federal Police." Neither men presented their hand. "This is Senior Detective Birgitte Vestergaard, from Denmark. She's helping us with a local investigation and we need to ask you a few questions."

Lao's eyes passed over Birgitte perfunctorily then returned to Tony. He didn't move.

Tony gestured to a chair. "It's an informal talk, at this stage." He turned to the maitre d'. "Could we have the room for a few moments?"

She nodded and directed the wait staff in Mandarin to leave through the door to the kitchen then she left through the main door, closing it behind her.

Lao took a seat across from Tony and Birgitte. He exuded blunt authority – a man who wasn't in the habit of being questioned. He could have been sitting before a Senate Committee with no intention of admitting malfeasance. His back was straight and his head was tipped back, forcing him to look down his broad, flat nose at the two detectives.

Tony did his best to ignore the man's arrogance. He needed to remain impartial until he knew for sure who he was dealing with. "You may have seen in the news recently two people have been murdered. A Danish gentleman by the name of Hans Thostrup was found outside of Alice Springs a couple of weeks back. And Salina Heysmith, a corporate lawyer, was discovered in the Murray River near Mildura. We believe the two events are connected."

Lao listened but gave no indication that he was familiar with the news.

Tony waited for some sort of response then continued. "In the past few days a young man by the name of James Freedmont has gone missing. We are obviously concerned for his safety and we're hoping you may have some information which might help us locate him before it's too late."

The businessman considered the detective and eventually responded. "I don't know any of the people you've mentioned." His English was clear enough to be understood despite the thickness of his Mandarin accent.

"Okay," Tony said, thinking of a wooden puzzle box he received one Christmas as a child. He knew there was an art to getting inside but he hadn't the patience so he'd smashed it against a brick wall. "So you didn't know Hans Thostrup or Salina Heysmith?"

Lao shook his head slowly.

"Have you heard of any of these people in passing? Their names being mentioned by a colleague perhaps?"

"No," he said, with barely a note of concern.

"They're each connected to the mining industry, which I believe is your field of expertise. Thostrup used to be the head of an energy agency for the European Union. Heysmith was a lawyer who specialised in corporate mining. And young James just happens to be friends with someone whose father is involved in mining."

Tony waited and was about to get firm with the CEO when he answered.

"Xancorp is not a big operation," he said. "We don't have any dealings with the more established corporate entities in this country, which is why I don't know many people in the industry. I can confidently say I have never come across the people you have mentioned."

Tony stared at the puzzle box in his mind. He turned it over and tried a different angle. "What can you tell us about the proposed off-shore gas mining deal in the Timor Sea that's been in the news recently?"

"Only what has already been covered publicly."

"You weren't involved with the group lobbying the Northern Territory Government?"

"Even if we wanted to," he said, "Xancorp couldn't operate on that scale, so there was no point in us being involved."

"If Katercorp and Barclay Industries were to back out of the tendering process, you wouldn't throw your hat in the ring, so to speak."

"Without divulging too much of our financial position, Detective, we don't have the capital or the man power. Is that what this is about?" he asked flatly. "The two murders... the missing young man?"

Tony persisted. "Do you know Nils Brekman?"

"He's the CEO of Katercorp. We've never met, but I am familiar with his work."

"Hans Thostrup, the Danish gentleman found in Alice Springs, was an old friend of his. And Salina Heysmith, the lawyer, was representing his company – she was also involved with the Lead Counsel of Barclay Industries. I take it you know of Reginald Barclay?"

Lao offered a subtle nod, processing the information as if hearing it for the first time.

"The young man," Tony continued. "James Freedmont, is good friends with Reginald Barclay's eldest son. If those two companies were encouraged to back out of the tendering process through less than legal means, that would open the way for smaller players, not unlike Xancorp. We're questioning anyone who could be seen to benefit from such an outcome."

"I understand."

Tony decided it was Lao's turn to wait. He stared the man down, looking for some semblance of concern or anxiety, but there was nothing. When it began to get awkward, he tried again.

"Now you've said it's not in your interests to compete for the Timor Sea deal. Yet you have donated considerable funds to some major institutions in the Northern Territory in the past 18 months. If you don't mind me saying, you seem quite eager to ingratiate yourself with the Minister for Trade, a Mr Frank Howard."

The businessman inhaled through his nostrils and slowly sat up in his chair. "I have contributed modest sums to what I believe are worthy causes – universities, research facilities. It's common practice in the industry."

Tony's observation had obviously rankled him, but it wasn't enough and he didn't have any other angles to pursue. The CEO gave a barely perceptible grin when he realised Tony had run out of questions. He stood up.

"Now, as I've already stated, Detective" he said as if talking to a stubborn child, "I don't know the people you have mentioned. Xancorp don't intend submitting a tender for the Timor Sea deal, so I don't think there is any way I can help with your investigation. However, I do hope you find the young man who has gone missing. It must be very concerning for his family."

Tony didn't move. "I suggest you sit back down. We're not done here."

Birgitte could see Lao was reassessing the relationship between himself and Tony. The businessman stood his ground. "I would be more than willing to continue this conversation at the police station, Detective. In fact, I would prefer it."

"What can you tell us about Sam Westlake?"

"He works for Katercorp. We have met on occasion."

"I thought you said you don't socialise with other miners."

"Detective, I do know some figures in the industry, just not the ones at the centre of your investigation."

"How well do you know Westlake?"

"Not very. We've met at a few functions."

"And Jason Pender?"

He shook his head. Tony couldn't tell if Lao's reaction was contempt for his line of questioning or a straight answer.

"Yes or no."

Birgitte reached across and touched Tony's arm. He barely registered, so she stood up as well. "We'll be in touch if we have any further questions, Mr Lao."

Tony got to his feet slowly. Birgitte could see he was struggling to control his anger and gave him a look as if to say, "Please, let me handle it."

She turned to the stone-faced CEO and said, "You're obviously very busy. I struggle myself to keep up with all the news. I'm sorry if you felt we expected you to be across the latest stories."

He nodded and offered a conciliatory smile as he guided them toward the door. "I wish I could be more helpful."

"Just one more question, if you don't mind."

He stopped and gave her his full attention, confident that the interview was over.

Birgitte smiled warmly at him and asked, as if in passing, "How do you think Wan Bi will react when he hears the Federal Police are interested in possible connections between your company and the two murders we're investigating?" Tony quickly looked at Lao, whose cheeks had reddened slightly even if his face remained perfectly still.

"Wan Bi is as busy as I am. I have no reason to believe he is in any way concerned with what takes place in Australia."

"Really, Mr Lao? He strikes me as someone who would be very interested indeed."

The CEO stepped forward, inhaling deeply, as he chose his words. Before Tony could get between them, Lao was in Birgitte's face, crimson with anger. "I don't like what you are implying, Detective. I assure you I have a legal team that will make your life extremely difficult if you attempt to cause more trouble than you're worth."

Tony place his hand on Lao's chest and applied enough pressure to get the man's attention. He glared at Tony, held his ground to show that he could, then stepped back, breathing heavily through his nostrils. Tony couldn't tell if the guy had merely revealed he had a short fuse and contempt for women, or whether his reaction was evidence of his involvement in the murders. He held up a finger to Lao's face. "Do anything like that again and I'll be advising you to call your lawyer."

Lao moved away like a sullen gorilla. The maitre 'd came back into the room unannounced, which startled the CEO. He yelled at her in Mandarin so violently she flinched. His blood was up now and he was struggling to control his rage. He stood at the opposite side of the table and hurled abuse at Birgitte, but neither she nor Tony could understand a word he was saying. He was almost apoplectic with rage.

Tony turned to Birgitte, who stood calmly, taking it all in. When Lao had expended all his energy and was breathing heavily, she said, "Thank you again for your time, Mr Lao. We'll speak again if we have any further questions."

As they left the restaurant they could hear a plate smashing against a wall.

Down on the street Birgitte walked purposefully back towards the car. Tony struggled to keep up. "Do you intend sharing what just happened in there?"

She kept walking, deep in thought.

Tony called after her, "Who the hell is One Bee?"

She stopped and looked back up the street towards the restaurant. "Wan Bi is the Chairman of Shanghai Consolidated Holdings, one of the biggest state-owned mining companies in Asia, making him one of the most powerful mining figures in China. He is worth billions – 26.3 to be precise."

"Good for him," Tony said, still fired up by the altercation in the restaurant. "What's his connection to Captain Arrogance back there?"

"Wan Bi Lao is Xian Lao's uncle."

Tony scoffed in disbelief. "Jesus."

"I spent some of my time over the past 24 hours researching the global mining scene, too, trying to find out who the main players are, to put this local drama into some sort of context."

"And?"

"It would appear Xian Lao is keen to impress his family back in China. Perhaps he's trying to secure this deal to get Wan's attention, hoping his uncle will make some sort of investment, perhaps similar to the agreement struck in the north west of Australia. If there is as much gas as he's hoping in the Timor Sea, he'll need a lot of capital to access it."

"So he butters up the Northern Territory Minister for Trade, knocks out the competition and then bids for the rights, hoping his uncle will come to the party."

"Something like that."

"And you couldn't have told me any of that before we went in there?"

"I couldn't be certain," she said. "I wanted to see how he'd react. He appeared to be telling the truth up to that point."

"Do you think he's lying about the murders?"

"To be honest, I can't tell."

"Shit," Tony said, rubbing his face. "This is doing my head in. So where does that leave us in terms of James Freedmont?"

"Can you organise surveillance on Lao?"

"Based on what exactly?"

"What you just witnessed. Despite what he said, Xancorp will be in a position to bid for the deal if Katercorp and Barclay back out – that's motive."

"Based on that logic, we'd have to put surveillance on every CEO in the lobby group. I'm sorry, Birgitte, but a judge isn't going to authorise a warrant based on your intuition, as sound as it appears to me. We'll have to do some more research on both Xian and his uncle in the morning."

"Or we could see where he goes now?"

Tony checked his watch. It was past midnight. "Do you ever sleep?"

"That boy is being held and the only two people who are able to do anything about it are you and me."

Logic was telling him the boy was already dead, but Birgitte was right. If there was any chance of saving his life, it rested with the pair of them. "Stay here and keep an eye on the front of the restaurant and the entrance to that parking station next door. I'll head round to the back – there's an alternative entrance on Dixon Street. Call me if you see anything."

She nodded.

Tony paused. "There's a chance he's already left so let's give it one hour then call it a night. Okay?"

"Okay. And thanks, Tony."

He shrugged, knowing full well he never had a choice in the matter, then set off down a laneway towards Dixon Street.

They didn't have to wait long. Birgitte noticed a dark hire car emerge from the parking station. Lao was in the back. She called Tony and he came running back up the laneway. They followed the car out of Chinatown, around Darling Harbour to Star City Casino.

The watched Lao stride through the main hall, nodding to several croupiers as he made his way to the elevators. He emerged on the third floor and disappeared into a room for high-end baccarat players. They waited 20 minutes to see if anyone else they recognised arrived – it may have been a subtle way of meeting with his colleagues away from prying eyes. But aside from staff, nobody else entered the room or left.

"He could be in there all night," Tony said, looking at his watch. "It's 2.30am. Let's call it a night. I'll speak to a judge in the morning and see if we can swing some surveillance."

Birgitte offered him a tired smile. "Thanks, Tony. I'm sure something is going to come of this. I can feel it."

"I'm just glad you came back." He didn't realise how it sounded until the words were out and he was too damned wrecked to care.

The sound of the rushing river was soothing. Not quite the Madikwe, he mused, but at 4am he wouldn't have been standing by those banks if he valued his own life. The muddy brown water of the Darling River flowed past steadily. Occasionally the lights and distant rumble of a road train travelling along the highway into Bourke would disturb the pre-dawn stillness. He was a few kilometres out of town and parked deep into the bush. There was no chance of him being seen, but he paused in his work each time a truck passed because it hampered his senses.

He opened the back of the SUV. He was about to drag the refrigeration unit onto the ground, with the intention of dumping the boy's corpse, when his mobile bleated. He pulled it from his pocket and checked the message. It was from his client:

Your excessive behaviour has brought unnecessary attention on me and my company.

He considered the message carefully before responding.

Third parcel is on its way, as agreed.

He sent the text and rested the phone on the tray of the SUV. This wasn't the first client to get tetchy in the middle of a job. He drew out the keys to the lock on the fridge and looked over at the river. If he pushed the body out far enough, he had calculated it should float down and get snagged at the turn in the river on the outskirts of the town, where it would no doubt be found once the sun was up.

His phone bleated again.

Deal off. Police asking questions.

He started to type:

Deal is no longer yours to break. Send names of officers involved.

This time he waited for a response. The reply came through:

Detective Tony Kingsmill with the AFP, and a woman from Denmark, Detective Birgitte Vestergaard. She is the problem. Can't take the risk. You failed. Broke word. Promised no connections. Deal off. Don't contact again.

Zachary wrote back:

Police will be dealt with. Final instalment must be paid by COB tomorrow as agreed. There is no backing out of this deal.

"Silly little man," he thought, as he pushed the fridge back into the SUV and closed the door. He was disappointed he wouldn't be completing the job as originally planned, but it was time to consider the alternatives. He recalled one of the lessons his father had taught him early on – those who couldn't be made to comply could always be used to ensure that others did.

With this in mind, he went to the cabin of the SUV and drew out his laptop. Once online he opened a search engine and typed in three words:

"Detective Birgitte Vestergaard"

By the time he pulled the SUV back onto the highway there was a soft white glow on the horizon and he knew exactly what he needed to do.

CHAPTER TWELVE

Superintendent Miller sat across from Tony, in her full dress uniform, staring at him in disbelief. She was supposed to be preparing for an awards ceremony with the Premier of NSW, instead she had spent the first two hours of her Thursday morning dealing with a terse letter from the legal department of Xancorp threatening to sue the AFP for harassment. She'd called Tony into her office as soon as she'd spoken with the AFP's legal team.

"What the hell were you thinking?"

"Despite how it looks, Birgitte's definitely on to something," Tony said, trying to sound more awake than he felt. He was running on three hours' sleep. "The more I think about it, the more it all makes sense. Xian Lao is trying to impress his uncle in Shanghai. He's hired a contract killer to scare off the executives of the two majors so he can step in and win the deal."

"What she did was incredibly reckless. Jesus, she shouldn't even be here. I told you to take her to the airport."

"I did. She obviously had other ideas."

"Why did you even go with her to the restaurant in the first place?"

"She had a hunch about Xancorp's involvement. We were really just extending the questioning beyond the companies at that mining conference in Darwin because we'd hit a dead end. But I admit, it got a bit out of hand."

"I specifically told you not to pursue this line of investigation," Miller said. "Her actions could have set off a whole new train of developments that we don't have control of."

"Yeah, but without her, we'd still be none the wiser about any of this."

"That's beside the point. How many times have I told you to stay out of this? And whether you like it or not, I am your superior officer."

Commander Barton's soft, craggy face appeared in the doorway. He was tired-looking on the best of days but his eyes were sharp. It seemed the closer he got to retirement age the more engaged he became. He was also wearing his full dress uniform.

Miller slightly paled at the sight of him, hoping he hadn't overheard her desperate attempt at reining in her own staff. "Sir, there have been some developments in the Thostrup and Heysmith case."

He stepped into the office. "You'll have to remind me again."

He took a seat across from Tony. She spent the next 15 minutes walking him through what they knew so far with Tony filling in a few details where needed.

When she finished Barton turned to Tony. "So where to next?"

"We need to get a wire and surveillance on Xian Lao as soon as possible. He's bound to contact the killer, if he hasn't already done so. I don't think we can pull him in and access his computers as yet. Detective Vestergaard thinks the reason he might be so cool about it all is that he's given this contract killer free rein to do what he likes so long as it meets the brief – the less he knows of the details, the better. So he's right when he says he knows nothing about Hans Thostrup or Salina Heysmith, or the whereabouts of James Freedmont."

"And none of the executives at Katercorp or Barclay Industries admit that they are being targeted?"

"They're obviously terrified of what this killer can do to their families. I'm guessing that both companies will pull out of the deal in the days ahead, particularly when Freedmont turns up."

"You think he's dead?"

"It doesn't look good – it's been seven days."

"Surely we can pull in Lao based on the evidence so far?"

"It's really just a hunch. And if we're wrong about any of the details, he could slip through our fingers in court and Freedmont will have died in vain." He turned to Miller. "Have the local guys in Alice or Melbourne come up with anything new?"

"They're not convinced about the tape residue," she said.

"They're not convinced about the forensic evidence?" said Tony. "That's fucking ridiculous. We need to get everyone together and fill them in on Xian Lao."

Miller cut in, "Tony, we've discussed this."

"He's right," said Barton. "I'll organise a conference call with the heads of both the teams. Make sure Detective Vestergaard is available. I want her input on this."

He stood up and went to the window. "Form a task force, Carolyn, with whatever staff you have available. Tony, are you free to take charge of it?"

He looked at Miller who sat stone-faced, clearly aware of what was happening but unable to prevent it.

"I am," said Tony.

"Excellent. Keep me updated each day please. Thanks, Carolyn."

Barton strode out of the room.

"I'm not happy about any of this," she said to Tony.

"I understand that, but right now I really just want to find James Freedmont as quickly as possible. You can drag me over the coals when we're done."

She suddenly looked smaller in his eyes. As he stepped out of her office he realised that Birgitte had played it perfectly. Without her willingness to unsettle Lao, Commander Barton would never have seen the connections between the killings.

The conference call was organised for 3pm, Sydney time. Tony had managed to update Birgitte on developments as she arrived at Goulburn Street. He took her to Commander Barton's office. She was grateful that they were both being listened to by someone who was willing to move the investigation forward. She was introduced to the Commander and Superintendent Miller, both of whom had just returned from the awards ceremony. Miller made a pointed reference to Lao's harassment claim, but before she could make an issue of it Barton suggested it supported Birgitte's theory that he had something to hide.

They moved into the conference room where a large screen was set up against the wall at the far end of a mahogany boardroom table. A young IT staffer made two video calls via the keyboard and soon enough the screen was divided in two. Senior Sergeant Frankston was peering into his computer screen in Alice Springs, trying to adjust the brightness. He stood up and drew the blinds over the window that looked onto the main street. It looked like another blisteringly hot day in the Red Centre. Beside him, in a police station in Mildura, Senior Sergeant Braithwaite was sitting back at his desk with his arms crossed, clearly not happy with the arrangements. His office looked bare, grey and bureaucratic – not unlike the man himself, thought Tony. He had to remind himself to keep his cool when talking with these two. Barton's presence would keep them in line to a certain degree, but he wouldn't always be around to back Tony up.

The Commander got the ball rolling with general introductions. Aside from Tony, Birgitte and Miller, the rest of the investigative team had assembled round the table. Tony was adamant that Harris and Donleavy should be included. He trusted them both and knew that at least Harris was keen to impress. Donleavy was good for muscle if it was ever needed. They sat together in uniform at the far end of the table. There were three other Federal officers in civvies, whom Miller had selected. They were all young and inexperienced. Birgitte wondered if Miller was attempting to hobble their efforts intentionally. It was hardly a crack squad with collective experience. But Birgitte had faith that Tony would bring out their best.

Barton said, "I just want to start by thanking both Jack and Ron and their respective teams for their work to date. It's much appreciated, gentlemen."

They both nodded.

"The key thing at this stage is that James Freedmont is still missing and presumed alive until we know otherwise. The other thing is we have to keep a lid on the media. If Detective Vestergaard is correct, then this is going to get out of control as soon as the major outlets get wind of it."

"What exactly does Detective Vestergaard think is happening, Sir?" asked Braithwaite, making no attempt to hide the contempt in his voice.

Barton turned to Birgitte, but Tony interjected. "Mind if I take it from here?"

She nodded.

"Right, as far as our research can verify, the murders of Thostrup and Heysmith are linked to a potential off-shore mining deal in the Timor Sea. You may have been following it in the press. The Northern Territory Government approved the project earlier in the week. It will be worth billions to whoever lands the tender. The two main companies involved are Katercorp and Barclay Industries. Hans Thostrup was an old friend of Nils Brekman, the CEO of Katercorp," he said, addressing Frankston. He then looked at Braithwaite. "The woman found in Mildura was Salina Heysmith, a senior lawyer for Blake, Patterson & Walker, a firm that has been representing Katercorp for this deal."

Braithwaite looked unimpressed. Tony ignored him and delivered the rest of the summary to the room as a whole. "What we soon learned was that Heysmith was sexually involved with the lead counsel for Barclay Industries, a guy by the name of Jason Pender, so there may be a double connection, linking both firms. Since then, James Freedmont has gone missing. He's the 22-year-old friend of Tom Barclay, the son of Reginald Barclay, the CEO of Barclay Industries. We don't know specifically why these people have been targeted but we're confident it has something to do with the Timor Sea deal."

Frankston spoke up. "Why haven't you interviewed Brekman and Barclay?"

"We have, a couple of times, but at this stage they're all adamant they know nothing about any of this. Now I'd like to hand it over to Detective Vestergaard to explain the Lao connection because it was her nous that gave us the lead."

Birgitte said, "It occurred to me if Katercorp and Barclay Industries were being pressured to back away from the deal, we had to ask ourselves who would benefit. Detective

Kingsmill and I then started to look into the mining conference in Darwin that Heysmith and Pender attended before she was abducted. Most of the main mining companies in Australia sent representatives but there was a particular company who didn't attend, Xancorp. It's a new operation headed by a Chinese Australian gentleman called Xian Lao. He's a relatively small fish in Australia but his uncle, Wan Bi Lao, is one of the biggest mining figures in China. He is Chairman of a state-owned company called Shanghai Consolidated Holdings, which dwarfs any of the firms involved in Australia. We decided to talk with Xian Lao to see if he knew anything about Thostrup, Heysmith or Freedmont. His reaction was very telling. He denied knowing anything about the murders but lost his temper when it was suggested that his uncle wouldn't be impressed if he was connected in any way to these events."

"You threatened him?" asked Braithwaite flatly.

Miller looked at the camera with smug satisfaction. Tony wondered if the two bureaucrats had met.

Birgitte addressed the Commander. "I simply made him aware that if there was a connection, we were across it."

"To force his hand?"

"To give him the opportunity to reassess his position."

"Have you brought this Lao character in for questioning?" asked Braithwaite.

Barton thanked Birgitte for her summary. "Gentlemen, we are in the process of organising warrants to tap his phones, and access the computers in his office and home. We should have authorisation later today. What I want to start focusing on are the potential links between Thostrup's and Heysmith's murders. What do we know about both that can be used to get a picture of the killer ASAP. There's still a chance we could save James Freedmont if we work together."

Frankston looked uncomfortable. "Most of my resources are tied up with a sting operation that is set for dawn tomorrow morning."

"Who are you attempting to sting, Ron?" Barton asked with a hint of irritation.

"The Phoenix Rising bikie gang. We believe they may have been attempting to extort money from Thostrup."

"Bin it. Work with Braithwaite on this, please. And use all your resources."

He went to protest but Braithwaite cut in. "I'm not convinced the two murders are connected. You said yourself that Thostrup hadn't been here since the 70s and basically had nothing to do with Katercorp."

Tony stood up and peered directly into the camera so Braithwaite would be under no illusion as to who he was talking to. "We sent you and your team the forensic reports from both Alice Springs and Melbourne. The same electrical tape was used on both victims. That's proof enough. The MOs may be completely bizarre but there are strong similarities that can't be ignored: both victims were fed to wild animals and dumped interstate."

"At this stage," said Barton, "these are the strongest leads we have and I want you to pursue them without interruption."

Birgitte tried to get the conversation back on track. "We're looking for a male who drives an SUV or a van large enough to hold a refrigeration unit for transporting the bodies. He's obviously comfortable around sharks and crocodiles and is fairly brazen in his approach, but confident enough to be unnoticeable as he drives across the country with a dead body in his car."

Harris put her hand up. "Do we think Freedmont has already been fed to an animal?"

"If he hadn't before Detective Vestergaard harassed Xian Lao," said Miller, "he probably has now."

"That's crap, Carolyn," said Tony. "To be brutally honest, chances are James Freedmont is already dead. The first two victims were killed within 48 hours of being abducted, but we can't lose hope. If for whatever reason, he is still alive, we have a chance to save him."

She stared him down but chose not to pull him up in front of the Commander for not using her full title.

Barton stood up. "Okay, we know what we're doing?"

Everyone nodded.

"Detective Kingsmill is in charge. Any problems, go through him, he'll come to me if it's warranted. Got it?"

Again, they nodded. Braithwaite reached forward and severed the call, while Frankston fumbled with his keyboard, muttering under his breath. Eventually the screen in the conference room went blank.

Barton moved around the table to Birgitte. "I can't thank you enough for your input on this."

She smiled. "I appreciate the chance to work with you. And honestly, I couldn't have done any of it without Detective Kingsmill's hard work."

"I'm confident he'll bring this to a satisfactory conclusion. Given the amount of experienced officers involved and the egos, it might be best at this stage if you pull back a little. Perhaps Tony can update you at the end of each day."

"I understand."

"And of course, if anything occurs to you that might help the investigation, be sure to get in touch immediately."

"I will. Thank you."

She liked Commander Barton. He reminded her of Sven. She was relieved that common sense was finally prevailing. And although she was concerned for Freedmont's safety, she was realistic enough to know there was little they could do for him. The most important thing was getting as much information as they could on the killer before he struck again.

Westlake stared out of his hotel window down onto the afternoon traffic in the city below, thinking about the footage he'd been sent the day before. He had to admit, he was horrified at first; it would be inhuman not to be. He sipped on his scotch as he remembered having no idea what to expect from the movie file before he opened it – certainly not footage of an execution. As violent as it was, it made for compelling viewing. When that Federal officer, Kingsmill, turned up again shortly after, it only compounded the situation. It hadn't taken Westlake long to work out the identity of the man in the clip, nor what was expected of himself. What bothered him more than anything was not knowing who was behind it all. It couldn't be Pender – the guy simply didn't have it in him, but he had hoped he might know something, which was why he'd arranged to meet him in the Botanical Gardens as soon as he'd got rid of Kingsmill. Their meeting in the park had proved fruitless. Of course, when Pender contacted him later that day to say that he'd received a similar clip, only his was of Salina Heysmith, he realised they were both being played by a third party – someone very clever indeed. Pender was a mess by that point – terrified for his own safety, tortured with guilt for his involvement with Heysmith, and frightened for his family – typically, in that order. He was a soft target, as Westlake had always known. But why would anyone consider himself a soft target? Extortion was a simple game – find a target who may disrupt your plans, make a credible threat to eliminate their involvement, get on with your plans. As threats went, these were spectacular. Pender was babbling something about a crocodile – Westlake found himself admiring the killer for his inventiveness and audacity. At least Heysmith wouldn't be plagued by her demons anymore. So someone wanted Katercorp and Barclay Industries out of the tender process. Fair enough. He wondered if anyone from any other mining companies had received clips recently in order to eliminate them from the list of possible extortionists.

He poured himself another drink and considered his options. Backing off from the tender process was one he didn't care for from the outset. Finding the paymaster and making a deal that would work in both their favours was a possibility. As was finding the killer and doing the same. It was a hell of a risk but he was confident so long as he could enter negotiations he could get the upper hand. The first thing he had to do was send a clear message that Katercorp would continue with the tender, that way the extortionist would be forced to up the ante and perhaps contact him directly. Pender's blubbering would only work in his favour. With the Freedmont boy still missing, there was a good chance that Barclay Industries were receiving a double threat. The chances of them playing hardball were close to zero, which meant the extortionist would have little reason to panic; they'd just have to apply more pressure on him. He didn't care how dangerous it was so long as he was in the position of forcing someone's hand not the other way around.

But he wasn't stupid. He had sent a wire to Brekman stating he was going offline for a few days for personal reasons. Brekman knew well enough not to pry. Westlake had given instructions at the office to continue organising the tender. He then reached out to a guy he knew who could delete any trace of the movie file from both his laptop and his email account without asking any questions. It wasn't cheap but it was necessary. Then he booked himself into a different hotel each night, paying cash. It was now simply a matter of time.

Tony went to work on Friday with a new lease on life. He felt that all the resources at his disposal were working efficiently. He arrived at Goulburn Street to the news that the taps on Lao's phones had been authorised and a Mandarin-speaking officer was dedicated to translating every conversation as it happened. By mid-morning they'd learned that Lao had a penchant for Korean prostitutes and considerable passion for high stakes gambling. But there was no discussion about the Timor Sea deal or any hits put out on competitors. Tony wasn't surprised by this. Birgitte had suggested that Lao probably used a private, secure mobile and possibly another laptop for his shadier business dealings. If Lao still intended to bid for the Timor Sea licence, he would obviously wait for confirmation that Katercorp and Barclay Industries had both backed out before making a move.

As yet none of the CCTV footage from Alice Springs, Adelaide or Mildura had turned up anything definitive. They had pulled the plate numbers of several SUVs and utility vans but had come up with false leads each time. There was a chance the killer was changing vehicles every few days which would complicate the investigation further. What Tony really wanted to know was how much Lao was paying for the job. It would give him some indication of the resources the killer had to hand. Could he afford to change cars repeatedly? Did he have hi-tech equipment? Did he own the boat that was used to murder Thostrup? All of which suggested that somewhere along the way he was leaving a footprint, some evidence of his identity, anything that would give Tony the upper hand.

What did surprise him was how well they had kept the media at bay so far. Thostrup's murder had hit the headlines the previous weekend. It was reported as a murder of a Danish national but no cause of death was released. So far it hadn't broken in Denmark either. Heysmith's murder also received limited coverage because her identity was kept a secret. Dead bodies don't always turn up in the Murray River but without many details the journalists were at a loss for what to report. Freedmont was making press as a missing person – his parents had made several public appeals for him to come home – but no connections had been drawn to any of the mining companies linked to the Timor Sea deal. Now that the Northern Territory Government had given the green light, political and business commentators were devoting quite a few column inches to the possible players and potential ramifications of the deal to the economy, the environment and the cultural heritage of Arnhem Land. Tony prayed that he would get a few more days reprieve before the it all went to hell. He'd had a hard enough time from the media when he was working on the Middle Eastern Task Force. The fourth estate was a necessary evil that was beyond his control.

The clouds were swirling and would inevitably break but so far so good.

As soon as he could secure the warrants for Lao's computers he would descend on that creep's office like a force of nature. But until then he had no choice but to wait as his team continued to compile evidence and gather possible leads. Occasionally he'd look up from his desk to see Miller in her office talking on the phone or angrily writing emails. He knew this was his one and only opportunity to make a positive impression on Commander Barton. If it didn't go well, he would definitely be transferred into obscurity.

For several moments Birgitte was lost in the landscape – a vast expanse of desert, barely scattered with trees, a scene void of a horizon, burnt ochre that warbled and buckled in the heat. It was mesmerising. The isolation. The oppressive heat. A horrid place to die.

A voice over announced to gallery visitors that a guided tour of the permanent collection would be starting from the information desk in a few moments. Birgitte stepped back from the enormous abstract painting and looked about the main court of the Art Gallery of New South Wales. She had left her room at the East Wind a few hours ago, unable to sit still but equally unable to switch off from the case. Despite valuing her input, Tony had agreed it would be best if she stayed clear at this stage. He'd promised to update her each evening and discuss any relevant developments with her as they arose. She had already called Sven from the airport on Wednesday and told him that she had decided to take some annual leave, then lied to Miller that she had Augerson's approval for an extension. She could only hope that Miller would make no attempts to contact him directly.

She had decided to do at least one touristy thing while she was in Australia. She remembered enjoying the Gallery on her first visit there 20 years ago. There was reassuring sense of the familiar as she crossed the lawn of The Domain, beneath the swollen limbs of the Moreton Bay fig trees that lined the park and looked on to the monumental stone facade of the Gallery. It reeked of 19th-century pomposity but had since taken on a life of its own as a valued cultural institution. Banners for a Picasso exhibition hung between the fluted columns. She had walked into the cool air of the main court and as much as she loved Picasso's work decided to avoid the crowds and explore the 19th- and 20th-century Australian collection. As she wandered past paintings of remote country towns, mining sites and bleak but beautiful arid landscapes she couldn't stop thinking about James Freedmont, a young man who was caught up in a ridiculous game of big business. Did he even know why he had been abducted? Would it make his situation any easier to handle? She had stopped at Fred Williams' The Yang Yangs. It reminded her of the view from the plane as she and Tony had flown from Adelaide to Alice Springs.

She thought of Constable Smith, doing the rounds of a remote community when she received the call that a body had been found near Harley's Bridge. Why was she there? A domestic dispute, she had said. A domestic dispute that had never eventuated. The boy who found the body, Cody Dunbar. He always skipped school to play football in the creek. The killer knew that the body would be found within 12 to 24 hours. Salina Heysmith. Her feet sticking out of the Murray River at mid tide. The killer knew that The Eureka did its first run at about that time. If the captain hadn't spotted the feet protruding from the waterline, one of his passengers would have soon enough. Again, the killer knew that the body would be found within 12 to 24 hours. But what was the significance? Was it just to give him more time to get further away? He could have hidden the bodies more thoroughly. He was dumping them in remote enough places – he could have buried them anywhere. They were staged but not so obviously that their corpses could make a big enough statement to their intended viewers. The people he was trying to scare wouldn't even get to see the bodies and it might be weeks before they were told how they died, so why go to so much trouble? As the horrible realisation occurred to her, her phone bleated in her handbag. It was a text from an unknown number.

Howdy, Stranger. I heard you were in town. Fancy catching up with an old face? Daniel Hattersly.

Birgitte was baffled. She hadn't spoken to Daniel in several years. They had met on her first trip to Australia and vaguely stayed in touch over the years. She never regretted sleeping with him and was glad he made the effort to remain friends over such a long distance but she also knew he had always wanted to pursue a more meaningful relationship with her if he had the chance. It had never occurred to her to call him while she was in Australia. She toyed with the idea of ignoring the text but then thought that it might be nice to have a familiar face to talk to, one that wasn't connected with the case. She began to type:

Hey there, Daniel. In Australia on business. Flying out soon. When would you like to meet up?

She sent the text and continued through the Gallery. He responded almost immediately. She could almost sense the eagerness in his typing.

Tomorrow okay? I can book a table at Sebastian's Restaurant in Chowder Bay for 1pm, if that works for you?

She replied that it was and he sent her the address details. It was a restaurant on the north side of Sydney Harbour. She opened the link to the website which showed views of a pretty beach lined with a sandstone wall that extended from a tree-lined headland. It looked very similar to some of the paintings she had seen in the 19th-century gallery. The thought of catching up with Daniel pleased her, but the feeling only lasted momentarily. She tried to call Tony to explain her theory but only got his voice mail. She left him a message to call her when he had a chance.

"He's filming them," she said.

It was 8pm on Friday night. Tony had just arrived at her hotel room, his face was sagging with fatigue. He had spent the past two days trying to process the minutia of three cases consecutively. All the while knowing that a young man's life was possibly being held in the balance. He refused to accept that James Freedmont might already be dead. Birgitte's theory was almost enough to tip him over the edge.

"What for?"

"Think about it," she said. "Why do you think Westlake and Pender both changed so dramatically within 24 hours?"

"I have no idea."

"Were they both at their computers when it happened?"

Tony tried to remember. His mind was a jumble of tiny details, images of dead bodies, crime scenes. He eventually replayed in his mind his meetings with both men. "Westlake was in his office, not wanting to talk to anyone. And Pender went into his home office to take a phone call. He was at his laptop. I could see him through the door."

"Then there is a chance that the killer had sent them footage of the actual killings with some sort of note warning them off putting in a tender." Birgitte stood up and began to move around him like an American lawyer trying to convince a jury of her version of events. "There was no point in sending the footage any sooner. They were all waiting on the Northern Territory Government to give the green light on the deal. Once it came through, Lao could start pushing to get Katercorp and Barclay Industries out of the picture. It makes perfectly good sense."

"It's still only a theory."

"Are you able to requisition their laptops?"

"At the very least we can call them in for questioning as soon as we can reach them."

"We need to contact the CEO of Barclay Industries – is it Reginald Barclay? – and see if he's received messages on his office or home computer."

"Good idea."

Tony sat back in the arm chair by the window and rubbed his face. "This is doing my head in. It's one thing to be frustrated with the pace of an investigation. It's another to be thrust into the hot seat with no warning."

"You're doing fine," Birgitte said.

"Thanks for the support, but most of the time I feel like I'm flying blind."

"You're ensuring all the detectives involved stay on the right path and that is what a good lead detective does, Tony, use your resources. This may not be what you want to do in the long run but it is an incredible opportunity."

He looked up at her. "I feel stupid for judging Miller for being promoted on a whim, when my career could be enhanced because I happened to be given the job of being your liaison."

"Perhaps both of you deserve to move ahead for different reasons. Just don't let it rattle you. Stay focused."

He nodded and smiled. "How did you get to be so sage?"

"I've got plenty of scars for my trouble, believe me."

"Seriously. You have a much better handle on the office politics."

"My father was a diplomat. It runs in the family. If anything, I've always felt like I'm constantly having to prove myself to him and everyone else. It gets exhausting after a while."

"I think I've done a good job of keeping myself out of it – to the detriment of my career, but sometimes it just seems to find me anyway."

"Maybe it's time to stop running from it." She looked away from him because the statement made her think about her approach to the whole Max Anders horror show, her failed marriage and her own atrophying career.

"Are you okay?" Tony asked when she hadn't said anything for several moments.

She smiled. "I think the saying is 'Do as I say, not as I do'."

"I was kind of hoping we'd have at least one night, while you are still in Australia, where we could talk about anything but the case."

"I'd like that. Do you think it's possible?"

They both laughed.

She looked at her watch then opened the directory beside on her bedside table. "How does a bottle of cabernet sauvignon from the Margaret River sound?"

"As if it was made for forgetting our jobs."

She called reception and ordered an antipasto plate and the bottle of wine. When she hung up she opened the doors onto a small terrace that overlooked Circular Quay and the harbour. Tony hadn't even noticed that she had been upgraded to an executive suite on her return visit.

"Do you remember our friend the Head Concierge?" she asked.

"Really? He does like you."

They stepped out into the cool night air. There were two faux-wicker armchairs either side of a low glass table. Below them the lights of the city bowed around the edge of the Quay

236

and reflected off the black surface of the water as ferries bobbed about on the edges of the finger wharves. It was peaceful, serene. They stood in silence for several minutes. Tony took a seat and crossed one leg over the other knee. It was the first time she'd seen him relax in several days.

"I could get used to this," he said.

The wine and the platter arrived 20 minutes later. The hotel staff brought it out on to the balcony for them and wished them a good night. Tony opened the wine and poured two glasses. Birgitte sat beside him and sighed contentedly.

"You don't mention your family much," Birgitte said. "What are they like?"

Tony told Birgitte about his father, who had started a construction business back in the 60s with his two younger brothers. He was very much the self-made man, humble but hardworking, but he also was quick to point out his father wouldn't have been half as successful as he was without Tony's mother. Birgitte listened quietly, impressed by the warmth and high regard he felt for his parents. He described his mother as a strong woman who had held the family together through their fair share of personal dramas. One of his uncles had a drinking problem, the other had a thing for the pokies and had almost sent the family business under. He shared a few stories of how she had no fear going toe to toe with the men of the house, which made Birgitte laugh and think of her own mother.

Tony became a little distant when he mentioned his mother passing from cancer when he was still at high school. She had high hopes he would go to university and study economics but he had struggled through those years without her. The thought of working for his father made his head ache – they were both too pig-headed to work together – so he ended up at the Police Academy. His father had slowly closed down over the years, never really got over the loss of his wife. He eventually sold his business to Tony's uncle, who was by then in recovery, and he retired. Tony said he visits him when he can but he could be a difficult SOB when it suits him.

"Does he know about Hana?"

Tony shook his head. "I'm pretty sure he thinks I'm gay."

"Not possible."

He laughed at this. "My father isn't one to ask questions about my love life. That being said, if he knew I was working with you, he'd be nudging me in the ribs every five minutes, telling me to ask you out."

"And your mother?"

He looked at her with a mistrusting grin. "What's with all the questions? Feel like I'm in an interview room."

She shrugged and gave him a sideward glance. "Just want to get to know the man behind the gruff exterior."

"Gruff?"

"You can be a little grumpy."

"Thought I was being charming and mysterious. What about your family then?"

"As you know, my father was diplomat, and like you, he wanted me to follow in his footsteps. My mother met him at a point in her career when she could have gone on to achieve great things, but she chose to support him instead and raise a family."

"What was she doing when they met?"

"She was developing policies for Denmark's Department of Foreign Affairs."

"Clever lady."

"In some ways she's smarter than my father, but we don't let on."

"Did she adjust to married life and being a mother?"

"Surprisingly well, it would seem. She even enjoyed the travel. By the time I was 16 I'd lived in four different countries and attend six different schools. I think one of the reasons I've enjoyed being in the police is it makes me feel grounded."

"How was she with your choice to become an officer of the law instead of an arbiter?"

"Again, I expected more of a fight, but she knew my mind was made up when I announced it, so she sensibly got on board and did her level best to make my father understand, which wasn't entirely successful."

"I'd love to meet your father and tell him what an amazing detective you've turned out to be."

She smiled at this and said, "Thank you, that's very sweet."

"Seriously. You have a way of seeing things that is almost unnatural... I mean it's a talent. It's been incredible to watch you work."

"You've been watching me?" She arched one eyebrow and stared into his eyes, challenging him to take another step towards her.

"When I first saw you, in the lobby downstairs, I was convinced you couldn't be the detective I was waiting for."

"Why not?"

"Too hot. You looked smoking as you came out of that elevator..."

Before he could spoil the moment any more with his teenage observations she reached across and kissed him on the lips. He tried to keep talking so she kept kissing him harder, running her hand across his chest, something she had wanted to do from the first moment she had seen him in the lobby that morning. The laughed as they kissed and in her efforts to sit on his lap they both fell off the chair in a fit of laughter. Maybe it wasn't so bad being a bit of a teenager after all.

He lowered the boy's corpse into the water. The channel markers further out glowed red and green, casting thin lines of colour across the blackness. The moon, now sitting low in the night sky, was concealed behind clouds, enabling him to work at a reasonable pace without being seen from the shore. The water was warmer than the chill night air.

He stared at the boy's face as it sat up out of the darkness. The brilliant blue eyes once filled with hope and promise now stared into a different world. There was no pain. No anxiety. He brushed his fingers across the boy's cheek, across the sun-ravaged skin. He saw himself in the reflection of glassy dead eyes. It stirred in him fresh awareness of his own youth. As he ran his thumb slowly across the boy's cracked lips he was overwhelmed by memories of who he once was.

South Africa was a maelstrom of violence back then. Through a teenager's eyes his father was simply maintaining a semblance of order in an animalistic society. With the killing of the cripple he knew he had reached an age when it was time for him to contribute, to do all that he could to ensure the order of things was not turned on its head. It steadily evolved into an apprenticeship of sorts. His father was providing an education in power. Brutal though it was, it was a language he understood and quickly became fluent in.

But as Zachary became more adept at his father's ways he soon came to realise the old man's actions were only ever an end in themselves. He was satisfied to lord it over the villages around Rustenburg, where the idea of the Captain contained almost as much power as the man himself. Zachary suddenly became aware of an earlier time when his father had appeared simply too much of a giant for a child to comprehend his actual size. But as the edges of his being came into focus so too did the scale of his stature begin to diminish in Zachary's eyes.

Questions had begun to occur to him he knew his father couldn't answer, such as what came next? His father had assumed Zachary would join the police academy, work his way up through the ranks then work alongside him. But the laws he was supposedly enforcing made no sense in themselves, as Zachary had only ever known how to live beyond them; that was where real power lay. The thought of living out a pale parody of his father's life in Rustenburg repulsed him. He wanted more. But, thanks to his father, he was only good for one thing – killing. Exceeding his father's abilities wasn't enough to extinguish the fire already burning inside.

When the subject was first broached, in the back room of a mechanic shop on the edge of town, it wasn't raised by Zachary, although the thought had occurred to him on more than one occasion. The untidy group of local merchants, who stank of fear and cheap labour, hadn't come to him to appeal to his sense of compassion, nor even to reason with him. By that stage his reputation was rapidly becoming as fearsome as his father's. But a few of the more astute merchants had noticed particular differences in the two men. Where the Captain was driven by rage and malice, and could lash out without warning, punishing anyone within striking distance; his son was more measured, calculating. One of the men had referred to him as a dead soul. The reckoning would come, but the damage was controlled with meticulous efficiency, and once committed, nothing could disturb him from his course. They also realised he possessed a keener business mind than his father and would respond to financial incentives.

He had been surprised at first at the sum they had mentioned. Then mistrusting. How could they possibly get that sort of money? But once he had seen they were good for it, what did it matter to him where the money had come from? It was more than enough to get him out of Rustenburg, to get him started in a new life, on his own terms. What was already his desire became a binding clause in their agreement. He had to leave and never come back.

Zachary learned a lot from his first contract killing: the importance of research, planning, timing, the need to be flexible enough to incorporate last-minute changes. It was by no means a perfect execution but it had served his ends admirably.

He had waited in his room for most of the evening, occasionally drawing out the thick wad of notes from under his bed – the first instalment. The second half would come on completion of the job. While his mind was completely calm, rational and prepared, his subconscious was swirling wildly. He would need to learn to control this aspect of his nature if he was to succeed.

He heard the latch on the front gate. It slammed shut. There was a pause before the sound of heavy footsteps scraped across the boards of the verandah. The old man was already drunk. That could be a good thing or an unwanted element. Zachary couldn't tell at this stage. The tumbler in the lock turned and the door was thrown open against the wall. He'd obviously had more than a few. Zachary waited. His father's usual routine on nights like these was to go to the pantry in the

241

kitchen, pull out a bottle of scotch and then retire to his armchair in front of the TV.

He could hear the pantry door, the clinking of glassware, muttering. The TV was turned on and the springs in the armchair gave way as the Captain fell back heavily, spilling part of his drink as he landed.

"That you, Boy?" He peered into the darkness of the living room back towards the hallway to the bedrooms.

Zachary emerged from his room, determined, resolute, calm.

His father peered in his direction, trying to focus. What he saw he didn't like – a distorted version of himself, a constant reminder of the woman who had rejected him. There was something missing from the boy. Didn't know what. There had been times when he wished for the boy to become everything he was, but now he wasn't even sure he wanted him to join the police. He didn't need a reflection of himself, a reminder of his shortcomings haunting him, smearing his good name in front of his colleagues. Perhaps they'd both be better off if he enlisted in the army.

He'd spent the evening in a bar with an old colleague from his security forces days who was now a military officer. He sounded him out about placing the boy, suggesting that he was good with his hands and completely without fear. But he was still a little soft if the Colonel knew what he meant. The Colonel had nodded and promised to look into it.

"We'll make a man of you yet, Boy," he muttered into his scotch.

Zachary took a seat in the armchair set at an angle to his father's. His old man was dressed in his uniform but he had shrunk inside of it. His gun belt lay across the coffee table at his knees. He had aged considerably these past two years. His skin was sagging on his jowls, his eyes were becoming cloudy. It was possibly the drink, but it was also time. His father couldn't stop time and it was beginning to kill him in daily increments. Zachary considered for a moment what it would be like to watch the old man die slowly, over many years.

Would that have been a crueller demise? More satisfying perhaps?

"Spoke to the Colonel," he spluttered. "He's good for it. We'll get you sorted."

Zachary had no idea what he was talking about and no longer cared.

"I'll never be the man you are."

His father leered at this. "That's the truth. Too much of your mother in you."

It was a tired old criticism the old man always wheeled out when he was onto his second bottle of whiskey. Zachary knew nothing of his mother, so it was private joke that the Captain pretended to share with her at his expense.

"She must have been some lady," Zachary said slowly.

"What's that, Boy? Are you trying to be smart?"

Zachary stood up and went into the kitchen. His old man twisted in his chair, watching him carefully. He didn't like the boy's attitude. There was something about him that was alerting his senses but he was too drunk to respond to the signals flickering through his addled brain. He realised the boy was just getting himself a glass of water. There was nothing to worry about. He settled back into his seat. Perhaps it was time they had a chat, as men.

"Scotch, Boy?" he called out over his shoulder.

"Not tonight, Old Man."

"Where are your manners, Boy?" he snapped.

"No, thank you," Zachary replied.

He picked up a stool from the kitchen and placed it quietly behind his father's armchair. Without a sound he stood on it and reached up to the rafters where a rope was tied and lain lengthways along the strongest beam. The end of the rope formed a neat noose, a knot his father had taught him how to tie when he was only 12. Back then he'd practiced it on stray dogs, listening like a safe-cracker for the moment when the neck would snap.

In one swift, silent movement, he stepped down from the stool, threw the noose around his father's neck and tightened the knot against the back of his head. Before the Captain had realised what his son was doing, he could feel himself being lifted up over the back of the armchair. Zachary had the other end of the rope and was hauling his father into the air. The old man swung past the chair, his arms flailing, his legs kicking erratically. Zachary slid the stool to one side with his foot then climbed up and tied the rope off around the beam.

He stepped down and stood back to admire his handy work. He had expected the crack to be louder, more telling in its finality, but the twitching of the old man's limbs signalled the job was done efficiently. The minutes passed slowly, steadily. Eventually his father's tongue protruded between his teeth and his eyes bulged almost from their sockets. As the old man shuddered and spun, he shat his pants. His final statement to the world. Zachary felt nothing, but knew it was time to leave.

He placed the stool underneath the swinging feet then tipped it on its side. He ran from the house, jumped the back fence and made his way across the fields to the outskirts of town. Twenty minutes later he was at the back of the mechanic shop where the contract had first been discussed. Two of the shopkeepers were waiting for him.

"It's done," he said.

They looked at him nervously.

"It's done, I tell you. Check for yourself."

They looked at one another, uncertain how to proceed.

"Meet back here in an hour. And bring what you owe me."

The two men ran back towards his house. He kept himself out of sight for the next hour. Close to 1am they ran back into the shop.

Out of breath, the taller of the two, pulled a wad of notes from his pocket and handed them to Zachary.

"Who was the man in the car?" the other man asked, looking about into the darkness outside, frightened that they would be seen together.

"What man?" asked Zachary coolly.

"In the car at the back of the house."

Zachary grinned. "You wanted me to disappear, didn't you?"

The two men backed away from Zachary, the fear on their face growing every second. Zachary laughed.

"He's nobody, an itinerant worker I found in Jo'burg. No one will miss him for a year or two. And by the time I'm done with him my father's colleagues will be convinced it was me in the car, and the only bullet they'll find is from the gun of my grief-stricken father. The old man wasn't completely without redeeming qualities you know. Frankly, I've done him a service, although he probably would have hated me even for that."

They shook their heads then realised that their dealings with someone they could never understand were complete so they wrapped up the meeting, shut the shop and set off hurriedly in different directions as they'd previously agreed.

He ran back to the house, doused the car at the rear of the property in petrol and lit it. The faceless body in the front passenger seat was consumed by flames within less than a minute. And with that Zachary de Graff was dead. What remained was a non-descript young man devoid of identity – without his original name he couldn't be defined, associated or known. He had finally become the ghost he needed to be.

He was well across the field when the tank exploded. The house was far enough from any neighbouring property that it would be the glow of the flames that would alert them rather than the explosion. It would give him enough time to get to the car he'd stored on the other side of town.

For the next two years he lived in Zimbabwe, under different names, working as an enforcer of sorts for rich white farmers frightened of being expelled from "their" land. He learned to terrorise the local black population by turning their violence against them in ways that shocked the most hardened gang leaders. The chaos, although different, was certainly familiar. No one ever asked about his background and no connection was ever made with the suicide of the Captain back in Rustenburg, whose reputation as a psychotic killer had been sealed with the murder of his own son.

By the time the order of things in Zimbabwe collapsed, as he knew it would, he'd earned enough money to move on.

Soon enough he was travelling the continent, providing services few people were willing to perform. He developed his own philosophy of survival, drawn from what he had experienced growing up and his more recent misreadings of Nietzsche. It fed his twisted understanding the will to power and the limitations of morality. With the advent of the internet he was able to disappear, remove himself from the grid, existing only through VPN-protected sites, paid in cryptocurrency. His income increased 10-fold as he began to work internationally, which allowed him to extend his network of forged papers and set up hi-tech safe houses in several key cities. He felt invisible and omniscient.

It wasn't often he would recall his last night in Rustenburg, the first contract that set him on a path to being a willing executioner. Now, staring at the young man in his arms, he realised that had been a turning point. As he bent to kiss the lips, the clouds that had swirled on the periphery of his mind since that crucial night began to gather around him again. It came in the form of doubts when he felt that his greatest achievements had been that of his father all along. The resentment welled up within him, a blinding storm that suddenly consumed him. He bit into the lips of the boy and tore them from his face. His heart beat so fast and his blood rushed around his limbs in a torrent of energy that threatened to overwhelm him. He breathed heavily through his nose and closed his eyes. After a few moments, his mind calmed. He spat the refuse into the water, then slowly pushed the body ahead of him, deeper into the darkness.

CHAPTER THIRTEEN

Tony had barely slept. Birgitte lay beside him in her hotel bed. The sheet had fallen from her body. He wanted to touch her without waking her. The warmth that came off her body was melting his resolve. He pulled the sheet over her and carefully slipped out of bed. He stood by the window looking down on Circular Quay. Behind him were three empty bottles of wine and two glasses. What started as a research session had ended with them in the shower, on the bed, across the armchair, up against the window, on the desk and eventually back in the bed. He hadn't done anything like that in as long as he cared to remember. He expected to be troubled with remorse or guilt over Hana, but instead he was just savouring the memories of the night before that were flitting though his mind. He also hoped it wouldn't complicate the working relationship – there was too much at stake. He trusted Birgitte to be professional to the end.

The sun had just risen over Macquarie Street but, as it was Saturday, the city was yet to wake up. Tony dressed quietly and gathered his things. He considered kissing her forehead before leaving but decided to let her sleep. He slipped out the door with barely a sound.

As the latch clicked shut, Birgitte rolled over with a contented smile on her face. She felt well taken care of and well rested. Her mind was clearer than the night before. Tony had proved to a be a bit of a dark horse, a pleasant surprise for someone who seemed so tightly wired at times. Maybe it was a front. Men were such strange creatures.

She slipped out of bed and took a long hot shower. She savoured the memory of him pushing her against the tiles, having torn off her clothes with a hunger that alarmed and aroused her. He teased her with his cock at first, for longer than she normally would have liked considering how eager the rest of his body was to proceed. But he obviously felt he knew how to read her, which she liked. When he eventually pushed his way inside her she had felt her feet lift slightly off the ground. He had moved so smoothly and powerfully that she thought she might come all too quickly but he suddenly withdrew and teased her with his fingers. The memory was exciting her again. She turned off the water, stepped out of the shower and began to dry herself with the only dry bath sheet. The others were strewn all over the hotel room.

A few hours later Birgitte sat in the back of a taxi as it drove over the Sydney Harbour Bridge. It felt good to be meeting up with Daniel Hattersly for lunch. It brought back memories of her backpacking days, when she was young, confident, curious, but in hindsight, ridiculously naive. She had kept her wits about her on the road, and her eyes open, as any young woman travelling alone would, but she lacked the deeper understanding of the human mind and the tensions that bristled within any society that would come with her time on the Force. She envied her younger self for all that naivety. As she noticed her own reflection in the window, she wondered if Daniel would see much of a difference. She took a tube of lipstick out of her bag and holding a hand mirror up, applied a neat line of colour. Of course, she felt she no longer possessed the lithe body that had once turned so many boy's heads, despite what Tony had said the previous night, and the skin around her eyes was beginning to resemble the photos of her own mother in her 40s. She chided herself for her vanity. It was just nice to catch up with an old friend while overseas.

The taxi pulled off the expressway and headed east along Military Road, the arterial road that cut through the North Shore towards Middle Head. Birgitte did her best not to think about the case. She was glad Tony was in charge, and was therefore satisfied her input had been acknowledged. She thought about their night together. It was wonderful and passionate and heartfelt, but deep down she wasn't ready for the complications that often come with even a casual liaison – the use of the word made her smile. It wasn't what Sven had had in mind when he sent her to Australia. As much as she enjoyed the thought of Tony's loving, she couldn't bear the weight of any emotional need he may feel, nor her own hurt if he didn't feel anything at all. It was one night and that was all she wanted.

For the first time in months she thought of Jurgen and wondered how he was getting on. Was he still with his wife and kids? Had it all worked out for the best as he hoped it would? Theirs had been an affair of physical and psychological need, both alienated from the own partners, set adrift from all they knew by circumstances neither of them had control over. Or at least that is what they had convinced themselves at the time. She wasn't proud of the fact, but nor would she take back any of the precious days and nights she had shared with him. Tomas had every reason to despise her for this, but he had been part of the problem.

As the cab drove up over the crest of the middle of three headlands at the mouth of Sydney Harbour, Birgitte realised that it was time to stop blaming Max Anders for everything that had gone wrong in her life these past two years. He may have created an unbearable situation in her career that tested her resolve to breaking point, but he hadn't controlled her behaviour. She had made choices that impacted on her own situation as dramatically as Anders had.

She paid the driver and stepped out of the taxi into the warm summer air. She didn't know at what point her relationship with Tomas had begun to crumble nor who was responsible, but it had and she had reacted in a way that would ensure its demise, perhaps subconsciously, perhaps not. But it was over now. And for once she was okay with it.

Sebastian's Restaurant was housed in a former military mess hall that overlooked Chowder Bay. The sandstone walls caught the midday light and the gabled roof harked back to the 19th century. Birgitte was greeted at the door by a young female maitre d' in a crisp white shirt and striped tie. Birgitte explained she was meeting a friend for lunch and she was led out on to a wide terrace of wooden boards and glass railings. The tables, covered in white cloth, were mostly empty and there was no sign of Daniel. The maitre'd pulled out a chair at what must have been the most coveted table in the restaurant, perched as it was on the edge of the terrace, with an unimpeded view of the bay and the jetty below. Birgitte sat down and asked for a glass of mineral water. She checked her phone. It was still only 11.50am.

The restaurant steadily filled with the lunchtime crowd. A waitress brought Birgitte a basket of fresh sourdough and a small tray of handmade butter. A few moments later, a young man with long blonde hair who had noticed her as she arrived, introduced himself as the restaurant sommelier. He had an easy-going manner and was keen to engage her in conversation. When he asked about her accent, she explained she was from Denmark. He said had once spent a few days in Copenhagen and really enjoyed it. The patrons at nearby tables were trying to get his attention but he was too taken with Birgitte to care.

"Anything on the list you'd care to ask about?"

She gave it a once over and asked if he could make a suggestion.

"Do you like riesling?"

"I do."

"We don't have any Germans on the list but you might like a glass from the Clare Valley, down in South Australia."

She was about to mention that she'd been there only recently, but she checked herself. She'd rather not explain the circumstances. She looked down at the naval installations and the jetty in the bay. The sommelier told her it was once a facility for submarines and sea-mine research. It had been restored in the past 10 years and was now an historic feature of the harbour, along with the restaurant of course. It was a well-worn spiel tailored for tourists but delivered with genuine enthusiasm.

She commented that so much of what she had seen in Australia had been re-purposed but with respectful acknowledgement of its history. Of course, she hadn't mentioned the same couldn't be said for Forbes Creek. Some history was too painful or inconvenient to bear remembering. The sommelier eventually excused himself and attended to other tables.

By 12.30pm she began to wonder what was holding Daniel up. She checked her phone again but still there was no message. Perhaps he was your average Australian male – all the lovely weather made men complacent. She ordered a half dozen rock oysters and another glass of wine. Possibly within the week she would be back in Copenhagen. It was time, she realised, to give some proper thought to her career. Anders would fade from the public consciousness soon enough and she would have to get out of Fraud and back onto an investigative team where she could recapture the energy that was essential to her being a senior detective. If Sven didn't support her in this then she would consider leaving Copenhagen and starting up somewhere else, perhaps Arhuse or Odense. When she really thought about it there was nothing keeping her in the capital, except her obstinate need to prove that she belonged.

She was about to text Daniel to ask him what the delay was when she noticed a couple with a child down on the jetty. They were too far away for her to hear what they were saying but she could tell by their body language that something was wrong. The young boy, no more than six years old, had been exploring under the jetty and had come up in tears. The father checked to see if the boy was physically hurt in any way but the boy just kept crying. He gestured to the boy's mother who was on a phone call several feet away. The boy ran to his mother as the father climbed down under jetty to see what had upset his son. When he came up he was grey. He walked along the jetty and grabbed the phone from his wife who tried to protest. As soon as she saw his face and realised her boy was crying she began to panic. She swept the child up in her arms and headed to the point where he had first emerged but her husband barked at her to stop. She stood and swivelled on her toes, torn between her curiosity and fear and trusting her husband's good sense. The father hung up the phone and walked back to his wife. He hugged them both and spoke gently into his wife's ear as the boy held their legs and wept.

By this point several diners had noticed their behaviour and had stopped talking. Birgitte could feel her pulse racing as the woman pulled away from her husband and moved towards the edge of the jetty. Her child cried for her to come back but the father held him close. The woman disappeared under the jetty. Birgitte could actually hear her scream – a short, sharp howl like a frightened dog, quickly stifled by her own hand. She emerged pale and stricken. Several of the male dinners had leapt up from their tables and ran down a flight of stairs beside the restaurant that led to the jetty. Birgitte slowly took the napkin from her lap, folded it three times and placed it carefully on the table in front of her. She had witnessed enough horror on the job to know that rushing was now pointless. As she descended the stairs the police officer within her wanted to take control, to tell people to get back and mind their own business but it wasn't her place. She joined the throng along the jetty as more onlookers risked their own safety on the slippery wooden steps to sate their morbid curiosity. The bay filled with the crescendo of approaching sirens. An ambulance and two police cars cut across the park and came to halt at the start of the jetty. Uniformed officers ran along the pier and took the situation in hand. As the crowds moved back a police boat arrived on the scene. An officer was on the bow with a long pole that had a hook on the end.

What struck Birgitte at first was that the body in the harbour wasn't bloated at all and the skin had been blistered and burned all over. The crowd were silent as the officer gently guided the floating corpse out from under the jetty to the side of the boat. When the body turned in the water revealing the blistered face of a young man who seemed to be grinning maniacally at them all, several women screamed and began to weep. One man fell to his knees and vomited. Birgitte peered over the shoulders of the people in front of her, doing her best to take in as many details as possible. From what she could tell it was the missing boy, James Freedmont, and his lips had been torn from his face, but there were no other obvious injuries. Her own shoulders slumped momentarily. She had been too late again. The officers moved the crowd further back as the body was hauled up on to the deck of the police boat. The police on the jetty asked for the immediate witnesses to move to one side and that everyone else return to the restaurant. Slowly, and reluctantly, the crowd broke away and made their way back up the stairs to the terrace.

Birgitte sat at her table and phoned Tony.

He answered by cursing that Frankston and Braithwaite were both dragging their heels on the investigation, refusing to acknowledge the national nature of the murders, in the hope that they could solve them within their own respective states.

Birgitte listened, waiting for a pause in his monologue before quietly saying, "They've found the boy Freedmont."

"Seriously? Where?"

"Chowder Bay."

"How do you know?"

"He's washed up under a jetty where I am having lunch."

"Are you okay? What the hell happened?"

"He hasn't been in the water long, a matter of hours. He was naked and his skin was badly burned and his lips have been removed. That was all I could see before they covered his body."

"Jesus, what are the chances?"

They both fell silent.

Tony yelled into the phone, "Where are you exactly?"

"Sebastian's Restaurant. On the terrace."

"Are you in a crowd?"

She looked about at the other diners, unsure of where he was heading with his questions.

"Yes. I am."

"Can you see anyone around you who looks suspicious?"

"Aside from the corpse in the harbour?"

"Stay there. Don't move. I can be there in 20 minutes. Stay with the crowd."

"I don't understand."

"He knows you're there. The body was sent to you."

Birgitte didn't hear the rest of what he was saying because she had dropped the phone on the table. Her skin crept with a coldness that bristled up from deep within her bones, sweeping over her limbs like the first wind of a European winter. It was happening again.

She quickly checked the message that Daniel had sent through the day before. Why hadn't he called yet? She considered dialling his number to tell him to stay away when a hideous thought occurred to her. She jumped online and searched for his name, found his LinkedIn account and the number for the company he worked for. It took a few minutes but she was eventually put through.

Down on the jetty a canvas screen had been put up as forensic teams arrived. Overhead a chopper hovered as a TV cameraman leaned out over the landing rail to film the scene for a live cross straight into millions of homes across the country. Birgitte could see a small army of camera crews running across the park to set up on the perimeter of the scene. The media circus had arrived.

"Daniel Hattersly speaking."

"Daniel, it's Birgitte Vestergaard... I mean Birgitte Sorenson."

She waited for him to answer.

"Wow," said the voice, slightly awkwardly. "Birgitte... What a blast from the past. What can I do for you?"

"I'm at Sebastian's Restaurant, waiting for you."

"Seriously? Why?"

"You didn't text me yesterday?"

"What? God no. I haven't spoken to you since... Jesus, it's been years. I didn't somehow arse-dial you by mistake?" he asked laughing. "That doesn't make sense – I don't even know your number."

He was about to suggest they meet up anyway but she hung up. The realisation that the killer had hacked into her life in such a knowing way was terrifying. How much did he know about her? She looked about the crowd. Was he watching her now? The faces around her seemed benign, still processing the dreadful nature of what they had witnessed. Some were on the phone to friends relaying what had happened, leaving no gruesome detail unexplored. But there was no one who looked like a killer. She thought of Max Anders, his soft, corpulent features, his look of resigned fate that belied a calculating mind and realised that it meant nothing. The killer could well be the most non-descript person in the restaurant. She tried to reason with herself – to think back to what they had learned so far. It was in his nature to abduct and kill a victim in one state and dump them in another, ensuring the body wouldn't be found for 12 to 24 hours. She began to breathe more easily. There was a good chance the killer was long gone. But why had he changed his MO so dramatically? What did it mean?

Tony ran into the restaurant as most of the guests were being encouraged to pay their bills and leave. The maitre'd attempted to block his path but he stepped around her holding up his identification.

"Are you okay?" he called out to Birgitte.

She nodded and motioned to the seat opposite. He sat down and looked at the chaos in the bay below. "We need to get you out of here."

"I'm quite certain he's not here, Tony."

"I don't want to take that risk."

She looked at him coolly and kept her voice even so he would understand exactly where they stood. "It's not your risk to take."

He stared at her dumbfounded. "You do realise what is going on don't you?"

"Not entirely, and neither do you, so let's not get ahead of ourselves."

"I would feel a whole lot better if we had this discussion back at Goulburn Street."

She resigned herself to the fact that Tony wasn't going to let her out of his sight. She was flattered but already irritated by his need to control her. Right now, they needed to think clearly about the killer, try to pre-empt his next moves, not panic about the safety of one detective – that was what he wanted.

They left the restaurant without another word. Tony was parked up where the taxi had dropped her off earlier. On the way to the car he guided her with his hand on her lower back, looking over his shoulder into the trees that lined the property. She felt like the First Lady being shunted to safety and she didn't like it. Once they were inside the car she said, "Is all this Secret Service behaviour necessary, Tony? I am a senior detective. I know how to handle myself. And I have been in far more dangerous situations than this back home."

He turned the engine over and pulled out onto the street. "I'm sure you have, but the fact is you are only connection we have to this guy so we need you alive."

She muttered under her breath. "You wouldn't have had that connection without me..."

He braked heavily at a Stop sign, causing her to lurch forward in her seat. He glared at her. "Damn straight! The only reason he's targeting you is because you were rash enough to provoke Xian Lao. Now the Freedmont boy is dead and this nut job has a hard-on for you. Well done."

"I didn't kill the Freedmont boy. I'm confident that an autopsy will show that he was already dead before we met with Lao."

Tony laughed mirthlessly. "It must be fucking brilliant being so confident all the time."

"Think about it, Tony. Everyone this guy has picked up has been dead within 48 hours. Why would it be any different with the third victim. He's incredibly well organised, and exceptionally calculating. Everything has gone smoothly, until now. He is flustered. He's trying to regain control but he's had to alter his arrangements, which could work to our advantage. James Freedmont's body would have turned up at around the same time, I'm sure of it. It just would have been in some other location designed to scare someone at Barclay Industries."

Tony looked again for oncoming traffic, struggling to come up with an alternative line of reasoning. "Still, you shouldn't have ruffled Lao."

"I disagree."

"Christ, you're annoying. Can't you see that I am just trying to keep you in one piece long enough for us to get to the bottom of this."

She looked at him warmly and touched his hand. "And I appreciate it, but you need to give me enough room to do my job."

The touch of her hand was more disarming than what she said. He shifted it out of reach along the steering wheel and pulled the car into the main street.

"Well, you can't stay at the East Wind Hotel anymore. We'll have to set you up somewhere else."

"What about my things?"

"I'll get Harris to swing by and collect everything."

As they headed west along the headland she asked, "So where will I be staying?" Suddenly a thought occurred to her which made her smile. "You're weren't thinking of taking me to your place, were you?"

He looked embarrassed. "Why the hell would I want you in my house?"

"I don't know," she said, watching him. "To be chivalrous ... just so you can say the words 'there's only one place I know where I can really protect you'."

He laughed out loud. How the hell did she know what he was thinking? It was worth a shot, he figured, but there was no point pushing the idea.

"There's a boutique hotel in Surry Hills near the Goulburn Street office – keeps you close to all the action so you won't miss a thing."

"I feel safer already."

"You'll have to make a statement at the office first."

They arrived at Goulburn Street 20 minutes later. Tony had flicked the radio on in the car to get the 2pm bulletin. The media were already reporting a body had been found floating in Sydney Harbour, but there were little details.

The office was buzzing with the news. Many of the staff turned to watch Birgitte as she walked with Tony towards his desk. Across the floor they spotted Miller as she stood up in her office and signalled for them to come in. She looked grave and was clearly doing her best to mask her anger.

Birgitte said, "I need the bathroom. You can start without me."

Tony nodded and headed for Miller's door.

Miller looked over his shoulder as he entered, her brow furrowed.

"She's in the ladies," Tony said. "Any news?"

"It's definitely James Freedmont," she said. "An autopsy is underway. Forensics haven't found anything at the scene as yet. Do you have any ideas?"

"The killer is sending her a message."

Miller stared at him blankly then said, "That's utterly ridiculous. I'm getting sick and tired this."

"She was at Sebastian's Restaurant overlooking the jetty when the body was found."

"What was she even doing there?"

"She said an old friend had texted her yesterday and invited her out to lunch."

"It could still be a coincidence then."

"That's what I thought as well, but she phoned the guy direct when the body was hauled up and he had no idea about any lunch meeting. The killer organised for her to be at the restaurant so she would see the body. He knows we're on to him."

Miller looked down at her laptop while she processed the information. "This is exactly why she shouldn't have harassed Xian Lao," she said mostly to herself. "It's her fault this is getting out of control."

"I've been through all that with her," Tony cut in, "but I think she's right – Freedmont was already dead when we went to the Floating Lotus. The autopsy will hopefully verify that."

"Are you trying to tell me she knew that at the time?"

"So far her judgement has been sound."

"Judgement? Sounds like guess work to me." She was about to say more when Birgitte appeared at the door.

Miller feigned concern. "Everything okay?"

"I'm fine, thank you." She came in and took a seat beside Tony.

Commander Barton strode in behind her. "What do we know?"

Birgitte spent the next hour walking them through exactly what happened. Miller said very little but the Commander prompted Birgitte with pertinent questions, carefully considering her and Tony's answers.

Eventually, he said, "I'm going to have to talk to the media."

"I wouldn't let them know too much," Tony said. "Essentials only."

"Can you talk to the family this afternoon?" he asked. "Get anything you can on his whereabouts before he was abducted. And speak to Reginald Barclay, see if he's had any contact from the killer." He turned to Miller. "Anything else you need?"

She shook her head.

"Okay, keep me in the loop." He stood up and looked at Birgitte. "I'm not sure if it's a good idea you remain too involved with this."

"I'm capable of dealing with the situation."

"I've no doubt you are, but we have to think of the broader context. We can't put the case at risk, or your safety. If this guy is coming for you, I want to know you're in good hands."

Tony said, "I've got a place in mind. Harris is collecting her things from the East Wind as we speak."

"Try not to let too many people know where she's staying."

Birgitte could feel the blood flushing her cheeks. *This is what the killer wants – to isolate me from the case.* "I don't want to cause any concern or get in the way, but I think it's important I stay involved in the day-to-day operations."

Barton rubbed his face slowly. "Tony, I'll leave it up to you as to how involved she needs to be. We wouldn't have got this far without her, but I'll be held responsible if this gets out of hand."

Tony nodded. "How about I meet with her at the end of each day to go through any developments, share ideas?"

Barton was satisfied and thanked them for their efforts. Birgitte wanted to scream at both of them but contained herself. She smiled at the Commander and reassured him they were on the right track.

When he was gone, Miller said, "I'll need the name and address of the hotel and a contact number."

"You heard the Commander," Tony replied, "The less people know her whereabouts the better."

"How can I get in touch?"

"Through me. Birgitte is no longer an active member of the team anyway."

Miller held his stare and chose not to pursue it. Tony suggested it was time they made a move.

On their way out of the building they saw Commander Barton on the front steps surrounded by a scrum of eager journalists.

It was almost 4pm when Tony pulled up on a narrow street on the east side of Surry Hills that was lined with plane trees and terrace houses. Halfway along was a former warehouse that had been converted to a hotel for business people and middle-aged tourists. As they got out of the car he looked across at Birgitte. She hadn't said a word since the meeting with Miller and Barton. He could tell she was fuming with how things were playing out.

They checked in with the young woman on the front desk. She told them an officer had already brought Birgitte's belongings and left them in her room. Tony thanked her, took the key and followed her directions to the stairs. They climbed three flights which led onto a narrow corridor that seemingly took them away from the main section of the building. They turned several times until they reached a single door.

The room was quite small but there were no street-facing windows. It had a limited view of a quiet internal courtyard down below. Birgitte's bags and laptop had been placed neatly on the bed.

Tony quickly scouted the room then moved to the window. He searched the roofline and the courtyard until he was satisfied no one could enter from the outside.

Birgitte had taken her toiletries into the bathroom and closed the door behind her. He could hear the tap running so he took a seat at the desk by the window and tried to think of what their next move should be.

Birgitte stared at herself in the mirror. Her hands were shaking violently. She gripped the basin and grit her teeth to hold back the tears. The shock of the day's events was rising up to overwhelm her but she was determined to hold herself together. The image of James Freedmont's burnt skin and death's head face was seared across her consciousness. She told herself over and over again that it wasn't her fault, but she was steadily losing confidence in her own reasoning. What if the boy had still been alive and the rashness of her actions had tipped the killer over the edge? Her breathing became shallower and faster as Max Ander's laughter peeled through her mind like church bells. The faces of the three dead Svedbo children taunted her from her nightmares. This wasn't her fault, she told herself. She couldn't let either killer undermine her ability to do her job. She took a deep breath, turned off the taps and opened the bathroom door. Tony was sitting across from her with a slightly perplexed look on his face. He was obviously worried about her but couldn't read her mood.

Without a word, she stepped across the room, took his face in her hands and kissed him hard on the lips, pushing her tongue into his mouth, allowing the endorphins to race through her brain, willing them to wash away her anxiety, to make her forget everything she had seen in the past two weeks. Tony responded in kind. His hands came up, grasping her hips as she straddled his lap and lowered herself onto him. She continued kissing him, hurriedly undoing her blouse. She tore off one strap of her bra, releasing her breast and pulling his head downwards.

"Suck them."

She pulled off her shirt and undid her bra as he took her in his mouth. She closed her eyes and arched her back, then pushed his head across to the other breast.

"Don't stop," she murmured. She had already kicked off her shoes and was undoing her trousers when Tony stood up, lifting her with his hands under her arse as he continued to flick and provoke her nipples with his tongue. He kicked her luggage off the bed and threw her down on her back. Before her body had settled into the warmth of the quilt he had pulled off her trousers and panties. He began to kiss her stomach, tracing a steady trail down her belly until she was moaning with pleasure. For the next 20 minutes they barely moved as her fears and nightmares faded away into a sensual oblivion.

She came twice more before Tony eventually fell from her body exhausted. He instantly sank into a deep sleep beside her. Her legs were still shaking with pleasure as she rolled onto her stomach, gripping the sheet and burying her head into the pillow. For more than two hours she had been able to forget the case, and her past, and just exist in the moment. And it felt glorious, as if she'd been cleansed in a river of the purest water. Slowly and securely she drifted off to sleep.

CHAPTER FOURTEEN

Birgitte awoke with a start at about 3am. The room was foreign and off-putting. It bothered her that she didn't automatically recognise where she was, but the sight of Tony's bare shoulders in the bed beside her and the sound of his low, steady snoring reassured her. She slipped out from between the sheets and turned on the desk lamp. She rubbed her face and struggled to comprehend how she had slept so deeply for eight hours. She'd obviously needed it.

As she opened her luggage and found a pair of yoga pants and a crew neck, she recalled the previous day's events. The image of James Freedmont's face came to mind and with it the unsettling feeling of being watched by an unknown killer. She had to stay focused, not allow fear to govern her thinking. It would be rational police work that would keep her safe more than anything else.

She set up her laptop on the desk. As it warmed up she made herself a cup of coffee, then settled down to check her emails. She scrolled through the usual smatterings of spam, spotting a message from her mother asking her if she would be back in Copenhagen in time for their father's birthday, a request from Sven to get in touch when she was back in the country and a few group invitations from former colleagues for Christmas drinks, which she knew she wouldn't be attending. But further down she recognised a name on an email that made her heart leap into her mouth. It was a message from Hans Thostrup entitled "Greetings from Adelaide". It had an attachment.

Birgitte's mind was already racing. She looked at her inbox then across to the bed, where Tony continued to sleep. Should she open the email? Should an IT forensic team check it first in case it deletes as soon as she finishes watching it, leaving them no way of tracing the file? Should she wake Tony? A voice inside her said, "You don't have time. The killer is reaching out to you. This could be the only chance you have to discover what he wants."

She opened the email but there was no message, only a single movie file. She double clicked the icon and waited in anticipation and dread as the media player start up.

A close-up of Hans Thostrup's face appeared on her screen, dishevelled, pale, exhausted. He was staring behind the camera with a look of disgust. His mouth was taped with the same silver electrical tape that was also used on Salina Heysmith.

The camera slowly zoomed out as Thostrup's head lolled forward. His arms were suspended over his head. He was hanging by his wrists – an uncomfortable position for a young person, but for a man in his 70s, his shoulders must have been in excruciating pain. It was shot outdoors. He was hanging from a metal arm. Sea gulls flapped in the background. The image lurched to one side revealing a vast expanse of dark blue ocean that tipped out of view just as quickly. He was on the back of a mid-sized commercial trawler somewhere out to sea.

There was only the sound of gulls and water slapping the hull. The camera was hand held. The operator moved to the back of the boat. A dark rubber-gloved hand grabbed a metal scoop from a cutting station then it plunged into a plastic garbage bin. When the scoop came out it was filled with a red-brown mixture of decaying fish guts and blood that must have been putrid to smell. The gloved hand flicked the chum over the side, then threw the severed heads of several tuna into the water as well, being careful not to allow the camera to capture any more of the operator than was necessary. The gulls were flapping wildly, swooping down into the dirty water. The camera was being held over the side focussing on the chum swirling with the deep blue. The water changed colour again as a large shadow moved beneath the boat. Birgitte could feel the blood drain to her feet. She wasn't sure whether she could watch all of what was about to occur, but knew she had to.

The camera was attached to the canopy and gave a clear view of the back of the trawler and the water behind. The killer and Thostrup were now out of view. The boat engine started up with a noisy, then deafening rattle. Then another sound could be heard – an electrical whirring. Soon Thostrup's narrow hips came into view, then his knees and pale feet. He was being winched into the air. The mechanical arm extended out over the water lifting the Dane over the stern.

Thostrup was now fully alert and cognisant of his fate. He began to try to lift his knees up but he was too old and didn't have the muscles in his stomach to achieve much more than desperate wriggling. Birgitte couldn't hear his screams through the tape over the sound of the engine but the sudden redness of his face and the wideness of his eyes suggested he was screaming for mercy. His body suddenly plummeted into the water. He thrashed about hysterically as the winch was slowly retracted. He was lifted out of the ocean so slowly Birgitte found herself wanting to scream at the computer.

When the great white breached the surface it's eyes were rolled back, its tremendous maw was ingesting litres of bloodied water, its jagged teeth bared. With a kick of its powerful tail the head lurched violently to one side. Thostrup's feet kicked at the nose. The huge bulk of the shark's head receded into the dark, disappearing entirely. Thostrup looked back into the boat for a moment but then he stared about into the water wildly, unsure of where the next attack may come from.

The electrical whirring started up again. Thostrup was raised high over the water, his feet dangling at a safe distance from the depths. The mechanical arm was drawing him in towards the stern. His body relaxed. He looked into the back of the boat with a mixture of hope and relief. Whatever the killer needed to know, he'd tell him as soon as he was on board. He had no idea what this lunatic could possibly want from him but there had to be a sound reason for his abduction. As long as there was reason, there was hope that he could talk his way back to safety.

Thostrup kicked his legs in an attempt to reach the stern with his toes but every time the boat lurched with the movement of the ocean, he swung in the opposite direction out over the waves. He managed to get one foot onto the stern but it was slipping across the wet wood. With all his might he tried to lift his body upwards, away from the water.

The engine stopped. He had just enough time to look into the back of the boat to see the killer release the winch.

Thostrup was dropped into the water up to his waist.

Birgitte stood outside Miller's office staring out the window on to the street below. Behind her, beyond the closed venetian blinds Commander Barton, Miller and the officers on the combined task force, including Tony, were watching the footage of Thostrup's murder on her laptop. The IT team, irritated at having been called in on their Sunday, were waiting to inspect the file which hadn't deleted after the first viewing. Birgitte didn't need to see it twice.

In the office Tony stood with his arms crossed, coldly fixated as Thostrup was winched up a second time above the water. His feet were no more than a few inches out of the chum when the great white hit him with such ferocity that the old man could barely register what was happening. For just a moment the jaws clamped around the man's thighs and the two-tonne behemoth was suspended. The metal arm bent slightly with the weight and the stern tipped into the ocean, pushing the gunwale down to the surface.

"Christ," Barton muttered breathlessly.

With a ferocious twist of its enormous dull nose, the shark's jagged teeth finally came together. The stern lurched upwards. The metal arm did the same. Thostrup rose in the air. The shark sank back into the water, satisfied with its catch. Thostrup swung back and forth like a lantern in the wind as the blood pumped from the fleshy stumps of his thighs. His eyes no longer registered anything resembling reality.

Tony closed the media player. Miller looked slightly green and her hands were shaking. They stood in silence for several minutes.

Birgitte was at the white board in the main meeting area, writing rapidly.

Hans Thostrup, former exec for EU energy agency
In Australia on holiday, possible intention of catching up with Nils Brekman (Katercorp).

Abducted in Adelaide, SA
Taken off shore, fed to shark, filmed while dying
Dumped in Forbe's Creek, NT
Footage sent possibly to Westlake (Katercorp) and Pender (Barclay
Industries), Vestergaard

Beside this she wrote:

Salina Heysmith
Lawyer representing Katercorp (run by Brekman)
Involved with Pender (Barclay Industries)
Abducted in Darwin, NT
Taken to jungle, fed to crocodile, filmed while dying
Dumped in Mildura, Vic
Footage sent possibly to Westlake (Katercorp) and Pender (Barclay
Industries)

And in a third column she wrote:

James Freedmont
Uni student, friend of Tom Barclay, son of Reginald Barcly (Barclay
Industries)
Abducted at Melbourne University, Vic
Cause of death??
Dumped in Sydney Harbour, NSW, where Vestergaard would find him
Footage??

She stepped back and considered the board carefully. Most
of the team were still processing the violence of what they'd
just witnessed, but Tony had moved out of the office and was
now standing behind her.

"The first two murders make sense in terms of the MO,"
she said under her breath. "He probably has an SUV or a van
with a chest freezer or a refrigeration unit. He has the time to
drive from Adelaide, to Forbe's Creek, up to Darwin, across
the Kakadu, down again to Mildura, across to Melbourne. But
the Freedmont boy didn't look like he'd been attacked by an
animal. He looked, emaciated and badly sunburned."

"Maybe it was somewhere remote," suggested Tony, "and he escaped from whatever was supposed to have attacked him…"

"Then perished in the sun…" Birgitte thought out loud.

"The killer caught up with him?" he suggested.

"Seems a long shot," she said. "Unless having him perish was always the plan. Let nature takes its course."

"How would the killer film that?"

She shook her head. "No idea. And why is he making such a blatant attempt to involve me?"

"What do you mean? He's obviously trying to warn you off. He drew you to the body and sent you footage of Thostrup's murder."

"But why now?"

Tony looked at her with incredulity. "You made the connection between the first two killings, and you questioned Westlake and Pender before he'd had a chance to contact them."

Miller was now behind them. Her voice was terse. "How would he know any of that?"

"He wouldn't, directly," replied Birgitte. "The point I'm trying to make is that his MO changed dramatically between the abduction of James Freedmont and the dumping of his body."

Tony said, "Which confirms he didn't know we were on to him until…"

"…after we'd spoken to Xian Lao."

Miller could see the reasoning but didn't like it. "Mr Lao already threatening legal action for your behaviour at the restaurant the other night. If you go after him again without cause, we'll be up for harassment."

Birgitte turned to her, "Without cause? His mining company will directly benefit from Katercorp and Barclay Industries backing out of the Timor Sea deal."

"As would every other mid-size mining firm in Australia," she retorted. "You don't have enough evidence."

Barton had joined them. "We need to speak to Reginald Barclay – see if he's received any footage of Freedmont boy dying."

"And Sam Westlake and Jason Pender," added Tony, "to confirm they also received footage the other day."

"It still doesn't prove Lao was responsible," Miller said.

"It will prove beyond doubt there is a connection between each of the killings," said Tony, "and that it is motivated by extortion, which means we're dealing with a contract killer, whose own motivation is purely financial."

Harris called out from across the room. "I've just spoken to Reginald Barclay. He's on his way in."

"Did he say he'd received any emails or contact from anyone?" Tony asked.

Harris shook her head.

An hour later, the CEO of Barclay Industries arrived at the Goulburn Street office. He had brought his laptop in as requested. Harris directed him into Miller's office, where he sat with the Commander, Tony and Birgitte.

Reginald Barclay was in his mid 50s. He had the look of the Irish to him – thick curly black hair, greying at the temples, clear blue eyes, thick neck and shoulders. Tony had read his profile on the Barclay Industries website. He had a degree in engineering from the University of Sydney, had played second row for the Waratahs and still followed the game like it was a religion. He had started his career with a leading multinational – Tony figured family connections. The bottom rung Barclay had started on was 30 stories higher than most could ever hope for. And he'd proceeded to climb without fear of falling. Now he ran his own multimillion dollar company.

The events of the past few days, however, had taken their toll. Barclay looked like he hadn't been sleeping. His eyes were furtive. He wasn't bothered being in a police station but didn't like not having all the facts at hand before walking in. And of course, anything that came close to hurting his family was unacceptable.

"I can't believe what happened to James," he said to the room. "He was such a great kid."

His large pale hands shook in his lap. They were talking to a father more than a company director. "My son's a mess."

"And you haven't received any emails?" the Commander asked.

"I really haven't had a chance to look properly. My EA has been on holidays and her replacement is having trouble keeping up."

"Would you mind taking a look with us here?"

"Of course." He opened his laptop. He began scrolling through his inbox. Birgitte could see over his shoulder there were 176 unopened messages.

"What am I looking for?"

"Anything that looks odd," Tony said.

"Perhaps a message from James," added Birgitte.

He looked up, slightly puzzled. "He wouldn't write to me. I've only met him a few times, even though Tom and him have become good mates over the past year or two at uni."

"It wouldn't be from him."

The realisation of what that meant took several seconds to register. His faced tightened.

"Would you like us to check for you?" offered Miller.

"No, it's fine."

Several minutes later, he looked up again anxiously. "Nothing. There's nothing here that looks out of place. All work-related emails."

Birgitte could sense the group exhaling with relief. "Your spam folder – is it empty?"

He checked. "There's a lot of stuff here. Just rubbish, really. Hang about. Oh Christ."

Halfway down there was an email entitled: "Greetings from the Outback".

"Mr Barclay, probably best if you wait outside for this," said Tony. "This is now evidence and we need to take a look in private."

He nodded and placed the laptop on Miller's desk and excused himself. Miller closed the door as they huddled around the screen. As with the other email, the message contained a single movie file. Tony sighed heavily and clicked Play.

The screen filled with a mottled ochre and white pattern, which slowly appeared to expand. It was hard to discern what was being shown, when Birgitte said, "Satellite camera, GPS."

It suddenly made sense as the camera steadily zeroed in on the black dot at the centre of the screen. As it came closer the dot faded in colour and moved around hesitantly. The zooming stopped at the point where it was obvious the focal point was a human being, naked, shuffling around aimlessly. The footage then sped up. The figure moved like an ant towards the top of the screen but slightly to the right. The camera zoomed back to show the figure hobbling in a large, ungainly circle, stopping occasionally, then setting off with more purpose in another direction. You could see the frustration and exhaustion in his body, which moved slower and slower and eventually stopped. When the body was completely still, the camera zoomed in closer than before. You could clearly see it was the body of a young man. He rolled onto his back, his face hidden behind the crook of his arm, his mouth open in a silent scream. When his arm moved away it was obvious they were looking at James Freedmont, alone in the middle of a desert, slowly but steadily succumbing to the elements, absolutely aware of his own fate. He was weeping like a child. The screen went black.

"I'll cancel the tender," Barclay said, staring out the window of Miller's office. They'd brought him back in and confirmed that he'd received footage of the boy's murder. "I want nothing to do with this. That poor kid. Tom and him were like brothers."

"Do you have any ideas as to who might be behind it?"

He looked at Miller in disbelief. "Who do you think I knock around with?"

"We understand you're upset, sir, but we need to know if you've been approached in the past few weeks or if you've seen anything that would help us out."

"I've got no idea. Whoever it is, they'd have to be insane to think they could pull this off."

"What do you mean?"

"If we back out, and Brekman does the same, which he bloody well should, it's safe to say whoever gets the deal is probably behind the killing."

"But that won't matter if we can't physically link the killings to any one company. Do you mind if our IT department work on your laptop?"

"Of course not."

Miller closed the screen and signalled to Harris who was waiting outside her door. "Get this to IT. Tell them the email is in the spam folder."

Harris nodded and left with the laptop.

Birgitte asked Barclay, "What can you tell us about Jason Pender?"

"He's my lead counsel, worked for me for the past five years. He's bloody good at his job." He stopped. "You don't think he's behind James' death?"

"It's not that," said Birgitte, flashing a look at Tony to determine how much she should reveal. Tony nodded. "We believe Jason may have received a similar file earlier in the week."

"On Wednesday," said Tony.

"Of James?"

"No, probably of Salina Heysmith."

"Why?" he asked, trying to understand.

"We believe he was in a physical relationship with Salina until recently. And whoever is trying to threaten you tried to reach Jason the same way, but using Salina?"

"She's a lawyer for a competitor... and I know his wife... he wouldn't be that stupid."

As if on cue Harris knocked on the door and leaned her head in. "Jason Pender has arrived, Sir."

"Bring him in here."

Barclay's face had darkened. He clearly wasn't used to being the last to know about anything, especially dealings within his own firm.

Pender appeared hesitantly at the door with his laptop slung over one shoulder. He looked a wreck, as if he hadn't slept for a week. His confidence had vanished and as soon as he saw his boss he almost backed out of the room.

"Take a seat, Mr Pender," said the Commander.

Barclay glared at him but didn't say a word.

"Mr Pender, I'm Commander Barton. This is Superintendent Carolyn Miller. I believe you've met Detectives Kingsmill and Vestergaard."

He nodded like a school boy before the principal.

The Commander was comfortable with the dynamic that was weighted heavily in his favour. "Now I'm going to ask you a few questions and I need you to answer honestly. I know you've been interviewed by Detective Kingsmill on two occasions and he was of the opinion you weren't exactly being forthright. This is your one opportunity to get on a better footing, shall we say. Do you understand?"

He nodded and swallowed, then ran his dry tongue across his lips. "Okay, we asked you to bring in your laptop because we believe you may have received an email of a disturbing nature in the past few days. Is this the case?"

He paused, looking furtively about the room, then his eyes finally met Barclay's. "I had no idea it would end like this, Reg. I'm so sorry."

"Answer the Commander's questions," Barclay said flatly.

He began nodding. "Yes, I did receive an email."

"While Detective Kingsmill was at your house on Wednesday?"

"Yes."

"What did the email contain?"

"It was a movie file. It showed Salina…" His bottom lip began to tremble. "It showed Salina… in a jungle, being eaten…" The air evaporated from his lungs as he was overwhelmed with sobs. "It fucking ate her. It dragged her into the water and ate her." He almost fell out of his chair, pushing the laptop at Tony. "Take it, get it off my computer."

Tony handed the laptop to Harris as she passed the office.

They waited while Pender wept openly for several minutes. When he contained himself, he apologised.

Barton leaned on the edge of Miller's desk hovering over Pender with his arms crossed. "What was the nature of your relationship with Salina Heysmith?"

"We had a short fling, only for a few months. I'd ended it."

"You stupid vain bastard," Barclay muttered.

"Had she mentioned anything about the Timor Sea deal prior to her trip to Darwin?"

"We were both a part of the same lobby group so we discussed it often enough," he said, then turned to Barclay, "but we're both professionals. We knew where the line was and we never crossed it."

"Who instigated the relationship?" asked Birgitte.

"I did," he said, then he paused. "At least I think I did."

"Think carefully, Mr Pender. Was there any chance she instigated the relationship in an effort to access information about Barclay
Industries?"

He shook his head. "She wouldn't have."

"Are you sure?" Barton said. "From what Detective Kingsmill tells us, she had an unhealthy gambling addiction, which could make her susceptible to making some questionable choices for pecuniary gain."

"Tell me you didn't blab about the firm, Jason," Barclay said, mortified by what he was hearing.

"I didn't say anything, Reg. I promise."

"And to think I was going to offer you a greater stake in the shares, you fucking dog."

Pender stared at the floor, his breathing shallow. "Oh Christ, Westlake might have put her up to it."

"Westlake? That wanker at Katercorp? What the fuck's he got to do with this?"

"I've known him for while, see? We went to uni together, back in the day. We caught up a few months back and got to playing squash occasionally."

"He's the fucking 2IC of our closest competitor. What the fuck were you thinking?"

The Commander stood up. "Mr Barclay, I'm going to have to ask you to ease up please. We have a lot to get through."

Barclay was glaring at his lead counsel. "If that boy died because of something you've done, you smarmy little turd, I'll fucking ruin you."

"Enough," barked Barton. He turned back to Pender. "What was the nature of your relationship with Sam Westlake?"

"We were just friends… or colleagues, I guess. We'd play squash but we wouldn't talk about work. Ever."

"Did he introduce you to Salina Heysmith."

"He did." Pender's shoulders slumped as he realised how much he had been played.

"Have you spoken to him since you received that email?" asked Birgitte.

He looked up at her almost wishing she might offer some solace in a room full of accusatory stares. "He contacted me just before, upset. He wanted to meet in the Botanical Gardens where we wouldn't be seen together. He was furious, yelling at me about some Danish guy. I told him I didn't know anything and he stormed off. Then when I got home and Detective Kingsmill turned up, I received that email. I figured Sam must have got something similar, but I haven't been able to get a hold of him since."

One of the IT department appeared in the doorway. "It's another clip."

Barclay and Pender were sent to different interview rooms to wait while the team watched the clip of the second murder – Salina Heysmith sitting by a creek in an eerie grey light of a night vision camera. The attack was sudden and brutal, four seconds of ferocity that was so violent it was almost impossible to see what was actually happening, then stillness.

Tony stood up and stretched his back. "We need to find Westlake."

"And Nils Brekman," said Barton. "We need to know where he stands on the tender. If they go ahead, more people are going to get hurt."

"What about Lao?" asked Birgitte.

"Harris has been trying to get a hold of him but apparently he's on a business trip and no one is saying where."

"Interstate? Overseas? When is he due back?"

"We don't know," said Barton. "I'll try to rustle up a warrant for his house and his office." He checked his watch. "I want Brekman and Westlake in here within the hour."

It was after lunch when Nils Brekman and Sam Westlake arrived at Goulburn Street, both carrying their laptops. Tony noticed the CEO appeared older in person. His dirty grey hair was combed back from a face that had become more gaunt since his photo was taken for the Katercorp website. His tall, angular frame still possessed a certain energy, like a marathon runner between seasons, but clearly he was beginning to fade inside his own skin. He looked tired and out of sorts. He stood slightly behind Westlake, who had entered the reception area as if it was a part of his asset portfolio.

As they were signing in they noticed the bulky figure of Reginald Barclay sitting to one side. He stood up, seething with anger. He glared at Westlake. Brekman offered his hand, slightly perturbed by Barclay's demeanour. Barclay shook his hand then sat back down without a word. Westlake ignored both of them, almost exuding an air of authority that exceeded his position.

Commander Barton came out and introduced himself to the two men and directed them into separate interview rooms. He signalled to Tony, Birgitte and Miller to join him in the first room with Brekman.

The CEO of Katercorp sat upright at the single table, his hands in front of him. It could have been a boardroom meeting he was chairing. "Would someone mind telling me what is going on?"

Barton nodded to Tony who took the seat opposite. "We believe someone is attempting to extort Katercorp and Barclay Industries, to get them to reconsidering submitting a tender for the Timor Sea deal."

"First I've heard of it," he said bluntly. "Surely, if someone wanted my company to do something, they'd threaten me directly."

"Not necessarily, said Tony. "Has Mr Westlake mentioned receiving a movie file from an anonymous source?"

"No, he hasn't. Did he?"

"We think he might have but he hasn't come forward about it as yet."

"What's on this movie?"

"The murder of Hans Thostrup."

"Christ." The resistance in his eyes evaporated. "I had no idea."

"We think it was sent to your 2IC so he could influence your decision-making. Has Mr Westlake intimated that you should pull out of the tender process – say, since last Wednesday?"

He thought for a while then shook his head. "Quite the opposite. He's more fired up than ever. Are you sure he got that email?"

"We'll question him shortly," Tony said.

"Well I definitely haven't received anything," he said, looking around the room at the team. "Does this have anything to do with the body they found in the harbour yesterday?"

"James Freedmont was a friend of Tom Barclay, Reginald Barclay's eldest boy. A clip of his murder was sent to him also. Further to that, your counsel, Salina Heysmith was found murdered in Mildura and a clip of her killing was sent to Jason Pender, lead counsel for Barclay Industries."

"Why him? I don't get it?"

"They had been having an affair until recently. It would appear Mr Westlake may have put her up to it to get information about Barclay Industry's intentions – in regards to the Timor Sea deal."

"She wouldn't do something like that just because Westlake told her to."

"Apparently, she had debts, thanks to a hefty gambling addiction," said Tony. "He may have offered to make the problem go away."

He shook his head in disbelief. "So three people have been killed to prevent my company or Reg's from submitting tenders?"

"We believe so."

"I don't know what to say." He looked genuinely perplexed. "What do you suggest I do?"

Barton stepped in. "We can't force you to pull out of the tender, but you may want to hold off for the time being, at least the next few days."

"Surely the whole deal should be canned."

"We're only just getting our heads around it ourselves, Mr Brekman," Barton added. "I assure you we'll be getting in touch with the relevant authorities as soon as these interviews are over."

"Do you have any ideas who's behind it?"

"We'd rather not say at this stage," Tony replied. "Do you have any reason to believe one company over another might benefit from you and Barclay backing out of the deal?"

"Any and all of them. Has Reg made a decision about how he's going to handle it."

"That's up to him, sir," said Tony. "Do you mind if we go through your emails on your laptop?"

"Of course not," he said, putting the computer bag on the table.

"If you go with Constable Harris, she'll work with the IT team."

He nodded slowly, suddenly looking much frailer than when he arrived, as if he was beginning to realise the corporate race he'd been competing in for so long no longer made sense. The rules had changed and no one had bothered to tell him.

The team left the interview room, walked down the corridor and Tony knocked on the next door. Westlake was sitting back in his chair with his legs crossed at the ankles. He sat up as they came in. As before, Tony took the seat opposite. The others stood behind him.

Tony rested his elbows on the table and locked his fingers. "Mr Westlake, since we last spoke, has anyone tried to contact you in regards to the disappearance of either Hans Thostrup or Salina Heysmith?"

Westlake shook his head slowly then raised his eyebrows. "Should I have heard something?"

Tony studied his features carefully. "You haven't received any emails then, possibly with a movie file attached?"

"No, I haven't."

"Are you certain?"

"What's this about?" he asked innocently.

"Do you mind if we check your computer?"

"Of course not. I've written the login details on a sticky note," he said lifting the laptop case onto the table. "You'll find it inside."

Constable Donleavy took the computer and left the room.

When Westlake had settled back into his seat, Tony resumed the questioning.

"You recall me visiting your office last Wednesday?"

"Of course."

"You seemed… out of sorts. Is that a fair assessment?"

"I was having a difficult day – work-related issues."

"After I left your office, what did you do?"

He thought for a moment. "I had a few meetings, out of the office."

"With anyone in particular?"

He sighed. "I met with Jason Pender in the Botanic Gardens."

"What about?"

"I was angry with him and needed to clear the air."

"Business related?"

"Sort of, but not exactly. Well after you and Detective Vestergaard visited me the first time and suggested he may have been involved with Salina Heysmith, it dawned on me how inappropriate it was, and how dire the consequences could be for both our businesses. He'd told me that it was over but I had to be sure. There is a lot of money riding on the Timor Sea deal as you know. I simply couldn't afford to let his need for attention get in the way of it all."

"You introduced the pair, didn't you?"

He looked around the room and chortled. "I might have, I really don't remember, but I certainly had no idea they would become an item."

Tony made some notes then asked, "What do you know of Hans Thostrup?"

"Only what Nils has mentioned over the years."

"But you knew they were friends?"

"Yes."

"Did you know he was in Australia?"

"Nils had said as much but that was it."

"We're you aware he'd been murdered recently?"

He nodded. "It was on the news."

"But you are certain you didn't receive any footage of his murder via email?"

He nodded. "Have people been receiving footage?"

"Jason Pender and Reginald Barclay have both received emails," said Tony. "And to be frank, Mr Westlake, I'm not entirely convinced you haven't."

"Well, you have my laptop. Surely, if someone was trying to threaten me, I'd be the first person to draw your attention to it. A person has been murdered."

"Three people, Mr Westlake, and they're all connected to either Katercorp or Barclay Industries."

"Has Nils suggested what he intends doing?"

"We can't say either way, in as much as it is his decision how to proceed in regards to Katercorp and the tender. However, we will be speaking to the relevant authorities in the Northern Territory to put a stay on this deal until the matter is resolved."

Westlake shook his head. "Good luck with that."

"What do you mean?"

"I don't think it's in the Government's own interest to delay on this deal."

"Even if three people have been executed in the past few weeks?"

"That situation has to be addressed of course, but it should be a part of the overall plan to see this deal through. Government's don't negotiate with terrorists, do they Detective?"

"This is hardly a case of terrorism, Mr Westlake."

"Not in the conventional sense, but I think you'll find the same principles apply."

Tony couldn't believe what he was hearing and struggled to keep the frustration out of his voice. "So what do you suggest we do?"

"Find the killer, Detective, or the person paying him, and do it quickly."

"What do you think we're trying to do? Perhaps if you were a little more helpful with information, we could resolve all this to everyone's satisfaction."

Westlake held up his palms in supplication. "What exactly are you implying, Detective?"

Barton decided to make his presence felt. "Mr Westlake, I'm sure we don't need to spell out that if you haven't been telling the truth or have been getting in the way of the investigation, you will be held accountable. And that could involve jail time."

"Commander, I have been very generous with my time. I've given you access to my laptop. And I've answered all your questions to the best of my ability. I'm sorry if they are not the answers you want to hear. What more do you want?"

The Commander looked at Tony, gave him the chance to ask further questions but when none were forthcoming, terminated the interview.

After the four interviewees had left the Goulburn Street office, the team reconvened to discuss the outcome. They were all convinced that Westlake was lying.

"We could get a search warrant to search his office," suggested Tony.

"If he's cleaned his laptop of any files," said Birgitte, "I'm sure he's cleaned his office as well. But he may not be as careful as he thinks he is."

"I'll look into it," said Barton. He looked at his watch. "We'll there's not much more we can do today."

Tony rubbed his face then ran his hand through his hair. It had been a long day. He turned to Birgitte, "How about I give you a lift back to the hotel and we can pick it all up tomorrow."

"Thanks, Tony," said Birgitte. "But Kate's already offered me a lift."

He tried to hide his querulousness. "No problem. I guess I'll see you both in the morning then."

He paused, not entirely sure if there was some signal they were supposed to be sharing for catching up later in the evening. He knew well enough not to make any overt suggestions in front of the others.

Birgitte had already grabbed her bag and was motioning to Harris she was ready to go.

"Women," he thought. "I'll never understand them." He had nowhere to be, so he walked back to his desk feeling a bit foolish and rudderless.

Down in the carpark, Birgitte said to Harris, "Do you mind if we take a short detour before going back to the hotel?"

"Certainly. Where are we headed?"

"The University of Sydney."

"Okay. Which part?"

"The main library."

"No problem."

It was early evening as they pulled out onto Goulburn Street. There was hardly any traffic so the trip across the southern end of the city was brief, but still long enough for Harris to break the ice on a certain subject.

"What's it like working with the elusive Tony Kingsmill?"

"Elusive?" Birgitte replied with a questioning grin. "He's a very good detective, bit gruff at times but he knows what he's doing. We could do with a few more like him in Copenhagen. How do you find him?"

Harris pretended to watch for traffic coming past Central station to avert her face. "He's all right, I guess. I mean, I admire him and would like to learn more from him if I had the chance."

"Are you planning on pursuing that path?"

Harris suddenly looked at her defensively. "I wouldn't suggest that he'd want to. He hardly knows I exist. I just like working with him."

"I meant about being a detective."

She blushed and coughed, gripping the wheel a little tighter. "Maybe."

Birgitte sensed what was happening and didn't want to let on about her involvement with Tony. "I'm sure you'd make a very good detective. And this case is certainly a good opportunity to learn a few things."

"Are you going to the library to do some research?"

Birgitte thought for a moment. "Yes, I am. Do you mind waiting for me? I shouldn't be more than 45 minutes."

"That's fine. Is there anything I can do to help?"

"I'll let you know."

They drove past Victoria Park and pulled into the grounds of the university. At the top of a small hill, Birgitte took in the dramatic roofline then stone walls of the main hall. Harris turned left before a manicured lawn then pulled over.

"The entrance to the library is just up there. I might stretch my legs if you don't mind, been sitting at my desk most of the day."

"Of course."

The two women approached the glass doors of Fisher Library. Birgitte thanked her for being helpful and entered the building. Harris stood at the door and checked her phone. The few students who were studious enough to be on the grounds on a Sunday night looked her warily, peering around her to see what drama had attracted a uniformed officer to the library.

Birgitte didn't have to go far. The person she was looking for was just leaving the information desk clutching a pile of books.

Cerina Ming didn't recognise Birgitte at first, but when she did, she didn't have time to react.

"Cerina?"

The young woman stopped. Her dark hair sat neatly around her face, in a conservative trim. Birgitte guessed she probably still lived at home with her parents and judging by the way she held herself she didn't have a boyfriend. This was why Birgitte hadn't brought Tony along. She would be less likely to talk in the presence of a male authority figure. And at this stage, there were no guarantees this would be a productive line of inquiry so Birgitte had decided earlier to wait until after the interview to tell Tony about it.

She approached the young woman, smiling warmly. "You're not in any trouble. I just want to talk to you briefly about the other night."

"I don't know anything," she said quietly.

"I know you don't, but I would still like to ask you a few questions."

"How did you know I was here?"

"One of the staff at the Floating Lotus mentioned you had a paper to finish and that you'd dropped a shift to be here. I actually didn't expect to find you so quickly."

Cerina considered this then said abruptly almost petulantly, "I don't have to talk to you." She set off back towards the main entrance. Birgitte followed her at a safe distance.

As soon as Cerina turned at the foyer she saw an officer in uniform standing just beyond the glass doors. She froze, then turned on her heel and walked briskly back inside.

"I don't know anything," she said desperately.

Birgitte realised what had just happened and decided to use it to her advantage. "Then a quick, private conversation won't do any harm, will it."

She led the reluctant student to a vacant study room and closed the door behind them. Birgitte gave her a moment to get settled.

"Cerina, how well do you know Xian Lao?"

"Not very."

"Is he a regular at the restaurant."

"I guess."

"How often does he come in?"

"It depends."

"On what?"

"I don't know. Sometimes he might be there twice a week and sometimes I don't see him for a month, but I only work four nights. He may come in other times."

"Have you seen him since the other night?"

"No."

"Does he know who you are? Outside of your role as maitre d'?"

She shook her head.

"What are your impressions of him?"

She looked through the glass wall at the other students. "I don't like him. He is very wealthy and very powerful and doesn't treat the staff very well."

"Okay. Has he ever said anything you that bothers you?"

She shook her head again, but was slowly beginning to trust Birgitte. "He has many mistresses," she said with distaste. "I think he pays for some of them to be his friend. They behave badly in the restaurant, worse than him."

"The other night, Cerina, when I was there with the other detective, Mr Lao got quite upset with us. Do you remember?"

She nodded.

"He started yelling at me in Chinese."

"He was very angry. I don't think I've ever seen him that mad."

"Is there any chance you can remember what he was saying?"

"What did you say to upset him?" she asked, clearly wanting to know what you could say to rankle such a powerful figure, and a source of discomfort in her own life – as if it might be a potion she could use against him some time in the future.

"It doesn't matter what I said. But I do need to know what he said."

"He called you names."

"Such as?"

"Dog, a street dog that should know better than to sniff around him like a horny bitch." Her eyes flashed as she recounted the incident. Using that sort of language was new to her. "He said dogs like you get what they deserve, and it wouldn't be long before you would be nothing more than shredded meat in a roadside cart."

Birgitte watched her impassively. It was important the young woman understood that she wasn't frightened by Lao's threats. "That was all he said?"

"That was all I heard. When he started throwing plates, I ran back into the kitchen."

"And you haven't seen him since?"

She shook her head again.

Birgitte stood up. "Thank you, Cerina. I appreciate your honesty. And I assure you, he doesn't know I'm here with you so you have nothing to worry about. If anyone asks you at work what the call was about, just tell them it was a family matter."

Cerina gathered her books. They both walked out through the stacks of books to the main foyer. When Cerina spotted the officer again she suddenly said, "I went to his house."

"Sorry?" Birgitte stopped and held out her hand to hold her up.

"A week ago. He had a private function at his house in the Southern Highlands. A few of the staff had to cater for him and his guests. We were paid very well. I needed the money."

"How many guests?"

She tried to recall. "A table of 12. Businessmen mostly, from mainland China, and a few mistresses."

"If you saw photos could you remember who was there?"

She shrugged.

Birgitte ruffled through her bag and drew out a black and white copy of a magazine article. She showed Cerina the image. "It's not very clear, but was that man in the front row, second from the left, was he there?"

Cerina looked at the photo carefully, then nodded. "He was there. I think he's related to Mr Lao."

"Did you overhear him saying anything?"

"Not really but I got the sense that Mr Lao was doing everything he could to impress him."

"Can you remember the address, Cerina. This is really important."

"I don't. One of the waiters gave me a lift. It was on a large property off the highway. We turned right a few kilometres passed Berrima, on the edge of a state forest. We turned right again onto a gravel road that led up through the trees to an enormous old house."

She pulled out her phone and brought up a map. A few minutes later she said, "I can't be certain but I think it was around here somewhere."

Birgitte stared at the map, committing it to memory. "You've been incredibly helpful, Cerina."

"He doesn't know you're here?"

"No, he doesn't. Was there anything else you can remember that struck you as odd or worth remembering about that night?"

"I'm not sure. I think they were all talking business. Then they started to drink a lot and we left. But the older man that Mr Lao was trying to impress had his luggage with him. I think he might have been flying back to China the next day."

"That's terrific. I can't thank you enough."

"Is that all?"

"It is."

Birgitte watched the young student walk hesitantly through the main doors, quickening her pace as she passed the officer who was still playing with her phone. If it wasn't for the uniform, Harris would have looked like any other student.

Birgitte turned back to the information desk and was directed to the energy resource section of the library.

Half an hour later she came out into the cool night air looking slightly triumphant.

"All okay?" asked Harris.

"Yes, Kate. All is okay. Thanks for waiting."

CHAPTER FIFTEEN

The conditions were acceptable for the task: low cloud cover, muted light, a slight breeze from the north-west, no more than five knots. He checked his watch again. It was 10.32am. The traffic on the motorway was moving at a steady 110km/h in either direction – sedans, SUVs, trucks – the occasional vehicle speeding up the outside lane at 120-130km/h to get clear of the sticklers.

From where he was lying, 300 metres back from the western shoulder of the highway, he had a clear view of the grazing land that stretched out from the edge of a vast state forest. His position was suitably elevated, the crest of a low-lying hill. Behind him the ground fell away but the bush thickened. He was concealed beneath a sheet of mottled mesh, military camouflage, a high-powered rifle nestled comfortably against his shoulder. He adjusted the sight ever so slightly, then peered once again through the glass.

The cross hairs were aimed midway between the centre line of the highway and the broken markings of the outside lane. Within the instant it took for a dark sedan to enter his field of vision, he watched a woman in her 30s talking animatedly to her hands-free phone, her hands flitting about on the steering wheel. Behind her, in a raised seat, a curly-haired child of three stared dolefully out the window at the inexplicable world rushing past.

He took a deep breath and steadied his mind. The pressure of his index finger increasing in measured increments – a gentle squeeze. This is how it needed to be. A gentle squeeze to send a clear message of exactly what was at stake. Other clients had attempted to renege on previous contracts and they were made to see the error of their ways. It didn't take long, but it really was unnecessary. He would rather be preparing for a new assignment.

The body in the harbour should have been enough. Perhaps it wasn't. A scenario was playing out, a meeting had been arranged, a remote property, a suitable location for a frank and private conversation. A realignment of expectations.

But unfortunately, the implied trust between partners to a reasonable deal had been misplaced. Counter measures were required, if only for his own self-preservation. He would always give his clients the benefit of the doubt, but that didn't mean he would leave himself exposed.

As he raised his head to stretch the muscles in his neck, he spotted a bright white truck speeding down the outside southbound lane – a tanker emblazoned with the logo of a natural gas company. The irony pulled at the corners of his mouth. The driver was taking an unnecessary risk, overtaking a cattle truck who was already doing 115km/h on the flat, but it kept him on the outside. For a moment, there was a break in the traffic coming the other way.

This was it. He lowered his head, pressed his eye to the sight and inhaled a lungful of air. The front bumper of the rig entered his field of vision, but he waited. Front wheels, the length of steel that held the bulbous tank of compressed energy, the bottom of the letters of the logo, too fast to register, then the focus of all his concentration – back right tyre.

The shot cracked and rang out across the plain, but the truck was already fishtailing across the bitumen. The back-end of the tanker clipped the rig of the cattle truck, whose driver didn't have time to react. The force of the collision shoved him away from the wheel and brake. His rig crossed the shoulder and tipped into a gully, his load of startled animals leaned precariously over the left-side wheels then tipped back suddenly to the right. The gas tanker had swung violently across the highway, jack knifing. Fifty metres away, travelling north at 120km/h, a salesman in a luxury sedan was listening to a podcast about the latest trends in internet wealth creation. He didn't consider the safety of the passengers in the minibus beside him, nor even their age. He jerked his steering wheel to the left and prayed to a god whose existence he had vehemently denied up until that moment.

The view from up on the hill was satisfying. It was a clean shot. He slipped from beneath the mottled netting, disassembled the rifle then cut down through the trees to the fire trail where his SUV was waiting.

He drove three kilometres south east, through to where the native bush met the plantation of pine trees. He pulled off the road and made his way carefully through the even lines of thick trunks. The ground was soft and pitted, the unevenness hidden beneath the bed of pale brown needles. He negotiated a path up and down gentle hills. He checked his GPS then slowly came to a stop. He killed the engine. On his screen, the plantation encircled a solitary property with a one lane driveway that pointed north-east back through the native bush towards the highway.

He got out of the SUV and checked his watch. It was 10.55am.

Xian Lao sat at a large oak desk in what was once a sitting room. The walls were lined with floor-to-ceiling bookcases, stacked with books he would never read. The French doors to his left looked out over the sprawling lawn that gradually fell away to a thick wall of pine trees. It was the solitude of the property that had attracted him, and the stateliness of its proportions. Eight bedrooms, two kitchens, three living rooms, a library and a billiard room. Despite all this, whenever he was there, which was never as often as he would have liked, he spent most of his time in the "office". Perhaps because it was shut away from the rest of the house, accessed by a long dark corridor. There was a discreet ensuite bathroom, and he had installed a small kitchenette for coffee. The bar behind one of the bookcases was always fully stocked with whiskey.

He had several monitors set up across the desk, each was now relaying market information from across the globe. His stocks in China were doing well – a conservative mix of mining, research and energy, with a few smaller, riskier ventures scattered through to keep it interesting. It was Shanghai Consolidated Holdings that sustained most of his wealth; a fact that continued to grate on his nerves. He appreciated everything his uncle had taught him when he was younger but it was high time he made his own mark, his own money, his own moves.

His uncle had built Shanghai Consolidated Holdings over several decades into what was now one of the biggest mining conglomerates in Asia. It was Wan Bi's foray into Africa in the 90s that had underpinned its exponential growth. It had been a difficult time, but it had proved to be the makings of the old man. He had gambled on the greed of several government ministers across three nation states, and pandered to the egos of more than one delusional president. Memorial hospitals and schools were built, highways extended across deserts in lands where few could afford to drive – infrastructure on a grand scale. All Shanghai Consolidated Holdings required in return was access to certain pockets of land. Deals were struck that filled the government coffers at a rate not seen for many years. But the brilliance of the short-term returns had blinded the ministers to the potential long-term riches they had willingly signed away.

Africa wasn't the only continent to fall prey to this method of business. Shanghai Consolidated Holdings had made significant inroads into the South American market and in several lucrative valleys in southern and central Europe. Xian had hoped to head up one of their recent ventures in Brazil, but that had gone to his cousin. As had the copper mine in Angola before that. Every time Xian believed his time had come, his uncle had favoured one of the others.

Moving to Australia had been Xian's own idea. His uncle did little to stop him. He made conciliatory gestures so as not to offend his own sister, suggesting a deal in Gambia was in the offing, but Xian knew better to wait any longer. He had needed to make his move within the next five to eight years or throw away any plans to rise within the company.

Despite his elderly mother's reservations, he had started Xancorp with the proceeds of a sale in Mali, and made the move from Shanghai to Sydney. It was one of his greatest regrets that he hadn't acted sooner. He had wanted more than anything to prove his worth to his mother, but she had passed away two years ago before his plans could come to fruition.

Since then he had been driven as much by spite for his uncle as actual ambition for his own business ventures. He resented relying on him so heavily for his fortune. If the Timor Sea deal came off as planned, it would be the last time he would need his assistance.

There was a knock at the door.

A heavy-set Chinese man in his early 20s, wearing a dark suit, appeared, pressing an earpiece with his fingers. He told his boss in Mandarin that the perimeter was secure. There were two other men in matching suits patrolling the outside of the house, all former elite soldiers of the Chinese army. They were armed with service revolvers, but could do as much damage with their bare hands when necessary. Xian told him to check all the rooms in the house then run the perimeter again. The man nodded and relayed the information to his colleagues. Xian checked his watch. It was almost time.

He liked to think hiring the Afrikaner was his own idea, but even that stemmed from the actions of his uncle. The blonde assassin had served his purpose well on several operations in Zimbabwe back in the early days. He was expensive but disturbingly efficient, and virtually invisible. Xian knew of several deaths that could be attributed to his work that were commonly accepted as accidental by the local authorities, and a few more hindrances who had just disappeared without explanation.

More recently, however, Xian's uncle had grown concerned at the assassin's increasingly gratuitous methods, which had been garnering undue attention. It came to a head in Sao Paulo, where the children of two government ministers were killed in what should have looked like a standard gangland kidnapping. When their tiny bodies were found, broken and abused, the police instigated an extensive manhunt for what they believed was a serial killer with a political agenda. The media went into overdrive. Shanghai Consolidated Holdings was forced to cut a discreet exit from several lucrative projects until the incident blew over – two more unsolved murders in a city of 12 million people. "Unhinged", was Wan Bi's assessment. He decided the Afrikaner could no longer be relied upon to act in the company's interests. His services were terminated. That was a year ago.

Xian had scoffed at his uncle's reticence. Of course, the man was unhinged. What contract killer wasn't? He likened them to pit bulls trained to fight. You had to keep them on a tight leash but once they were in the ring they needed to be free to do their job.

Xian had reached out to him through the dark web, inviting him to Australia for a one-off assignment, suggesting further opportunities to get back in with Shanghai Consolidated Holdings. After an interminable wait, the Afrikaner had responded, requesting an outline of the assignment. Xian offered $300,000 a head for three executions with the express purpose of scaring off two large mining companies interested in exploring gas reserves in the Timor Sea. The assassin had demanded $750,000 a head, payment in cryptocurrency. Xian tried to argue him down to $500,000 a head but he wouldn't budge. They agreed to terms. It was a reasonable deal in the broader scheme. If the Timor Sea deal came off, the initial outlay would seem inconsequential. Xian's mind had already started swirling with loose plans to use the Afrikaner for work of a more personal nature if his uncle didn't start showing him the respect he deserved.

The assignment had gone smoothly at first. Xian had wanted to know as little as possible about the arrangement so in the unfortunate development that he should be questioned by police, he could confidently claim ignorance of any dealings with each of the victims or even anyone at Katercorp or Barclay Industries. When he learned how the Afrikaner was operating, he was impressed – feeding people to wild animals sent an unambiguous message to his potential rivals. He didn't even mind being questioned by local police. It was the Danish woman who had unnerved him. She was the one who had made the connection between himself and his uncle. He couldn't afford to get on the wrong side of Wan Bi at such a crucial stage of the operation. The safest thing to do was to back out as quickly as possible, and hope the first two bodies were enough to serve his purposes. But the Afrikaner clearly had other ideas.

It was time to bring this particular pit bull to heel.

Xian had contacted him again, apologising for attempting to terminate the contract, then suggested they meet to resolve their differences. The assassin had refused. He reiterated that the final payment was still owing. Xian brushed over the amount as a trifle compared to his next assignment with Shanghai Consolidated Holdings. His ruse worked. The Afrikaner had agreed to meet with him in the Southern Highlands in an effort to realign their expectations.

Xian moved around his desk and poured himself a whiskey to still his nerves. He had cut it fine, but managed to secure the services of another 'pit bull' – an up-and-coming player from Shanghai. The former IT student with a penchant for piano wire had flown in the day before and was now waiting patiently upstairs for the signal to get to work. He came in at a fifth of the cost of the Afrikaner. Furthermore, he suggested he had the IT contacts to retrieve the monies already paid for the first two murders. It could be the beginnings of a lucrative relationship, Xian mused as he checked his watch once again.

The serenity of his rural hideaway was suddenly spoiled by the desperate and persistent wail of a car alarm. It was coming from the front of the house. One of the SUVs. He could hear his security detail moving through the halls. He waited a moment then rose from his desk. He peered through the French doors. The lawn outside and the surrounding forest looked peaceful, secure. He opened the door to the office and made his way along the corridor. It was so dark he had to run his hands along the walls until he reached the foyer. He slipped into the front living room and pulled back one of the curtains. His three staff looked bemused. One of them had retrieved the keys and turned off the alarm. The other two stared at the tree line unsure of what caused the alarm to go off in the first place. Xian lowered the curtain and walked back through the house.

When he reached the office, he closed the door behind him, and without thinking, locked it. He was slightly embarrassed his heart rate was up but then almost choked when he realised he was not alone. In the shadows by the French door, stood a tall blonde man in a white business shirt and dark suit pants. He was staring intently at Xian.

When Birgitte had arrived at the Goulburn St office that morning, she had almost been knocked over by plain clothes detectives and uniformed officers preparing for some sort of joint operation. She wondered if another body had been found during the night. It was difficult to determine who was in charge.

She had made her way through the crowd towards Tony's desk but had spotted him coming out of Miller's office looking furious.

"She takes the fucking cake," he'd muttered under his breath, running his hands through his hair in frustration.

"What's going on?"

"We've got the warrants to search several of Lao's offices and residential properties across the city."

"That's great news."

"Of course it is," he said tersely, "but Barton flew to Canberra last night for meetings with the Federal Minister. He won't be back until Wednesday. Apparently, he's left Miller in charge."

"You are still running the investigation. Aren't you?"

"Doesn't matter. She's running the operation today and has relegated me to god knows what. I'm stuck here, while that lot go out and search for evidence. It's fucking ridiculous." He looked at her. "I'm sorry. The main thing is they pull him in for questioning, but I don't like being manipulated by the people above me who should know better."

"It's okay." She pressed his upper arm. "I'm sorry I wasn't here for the briefing."

"You weren't invited either."

Her eyes widened.

"Miller's trying to minimise involvement from either of us."

"Can I see the list of properties on the warrants?"

"Sure." They went to his desk and he brought it up on his screen. He glared at Miller through her office window, but she was too busy working with special ops officers to care.

Birgitte eventually said, "It's not here."

"What's not?"

"A property in the Southern Highlands."

"What's the significance?"

"It might be nothing, but I met up with Cerina Ming last night, the maitre d' from the Floating Lotus. She mentioned a function she catered for off the highway past Berrima about a week ago, in a large house, which appeared to belong to Lao."

Tony finally understood why she'd left the previous night with Harris.

She noticed the look on his face. "I should have told you but I wasn't sure if it would amount to anything. I'm still not sure."

"It's fine. Walk me through what happened."

"I showed her a photo of Wan Bi Lao and she said he was there but was probably flying back to China the next day. Xian Lao may have the property in someone else's name or it's owned by a shell company perhaps, but it might be worth driving out there to have a look."

"That's great work," Tony said, grinning because they finally had an edge over Miller. "I could kiss you so hard right now."

Her eyes glinted. "Do we need permission to drive out there?"

"Not fucking likely. She won't even know we're gone."

"Should we bring some back up?"

"I'll see if Harris and Donleavy are free."

An hour and half later the four of them were sitting in a café in the country town of Bowral, clarifying their plans. Harris had brought a tablet, which showed a map of the surrounding area. Birgitte pointed to what she believed may have been the property in question. There was a single-entry drive from a narrow road that came off the highway. The house seemed to face on to a large pine forest – a plantation that spread for several hectares to the south and west. There were no ancillary buildings, which was reassuring.

"Okay," Tony said. "Birgitte and I will drive up and park out the front and make some general enquiries. You guys park back here and keep an eye out. I'll call you if we need you. If Lao is there, I don't want to alarm him. Miller said they're hitting his offices at 11am, so we should have 30 minutes or so where he won't be expecting us."

"And if he's not there?" asked Donleavy, who made no attempt to hide his irritation at being pulled away from the bigger operation.

"I'll call you in and you guys can scout around the property for a bit. If he's not there, he won't mind us taking a look around, will he?"

"Nothing may come of it," said Birgitte, "but it's best we have a look to be sure."

They were pulling back onto the highway when the announcement came over their radios that a serious multi-vehicle collision had blocked traffic for kilometres outside of Berrima. Within minutes they reached the tail the of the jam. Ambulances and other police cars with their sirens wailing raced past.

Tony reached out of his window with the flashing light, attaching to the roof. In the car behind, Donleavy hit his own siren and lights as they pulled onto the opposite side of the highway, which was empty. The frustrated passengers stuck in the two interminable lines of motionless cars watched them as sped towards the collision site.

Five minutes later they slowed down and proceeded through a makeshift barrier of police cars. The highway was strewn with twisted metal, flaming chassis, police and paramedics running between vehicles, working desperately to calm the people still trapped. In the centre of it all, the gas tanker, on its side, threatening to unleash a greater hell on an already horrific scene. The driver was slumped by the side of the road, shaking his head. He was flanked by two officers who looked agitated. The driver was oblivious to their presence. He still had no idea what had happened but he knew he had somehow killed several people.

Tony called Donleavy. "You'll have to stay and help. It looks like there are more troops on the way. We'll keep going."

Donleavy pulled over and he and Harris leapt out of their car as two fire engines arrived from the south.

It didn't feel right to Tony, to leave so many injured people, but he also knew that this could be their only chance to pin Lao down. On the edge of the scene he had noticed a former colleague taking charge, so at least the rescue efforts would be coordinated and effective.

Birgitte turned in her seat and watched the chaos recede as they sped up the highway. Deep down she knew it was no accident but she chose not to say anything to Tony. He was already reactive because of Miller's ham-fisted management style. She needed him to clear and switched on because she had no idea what they were about to encounter.

Eventually, Tony pulled onto Mason's Creek Road. The land on this side of the highway was rolling pasture on a gradual upward slope, which soon gave way to native forest of gum trees and bracken. About two kilometres in he turned onto a narrow gravel road. There was no post box or main gate. The bush seemed to close in around them.

Tony peered through the trees and slowed right down. He hadn't the heart to tell Birgitte that the nearby pine forest had been the scene of several famous killings over the past 30 years. It had developed its own creepy folklore. He didn't care for the myths – the people responsible were either locked up or dead. Donleavy had made a joke about it in the café – something along the lines of when people went there to bury a body they usually dug up someone else's. Tony had brushed over it and glared at him to shut the fuck up.

They came up over a ridge and continued to wind through the trees until they reached a clearing.

The house was huge – three stories, probably built in the turn of the previous century. Two dark SUVs were parked in an open garage, a third was on the lawn to the south. The grounds were well kept. Tony swung the car round front and killed the engine. They got out and waited a moment, listening. It was hard to believe that not far away the air was full of sirens. All they could hear were the birds from the surrounding bush. It felt isolated, the silence was almost eerie. Tony looked at Birgitte. She nodded towards the front door.

They stepped up onto the verandah. The curtains were drawn across all the windows.

Tony rang the bell. They waited.

He pressed the bell again, then checked his watch. He looked back towards the car then at the lawn that led around the southern side of the house.

"Do you want me to go around the back?" Birgitte asked. "I might be able to see something."

"Not yet."

Tony tried the door handle. It worked. He pushed the front door open carefully, peering inside.

"Mr Lao?" Tony called out from the stoop, "It's the Federal Police. We'd like to have a word."

He held up his hand for Birgitte to step back, the he crouched down, drawing his gun. A few feet in from the door was the body of a man, face down in a pool of blood.

"Wait here," Tony said.

He stepped inside, his eyes slowly adjusting to the dimness. He was in a large tiled foyer with a staircase leading to the upper floors. He could see a library off to the right. To the left was a living room. Slumped against the mantle of a large fireplace was the body of another man, his lifeless hands pressed against his stomach, which was stained with blood. Beside the staircase was a dark hallway that led through to the back of the house. Several metres in he could make out the figure of third man who appeared to be floating. He approached carefully. A young Chinese man was suspended from the balustrade midway up the stairs by a thin metal wire that had cut deep into his throat – a garrotte. The other two bodies were dressed in suits. This guy wore black pants and black shirt. They all looked Chinese.

"Tony," Birgitte called out in a barely audible hiss from outside.

"Give me two more minutes. Let me know if anyone approaches."

He moved through to the back part of the house. As he walked carefully down a long dark corridor he almost discharged his weapon tripping over a fourth body. The guy at his feet was bigger than the others. His head was twisted at an awkward angle to his body, his neck was obviously broken.

The corridor split off to the back rooms of the house. Tony continued to the door at the end. He held his ear against the wood but couldn't hear anything from inside. He turned the handle and stepped back. Across the room, behind a large timber desk sat the body of Xian Lao. His throat was cut from left to right, pitching his head oddly to one side.

"*Jesus Christus*," whispered Birgitte. She had slipped in behind Tony.

He turned to her angrily. "I haven't finished sweeping the house. Whoever did this could still be here."

"I think they've gone, Tony."

"We'll I'm not willing to take that risk. You're unarmed. Stay here."

He left the room.

Birgitte stared at the body. Part of her was relieved. With Lao dead, the killing would stop. But it also meant the window for finding the killer was closing – fast. They had no idea who he was, or what he looked like. They didn't even have the make of car he was using.

She moved across the room, careful not to touch anything. Suddenly, she heard Tony call out. "Christ, he's still alive."

His footsteps echoed through the house.

She knew she should run back to help him but she needed to check something first. She stepped through the French doors and scanned the line of trees from the north, across the west down towards the south. Through the thick wall of established pines, she spotted a figure running deeper into the forest.

It was him.

She called out to Tony. "He's in the trees."

She waited a moment but all she could hear was scuffling. "Tony, we have to follow him. This could be our only chance."

She set off across the lawn, hoping Tony would follow her as soon as he could. She had no intention of stopping the killer; she just needed to get a good look at his face or at least get a licence plate of his car.

Tony hadn't heard Birgitte call out. He was midway up the stairs, struggling to lift the young man who was tied by his throat to the bannister. He'd stepped past him on the way to searching the rest of the house, when he'd suddenly grabbed Tony's hand. Reflexively, Tony had leaped back and turned the gun on him then realised he was reaching out for help. Tony was now doing his best to take the pressure off the guy's throat but it was awkward trying to lift him with the bannister in between them. The man's arms were flailing wildly, as blood gushed from his mouth.

It was no use. The garrotte was cutting deeper into his throat.

"Don't struggle. I'll get something to cut you down."

Tony gently lowered the man back down, shuddering at the pain it was causing him, then bounded down the stairs. He ran through the library and billiard room, then through several more rooms until he found a large kitchen. He called out to Birgitte again, "I could do with a hand. The guy on the stairs is still alive."

He rifled through drawers until he found a pair of secateurs, then ran back the way he had come. The young man had managed to get one foot up on the stairs to take the weight off the wire. Tony leapt up to where it was tied around the bannister. He cut the wire. The body fell to the floor with a loud thud.

Tony descended the stairs, trying to catch his breath. When he got to the bottom, he felt a searing pain across his right upper arm. The man he had just saved was wielding a short-blade knife attached to the knuckles of one hand. It suddenly occurred to Tony that this guy could have been responsible for the deaths of everyone in the house. Had he also killed Hans Thostrup and the others?

The assassin's face was full of cold rage. His black shirt soaked in blood. He took another swipe but missed. He fell against the opposite wall, still in shock at being cut down and realising he had another chance to escape. With every breath, a fine mist of blood sprayed out from his mouth. His throat was an open wound. Tony could see by the look in the young man's eyes he had no intentions giving himself up.

Tony reached for his gun but it wasn't there. He looked up the stairs. It was sitting midway to the top from when he first tried to lift the man to safety. The young man lunged. Tony leaped backwards.

"Put down the blade," he said, "and I might be able to stem your bleeding.

The young man ignored him, his face turning a sickening grey. He kept slashing at the air between them with the knife.

Tony wasn't sure if the guy spoke English but he did his best to reason with him. "There are ambulances not far from here. I can get you the help you need."

Tony misjudged his step, falling backwards over a potted palm. The young man came at him with the blade raised. Tony managed to grab his wrist as they both fell to the floor. They struggled wildly in the dim light of the hallway. For a moment, the assassin had the weight advantage. He brought the edge of the blade down on Tony's throat – a swipe to the right and both of them would have been in trouble. Reluctantly, Tony jammed the webbing of his left hand deep into the open wound beneath the assassin's chin. The young man shook violently as if struck by a jolt of electricity. Tony maintained the pressure until he could feel the fight go out of his attacker. He used all his remaining energy to push the guy over onto his back. The knife hand fell back limply. Tony got up on one knee and watched the assassin's eyes glaze over as he aspirated a final jet of blood into the air. Tony checked his pulse. He was dead.

Tony slowly stood up and checked himself. The cut in his upper arm was long but not deep. He'd been lucky.

He climbed the stairs to retrieve his gun, then called out to Birgitte again.

The house was silent. He felt a sense of dread creeping over his skin as he ran back to the room where he'd last seen her.

Xian Lao's corpse was still sitting behind the desk but Birgitte was no longer there. Tony ran to the open French doors and looked out across the lawn. Nothing. Perhaps she'd moved through the rest of the house and was out of ear shot. He retraced his steps and headed up the stairs to the upper floors.

Birgitte had reached the line of pines. It was disorienting to enter the plantation. The trees had been planted 10 metres apart but the rows weren't exactly even, nor was the ground on which they were planted. Now they were fully established, the trunks were thick and tall. It created an optical illusion of depth and continuity that shifted with every step. The soft, dappled grey-green light of the forest continued to dim the deeper she went. Occasionally, some of the lower branches jutted out at shoulder height, obscuring her vision and forcing her to walk on her haunches. The foliage would clear and 300 metres a head she would see the figure in dark pants and white shirt moving purposefully through the trees, disappearing for seconds at a time then reappearing suddenly. He looked tall, Caucasian, blonde. At this distance, it was hard to say, but she guessed he was in his late 30s, early 40s. He moved with a swiftness and agility that was almost feline. She had to pick up her pace to keep up with him.

The ground fell away to a low gully then rose unevenly across a broad swathe of land that suggested she was on the edge of a steep hill. It was hard to determine how high it rose but it suddenly became a challenge to keep her footing. There were now rocks to contend with, large soft-looking boulders that interrupted the lines of pines. The landscape felt surreal. She could no longer see her target but decided to simply follow the line of when she last saw him. As she scrambled with her hands to the crest of the hill, she looked back in the hope Tony was somewhere behind her, but all she could see was the thick mesh of thousands of pine branches.

She was on a ridge. She spotted her target again. He had also slowed down. He was only 100 metres away. Further on,

303

deeper through the trees, she saw his dark SUV. If she couldn't get a good look at the killer, she had to at least get the licence plate number on the vehicle.

He placed his hand against a trunk to catch his breath. He could feel his heart rate steadying. The distance from the house had allowed him to burn off the adrenalin from what had taken place inside. He knew Lao would have protection, but the little guy in black was a surprise.

He looked down at the back of his hands, which were still bleeding from the garrotte. Thankfully, most of the weight was taken on his watch. Otherwise, it would have cut him to the bone. A tricksy little fucker, he thought – but too light for the task. He had been able to lift him quite easily. He'd struggled to get a firm grip on him but once he had him in his grasp it was like strangling a cat. Tying him to the stairwell was just for kicks. The other three were military trained so dispatching them had been more straight forward. He could read their moves before they'd even considered their options.

And Mr Fucking Lao – that pathetic lump of a man, begging for his life like a little girl. Brought an amateur in to do a professional's job – that was his first mistake. If he'd just paid his bills on time, he'd still be here.

The clouds had begun to swirl on the periphery of his consciousness once again, obscuring his thinking, dredging up thoughts of his father. The Captain always said, "Pay your bills on time and you'll have nothing to worry about". He wondered for a moment what his father would have thought of his handling of the situation. Inspired, he told himself. The look on Xian Lao's face when he sent greetings from his uncle in Shanghai. Beautiful. It had only taken a single phone call to put things to rights. Wan Bi Lao was more than willing to cover the cost of the third killing then offered a very respectable sum to eradicate his nephew immediately.

But "inspired" was not the word his father would have used. "Eh, Boy," he could hear his father say, "think you're smart then. It could have gone very differently, couldn't it?" He laughed nervously, quickened his pace and tried to shut out the voices in his head.

By the time he reached the SUV, the clouds in his mind had receded. He stopped to open the backdoor, and heard a crackling of pine needles some way off behind him. He turned and was genuinely surprised to see a woman in jeans and white blouse 50 metres away suddenly stop in her tracks, watching him. Where the hell had she come from? There wasn't another house around there for miles. Then he recognised her from the internet – Detective Vestergaard. He liked what he saw. There was something animal about her demeanour, poised on the balls of her feet, her long slender legs ready to engage – fight or flight, he wondered. He scanned the trees for signs of other police and when he realised she had come alone he couldn't help but smile. She was game. He had to give her that much.

He considered retrieving the rifle from the back of the car, but getting a clear shot through the trees at a moving target could prove cumbersome. He took a step towards her. She stepped back and moved behind a tree. He took another few steps, and she responded in kind, maintaining the same distance between them. He dodged to the left, off the crest of the ridge. She moved to her left but held the higher ground. He didn't want her near the car so he moved swiftly back up onto the ridge and broke into a run that sent her scarpering back through the trees. She was obviously fit. He watched her body move lithely through the trees. Occasionally she checked over her shoulder and altered her pace so she didn't get too far ahead. He tried to move round to her right in the hope of forcing her down into the gully, but she held her line, swinging from low branches when the pine needles beneath her feet threatened to bring her down.

They were now several hundred metres from the SUV, both pausing to catch their breath. She was no closer or further away from him than before. He stepped behind a tree, waited a moment then moved diagonally back through the pines, shifting swiftly from cover to cover. He cut a ragged path, hiding for seconds behind one tree then flitting past several others. When he looked back he could see she was struggling to guess his next move, waiting longer between each short chase. It was tiring work but he was increasing the gap between them. Then he saw he had a clear line back to the SUV. He broke into a sprint.

He got back to the car and quickly started the engine. He checked his rear-view mirror. Perhaps he could hit her with the rear bumper, if she came close enough, but he couldn't see her. Fuck it, he'd just have to leave it be. Not ideal but not worth wasting time over.

As he put the SUV in gear, the windscreen exploded inwards with an almighty crash. A rock the size of a small basketball stopped short of crushing him when it hit the steering wheel and was wedged against the dashboard. He hadn't seen it coming and was momentarily stunned. He tried to lift it out but it wouldn't budge and he couldn't turn the wheel in either direction. Through the shattered glass he could make out the fractured image of the detective moving back from the car.

He leapt out of the front seat, furious. She was waiting for him, her knees bent, shoulders forward, ready to run. Her eyes blazed. He went to the back of the SUV and withdrew a crowbar, but when he looked up again, she was gone. He moved back to the front of the car, leaning over the bonnet and began prying the windscreen out of its frame.

The next rock was smaller but it found its mark. The back of his head erupted in searing pain. The crowbar slid across the bonnet and fell to the ground. He made a flailing attempt to grab at it but could only see stars. He felt the back of his scalp. The gash was deep enough to require stitches. His fingers shone brilliantly with his own blood. The sight of it enraged him further. He stepped back from the car, trying to think.

Birgitte stood a few feet from the bonnet, wielding the crowbar like a baseball bat.

He shook his head slowly. "You're a feisty little thing, aren't you?"

She moved around him in a wide arc, not saying a word.

"Why don't you put the bar down, Missy. I'd hate to have to hurt you."

Birgitte stepped lightly around him, close enough to strike. He suddenly lunged, but she danced back across the pines needles, maintaining her distance. He stood up straight, defiant. "Sizing me up are you, Sweetheart?"

She didn't answer.

"Tell me, Detective, what do you see?" He paused, motioning to his white shirt that was smeared and smattered with wet blood, none of which was his own. "Do you see someone who is just going to give up and hand himself in?"

His accent was thick Afrikaan. She figured South African or perhaps one of the countries on its borders. For the first time, she took in his features, the length of his face, the line of his nose, his small but piercing eyes. There was no warmth to any of it. He looked – nasty and soulless.

The gravity of her situation was not lost on her. She was alone in a remote forest with a man who had brutally tortured three innocent people, and possibly just executed five more without barely a scratch. She was the only person standing between him and his escape, and she was only armed with a crowbar.

He grinned, revealing crooked grey teeth, his smile distorting his features further. "I'll tell you what you can't see, Missy – it's me driving out of here and not looking back on this stinking backward country."

He laughed with incredulity as he stepped quickly to his right just to force her to do the same. "Christ, I thought Zimbabwe was bad. These people, these stupid Australians, should know better. They're getting raped by the Chinese and they think it's fucking date night. They want to call their friends and tell them all about it."

He looked at her for some sort of response, complicity in his assessment, but she gave him nothing.

"But you're not one of them, are you, Birgitte Vestergaard?" He enunciated each syllable of her name, curling his thin lips as he spoke. "Tell me, Detective. Do you still have nightmares about Max Anders?"

She was determined to conceal her emotions. She stared him down and let the words fall short of their mark. But he persisted. "Do you think maybe I could visit you in your sleep some night – just slip into that pretty little head of yours and swim about with you. Perhaps I could tell you some stories from my life – colourful stories, I assure you, full of characters that will swirl around your mind like nightlight animals on a nursery wall. Would you like that, Detective?"

He crouched down, moving around her, forcing her to think on her feet.

"Shall I tell you about the little girl I picked up outside Coober Pedy," he said. "The sweetest little thing. A real little vixen, not unlike yourself, only younger, sweeter." He considered her figure for a moment. "You must have been quite a catch at her age. Did you let them catch you? Or did you keep all that sweetness to yourself."

He lunged at her again. She swung the bar at him, missing his nose by inches. He chuckled at her attempt to hit him. "She was quite the temptress, my friend. But it was all an act. No virgin, mind you, but not far from it. I loosened her up good." His face softened all too naturally into a conspiring leer. "I loosened her up so much she discovered a voice she didn't know she had. Did you know, Detective, there's a scream a woman makes that stays with you? It comes up from the very depths of their soul. When I first heard that scream – years ago, it truly frightened me. Frightened me! Can you believe it? I felt chills. It was a sickening sensation I wouldn't wish on my worst enemy. But I was only young myself then; I came to like hearing it after a while. I've been searching for it ever since. Have you ever been made to scream like that, Detective?"

"What did you do with her?" Birgitte's voice was a low grumble, filled with rage.

His eyes glazed with the memory, his shoulders slackened. "I gave her knowledge of herself – showed her the limitations of her being."

For a moment, he appeared to be staring at the pine needles on the ground between them – lost in the memory of a brutal assault. Birgitte saw her chance. Without Tony to back her up she had to act now. She leapt forward and brought he crowbar down as hard as she could at the side of his face. If the bar had connected with his jaw, it would have crushed the bone and knocked him out cold. But he'd tricked her. He'd pretended to vague out. The bar stopped dead an inch from his jaw, clasped in his large thick hand. They were both now connected with all their strength on either end. He grinned again.

"I thought you were smarter than that."

With a sudden twist he retrieved the crowbar, spun it around and used the hook to pull Birgitte's leg out from under her. Before she hit the ground on her back, he was already on top of her. He pressed the crowbar across her throat and brought the weight of his upper body bearing down on her. He inhaled the scent of her skin. "Now you are going to listen very carefully. We are going to take a short drive and you will behave yourself. This was your choice, remember? You could have walked away at any point. You chose to be here. Consider yourself my insurance package. Now get the fuck up."

She slowly got to her feet, furious with herself. He drew out a roll of silver gaffer tape from the back of the SUV. She shuddered when she realised what it was.

"Wrap your ankles," he demanded. "Here – sit on the bumper, and wrap your ankles nice and tight. Now, put your wrists together." He snatched the tape from her hands and quickly bound her forearms.

"Get in the back and keep your pretty little head down until I let you out."

He slammed the door behind her, then used the crowbar to strip the windscreen away and dislodge the rock.

He began to drive the SUV carefully through the trees, down into the gully and up the other side. Birgitte was rocked back and forth with the motion of the vehicle, the sight of the refrigeration unit beside her made her feel sick. She thought of Hans Thostrup, Salina Heysmith and James Freedmont. They had all been transported inside that sleek white coffin. For the first time, she wondered if it would be her fate as well.

The sound of approaching sirens brought little relief to Tony. After calling for back-up, he'd searched every room in the enormous house twice over but there was no sign of Birgitte. It didn't make sense. He did find a kit bag in a bedroom upstairs. It contained an assortment of knives, syringes, a couple of hand guns. He figured it belonged to the guy who had attacked him on the stairwell.

Tony had gone back downstairs and tried to determine how events may have played out just before they had arrived. It looked as if the killer had executed Xian Lao at his desk then moved through the lower floor taking out the security detail one at a time. One of them must have used the garrotte on the stairwell, but suffered a fatal stab wound themselves. It was sketchy and not exactly convincing. There was no blood on the stairs. And if the assassin had a knife, why hadn't he cut himself down? Tony also couldn't work out how the guy got from the bedroom upstairs, down into Lao's home office without being seen by the three guys hired to protect him.

He was about to make a cursory search of the surrounding plantation when Constable Harris had phoned from the accident site to relay the message from Miller that the warrants had all been executed. Apparently, Miller had found a false wall behind Lao's desk at Xancorp but it only contained business papers. Other than that, she'd come up empty. Tony told Harris that Lao was dead and it looked like his killer was too. Harris was stunned. He then informed her Birgitte was missing. Harris told him the accident site was relatively under control so she would organise for several officers to follow her and Donleavy up to the house.

Tony had run back into the home office and while being careful not to disturb the body or any other potential evidence, soon found a false wall. This cavity held a laptop. He carried it out to his car. He was standing at the front door when three patrol cars appeared through the trees.

Two hours later the property was swarming with forensic teams, paramedics, uniformed officers and the investigative team. The air was filled with the sound of helicopters from the three major news outlets who had followed the patrol cars from the pile-up on the highway. Several officers with Alsatians were moving through the pine plantation searching for evidence of Birgitte.

Commander Barton stood at the front door peering into the house as Miller offered her theories on how the day had played out. Tony stood to one side trying to not lose his temper. He was angry at himself for not keeping a better eye on Birgitte.

"Lao must have known we were searching his offices," Miller said with finality. "Panicked perhaps. Got in an argument with guy he was paying to intimidate Katercorp and Barclay Industries."

"So you're on board with that idea now that Lao is dead?" Tony said. "You didn't seem so keen earlier. In fact, you were sure Birgitte had it all wrong from the outset."

"It didn't seem feasible at the time."

"And if you'd listened?"

Barton raised a calming hand. "What's done is done. The main thing now is we find Birgitte as quickly as possible. What are your thoughts, Tony?"

He looked into the surrounding bushland. "There had to have been someone else. She had no reason to go running off unless she'd seen something."

"So now you're saying the guy in there isn't the killer we're looking for?" said Miller.

"The guy in there is very possibly a contract killer – he almost succeeded in killing me despite having a gaping hole in his throat. But was he the guy who killed Thostrup, Heysmith and Freedmont? I don't know – and neither do you."

Barton stepped back as the first body was carried out on a gurney. "And you said there was no blood on the stairs?"

"That's right. If someone else was here, they could have killed Lao, his security detail, then taken out the other contract killer. Maybe Birgitte spotted him trying to escape."

Tony's phone rang. It was the search team in the forest. They'd found a smashed windscreen and tyre marks leading west through the trees. They'd lost the trail at the top of the next hill.

Tony turned to Miller. "Get a chopper here now."

CHAPTER SIXTEEN

Birgitte didn't like her chances of escape. She looked at the thick layers of gaffer tape binding her wrists, and the metal wire that ran from the tape to the base of a timber post. She was trapped in a run-down weatherboard house somewhere on the side of mountain in remote bushland. Nor did she like her chances of being rescued. She figured about eight hours had passed since she'd been abducted from the Southern Highlands. An hour of that had been spent jostling about in the back of the SUV. She had sensed they had been going uphill for the last few kilometres before they eventually came to a halt. The had engine stopped. The front door opened and closed. She waited. It was at least 20 minutes before the back door suddenly opened – too fast for her to lash out with her feet. He had grabbed her ankles and pulled her out of the SUV, allowing her to fall to the ground roughly. She had rolled over and quickly tried to take in her surroundings. Heavy bushland rising steeply behind a single-story house. A makeshift shed, little more than four posts and a sloping corrugated tin roof, cluttered with rusting engine parts and sheets of rotting canvas. A single dirt road leading into the property around the side of the mountain. She had looked up into the canopy of gums and realised that vision from a police helicopter would be extremely limited. And god knows how deep they were into natural bushland. Would a pilot think to come this far? Where ever "this" was.

He had thrown her over his shoulder in a fireman's lift and carried her into the house. There he quickly tied her to one of three timber posts that supported the roof.

"If you need to the toilet, it's through there," he had pointed to a door at the far end of the living area. She could see two other doors that opened onto empty bedrooms.

She looked at her feet, bound together. "I can't walk."

He walked out to the SUV and came back with a large bowie knife. He cut the tape between her ankles. "When you need it, I'll add a length of wire so you can get there and back, but no further. If you fuck me about in anyway," he said, pointing the tip of the knife at her face, "I will fuck you so hard you will wish you'd never been born." The playfulness had gone from his voice. She was now a hindrance he had no interest in playing with.

She had nodded and rested her shoulders against the post.

The house was sparsely furnished. The kitchen held an old fridge and stove. There was a dining table and chairs, a decrepit sofa in the living area but little else. It was dusty and stank of mildew. The place looked like it was used only rarely.

He had retrieved a first aid kit and a canvas bag from the SUV. "You're quite the pitcher," he said as he peeled off his blood-soaked shirt and headed for the bathroom. Five minutes later he came out with a neat patch taped across the back of his head, and another around his wrist. He had cleaned the blood from his neck and shoulders. His bare torso was thin and wiry. He pulled a clean dark t-shirt and a grey hoodie from the canvas bag.

Birgitte watched him. "Back in the house, were you the one who killed Xian Lao?"

He ignored her, pulling the shirt over his head.

She tried again. "What was he paying you?"

He zipped up his hoodie then stepped towards her. He crouched down and stared into her eyes. "We both intend getting out of here in one piece, yes? So how about you stop with the silly questions, because you'll only be cutting your own throat if you keep it up."

He stood up, considering her for a moment. The light had faded quickly. It was getting colder. He went back outside but came back with a thick blanket, which he threw at her feet.

He had turned on the lights and brought in more supplies from the truck then set about cooking a can of stew on the stove top. He gave her a bowl of it with a spoon, which she struggled to hold. "Don't fuss," he had said, "you're lucky to be getting that."

She had waited for the stew to cool then ate it quietly. She would need her energy. She had to stay ready for any opportunity.

When night fell, he had continued to busy himself around the house. He had brought in his rifle and some other equipment in boxes she couldn't recognise. He had also brought in a laptop – the one she was sure he used to stay in contact with Xian Lao. This gave her hope.

She figured it was now somewhere between 8pm and 10pm. He had been out once in the last hour, to move the SUV. When the engine had started, her heart began to race – was he just going to leave her there? But then she heard him reverse the SUV into the shed, shifting it away from prying eyes.

His movements were slower now. He was more relaxed. He'd said very little since they'd arrived at the house. She decided it was time to engage with him again.

"Thank you for the blanket." She had pulled it up over her shoulders. The casual act of consideration was at odds with his other behaviour. It was as if there was a part of him that wanted to show he cared.

She wasn't sure which line to take with him – get him talking about himself, bring up the girl he mentioned earlier, or keep it all about business. How do you engage with a person who devotes their life to torturing and killing innocent people for money?

"You're not what I expected," she said eventually.

He was checking his equipment, pretending to ignore her, but she knew she had his full attention.

"When I first saw Hans Thostrup's body, in the morgue in Alice Springs, I pictured something different. I don't know why."

She watched him shifting gear from one bag to another. "Perhaps I was confusing the damage done to his body with the physicality of the man behind the act. I pictured someone bigger, wilder, more animal."

He zipped up one of the bags and moved it to the front door.

"It was the same, only more so, with Salina Heysmith," she said. "Her body was so… crushed within her skin." She watched his face as she continued to talk, looking for signs she might be pushing him too far. "It suggested immense power. I was almost hoping you would be bigger, physically, I mean."

"It's not about size," he said bluntly. "It's about language."

He stopped preparing his gear for a moment, considering his words before he spoke. "My job is to deliver a message on behalf of my clients. The language must be clear, emphatic. There can be no misconstruing the intent. The means, as creative as they may appear to someone like you, on the outside, are neither here nor there. It keeps you lot at arms distance, chasing your tails, gives me the room to do my work. It is, I'm afraid, as simple as that."

He returned to his tasks, satisfied with his explanation.

Birgitte shifted under the blanket. The hard wood floor was unforgiving. "You must think we're pretty stupid then. It's taken us so long to catch up with you."

"My opinion of them is a far cry from my opinion of you," he said. "They behaved as I knew they would. The police are the same all over. It's mystifying how stupid they are as a breed of people. I should know, my father was police."

She could feel her breathing quicken. As much she needed him to talk, to give her something to work with, she knew if he said too much, he may be more compelled to kill her afterwards. Mother confessor wasn't a role she was necessarily going for.

"You, on the other hand," he said, pointing his finger at her, "you're something else. You have a way about you. I should be grateful. You've certainly made a routine assignment more interesting."

"Was the young girl outside Port Augusta routine?"

He got up from his chair, moved about as if unsure of what he was to do next, then he turned towards her. "I have to admit," he said. "She was a poor choice. I don't make them often. But then, she should have known better than to approach me."

"But you picked her up anyway."

"I picked her up. What harm done? I gave her a ride to the next roadhouse. She should have got out and left me alone."

315

He was pacing about, distracted by the memory. "My father warned me about girls like her. Said they'd undo my mind."

Birgitte did her best to suppress her imagination, which was racing with images of the poor girl's last hours. "Why didn't you let her go at the roadhouse?"

"She was a persistent little thing," he said. "Constantly whining."

"You could have said 'no'."

"It was her funeral – I warned her."

"How could she know who she was travelling with? You were just an older man to her, someone she probably found attractive, someone who she wanted to find her attractive. She was just being a teenager."

"I was never a teenager," he said defensively. "The Captain made sure of that. I had my childhood taken away from me. I spent those years learning skills no child should learn."

"Then why would you take hers? You weren't being paid for it. It wasn't a part of your job."

He rubbed his face with the heels of his hand, confused, frustrated. Then he looked down at her. "I don't know," he said. "I don't know why I had to kill her. She knew too much."

"You told her too much about yourself?"

He shook his head. "It wasn't that." He lowered his head. "She just got… too close."

Birgitte thought of the map detailing the kilometres he'd been willing to cover. He had spent so much time alone, unable to challenge his own thoughts, he struggled to communicate with anyone on a human level. She felt no pity for him, but at least she had a deeper understanding of who she was dealing with.

"Do you ever wonder why you do what you do?" she asked. "Do you ever question your own motives?"

He stood up, twisted his head from side to side, stretching the wiry muscles in his neck. "I don't have to answer to you, Detective. You are the one tied to a post, not me. Perhaps you should be answering my questions." He gave her a knowing smile. "When you're alone at night, unable to sleep, do you ever acknowledge your part in the deaths of the Svedbo children?"

It was meant to be a parting shot as he returned to his preparations, but clearly the idea gave him pleasure. "Of course, the court cleared you, but do you ever acknowledge the fact that if it wasn't for you, those three children would still be alive?"

"Anders was going to kill them anyway," she said, disturbed by how much he knew about her past.

"Do you really believe that?" he asked. "From my understanding, he could have just have easily let them go and continued on his way."

She looked away from him. Defending herself from the accusations of a contract killer who feed innocent people to animals was repulsive nonsense.

"It's your pride that will be your downfall, Detective," he said. "Clearly, I have my short comings, but you seem to think you know more than everyone else, that your blessed with some gift that sets you apart. I admit, you are very good at your job, impressively so. But you must learn when to put your ego to one side. At the very least, know when you're beaten."

With that he walked outside into the night air. Birgitte seethed with anger and disgust, mostly at herself. He was right – her pride had got her into this situation and she had no idea how to get herself out.

It was after midnight before she fell asleep. He had watched her head lolling, the internal struggle to stay awake manifesting itself in sudden jerks and gradual submissions. He looked at Birgitte more carefully. She was particularly attractive – that pale skin and dark hair, not a combination he encountered often in Africa. There was something about her that excited but also disturbed him – a strength only certain women possessed. It was alluring. He wanted to be closer to her but knew that desire contained a level of risk that could equate to his undoing. He went to move away from her but a button had come loose on her shirt. He took in the curve of her breast, the whiteness of her skin. He could picture himself slowly undoing the other buttons, releasing her as it were. Would he untie her for the act or would that add to the excitement?

He didn't know how long he had been staring at her before he snapped out of it. He couldn't afford to make the same mistake as he had with the girl.

He checked his laptop. The flight out of Canberra was booked for sunrise. It would leave from a small, private air-strip 60 kilometres away – a twin-engine plane that would get him to Cairns in the far north of the country, no questions asked. From Cairns, he would be on another flight out of Australia within 24 hours. He quickly looked up his cryptocurrency account and was pleased to see that Wan Bi Lao had been true to his word – a satisfactory outcome for all concerned.

It was 3am. He would hit the road within the hour. He knew he had to keep the detective alive until he was ready to leave. If anyone tried to stop him, he'd have to use her as cover until he escaped. Beyond that, she was unwanted ballast.

She awoke to the sound of his voice. It was still dark and felt much later, but it was hard to tell. She was groggy and stiff. She thought he'd said something to her, given her an instruction of some sort, but he was sitting at the dining table his back turned away from her. He was steadily sharpening the blade of a bowie knife against a whetstone, and talking to himself.

"It was your doing…. you asked for it. I would have let you be, but you wanted a ride… you don't ride with someone like me… you don't take that chance… silly little girl… I would have let you be, honest."

Birgitte struggled to understand what he was talking about.

The scraping noise of the blade against the stone, wet with his saliva was grating in Birgitte's ears. She had to think.

"I didn't want to do it…" he muttered, "…but he watches me, see… he wants to know that I can… you don't disappoint Captain De Graff… everyone knows that." He paused, scraped the edge of the blade across his cheek, then returned to the whetstone. "You were so pretty, even when you slept…

but you knew I had to cut you… wild dogs… you sleep better that way. No one to disturb you… trust me."

He stared at the blade in his hands as it moved in a circular motion against the stone. In his mind, he stood over the grave of the girl who had called herself Susie. It couldn't have been any different. The clouds had swept in and he had succumbed, the way he always did.

His father had joked with him early on that his eyes looked strange in the act. He had no idea what he had meant at the time – it was all new to him back then. But over the years, he became more aware of the clouds that would gather on the periphery of his mind before he committed to a killing. He reasoned with himself that it was part of the preparation; his subconscious protecting him from irrational fears that could put him at risk. But his father knew different, he knew something Zachary had refused to acknowledge.

He could suddenly hear his father's callous laughter from within the maelstrom of his thoughts. He tried to shut it out by scraping the knife harder against the stone, muttering more loudly to himself.

The old man's insanity had been a creeping form of death that had eaten at his reason, driving him to drink, making him careless. Zachary had hated him for this; it was an unforgivable weakness that had put them both at risk.

The sound of his father's laughter continued to grow more raucous. He knew the truth, but Zachary couldn't grasp it. The clouds were obscuring his reason. He hated to admit it, but ever since he had landed in Australia, he had felt himself losing control of his own thoughts with increasing frequency. He had ignored it at first, but now it deeply disturbed him.

His father's laughter became a scream as he realised the gene had been passed on. He was being consumed by the clouds of insanity that had destroyed the old man, and there was nothing he could do to stop it. He was steadily going insane himself. He felt a wave of pure horror flow over him, quickly followed by the bitterest resentment he had ever experienced. As the blind rage blotted out any light of reason he knew he had to kill the Danish woman. She had to die.

With a tremendous thunderclap in his own skull, he capitulated to the storm.

Birgitte watched in terror as her captor suddenly stood up and approached her with the knife before him. His face was blank, his eyes distant.

In an instant, she measured the distance between them, judged his pace, then with a single brutal kick, drove her heel up under his left kneecap. He screamed in agony, falling forward as his lower leg shot out uselessly underneath him. Birgitte rolled swiftly, pulled herself up on one knee and quickly wrapped the wire around his neck. She knew she didn't have the body weight to hold him for long, she just needed to hold him for long enough.

When he realised what she had done, he thrust backwards over his shoulder with the knife. It barely missed her ear then wedged deep into the timber post. He struggled to retrieve it but his hand was on an awkward angle and the wire around his throat was cutting deep into his skin. The more he wrestled against it the more he could feel himself needing oxygen. She had managed to bring her knee up between his shoulder blades, enabling her to pull the wire with all her might.

For a moment, it occurred to her that she could kill him there and then. She only needed to hang on for another minute or two, and justice for Hans Thostrup, Salina Heysmith, James Freedmont and the girl called Susie would be served. No one would question her actions. He had killed four innocent people in the most brutal of ways, for financial gain. He deserved to be wiped from the earth. He had no right to live. She leaned back and drove her knee in deeper, her arms were aching with the strain. She could feel his shoulders beginning to soften, as his body increased in weight. He fell across her, unconscious. She was suddenly repulsed by her own actions. She pulled the wire from his throat and checked his pulse. He was still alive.

Birgitte spent several minutes freeing herself from the timber post. She checked his laptop but it was locked. She ran outside. During the night, they had both occasionally heard the distant thud of helicopter rotors in the distance. It never came close enough to cause alarm for her captor, but it reassured

Birgitte to think that they were looking for her. She listened carefully but all was silent.

She looked to the shed. There was a tank of fuel near the SUV. She tipped the contents out on the earth in front of the house in a sweeping circle, then quickly lit it. Within seconds the flames were leaping up into the night sky. She threw sticks and leaves on the ring of fire to build it up. She didn't know what else to do.

Tony was sitting in the cabin of a small helicopter, directing the pilot to head further south. For the past eight hours, he'd been up in three times, scouring the forests within a 50 kilometre radius west of the house in the Southern Highlands. Miller and Barton had gone home at 10pm but he was determined to keep searching, even if it took all night. Every time the chopper had needed to head back to refuel, he waited impatiently then demanded they take him up again. He was now firmly blaming himself for Birgitte's disappearance.

The pilot pulled the nose around the base of a large mountain, rising steadily over the windward face. "We're getting low on fuel again."

"Just get us round the other side."

"I don't think we can, Tony. We need enough to get back."

"Just get us over the ridge there."

The pilot glared at him. He was getting tired of his desperate attitude. "This is the last sweep, then we're heading back. If you don't like it, I'll let you out and you can search for her on foot."

He pulled the stick back and to the right, arcing the helicopter up at an awkward angle. The trees within the spotlight beneath them appeared to rush past. The ground suddenly fell away as they reached the crest and swung left around peak of the mountain. The both spotted the orange glow of a fire at the same time.

"It's her," Tony yelled to the pilot. "It has to be."

The pilot nodded and pushed the stick forward. Tony sat up in his seat, now oblivious to his own discomfort. The chopper dipped and accelerated over the trees. Tony had never felt so relieved.

He peered down through the thick canopy. Birgitte was standing by the circle of flames waving her arms. She looked exhausted but physically unharmed.

"Can we get down out front?" Tony yelled to the pilot.

"I can't land in the flames and there isn't much room outside of that."

Tony started signalling to Birgitte to douse the fire she had started but she kept waving at him. Then he saw another figure emerge from the house. It was a tall blonde man, limping with a rifle in one hand.

"Oh shit," said Tony. "Get us up, quickly."

The pilot saw the man raise the rifle to his shoulder and knew there was no chance they were going to get away cleanly at that distance.

The shot rang out over the noise of the chopper. Sparks flew from the rear rotor. The chopper suddenly lurched to the left. Tony lost all sense of direction as the tiny glass cabin began to spin wildly. He was thrown against the window then back the other way, his head colliding with the pilot's. The canopy of trees loomed closer and there was the hideous crack of metal against timber.

The pilot barely had time to yell "brace yourself", when the chopper careened through the upper branches and slammed into the side of the mountain.

Birgitte watched in disbelief as the helicopter that had come to save her spun helplessly around then cut through the trees at a hideous angle. She expected it to explode when it hit the ground, and she prayed that Tony wasn't on board, but the trunks had lessened the final impact. The helicopter ripped through the trees then crumpled on its side 200 metres from the house.

Without thinking she ran blindly through the trees, expecting another shot to ring out that would bring her down, but the shot never came. She reached the helicopter. The side door fell open and Tony tumbled out, bloodied and dazed.

Birgitte grabbed his shoulders. "Thank god you're okay."

He looked at her, disoriented, then peered back inside the cabin. The pilot was unconscious. Tony leaned through, and with Birgitte's help, they pulled him to safety. As they dragged him across the earth, they heard a large explosion coming from the other side of the house.

Tony checked himself quickly for injuries, drew his gun, then set off towards the house. Birgitte followed at a distance.

The SUV was a ball of flame inside the shed. The flames leapt up around the tin roof. Beside it there an empty space, a sheet of canvas strewn on the ground.

Birgitte appeared beside him. "He had another car. We have to stop him."

Tony looked up the road, there was no sign of tail lights. The only other vehicle was engulfed in flames. "We can't," he said, now exhausted by the night's events. "We can't chase him on foot. I'll call for help, but I barely know where we are myself."

Birgitte stared hopelessly down the road. "He can't get away."

Tony checked their location on his phone then called for patrol cars to block the roads to the south and the west at the bottom of the mountain. He knew they couldn't possible get there in time but he had to do something. Within a few kilometres of where they stood the roads splayed out in several directions. It would be impossible to know which way the killer was heading.

With more patrol cars and an ambulance on their way, Tony grabbed a hose from the side of the house to contain the flames that were threatening to catch the trees above. "Go check on the pilot," he called out to Birgitte. "Tell him an ambulance is on its way."

She ran into the house to grab blanket, and noticed the laptop was gone.

Deep into the bush, the pilot had come to and was staggering around with a deep cut to his head and a broken collar bone. Birgitte wrapped him in a blanket and slowly walked him back to the house. She sat him on the front step and began helping Tony douse the fire.

When it was under control they both slumped to the ground.

Tony put his arm around her and held her close. He wanted to tell her how worried he'd been but thought better of it. "Did you get the make of the other car?"

She looked bereft. "I didn't even know it was there."

He kissed the top of her, grateful she was still alive. "You did well."

"I'm sorry," she said, looking up at him. "I should never have chased him."

"You did exactly what I would have done. I just wish you were armed."

"He's completely insane."

"Did he give any indication of where he was going?"

She shook her head. "He mentioned a young girl he picked up outside of Mildura."

"Another victim?"

She nodded. "She didn't have anything to do with the mining deal. She was just a child. He said he did it because he needed to."

Tony watched her carefully. The look on her face disturbed him. He didn't want to press her for details about what she had experienced during the night but he needed to know. "Are you physically okay? Will you need the paramedics to look you over?"

"My wrists are sore from being tied but other than that I'll be all right."

He sighed inwardly with relief. She kissed his cheek and thanked him, her eyes glistening with gratitude and regret.

CHAPTER SEVENTEEN

For the next three days, Birgitte and Tony were questioned at length about the events in the Southern Highlands. She did her best to work with the Federal officers, who had been brought in to determine if correct procedures had been followed, but she was getting increasingly frustrated with the pace of the investigation. There had been no sign of the Afrikaner – on the road or at any international airport. Every day that passed decreased their chances of catching him. She pleaded with the detectives to forward on her description of him, and the name de Graff, to police organisations in other countries in the hope that someone might recognise him from another case. But she was given no answer either way whether this information had been acted upon.

She had also provided as much information as she could about the girl called Susie. At least in this instance, they had taken her concern seriously. Teams of officers in South Australia and Victoria were searching the bushland either side of the highway to the west of Mildura. And Missing Persons departments in both states were now involved. But so far, no sign of the girl had been found and no one had come forward to say she was missing.

Tony was having problems of his own. Until the coroner could confirm otherwise, the death of the young Chinese man was resting at his feet. This required a fresh team of Federal detectives to scrutinise his handling of the situation. He ran through the events of that day over and over again, at Goulburn Street and back out at the house in the Southern Highlands, steadily convincing them he had done all he could to save the guy, and had then done only what was necessary to protect his own life and that of his Danish colleague. He had barely spoken to Birgitte since they had been picked up on the side of the mountain and taken to a nearby hospital for observation. Occasionally, Commander Barton would pop his head in to keep him up to date with developments.

Despite witnesses claiming a shot was heard immediately prior to the accident on the motorway nearby, no direct link could be drawn between the crash and the murders so they were being treated as separate incidents. The Commander was doing all he could to tone down speculation of a connection in the media.

Tony had left Xian Lao's laptop with IT, asking them to focus on any activity on VPN websites. He and Birgitte were sure any contact between Lao and the killer would have taken place in the dark web. Each time he'd had a chance to follow up, the IT guy shook his head and said he was still working on it.

In Tony's absence, Miller had been running the original investigative team but even she had to admit – the case was by no means clear. The torched SUV driven by the Afrikaner contained a refrigeration unit, but it was too badly damaged to provide evidence it had ever contained the bodies of Thostrup, Heysmith and Freedmont. It was circumstantial at best. Birgitte had been the only person to get a good look at him, and at no time had he admitted to killing the three victims or that he was working for Xian Lao.

Until IT could exhaust all the possibilities on Lao's laptop, there was also not much evidence linking the CEO to the killings. There was argument to say there was motive, but so too for every other natural gas mining company involved. The fact that a young man carrying a small arsenal of weapons was found at the house in the Southern Highlands certainly suggested something untoward was taking place but without a definitive ID from China, there was little they could use in court. Not that any of this would get beyond a coronial inquest. Without the man who had abducted Birgitte, they had nothing more than a string of dead bodies and a lot of unanswered questions.

On the Wednesday night, Birgitte was in her room at the Grierson Hotel, sitting at the desk with her laptop. Her time in Australia was coming to an end. A flight was booked for the following evening. She wrote to Commissioner Holl, outlining all that had happened and her theories as to who may have been responsible. He had responded that he appreciated her efforts and would inform his sister of the outcome. Sven was looking forward to her returning to Copenhagen. He had intimated it was time to consider her future beyond her current role in Fraud. This brought her some solace.

There was a knock at the door.

Tony stood in the hallway with a bottle of wine. He looked tired but pleased to see her. "I thought you might want to celebrate getting out of this kooky country."

She smiled, genuinely glad he'd come by. An uncomfortable distance had been forced between them and she hadn't known how to address it. She hated the thought of leaving Australia without Tony understanding that he meant so much to her, but she didn't want to complicate things by saying too much.

She busied herself looking for tumblers. He shut the door and rested the bottle on the bedside table, watching her. She couldn't find any glassware and muttered to herself that the staff must have removed it for some reason. She checked the bathroom, the wardrobe and she almost bumped into him when she went to check the bedside tables. He took her in his arms. "We don't need glasses."

For a moment she struggled, but only slightly – her determination to solve the mystery of the missing tumblers was fading. He took her face in his hands and brought her lips up to his.

They kissed slowly, allowing all the familiar warmth to return between them. She softened in his arms. This was everything she had wanted to express since he found her on the mountain.

At some point in the early hours, she asked, "Are you awake?"

He hadn't slept at all. He'd been listening to the cool, steady rhythm of her breathing, wondering what she had been dreaming about as her feet twitched restlessly between his calves.

He kissed her forehead.

She said, "I can't help feeling I should have done more."

"In what way?"

"I don't know. More to save the Freedmont boy, more to catch de Graff, more to protect the girl Susie."

"Hey, we wouldn't have had a case without you," he said, pulling the hair away from her face. "You made the connection between the first two murders, which put us on to the Timor Sea deal. And you discovered Xian Lao's involvement. We didn't even know he had a house in the Southern Highlands. Sure, it would have been great if we got there a few hours earlier, but you can't blame yourself for that. You should be just grateful you made it through in one piece."

"I am, don't get me wrong. I just know that de Graff is going to continue doing what he's doing. There will be other innocent people, like Susie and Salina Heysmith, who will suffer because I didn't do more."

He didn't know what else to say. Perhaps that was the difference between them as police. His time in the Middle Eastern Organised Crime Unit had taught him a lot about himself as a detective, and more generally, as a man. He had accepted his limitations and knew his place in the greater scheme of things. He'd learned to walk away when situations became untenable – to protect himself – a pragmatic defence mechanism in the interests of personal sustainability.

He was under no illusions as to who was the better detective, but he couldn't help wondering how long Birgitte could go on with such persistence, and at what cost. He ran the tips of his fingers down the length of her bare back until his hand slipped smoothly over her behind. She nuzzled into his chest, lazily brushing her leg over his thigh until they were entwined again. Their thoughts and fears slipped away unnoticed and soon enough nothing else mattered.

The following morning, Commander Barton called the investigative team in to his office. Tony didn't like the atmosphere when he arrived. The Commander's face was grim and he was avoiding eye contact as they each found somewhere to sit or stand. Miller stood beside him, her shoulders back, her chin up as if she was on parade.

"I've just been in a meeting with the Minister of Police and the Commissioner. It turns out the Northern Territory Government has decided to reverse its decision to approve exploration licences in the Timor Sea, without which there can be no mining deal. Katercorp and Barclay Industries have been notified, both have signalled their agreement with the decision, given the nature of the events leading up to this. As no financial investment had been made by either party, no further action will be taken, legally speaking." He paused for this to sink in. "Now, I want to sincerely thank you all for your work on this. It's been a hell of an investigation. Many of you have put in considerable hours and that hasn't gone unnoticed. However, there has been a development." He cleared his throat. "I have been told by my superiors that a new team will be stepping in to manage the case moving forward."

They looked at one another in silence, then Tony said, "That's absurd."

"This has come from the Commissioner, Tony. It's not something any of us are in a position to argue about."

"What do we do with all the evidence we've gathered so far?" he retorted, knowing full well it didn't amount to as much as it should.

"Superintendent Miller will serve as the link between the two operations."

Tony almost broke his coffee mug in his own hand.

Miller nodded at her boss curtly and took the floor, responding to Tony's question. "If you could write up a report summarising the events to date, the others can box up the physical material."

Birgitte cut in. "Excuse me, Superintendent, has any consideration been given to the possibility the Afrikaner may have been hired by a third party?"

Miller's face tightened. "We are considering all possibilities at the moment. My superiors are across every aspect of the case."

"Including Wan Bi Lao?"

"I assure you we are pursuing every angle," she said with a note of false warmth. "Try to have a little faith in our abilities."

"Are you familiar with Wan Bi Lao, Superintendent?"

Before Miller could answer, Barton cut in, "I will brief the Superintendent on your theory, Detective. Please bear in mind, we are working with the Chinese Government directly on this so there are certain diplomatic protocols that must be followed. I ask each of you to direct any media enquiries to the Superintendent."

Birgitte looked at Tony, whose shoulders had slightly sagged. He stared at his feet then turned to her as if to say, "What's the point?"

The Commander nodded to Miller. "Again, I'd like to take this opportunity to thank you for all your hard work. In particular, Detective Birgitte Vestergaard, whose efforts have been nothing short of exemplary. It's been an honour. I've been on the phone to your boss, Sven Augerson, singing your praises. He's very keen to have you back in Copenhagen. Personally, I would have liked more time to work with you but circumstances don't allow it. So thanks again."

The team applauded nervously then broke away to walk back to their desks.

"Got time for a coffee?" Tony asked Birgitte.

"We have nowhere else to be," she said, trying to bring some levity to a bad situation.

They walked to a café across the street from the office.

As they waited at the counter for their drinks, they both turned to the TV screen on the far wall. There was a live news update, something about a Federal Government mining initiative.

Tony asked the waitress if she could turn it up.

The Federal Energy Minister was standing with a Chinese government official at a press conference somewhere in the desert. The minister was doing his best to wave the flies from his own face and that of his distinguished guest. Behind them was the familiar bloated figure of Frank Howard, the Northern Territory Minister for Trade.

The Federal Minister stepped forward to the line of microphones. "As the people of Australia know, the Federal Government has long been committed to fostering a healthy relationship with our northern neighbours, China. A relationship in which ideas and opportunities are shared to the benefit of both nations. We believe this new deal, which encompasses some of the most valuable land in the Northern Territory, will only strengthen the ties between us.

"I'd like to thank the Northern Territory Minister for Trade for his unceasing efforts in developing such a strong business proposal. Most of all, I'd like to thank the people at Shanghai Consolidated Holdings, whose investment in the region is unsurpassed. For the next 10 years we will be working closely together to develop mining infrastructure that will put Forbes Creek on the international map. It is with great pride that I can announce that this project will serve as a research station for the future of global technological advancement."

The three men shook hands, beaming at one another. Then the Federal Minister for Trade looked off camera, coughed into his hand and quickly added, "I'd also like to acknowledge the original custodians of the land, the Aranda people. Thank you."

Birgitte stared at Tony, "Shanghai Consolidated Holdings? Seriously?"

"That Howard doesn't miss a beat, does he? No sooner does the Timor Sea deal get kyboshed and he's involved in an even bigger deal." It took him a moment to realise the significance of the announcement. "Wan Bi Lao runs Shanghai Consolidated Holdings."

She offered him a look of resignation. "Xian lost out on the Timor Sea deal, but his uncle has started doing business here anyway. I don't believe it."

She couldn't tell if it was a cruel case of irony or whether something more sinister had occurred. Her mind raced with the possibilities. Had Wan Bi Lao somehow orchestrated all of this, or at least some of it, to work in his favour?

Tony shook his head slowly. "More than eight people are dead, and the machine just keeps rolling on. No wonder the investigation was taken out of our hands."

"Even if they make a connection between Xian and his uncle – the chances of them making any charge stick is close to zero. It's not like the Chinese authorities are going to listen to the Australian police, particularly when the man in question is Chairman of a state-owned conglomerate worth billions."

Tony burst out laughing despite himself. "We're working for the wrong side."

They stepped out onto the pavement with their coffees, slightly numbed by the pace and scale of the developments.

The IT guy ran across the road toward them. "I've found something."

"Have you told Miller?" Tony asked.

"Not yet. I thought you were in charge."

Tony felt no need to correct him. He said, "Show us what you've got."

The three of them ran back into the building.

For the next hour, the IT guy did his best to walk Tony and Birgitte through the lines of code on Lao's hard drive that had piqued his interest. He had found a conversation between two avatars on a deep web site. It was obscure and possibly in code, but it made reference to Barclay Industries and Katercorp. It wasn't much but it was a start. Reluctantly, Tony told him to let Miller know they may have a connection. Birgitte made a note of the user IDs and the site on which they communicated.

They drove to the Grierson Hotel in silence but once back in her room the discussion heated up very quickly.

"You can't," Tony said with finality, watching her pack her bags for a second time. "It's out of our hands."

"You're not listening to me." She collected her toiletries from the bathroom and tossed them into her suitcase. "It's out of your hands, not mine. I don't answer to the Australian Federal Police, Tony, you do."

"It could disrupt the investigation."

"What investigation? Your superiors are quietly hoping this all goes away. Xian Lao is dead and the man who killed him has vanished."

She moved around him to gather up her laptop and hand bag, furious he was being so pigheaded. "We have contact details for de Graff – a means of getting in touch. We'd be crazy not to use it."

Tony had had enough. For him the case was over. He had quietly hoped they could have spent their last hours together back in the bed. The thought of not seeing her again had been eating at him all morning. He was pissed that she didn't seem to feel the same way.

He took a deep breath and tried to sound reasonable. "I have no idea what happens next with my job, Birgitte. I know that sounds small-minded and selfish, but I can't afford to get on the wrong side of Barton. You know I can't."

She sighed. "I'm sorry, Tony. I don't mean to make it hard for you, I just desperately want to get this guy before I get back to Denmark."

She suddenly heard the Afrikaner's words accusing her of pride.

Tony's phone rang. He pulled it out of his pocket and stared at it.

"Who is it?" asked Birgitte as she did a final check of the room.

"It's the prison switch board," he said distantly. "I think it's Hana."

They stared at one another for a moment, then Birgitte said, "Talk to her. You know you need to."

He looked at her with uncertainty, then eventually pressed the green button and held the phone to his ear.

Birgitte watched him as he spoke tentatively into the phone. She felt a flood of warmth for him both as a detective and a man. The thought of him being hurt in any way by Hana Shakib brought her a pang of anxiety but with it came the realisation that she couldn't stay to help him. Whatever had happened between them was already past.

Before he could stop her, Birgitte kissed his cheek and left the room with her luggage. She didn't like to end it this way, but it was better than farewells at the airport.

She arrived at the Departure Terminal of Sydney International an hour later, feeling dissatisfied with herself and quite alone. The airport was crowded with families and friends sending off their loved ones. Some were heading off on exotic holidays, their faces beaming with excitement and anticipation; others wrapping up their tour of Australia, preparing themselves for the long haul back home to their other lives. It was hectic and awkwardly intimate – so many people embracing one another with tears in their eyes, trying to smile and laugh when they wanted to scream with envy, or saying, "All the best" when they meant, "Take me with you". Perhaps she should have allowed Tony to drive her out there, to say good bye properly. It seemed churlish to be suddenly leaving Australia without talking about what had happened between them.

She wheeled her suitcase through the crowds to a departure screen. The check-in desk for her flight was 100 metres to the right. As she adjusted the strap of her laptop bag on her shoulder, she did a double take. Through the crowd she had spotted the slicked back hair and gaudy braces of Sam Westlake as he queued at a nearby check-in desk. He was heading for China.

She thought of Salina Heysmith lying on a steel trolley in a morgue. The woman was by no means a saint from all accounts, but she never deserved to be exploited, to have her shortcomings used against her in such a cynical exercise of greed. Westlake was not responsible for her death but he had caused a lonely, vulnerable woman undue anguish when she desperately needed guidance and support.

After check-in Westlake headed for the departure lounge. Birgitte caught up to him at the entrance to a high-end duty-free shop.

"Shanghai, Mr Westlake?"

He turned and took a moment to register who had addressed him. "Detective," he said warmly as if they had agreed to meet at that precise moment. "Are you heading back to Copenhagen?"

"I hear you are no longer working at Katercorp."

He sighed through his grin. "Sadly, the creative differences between myself and Nils had become untenable. It was time."

"So he was unwilling to be associated with a man who lives in an ethical vacuum, and you were incapable of change."

His smile faded. "You sound a little resentful, Detective. If anyone should be bitter, it should be me. I stood to make a lot of money from that Timor Sea deal – a lot of money for a lot of people." He cleared his throat but never took his eyes of her. "That's how the energy sector works, Ms Vestergaard – it generates power, which flows out to everyone involved. But of course, you could never be a part of that, so how could you understand."

"Did you even care what you were doing to Salina Heysmith?"

"She made her choices, Detective. I simply provided the options."

"What about Xian Lao? Did you know what he was doing?"

"To be brutally honest, Xian Lao was a spoiled, inexperienced fool who ruined a good thing for everyone. I have no sympathy for him. And, for what it's worth, I am sorry how it played out for you and Detective Kingsmill."

"Do you know who had Xian Lao killed?" she asked. "Was it his uncle?"

The glint returned to Westlake's eyes. "Wan Bi Lao, unlike his nephew, is a highly respected and very powerful member of China's business elite. I'd be careful about making unsubstantiated allegations; he has a very efficient legal team and incredibly deep pockets. Political careers have crumbled for less. In fact, you should give him the benefit of the doubt. Thanks to his research teams in Shanghai, his company is now investing more money in Australia than the Timor Sea deal could have ever generated."

"Why now?"

"It turns out there are some minerals outside of Alice Springs that are of no use to anyone – yet. But these minerals are the key to a revolutionary development in digital devices: tablets, smart phones and the like, that will see that little patch of desert hailed as the epicentre of the next boom in global technology."

"Forbes Creek?"

"Biggest discovery since they found coltan in the Congo."

She shook her head in disbelief. "And what was your involvement in all of this?"

"Merely a humble consultant, Detective. I simply put the right people in a room together and encourage them to do what they do best."

"Even if it means uprooting an entire community from their land?"

He looked confused for a moment, then nodded. "It's unfortunate that a small number of people will suffer a temporary inconvenience..."

"...so an even smaller number can profit."

"Watch this space, Detective. Your high-minded empathy for our Indigenous communities will look very misplaced in a few years' time when Shanghai Consolidated Holdings have funded more state-of-the-art hospitals and schools in remote regions than the Northern Territory Government could ever promise in a string of elections."

"And you take your cut at every stage of the process," she said with distaste. "It's extraordinary to think, so many people have been hurt in only a matter of weeks, and somehow you've managed to come out on top, richer and more connected than when it all started."

"I'm a survivor, Detective. Can you really blame me for working the odds in my favour when the opportunity presents itself?" He looked up at the ceiling, listening to the overhead announcements. "Now, you'll have to excuse me, my flight was just called. It's been a pleasure working with you. I sincerely hope your time in Australia wasn't a total waste."

He turned and made his way to the departure lounge. Birgitte watched him walk away, stunned by what she'd heard. A deep anger, which had been welling since she'd arrived in this country, threatened to erupt there and then. She closed her eyes for a moment and made her decision. Someone had to be held accountable for all that had happened. Someone had to pay.

He liked Hong Kong. It was a cold-blooded, nocturnal city. During the day, the claustrophobic clusters of office blocks and high-rise apartments would sit perfectly still, conserving energy. Down in the shaded streets, the hordes of Chinese would scutter about, busy with their shopfronts and small businesses. But they were waiting for the night as well.

At night, the city breathed and pulsed and grew in stature; it threw brilliant glimpses of colour to attract or distract its predators. There was a warmth beneath the skin that invited closer contact. It was a city with which he could share in the hunt.

Since arriving in Hong Kong, he had spent his days in his hotel room in Kowloon, waiting. He had a view of Victoria Harbour. It didn't interest him except for its ability to offer terminals for movement between the mainland and Hong Kong Island. His new assignment was straightforward enough – a Swiss accountant, whose firm managed the finances of a particular mining company in Asuncion. This accountant needed to understand the benefits of withdrawing from the region. At this early stage, it was a simple recon exercise: take an initial cursory look at the subject.

Wan Bi Lao had advised him that nothing elaborate was required. The accountant was thoroughly conservative; he wouldn't take much convincing. The key was to ensure no one could verify the existence of a threat. The photo Lao sent through was of a middle-aged Caucasian man, who looked after his health. His thinning hair was worn short and neat. His shoulders were angular but broad – possibly a regular tennis player or a cyclist. He was married, with two teenage daughters. Lao's caveat suggested focusing on the subject not his family.

He conducted some light research on the firm in Geneva, just to check the scope of its operations, which other industries it dealt with, how the accountant pitched his firm to the market. He would conduct a more thorough examination in the days to come.

It felt good to be back in with the Chairman of Shanghai Consolidated Holdings. There had been no mention of Sao Paulo, nor even of the job in Australia. It was business as usual, which suited him fine. He had all the information he needed to get on with it. He wasn't one to believe in redemption but he was smart enough to know that second chances didn't come very often in this game. He needed to perform at a higher level. For a moment, he thought of Birgitte Vestergaard, her steely eyed determination to bring him down had almost succeeded. With his admiration came a tinge of regret for not taking greater advantage of their time together. An image of her pale translucent skin within her white blouse had lingered with him for days.

The flight from Canberra into Far North Queensland had gone smoothly. The pilot had kept his focus on the itinerary, refusing to engage in even the most basic conversation. Once in Cairns, he had made his way to a non-descript roadside motel on the edge of town. He quickly showered and had his hair cut at a barber nearby. He put on an expensive suit, ditched most of his belongings in a dumpster, then made his way to the International Terminal. Wheeling a small suitcase in one hand, with his laptop hanging from his shoulder, he looked every bit the corporate executive on his way to Asia for business. He looked nothing like the rough sketch of a fugitive that he was sure had been circulated across the country.

There had been a moment of concern when an over-zealous immigration officer took closer interest in his British passport. He quickly adopted an educated accent and held his nerve, dismissing his limp as a sporting injury. It hadn't been his best performance to date, but it worked. Within two hours he was out of the country, and thanks to both his clients, $3M richer than when he'd arrived.

He stood in the window of his hotel room, watching the skyline across the harbour. The sun had gone down. The scales of glass and steel dimmed in the approaching darkness. Then beams of brilliant colour suddenly splayed out from the tops of skyscrapers, hidden towers came to life. The light show had begun. It was his signal to move.

He slipped out of his hotel room and caught the elevator down into the street. The air was thick with humidity. He headed east, purposefully negotiating the crowds, silent, virtually unseen. A Star Ferry carried him across the harbour to the Central Pier, where he made his way up through the network of elevated walkways that cut across the financial district. He caught the Mid Levels Escalator up the mountain towards The Peak, alighting among the restaurants and bars in the heart of Central.

Lao had informed him, when staying in Hong Kong, the accountant frequented a certain bar in Lan Kwai Fong – The Blue Dragonfly. It provided ample opportunity to study his target, get a sense of his movements and behaviour when he was off the clock in a foreign city.

He settled in among the post-work crowd, moving along the narrow alley ways that fed into the city's famous entertainment quarter. Within a matter of minutes, he found the bar in question. Bi-fold doors were pushed back to reveal a large establishment catering to a range of clientele. Diners were enjoying light meals at tables that faced onto a long bar. There were booth seats for more casual drinking deeper in, and a dance floor down the back for the late-night revellers. It was just on 8pm. Dinner service was in full swing, and most of the booths were taken. It was a mix of Western expats – bankers, lawyers, advertising executives – and local Chinese. The place exuded style and money. Fortunately, it was also dimly lit. He ordered a scotch and took a seat at the far edge of the bar. From there he could watch the entrance and use the mirrors behind the staff to keep an eye on the booth seats.

He sat on his drink for as long as he could, then ordered another. He didn't usually drink scotch. The significance of the choice was not lost on him. His time in Australia had worn him down. On the flight out, he had slept deeply, but not soundly. Images of his father had continued to harangue him from distant corners of his mind. There was no escaping the Captain. In many ways, they were one in the same person. It was a fate he didn't care for but his resolve to resist the inevitable was steadily crumbling and he knew it. He wondered how many more jobs he could do before he lost his edge.

Just before 10pm he spotted the accountant entering the bar. He was not alone. On his arm was an elegantly dressed

Chinese woman – no more than 20, and clearly not his wife of 17 years. They chatted amiably to the maitre d', before being directed to one of the booths near the dance floor.

Turning his back to the crowd, he used the mirrors to watch his target as they drank red wine and flirted in the low light. When the DJ in the far back corner started his set, several patrons made their way to the dance floor. The young woman dragged the reluctant accountant out to join them. He was obviously fit but still danced like a father of teenagers.

He checked his watch and ordered another scotch. It was now getting very crowded in the bar. He was struggling to maintain a comfortable line of sight. He decided to move across the room to stand in the shadows of an alcove to the left of the DJ's decks. As he stepped down from his chair, he thought he saw a woman through the crowd who looked remarkably like the Danish detective. It was only a glimpse, but it jarred his entire being. The woman's hair was up and she wore a dark top that sat just off her shoulders. He couldn't recognise the line of her neck but the tone of her skin and the way she held herself looked familiar. He dismissed the idea as foolish. He needed to concentrate. He looked through the crowd for his target. They had left the dance floor but not returned to the booth. He was getting agitated. It suddenly felt too crowded. He pushed his way through to the restaurant area, searching the faces for the accountant who was nowhere to be seen. Then he spotted the woman again, from the back this time. He couldn't be certain but he had to know. Despite the pain in his leg, he moved back to the bar and joined the queues three deep. Through their heads he tried to catch another discreet look. He hadn't noticed the queue had shuffled forward. A drunken Englishman in a suit gave him a shove and told him to keep it moving. In a flash of rage, he almost punched the man in his throat. He could feel the clouds swirling in, reducing his ability to see straight. His breathing slowed but it was more laboured than normal.

A voice in his head told him to get out, immediately. If it wasn't her, it didn't matter, but it was better to be safe than sorry. If it was her, he was compromised and vulnerable. He was about to push his way back out of the queue, when he heard a familiar woman's voice in his ear. "You're not the ghost you think you are."

He froze. In the mirror behind the bar he caught his own reflection – the long face, the small eyes, the blonde hair combed back from his brow, not unlike his own father in younger days. Beside him was the porcelain face of the Danish detective. She stared at him with an equally cold look of defiance. He remembered that same look in the pine forest outside Xian Lao's house. Could it be she was stupid enough to hunt him down on her own again?

The thought didn't last long. Without any further acknowledgement of the man in front of her, Birgitte spoke discreetly into her wrist and the entire bar erupted in chaos. Three patrons who had been standing blithely in the queue beside him suddenly drew their weapons and took aim, screaming at him to get on the floor, as eight Hong Kong Police, wearing flak jackets and wielding semi-automatic weapons charged into the bar from the front and rear entrance.

This was not how he envisaged going out. He spun around wildly, staring at his captors, looking for any weakness. He lunged at Birgitte but was brought down by a swift strike of a baton across his shoulders. He fell to his knees. He lashed out at the legs around him but was quickly set upon by several police who sat on his back and wrestled his hands behind him. From deep down in the darkness of his soul he heard his father's laughter, and he howled like an animal at the injustice of it all.

When his screaming subsided, the house lights went up. Patrons stood nervously behind a human barrier of undercover officers. The assassin was cuffed and lifted to his feet. He continued to writhe in the grip of two tactical unit officers who virtually carried him towards the entrance.

Birgitte resisted the urge to openly gloat in front of him. He wasn't worth it. Instead she stepped back into the crowd, her heart still pounding. The accountant approached her with an exhilarated look on his face. "Excellent work," he said in Danish.

"You seemed to be enjoying yourself a bit too much," she replied.

Sven pressed her shoulder. He had flown out to Hong Kong in the days leading up to the operation. It was his only proviso – he had to be present to protect Birgitte if anything went wrong. It was Birgitte's idea that he play the role of the Swiss accountant. If the assassin had decided to act on impulse, Sven had the training and the strength to handle himself.

For the past fortnight Birgitte and Sven had worked closely with the Deputy Commandant of the Hong Kong Police. They had convinced him of the need to catch an international contract killer who was most likely in the employ of a high-profile businessman from mainland China with strong links to the government. Given the nature of the crimes and the corruption with which it was associated, secrecy was paramount. The Deputy Commandant had assured them he could provide his best tactical unit and most trusted detectives to work undercover.

Birgitte and Sven had then devised a back story so when she used the contact details lifted from Xian Lao's laptop it would serve as a plausible lure. Sven had had his reservations, but trusted her judgement. Now, as he watched the assassin being shoved into the back of an armoured van outside, he was glad he had. "We'll need to go back to their Headquarters in Wan Chai to wrap it all up," he said. "Are you okay if I go with the Deputy Commandant?"

She nodded.

"I'll let you inform the Australians," he said. "And again, well done."

Birgitte spent several minutes thanking the local officers involved before moving out into the stifling night air. She drew out her phone and found a quiet spot at the top of the lane.

"Tony? It's Birgitte... Yes, yes... I'm in still in Hong Kong...." His voice was distant, but she could tell he was pleased to hear from her. She listened patiently as he told her Barton had agreed he shouldn't be transferred to Identity Theft and that he couldn't stay working with Miller.

Fortunately, the Commander had found him a place in Human Trafficking. The new role would start in the coming week.

"I'm so happy for you, Tony," she said. "I also have some very good news... you won't believe this – but we finally caught him! ... Yes, here in Hong Kong. I wish you could have been here just to see his face."

She ran her hand through her hair and paced about, struggling to contain her excitement. "I couldn't say anything earlier, but we found out who he is... yes, we've identified him. It took a lot of research but we got there in the end.

"His name is Zachary de Graff. He was born in South Africa, outside of Johannesburg, apparently. His father was a police officer... a very corrupt, violent police officer. The authorities there were convinced his father had killed him and then hung himself back in the 90s. But it turns out Zachary may have murdered his own father then disappeared, gone off the grid as it were.

"We believe he was operating as a contract killer in Zimbabwe, which is where he may have come into contact with Wan Bi Lao.

"He'll be extradited to Sydney in the coming days. If you guys don't lock him away for the rest of his life, I'm sure he'll be sent on to either Zimbabwe or even China to answer to their authorities."

She took a deep breath. It was good to hear Tony's voice, to share the outcome with him. "I'm sorry we couldn't have brought him down together in Australia... It doesn't feel right... I know, I know. I can't thank you enough. Listen, I have to go, I need to debrief with the Hong Kong Police." She closed her eyes and tried to control her voice. She wanted desperately to ask him how he got on with Hana Shakib. Was she being released? Would he stay in contact with her despite all that she'd done? But Birgitte knew it was none of her business. "Perhaps, one day, if you're in Copenhagen, we can meet up for a drink and talk about anything other than work... I'd like that too... Take care, Tony."

She hung up the phone and watched the tactical unit officers seal the back of the van which held de Graff under the immediate guard of two senior officers. A diminutive female uniformed officer politely offered her a lift to the Police Headquarters. Her patrol car was around the corner. Birgitte thanked her and was about to leave but something was bothering her. Had it all gone too smoothly? The Deputy Commandant had repeatedly assured her his best officers were on the job but that didn't mean they couldn't be reached.

"Would you mind if we followed the van?" she asked.

The officer nodded. "Of course."

They walked around the corner to where the patrol car was parked but before they even opened the doors, they heard two loud, muffled explosions from back in the laneway. Birgitte broke into a run, heading back to the front of the bar where the van was still parked. As she turned the corner she saw the back door of the van swing open and a tactical unit officer stagger out with his gun hanging from his right hand. Uniformed officers had already drawn their weapons and had surrounded him, screaming at him in Cantonese. He didn't look frightened or defensive, just bewildered. One of the officers stepped forward and took the weapon out of his hand. Another peered inside the back of the van then pulled back, shaking his head.

Birgitte ran toward them with her ID card raised high. She stepped between the officers and looked inside the van. An officer lay in the centre aisle with a gunshot wound to the side of his head, his service revolver in his hand. De Graff was still sitting upright, his hands behind his back. A single bullet hole sat neatly in the middle of his forehead. His eyes were open and he appeared to be staring into a void that no one else could see.

Sven broke through the crowd. "Are you okay?"

"He got him," Birgitte said vacantly. She looked at the officer who had emerged from the van. He looked distraught and confused. Had he shot the assassin? Or was he part of the hit and was just playing the shocked officer?

Sven grabbed her arm, pulling her away from the van. "You're not safe here."

She struggled at first then allowed herself to be shuffled into an unmarked police car. Sven demanded to be taken out of the area immediately. As they drove through narrow streets then down into the tunnel that carried them beneath Victoria Harbour, he had a very terse phone conversation with the Deputy Commandant.

They were driven directly to a safe house on the outskirts of the city. Birgitte was certain that if Wan Bi Lao wanted her dead it would have already happened but the Deputy Commandant seemed determined to maintain an appearance of protection, if only to save face for losing de Graff.

For next three days Birgitte and Sven were shunted back and forth to the Headquarters in Wan Chai in an armoured car to oversee interviews with the officer who had survived the shooting.

Under intense scrutiny he argued persistently that his fellow officer had pulled out his service weapon as soon as the doors to the van were closed behind them. The prisoner was shot dead before he had had a chance to respond. He was also adamant he was going to be next, so he had drawn his own weapon and shot his colleague in the head. It had all happened in a matter of seconds.

Birgitte watched the surviving officer closely during each interview. She was eventually convinced he was not involved. There was nothing more she could do. The killer was dead and the man she was sure was behind his execution was beyond her reach. What was left of the investigation was in the hands of the Hong Kong Police.

On the Friday night, Birgitte and Sven reluctantly caught a taxi out to the airport. Neither of them spoke on the way out. They checked-in, had a coffee in the departure lounge then boarded a flight for Copenhagen.

After the inflight meal was cleared away, Birgitte stared out the window at the night sky but her reflection continued to distract her. She drew the shade and looked at Sven. "I feel so stupid."

He put his magazine down.

345

She considered her words before speaking. "It was something de Graff said, in the cabin back in Australia. He said pride was my biggest problem. I actually thought it was over – that I'd done my job. How could I have been so stupid?"

"You did your job, Birgitte. You brought him in. It wasn't your job to protect him."

"He was our only link to Lao."

"Your job was to find out what happened to Hans Thostrup and you did. I'm sorry it couldn't have panned out differently. For what it's worth, I'm impressed with the way you've conducted yourself. It was an incredibly challenging situation. Now, please, get some sleep. You're going to need it."

She gave him a querulous look.

"I didn't want to tell you before the arrest," he said, "but Commissioner Holl has signed off on your transfer back into Homicide."

She didn't know what to say. She pushed her seat back at an angle and closed her eyes. She thought of Tony's ambivalence at being placed in charge of a task force, because it felt as arbitrary as Miller's promotion. Did Birgitte deserve to be back in Homicide?

She wrestled with the question for several hours, at one point even considering declining the transfer. But she recognised self-pity when she saw it. She was just angry de Graff wouldn't see the inside of a jail cell. And that someone like Wan Bi Lao, whose criminal behaviour reached across the globe, was seemingly immune from prosecution. It hurt to realise the limitations of her own capacity as a detective. It was what she had admired in Tony, his ability to accept his place in the world and still get on with the job. Why couldn't she do the same?

When the plane began its descent through the thick bank of clouds towards Copenhagen Airport, Birgitte felt slightly better about it all. Sven was right. She had only been sent out to Australia to assist in the search for a missing Dane. Even if the trip was politically motivated, she had executed her duties with professionalism. She had not only found Hans Thostrup but had managed to arrest his killer. It wasn't the ideal outcome, as far as she was concerned, given how many people were involved and that Wan Bi Lao was seemingly beyond prosecution, but she had done her best and that was all anyone could ask of her. Perhaps she needed to learn to only ask that of her herself.

More importantly, she realised her transfer back into Homicide signalled the end of her involvement with Max Anders. It had been a horrific episode in her life but one under which should could now draw a solid line, demarcating before and after.

She lifted the screen on her window to see thick rain lashing the glass. Strong winds buffeted the plane from all directions but she felt secure in her seat. She was finally going home.

EPILOGUE

The ball shot up against the stark blue of the sky. Cody had given it every inch of his left boot. It hovered then fell. Yambo ran forward, leaping up over Teddy's shoulders to take the mark. It was a clean catch and they all knew it. He passed the ball to Teddy as they continued to walk out towards the creek.

"What are you going to do when you meet Adam Goodes?" Teddy asked, pushing the ball firmly against the dirt. "Get him to autograph your jersey?"

"Don't be bugging him for autographs," Yambo said. "Tell him to get you a job with the Swannies."

"He may not even be there," Cody said flatly. He shielded his eyes from the sun, which was sitting midway over the tallest gums along the bank. "There's a chance he won't even be in town that week."

"But the other guys will be," reassured Teddy. "The selectors. I reckon you're in with a big chance."

Through the glare, Cody spotted a pale wild dog sniffing about the base of a eucalypt. He thought of the old man who he'd found crawling from the creek several weeks before. Occasionally, he still wondered how he'd got there. He motioned to Teddy to pass him the ball. When he caught it, he could feel his mind clear. He punched it to Yambo.

"How'd they find out about you again?" Teddy asked, running around the back of Cody, putting his mate in defence. Yambo chipped the ball over Cody's head. Teddy caught it and pretended to dodge around him.

"Aunty reckons that copper phoned 'em," Cody replied. "The guy who said he played state."

"Not likely," Yambo said, stealing the ball from Teddy and tossing it back to Cody. "Coppers are dogs. It would have been last year's comp. Best and Fairest gets a lot of attention with selectors."

"Don't matter either way, Cody," said Teddy. "You're in. You've got a real chance of making it now."

"You'll probably turn in to a fuckwit, forget your mates," Yambo said with a big grin. He reached up and ruffled Cody's hair. Cody shoved him playfully then kicked the ball as hard as he could. It arced up over the barren creek, lingered for moment on the wind then veered west as it fell. Yambo and Teddy ran after it then broke into a kick and chase game of their own down in the rough sand.

Cody let them run on ahead. He wasn't up to it just yet.

Truth was, he was torn about the prospect of joining the Territory AFL Training Scheme, a recruitment drive that usually only drew teenagers from Alice Springs and Darwin. Sure, it was an awesome opportunity – a chance to travel, but it also meant leaving his aunty and uncle. Right now, they needed him more than ever. Aunty wouldn't say a word of it, but he knew she was worried.

Without thinking he stopped and looked over his shoulder.

It was unsettling to see his town sitting behind a cyclone fence, topped with barbed wire. Most of the houses were empty now. The buses had come in the day before, loaded up as many of his people as they could and taken them north to a bigger settlement, closer to Alice. It wasn't right, but nobody had listened when they spoke up. The government said they'd be better off in their new homes, more facilities, bigger schools, better hospitals. They should be grateful.

Cody resented the town, but his uncle was right when he said it was their land and it should be for them to decide when they came and went, not the government.

He picked up a rock, tested the weight in his hand and threw it angrily at a metal sign tied to the cyclone fence. It read:

"**Do Not Trespass**. This land is the property of Shanghai Consolidated Holdings. For any enquires, contact the site office. Trespassers will be prosecuted."

The sound of the rock clashing against the metal chimed in the heat for only a moment then disappeared.

Other novels by Connell Nisbet

The Ember Room

While visiting Hong Kong, Senior Detective Birgitte Vestergaard is drawn into a deadly game of manipulation in which innocent children's lives are held in the balance. She has no choice but to immerse herself in the sordid world of her tormentor. However, the closer she gets to the truth, the more she learns about her own father's dark past.

Some secrets are best kept hidden.

Connell Nisbet is a Sydney-based novelist specialising in crime thrillers. For more information about his current and upcoming novels, visit **connellnisbetauthor.com**. If you've enjoyed this book, be sure to visit Amazon or Good Reads and give it a star-rating and/or a review.